The Fictions
of
John Fowles

D1520635

The Fictions of John Fowles

POWER, Creativity, Femininity

Pamela Cooper

with a foreword by Linda Hutcheon

University of Ottawa Press
Ottawa • Paris

Canadian Cataloguing in Publication Data

Cooper, Pamela, 1955–

The fictions of John Fowles

Includes bibliographical references.
ISBN 0-7766-0299-3

1. Fowles, John, 1926– — Criticism and interpretation.
I. Title.

PR6056.O85Z56 1991   823'.914   C91-090461-8

 UNIVERSITÉ D'OTTAWA
UNIVERSITY OF OTTAWA

This book has been published with the help of a grant from
the Canadian Federation for the Humanities, using funds
provided by the Social Sciences and Humanities Research
Council of Canada.

Cover Design: Judith Gregory
Text Design: Marie Tappin

CONTENTS

ACKNOWLEDGEMENTS

The production of this book owes much to the hard work and energy of various contributors, to whom I should like to extend my thanks.

Linda Hutcheon has been a consistent source of critical wisdom and personal encouragement. Her enthusiasm for and commitment to the book sustained and inspired me throughout its production. John Baird was not only enlightening but supportive, generous, and wise — when the going got rough as well as when it was smooth.

For invaluable work on the manuscript and thought-provoking critical insights, I am grateful to Barry Olshen, Henry Auster, Jay Macpherson, and Sylvia Van Kirk. The commitment, professionalism, and good judgement of my editor, Janet Shorten, have been indispensable to me throughout the book's publication; I appreciate also the well-judged editorial work of Jennifer Wilson.

For the friendships that provided me with a sustaining context in which to work, affectionate thanks go particularly to Catherine Griffiths, Ginny Lovering, and Lally Grauer. And special gratitude goes unstintingly to my spouse, Keith Hayes, upon whose literary and linguistic acumen, patience, love, and knowledge of computer software the creation of this work has, at every stage, depended.

I am grateful to the University of Toronto, the Trustees of the Connaught Fund, the Government of Ontario, and the Canadian Federation for the Humanities for financial aid during the production of the manuscript and its publication.

● ● ●

This book is dedicated to the memory of my parents,
Mervienne Vickers Cooper and Clive Cooper.

Pamela Cooper
University of North Carolina at Chapel Hill, 1991

FOREWORD

Linda Hutcheon

Pamela Cooper's *The Fictions of John Fowles: Power, Creativity, Femininity* marks an important departure from other work on a major British writer who has managed to straddle the line between the popular and the academic in his appeal and success. This is not an introductory or descriptive survey; we have several of these already. Instead, it presents a carefully argued thesis that radically challenges the received wisdom, so to speak, or the now canonical reading of Fowles's work primarily from the perspective of his interest in how the artist comes to terms with existential freedom. Cooper has turned that relatively benign interest in freedom upside down and revealed its dark postmodern underside — power. In so doing, she has probably put her finger on at least one of the reasons for Fowles's popularity: the interplay and tensions between power and freedom aren't exactly foreign to the experience of any of us today.

Fowles has proved a particularly difficult author to write about with any degree of fairness. By this I mean that his novels certainly have their detractors (and their name is legion): paradoxically, perhaps, they are usually found either too ethically conservative or too postmodernly formalist, too "tricky." This study goes beyond such first-level responses to tease out the complexities and ambiguities — moral and psychological, as well as literary — of the power relations between author and character, between author and reader. In Fowles's world, creator figures can be both tyrants and liberators, masters and slaves. Fowles's consistent ambivalence is one of the reasons he can and does end up being the darling (or the bane) of what seem like mutually incompatible camps of readers. He seems in tune with the liberal humanist values of the British tradition (such as a belief in the individual creative imagination and ethical responsibility); at the same time he is exploring more current and problematic issues of class and gender, while deploying what are considered postmodern narrative and linguistic strategies of reflexivity. His novels have always openly challenged notions of genre, narrative authority, textual singularity, and closure.

The complexity of these kinds of paradoxes is explored in Cooper's study primarily through examining the representation of women and thus the relation between art and gender in Fowles's novels. Those strong, self-reliant, seemingly independent female characters appear to be empowered by their creator to combat their age's restrictions, but the argument here is a convincing one: they are, in fact, re-inscribed and re-confined in other ways by the texts' reflexive narrative techniques as much as by the plots. These women end up being rendered passive, manipulated by both the narrative and its narrator, their creative potential contained by its relegation to the "feminine" instinctual realm, their voice muted. The paradigm? From being a "master" fiction-maker, Sarah Woodruff (in *The French Lieutenant's Woman*) becomes, in the end, a model for a male artist. This critical study deconstructs the latent politics beneath Fowles's apparently feminist sympathies, and analyzes the contradictions that result in the final attribution of full and mature artistic "potency" only to the male in all Fowles's fiction. Though obsessively his subject matter and alleged inspiration, woman has no creative power here. The passive object of the male gaze, she is always the represent*ed*; never does she do the represent*ing*. In this her role differs little from the one she had been assigned by those male authors and artists of the past whose work forms the dense intertextual background of Fowles's writing.

Working from this point of view, Cooper rereads Fowles's use of the ethical and psychological principles of the traditional *Bildungsroman*. She also asks us to rethink the romance tradition upon which Fowles depends so much, but this time in terms of gender and control — psychosexual, moral, and aesthetic. In activating the concerns of feminist theory, she raises the questions of textuality and sexuality, of the politics of language and its usage. What is particularly original about this book's central thesis is its reading of *The Ebony Tower* as the moment of potential breakthrough, the moment when new ideas could have altered the carefully constructed and internally consistent universe of Fowles's fiction. However, the challenge was not taken, Cooper argues. The novels after 1974 are here read as retrenchment, as the retreading of safe and familiar terrain.

One of the many pleasures of reading *The Fictions of John Fowles: Power, Creativity, Femininity* is having one's former readings of these well-known novels turned on their head. But another is watching the author foreground in such an articulate way her own ambivalence towards the novels about which she writes. Her admiration and her suspicion, in about equal doses, shine through, and the mixture feels just right.

INTRODUCTION

The intensity of John Fowles's interest in power is matched by the ambiguity of his attitude towards it and the complexity with which he treats it in his fictions. Most of the significant relationships depicted in his work involve some sort of power struggle, for Fowles is at once suspicious of and fascinated by the efforts of individuals to control and influence each other. His first published novel, *The Collector* (1963), presents this struggle in its simplest form, as Miranda Grey's fight to wrest physical freedom from her jailer Clegg — although the spiritual antipathy between the two lends an important moral dimension to their clash. Subsequent works analyze more subtle, intricate or abstract power relationships. In Fowles's second novel, *The Magus* (1966, revised 1977), Conchis is a kind of psychological bully who tries to torment Nick Urfe into emotional growth. The ambiguously benevolent despotism of a teacher/magician is questioned here in the alacrity with which Conchis combines seduction and brutality. The sadistic but enlightened older man rapidly becomes a symbolically resonant figure for Fowles; he does in fact appear as far back as *The Collector*, in the form of Miranda's shadowy and rather sinister mentor, George Paston.

In *The French Lieutenant's Woman* (1969), Sarah Woodruff battles the conventional sexual attitudes of an era that seeks — mainly through Doctor Grogan as the representative of canonical scientific wisdom — to brand her a lunatic. Here Fowles's ambivalence about power is expressed in his authorial and narratorial refusal fully to grant Sarah the independent identity she seems to crave. This sense of literary characters as potentially and disruptively autonomous — despite their status as projections of the authorial imagination — reflects not only Fowles's awareness of the *nouveau roman*, but the more palpable influence of one of his older contemporaries: Fowles evidently admires Flann O'Brien's boisterous and anarchic *At Swim-Two-Birds* more than Robbe-Grillet's chilly and disengaged *La Jalousie.*

O'Brien experiments as energetically with the stylistic legacy of Joyce as Fowles does with that of *his* favoured modernist, Eliot. Expanding their predecessors' interrogations of literary form in explicitly metafictional directions, both O'Brien and Fowles use the strategies of fictional self-consciousness to explore the different possible freedoms available within and operating upon the text. Perceiving these freedoms as at once exhilarating and threatening, O'Brien and Fowles both experience the potential escape of characters from writerly control as less an intellectual fallacy than a metaphor of authorial impotence. The problematic relationship between the author as potential tyrant and the characters as questers after freedom is not only manifestly a subject of Fowles's third novel, but is more or less present in all the fictions he has published since *The Collector.*

The Ebony Tower (1974) reiterates the motif of conflict by exploring various different rivalries, both between individuals and between ideas. For example, in the title story, David Williams and Henry Breasley clash as artists as well as competitors for Diana's love; "Poor Koko" returns to the physical and class aggression of *The Collector* to present the power struggle between a bourgeois biographer and a working-class burglar. Here the writer (an apparent authorial surrogate) tries to reify and contain the violence of the intruder through the sustained narratorial act that constitutes the story. "The Cloud" broods suggestively over love and art in its delineation of the difficult relations both between Catherine and Peter and between Catherine and the very narrative that contains her.

The latter story is Fowles's most obscure and indeterminate fiction, expressing in extreme form his sense of narrative closure as itself a kind of authorial power-play. Like his younger contemporaries Graham Swift and Julian Barnes, Fowles often eschews closure in order to problematize the authority of narrative, to question its ability to frame and transmit meaning. But while they are concerned mainly with the epistemological and philosophical implications of closure, he is equally preoccupied with its various moral dimensions. In *The Magus* and *The French Lieutenant's Woman* as well as in "The Cloud," the refusal of closure is Fowles's way of repudiating the author's *force majeure* and safeguarding the freedom of characters and reader alike. While Swift and Barnes see closure principally as the author's betrayal of the fluctuating indeterminacies of history, Fowles also views it in the moral perspective of liberal humanism, as the betrayal of individual freedom. And it is typical of his paradoxical imagination that he should see the potentially dictatorial author as constantly and ironically threatened by the very freedoms he himself can inaugurate in and confer upon his text. Fowles's fictions seek repeatedly but uneasily to acknowledge and act out the author's ethical responsibilities to text and reader alike.

In this connection, the figure of Catherine in "The Cloud" attests implicitly to the dubiety of *any* repudiation of power, for her literal and unexplained disappearance from the text can be read as an arbitrary act of authorial control. Fowles's work recognizes and expresses the deeper paradox of the author who wishes at once to renounce and to impose his power. The fictions regularly externalize this dilemma in artist figures like Paston, Conchis, and Daniel Martin, whose professed belief in human freedom is indirectly vitiated by a fascination with coercion. These radically ambivalent humanistic despots (among whom Fowles would apparently count himself) express the contradictions of their own authority aesthetically or textually through the various artworks they produce.

In Fowles's later work too, characters often struggle for supremacy — not only over others, but over self and circumstances as well. Daniel Martin seeks control of his own life and he can achieve this only by breaking free of the moral influence of his father and the intellectual influence of Anthony Mallory (*Daniel Martin*, 1977). Here the search for self-definition requires liberation from destructive and hampering paternalistic forces. In this, his most conservative novel, Fowles draws on certain classic conventions of the *Bildungsroman*, which usually presents history and identity as both progressive and coherent. In the lurid *Mantissa* (1982), the relationship between Miles Green (whose name recalls another of Flann O'Brien's pseudonyms) and Erato is a kind of internalized, affectionate war. Rebecca Hocknell in *A Maggot* (1985) fights against Henry Ayscough and what he represents in an

effort to escape her age's reductive categorization of her as a liar
and a whore. But once again, Fowles's contradictory attitude
towards power leads him to stop short of unambiguously empowering his heroine. The novel which contains Rebecca, like that which
contains Sarah, acts strategically to free her from the presuppositions
of Ayscough while re-categorizing and limiting her in other ways.
Fowles's latest fiction also presents a central character who tries
quite literally to rise above the horizons of his time: like Charles
Smithson at the end of *The French Lieutenant's Woman*, His
Lordship belongs imaginatively to the temporally uninaugurated
twentieth century. Unlike Charles, he gains physical and tangible
entry into the future by means of the mysterious "maggot" or time-
travelling spacecraft.

● ● ●

This study does not seek to place Fowles's work either
precisely or exhaustively in the context of contemporary British
metafiction; to undertake such a project at this time seems to me
precipitate. But as the above references to Graham Swift and Julian
Barnes suggest, Fowles's influence on certain younger writers has
perhaps been overlooked, and is worthy of comment. Swift's
Waterland (1983), for example, explores the relationship between
the past and narrative — between history and story — which
Fowles began to scrutinize as far back as *The Magus*. Although
Fowles was by no means the first to examine this theme, his highly
self-conscious treatment of it makes an intellectual link with Swift
both possible and intriguing. Also, *Waterland*'s self-aware and his-
tory-obsessed narrator may reasonably be seen as a displacement, in
the direction of a more urgent and pessimistic uncertainty, of the
sometimes glibly confident narrator in *The French Lieutenant's
Woman*. Lacking the suavity of Fowles's impresario, Tom Crick is
too bewildered by the past either to play with it or to take possession of it as his personal terrain. Those issues of textual indeterminacy, which Fowles's narrator finds not only worrying but
stimulating, become a source of deeper anguish for Swift's, as Crick
tries to bring narrative into a viable balance with what he sees as the
essential intransigence of experience.

The reappraisal and effective rewriting of the past — a
major theme throughout Fowles's *œuvre* — is also the subject of at

least two other British novels of the 1980s: D. M. Thomas's *The White Hotel* (1981) and Peter Ackroyd's *Chatterton* (1987). Thomas, like Angela Carter in some of the *Black Venus* stories (1985), creates a kind of revisionary psychoanalytic fable. Ackroyd, more palpably Fowlesian, avoids psychoanalysis and problematizes historical truth through the dilemmas of an existentially tense male protagonist. Despite the element of Dickensian comedy in his characterization, Charles Wychwood, a poet, has all the apprehensive and directionless poise of the young Fowlesian hero — of Nick Urfe, Charles Smithson, and David Williams. *A Maggot* reanimates this figure in the context of what Fowles perceives as contemporary anxiety about genre; in this way his latest novel revises and updates the formal preoccupations of *The French Lieutenant's Woman*. Although His Lordship is soothed in both his psychic and religious yearnings by the metafictional "miracle" of the spacecraft, his transubstantiation is less spiritually authoritative than generically resonant. Disappearing into the craft as into a kind of aerodynamic paradise, His Lordship also vanishes into its metonymic equivalent: the modern high-technology science-fiction novel — a prose form as yet unborn in his own era, the eighteenth century. In a similar way, Ackroyd has Chatterton himself occupy and reoccupy not only different genres, but the wider realms of both narrative and visual art. (In *The Ebony Tower*, Fowles too is concerned with the interrelationship between these art forms.) At once inhabiting and vanishing from the texts of those who try to write and paint him, Chatterton is finally, like His Lordship, both present in and absent from a text inconceivable in his own time — Ackroyd's novel. Clearly Fowles shares with some of his younger contemporaries a preoccupation with history and narrative authority, and the artist's efforts to control the one by comprehending the other.

Like them too, Fowles is interested in language as both the basic component of narrative and the medium of historical fact: he interleaves *A Maggot* with pages from *The Gentleman's Magazine* of 1736. Both this novel and *The French Lieutenant's Woman* are conceived explicitly as experiments in literary ventriloquism: each re-creates an historically specific, self-consciously "authentic" period diction based apparently on Fowles's sense of the novelistic prose of the eighteenth and nineteenth centuries respectively. In *A Maggot* this means that the imagery of the science-fiction novel reaches the reader indirectly, through Rebecca's description of events in the Devonshire cave. But Rebecca's language, like her experience, is limited by its historical specificity; she lacks the resources, cognitive and linguistic, to recognize the spacecraft and name it as such. This disjunction between the character's knowledge of her experience and the reader's knowledge of it becomes in *A Maggot* an epistemological split between meanings withheld in one time frame and made available in another. It is basically a technique of the dramatic monologue brilliantly exploited by Fowles in the service of metafiction.

Angela Carter uses the same audacious strategy in at least two of the stories in *Black Venus*. (The appearance of this volume in 1985, the same year as *A Maggot*, suggests a congruence of thought rather than a relationship of influence between Carter and Fowles here.) In "The Cabinet of Edgar Allan Poe," Carter uses narrative diagnostically to psychoanalyze Poe. But while the reader can see Poe's suffering as (in Carter's terms) the manifestation and result of psychosis, Poe himself, and the other characters in the story, have no such access to psychoanalysis as a paradigm of comprehension. For Carter, as for Fowles, this historically inevitable privileging of reader over characters signals the constructedness of narrative by foregrounding its enmeshment in time. "Our Lady of the Massacre" presents eighteenth-century imperialist violence in the New World through a narrator, clearly based on Moll Flanders, who cannot grasp the full meaning of her tale for a contemporary reader familiar with the long-term consequences of such brutality. Carter's treatment of her female narrator here differs from Fowles's treatment of Rebecca, and "Our Lady of the Massacre" has no image of futurity comparable to *A Maggot*'s spacecraft. But both authors use temporal dislocation to indicate the text's constructedness by emphasizing the ambiguity of its meanings and the instability of its strategies. Clearly Carter shares with Fowles not only a flair for experimentation and historical mimicry, but a sense of metafiction as itself a commentary on, as well as a way of exploring, the involvement of narrative in time. These are issues that Fowles's work repeatedly examines; their echoes in the work of some other contemporary British writers help identify Fowles as a presence on the current literary scene and a strong contributor to the mood and character of the modern British novel.

● ● ●

My focus in this study, however, is Fowles's *œuvre* itself — in particular, its consistent engagement with power as both idea and structural principle. Fowles's work investigates issues of power in various ways and contexts, and this can be seen as the corollary of his acknowledged concern with freedom, individual choice, and the quest for identity. When Daniel Halpern asked him in a 1971 interview what has "remained important" for him in his work, Fowles described the obsessive hold which the idea of personal liberty has over his creative imagination: "Freedom, yes. How you achieve freedom. That obsesses me. All my books are about that. The question is, is there really free will? Can we choose freely? Can we act freely? Can we *choose*? How do we do it?"[1] But I do not propose to focus specifically on the theme of existential freedom in Fowles's work. This has long been a favourite area of critical inquiry for Fowles scholars and the existentialist emphasis in his thinking has often been discussed.[2] His interest in power as a conversely related theme has been less noted,[3] and the above summary

---

1   Daniel Halpern and John Fowles, "A Sort of Exile in Lyme Regis," *London Magazine*, 10 Mar. 1971, 45, emphasis in original.

2   The earlier monographs are particularly aware of Fowles's existentialism, perhaps because those interviews in which he stated his philosophical allegiance appeared in the 1960s and 1970s. See, for example, William J. Palmer, *The Fiction of John Fowles: Tradition, Art, and the Loneliness of Selfhood* (Columbia: University of Missouri Press, 1974); Peter Wolfe, *John Fowles, Magus and Moralist* (Lewisburg: Bucknell University Press, 1976); Barry N. Olshen, *John Fowles* (New York: Frederick Ungar Publishing Co., 1978). See also Jeff Rackham, "John Fowles: The Existential Labyrinth," *Critique* 13, No. 3 (1972), 89–103. The interview with Roy Newquist in *Counterpoint* (London: George Allen & Unwin, 1965), pp. 218–25, gives Fowles's views on his intellectual debt to existentialists like Sartre and Camus. The interview with Carol M. Barnum in *Modern Fiction Studies* 31, No. 1 (1985), 187–203, suggests how his conception of existentialism has changed and developed over the years.

3   For some discussion of the topic from different points of view, see Peter Conradi, *John Fowles* (New York: Methuen, 1982); Bruce Woodcock, *Male Mythologies: John Fowles and Masculinity* (New Jersey: Barnes & Noble Books, 1984); Rosemary M. Laughlin, "Faces of Power in the Novels of John Fowles," *Critique* 13, No. 3 (1972), 71–88.

of his work in terms of its preoccupation with power indicates briefly and generally those precise aspects of the theme which this study will highlight. For power in Fowles's work is never a question *only* of morality, ethics, or philosophy — just as it is much more than a necessary weapon of the ego. It is also, and for him most significantly, the property of art and it inheres by extension in the creative abilities of the artist.

The power of creativity intrigues Fowles. This is one reason for his commitment to metafiction, his concern to explore power by means of a dialectical interpenetration of form and content. For him the work of art is the index and vehicle of the artist's power; as a novelist, Fowles focuses especially on the text as artefact and the author as creative artist. Both the structures and the content of the text are expressions of the artist's power, and narrative design, like narratorial self-consciousness, thus becomes the legitimate focus of his scrutiny. Therefore the specific kind of power which the following chapters will analyze is artistic power and its implications, including the complex modes of creativity and the nature of artistic inspiration.

Repeatedly in Fowles's work, the artist finds that, in order fully to comprehend and express his creativity, he must come to terms with that of his artistic ancestors — those mothers and fathers of his art who are both inspiring and formidable. In questing for his independence in a postmodernist age, then, the artist must fight to discover a place for himself among the artefacts of his forebears. Fowles's fictions never promulgate any definition of postmodernism, and I do not intend systematically to generate one of my own in this book.[4] But in its preoccupation with those historical, narratological, linguistic, and sexual pressures which operate upon the contemporary writer, his work offers a composite portrait of the authorial consciousness in the era of postmodernism. It delineates at least some of the challenges and problems faced by the creative imagination in our time. In this way, I believe, his fictions contribute to our cumulative sense of what this controversial term

---

4   For extensive studies of the meanings of postmodernism, see Linda Hutcheon, *A Poetics of Postmodernism* (New York: Routledge, 1988), and *A Politics of Postmodernism* (New York: Routledge, 1989). The subject is also variously explored in Hal Foster, ed., *The Anti-Aesthetic: Essays on Postmodern Culture* (Port Townsend, Washington: Bay Press, 1983).

implies. They reveal, for example, a growing sense of postmodernism as requiring the artist to define his powers in opposition to those of his creative elders, whose productions occupy the aesthetic landscape in which he too must be accommodated. This draws upon modernist perceptions of the past and its artefacts as weighing heavily upon the creativity of the present. But Fowles updates the cultural apprehensiveness of writers like Eliot in the light of a more developed metafictional awareness. He resituates such anxieties of influence in a contemporary context by means of a textual self-reflexivity both highly evolved and fully articulated. This brings an element of irony, even parody, to the relation between artist and forebear which indirectly interrogates, in one sense, the authority of *all* artefacts and their creators, even as it seriously engages, in another sense, in the historically inevitable competition *for* that very authority.

This search for a place, by compelling the artist into a relationship with pre-existent artworks, also forces him to confront not only his artistic ancestors, but the role and function of the critic. In *The Magus*, *The Ebony Tower*, and *Mantissa* particularly, Fowles is deeply concerned with the interplay between art and criticism. Foregrounding criticism and the critical faculty as a kind of threatening alternative to art and the creative faculty, his fictions implicitly describe postmodernism as, in part, an ambiguous rivalry of discourses. Always professedly anti-critical in his own thinking about art in general and literary art in particular, Fowles finds the critic's role an obstructive and constricting one. He told James Campbell in 1976: "If there's one gang of people I'd like to see thrown into the sea it's the professors of English Literature."[5] But in the above three works especially, he acknowledges what is for him the troubling fact that the artist, working inevitably in the presence of older masters, is obliged to turn critic himself and play an uneasy dual role. Thus the following chapters in this volume also investigate the various strategies by means of which artistic self-

---

5   "An Interview with John Fowles," *Contemporary Literature* 17, No. 4 (1976), 460. See also Fowles's interview with Raman K. Singh in *Journal of Modern Literature* 8, No. 2 (1980/81), 193. It should be observed that, in pointing out this aspect of Fowles's thought, the critic places his/her own endeavours in an ironic and dubious light with regard to the opinions of his/her own subject.

discovery becomes the locating of one's own works in a contemporary landscape filled with the creative offerings of competing
talents.

● ● ●

        I have said that Fowles's ingenuity as a metafictionist can
be understood in terms of his concern with individual freedom and
his sense of authorial power as a moral and aesthetic reality. Despite
a certain diversity of subject-matter, his fictions consistently return
to images or processes of liberation, evasion, and escape. Very
often these processes govern the structural intentions of a work
while also describing or shaping its content. So Sarah Woodruff,
for example, seeks to escape the hidebound assumptions of
Victorian society in a novel which tries to free itself from the conventions of nineteenth-century fiction. Isobel Dodgson in "The
Enigma" approaches the riddle of Fielding's disappearance by
attempting to liberate Mike Jennings' mind from the rigidities of
ratiocinative inquiry into the imaginatively unbounded realms of
fiction. In both these works a generic or formal transformation
accompanies the liberating metamorphosis which the narrative
undertakes to describe. Thus *The French Lieutenant's Woman*
acquires a more contemporary flavour of romantic and existential
Angst, with the self-conscious modernity of the story shaped by a
series of indeterminate endings. "The Enigma" effects a remarkable act of narrative transmutation by freeing itself from the narrow
conventions of detective fiction and becoming a love story.
        But these two examples of Fowlesian metafictional tactics
are suggestive in other ways, for they underline that crucial ambivalence in his attitude towards freedom which my opening survey of
the theme of power in his *œuvre* has emphasized. Specifically,
Fowles's fictions repeatedly reveal that his commitment to notions
of personal freedom and independence is not always as unambiguous as it at first seems. This is particularly true when the quester
after liberation and self-determined identity is a woman. It is at this
point that Fowles's preoccupation with power meets his over-
whelming interest in femininity and sexuality; the result is a fascinating tissue of contradictions in his work which the ensuing
chapters will analyze and explore. For it is a singular feature of his
fictions that Fowles's major female characters, apparently so self-

directed and compelling in their strength, can be revealed on closer examination as virtually the opposite of what they seem. Beneath the aloofness which seems to signal a poised self-sufficiency, the Fowlesian heroine is a passive figure, invariably compromised and controlled by the strategies of the text that contains her. In the ambiguity of his response to her, the Fowlesian narrator is led to exercise, in indirect ways and apparently on his author's behalf, the kind of textual tyranny which he so frequently repudiates.

This can be illustrated in terms of the examples cited above: Sarah's quest for freedom and identity leads not to true independence, but to another kind of subservient confinement — albeit a more glamorous kind than that which she experienced at Mrs. Poulteney's. In Chelsea, on the fringes of society, she becomes the assistant and model of D. G. Rossetti, who has rescued her from a life of destitution. But, in many ways, her search for independent selfhood is in effect a change of masters, for she starts as secretary-companion to a punitive symbol of provincial respectability, and ends as secretary-companion to a Bohemian artist. Similarly, Isobel Dodgson's cool efficiency is deceptive: as she liberates the imagination of Jennings, the very generic transformation of the narrative effects the restraining of her talents by changing her, within the framework of the story, from creative fictionalizer to mistress. In both *The French Lieutenant's Woman* and "The Enigma," then, an apparently valorizing emphasis on freedom becomes in effect the subtle re-imposition of confinement. The present study sees Sarah and Isobel as exemplifying essential features of Fowles's presentation of his woman characters, and it traces the different ways in which the heroine is limited and controlled in his fiction.

These two examples also suggest that one method of controlling the heroine is by limiting her creativity. Sarah, like Isobel, is a spinner of fictions, but the novel shows her abandoning her efforts at narrative. Both of these women can be seen as incipient artists, and both are manoeuvred into positions whereby their creativity is effectively de-emphasized in favour of their sexuality. Modelling for Rossetti, Sarah takes her place within the frame as it were: her beauty becomes the subject for *his* art, and she is never an artist in her own right. Similarly Isobel, an aspiring novelist, appears at the end of "The Enigma" as a lover rather than as an artist. The story suggests that she cannot be both and she assumes her final place, as we will see, in the work of another novelist, John Fowles. Clearly the ambiguities which cluster about the Fowlesian heroine are closely related to her incipient creativity — or, more specifically, to the power which she herself, as a potential artist, could come to inherit and exercise. Here Fowles's concern with artistic power meets his somewhat uneasy investigation into what constitutes the power of the feminine. Subsequent chapters will show that Fowles's sense of femininity is defined in large part by his implicit belief in the power of the artist as quintessentially masculine and his reluctance to present women in terms of fully developed creative authority.

For Fowles, the relationship of women to this particular kind of power is always ambiguous. They are regularly presented in his fiction as art students, like Miranda and Diana, as potential or aspiring artists, like Sarah, Isobel, and Catherine. But the mature artist, a usually formidable and often magical individual in Fowles's work, is invariably male. It seems that Fowles will bring his women characters within reach of full creative capacity, but the dual role in which he consistently, if indirectly, valorizes them is as guardians of the flame of masculine genius and providers of the material for art. Thus the specific power of woman is for Fowles an indefinable and contradictory quality; unrelated to force and without self-determined efficacy, it is nonetheless presented in his fiction as somehow retaining its identity as power. This implies that for Fowles feminine power is a mode of being, a pervasive ontological passivity and materiality, known by its separation from aggressive action and its availability to the artist as both the substance of his art and the source of his inspiration. This passive power, a suggestive contradiction in terms, is constantly at the service of the shaping, defining capacities of the male artist.

● ● ●

It is clear that sexuality and gender relations play a vital role in the artist's efforts to own and exercise his power. Fowles's fiction emphasizes women as providers of the material for art and it confines them in different ways to ineffective positions relative to creativity. In his work the woman is literally an *objet d'art* and it is not surprising to find many references to paintings of women in his books: for example, in *The Magus* Julie Holmes is compared to the women of Renoir and to Goya's *Maja desnuda*; in "The Ebony Tower" Diana reminds David of a Gauguin maiden and a *baigneuse* of Manet; Sarah is associated with the conventions of Pre-Raphaelite art through her connection with the Brotherhood. Even Miranda in *The Collector* is presented in terms of pictures: Clegg assimilates her image to the inverted aesthetics of pornography, one of the metaphors in the Fowles corpus for the destructive potentialities of art. And this idea of a woman degraded by means of her own photographed image is reiterated in Daniel Martin's rejection of Jenny McNeil, a film actress.

This imagery serves a double thematic purpose which establishes the interdependency of art and sex in Fowles's fiction: it foregrounds the work (in any medium) of the artist's forebears as inevitably implicated in his own endeavours, and it identifies women as the objects of his contemplation rather than the contenders for his position as creator. We might argue that this identification implicitly associates Fowles with the traditional and conservative sexual politics of modernism, even as his metafictional bent allies him primarily with the formal and intellectual radicalism of postmodernism. In fictions like *The French Lieutenant's Woman*, these mixed loyalties are perhaps reflected in the use (not without sadistic implication) of a highly self-reflexive textual apparatus to restrain and confine the heroine. Increasingly in Fowles's work, as we will see, the artist's clash with his creative progenitors takes on the colour of an Oedipal battle with the competitive artist-father for symbolic possession of the inspiring model-mother.[6] Here Fowles's sense of postmodernism as an arena for rival talents comes together with his aesthetically oriented reification of women under the auspices of Freud. This conjunction gives to his work its characteristic tonal blend of anxiety, desire, and mysterious threat — an

---

6   Not surprisingly, the only critical model which Fowles sees as useful and relevant to the psychic life of the artist — particularly the artist as author — is a Freudian one. In a 1977 essay on Hardy, he developed a theory of creativity based on the male artist's unassuageable yearning for reunion with that mother lost to him during infancy by the processes of individuation: "Hardy and the Hag," in *Thomas Hardy after Fifty Years*, ed. L. St. John Butler (London: Macmillan, 1977), pp. 28–42. For an extensive analysis of this Oedipal relationship between the artist and his forebears, see Harold Bloom, *The Anxiety of Influence* (New York: Oxford University Press, 1973).

imaginatively and atmospherically rich mixture which Fowles himself has identified in terms of a passionate indebtedness to the conventions of mediaeval romance,[7] that is, a fictional sensibility compelled towards motifs of ordeal, quest, and erotic reward.

The presentation of the woman as effectively an artefact in Fowles's work further suggests that this object of the artist's voyeuristic attention is also the embodiment of an iconographic femininity which he yearns to colonize and control. For this reason, Fowles's women are frequently made available for incorporation into artworks like paintings and novels while maintaining a sexual aloofness from the artists who observe and depict them. In this way these women combine promiscuous accessibility to the artist's imagination with a sexual reluctance that recalls the talismanic chastity of both the romance heroine and the lost mother of Oedipal desire. The ambiguous availability of the Fowlesian heroine is thus a crucial part of her paradigmatic function as both the artist's inspiration and the very substance of his art. One of Fowles's favourite psychosexual configurations is that of a man forced to choose between two women who represent different existential and philosophical alternatives: so Nick is caught between Julie and Alison, Charles between Sarah and Ernestina, David between Diana and Beth, and Dan between Jenny and Jane. Subsequent chapters will show how the male protagonist's choice of a symbolically significant partner depends in large part on a sense — shared evidently by his author — of the desirable woman as sexually remote but available to the masculine imagination for assimilation into art.

If feminine power exists for Fowles as a sort of immanent, unformed resonance at the service of the artist's shaping and defining powers, it follows that the idea of the articulate woman is particularly problematic, for Fowles usually associates language and narrative with the male artist as author. The endeavour in his fiction to limit and contain feminine creativity is in effect an effort to colonize it by defining it only in relation to masculine needs. This effort is directed especially at those women who aspire to the power of words. Women narrators are the most seriously compromised

---

7   See the "Personal Note" preceding Fowles's translation of *Eliduc* in *The Ebony Tower* — a volume that represents his most powerful manipulation of romance elements.

figures in Fowles's work, their aspirations to linguistic creativity regularly thwarted by different textual and narratorial ploys. Here Fowles's implicit sense of gender as central to *all* art merges with his explorations of narrative art specifically, and femininity comes into complex relationship with issues of language and meaning.

Throughout Fowles's work — and particularly in his most art-centred fiction, *The Ebony Tower* — the inarticulacy of the female comes not only to inspire but also to guarantee and signify the supreme articulacy of the male artist as author — just as the creative immaturity of aspiring visual artists like Miranda and Diana becomes an index of the power of their infatuated mentors, G.P. and Breasley. Fowles's conception of language is a contradictory one, for he identifies it both with narrative art as a product of the creative imagination and with the kind of ratiocinative intellection that informs criticism and is thus, strictly speaking, anathema to art. This ambiguity manifests itself in his sense of the author as a man involved with words but aware of the sources of his power to manipulate them as mysterious, irrational and inarticulate. Extending this sense of inspiration as irrational beyond its specific applicability to narrative art, it becomes possible to say that for Fowles the power of the artist to formulate and express — that power which defines him whatever his medium — depends on a constant commerce with the instinctual, the creatively undeveloped, and (in relation once more to the narrative artist) the quintessentially languageless.

This numinous reservoir of sub-rational inspiration, this shapelessness which inspires supreme shaping, is identified in Fowles's work with women and their sexuality. The very nature of creativity as he conceives it requires a consistently maintained association between the feminine and the inarticulate. In the physical sexuality of woman, her inhibited or reduced creative capacity, and her separation from language, the artist finds the inspiration and sign of his own power. In Fowles's fiction the thwarting or compromising of the potentially artistic woman is designed to keep her within the confines of this role. Thus the linguistic virtuosity of the male as writer demands the linguistic ineptitude of the female as written. By locating her within his text (whether it be a narrative, a painting or, like Conchis's, a boundaryless phantasmagoria), the artist, functioning variously as author, narrator, and/or protagonist of a fiction, defines the woman as crucial to that text but never authoritatively in control of it. So the Fowlesian heroine, ambiguously pure and celebrated when she is innocent, preserves a separation from language identical with and as significant as her separation from intellect and talent. This aloofness (another aspect of her contradictory availability) protects her against that contact between language and reason which for Fowles debases words and *all* who manipulate them, while signifying the power of men to undertake those very manipulations, to shape and control language just as they shape and control her. Thus feminine ineptitude, a complex sign in Fowles's work, comes also to indicate the alliance between artistic power and moral dubiety — an alliance that is, for the simultaneously idealized and debased heroine, at once beneath her contempt and beyond her reach. It is through this ambiguous figure, then, that we perceive the full complexity of Fowles's vision of creativity, including his sense of the artist as both paragon and brute, aesthete and pornographer, magus and monster. The following chapters will show that, in Fowles's thinking about femininity in general and about its relationship with language in particular, textuality and sexuality, art and gender, are inextricably linked.

The artist, in grasping and wielding his own power, is thus engaged in a struggle on two related fronts. He must stake out his own imaginative territory in relation to the work of his creative forebears. This usually entails, as will be seen, the reworking or translating of pre-existent texts in order symbolically to repossess or reconceive them. Here Fowles's work again intersects strikingly with that of Swift, Barnes, Ackroyd, and Carter, all of whom borrow and self-consciously re-present elements from the works of literary ancestors like Dickens and Shakespeare. In addition to this, the artist must confirm, guarantee, and signify his power by confining the women who inspire him to the passive, mutually reinforcing roles of muse and model.

• • •

In structuring this study, I have followed the chronology of Fowles's *œuvre* and devoted a chapter to each of his first four fictional works. My decision to treat his last three novels in a single concluding chapter is related partly to necessary limitations of length, but more importantly to the ideas which the study explores. As such, the telescoped conclusion clearly expresses both my sense of the development of Fowles's interest in language and meaning and, even more significantly, my own view of *The Ebony Tower* as a work whose importance to his corpus has been underestimated by critics. From at least as far back as *The Magus*, Fowles's work is concerned with narrative as an aesthetic formulation of language. His explorations of the relationship between language, narrative, and meaning mark him, once again, as an heir of the modernist tradition coming to terms in his own way with the imperatives of postmodernism. *The Ebony Tower* represents his most intense engagement with linguistic issues, as well as his most complex expression of the relationship among these issues, art in general, and sexuality. Here Fowles negotiates the outermost limits of authorial power, fictionality, and language, while scrutinizing the self-destructive and self-defeating tendencies of narrative art in the frequently directionless, fragmented world of postmodernism.

This study contends that *The Ebony Tower* is Fowles's most radical fiction. It argues that, whatever his influence on other novelists has been, Fowles's work after 1974 is an effective back-tracking from the prospect of the annihilation of narrative — what Catherine in "The Cloud" refers to as "the death of fiction" — which *The Ebony Tower* discovers and confronts. *Daniel Martin*, *Mantissa*, and *A Maggot* can be seen as collectively illuminating a "road not taken," and this description applies equally to the kind of gender relations depicted in these last three novels: Fowles's later work continues to flirt with and reject that conjunction of femininity and creativity which both fascinates and repels his imagination from the start. In *The Ebony Tower*, Fowles reaches a peak of technical originality and sophisticated insight; in the late 1970s and 1980s, he preferred to direct his artistic energies towards an effective retreading of the thematic and structural turf which his *œuvre* had previously explored. The ensuing chapters will consider the stages in his artistic development, and the processes that have brought his work to its present position of retrenchment and reconsideration.

1

THE COLLECTOR

Fowles's first published novel, *The Collector* (1963), provides a suggestive introduction to those issues of power, creativity, and gender so crucial to the rest of his *œuvre*. It explores these within a flexible generic structure that combines an awareness of novelistic trends in the 1950s with elements of detective fiction, the thriller, and the Gothic novel. In this context Fowles investigates, with a frankness perhaps unequalled until *Mantissa*, the artist as potential pornographer and the reified woman as pornographic artefact. Despite this openness, however, *The Collector* is technically and intellectually Fowles's least ambitious novel and, while its treatment of power is not without complexity, it engages with this theme in a particularly literal way. Later fictions would show Fowles exploring more subtle forms of power than the brute force which dominates his first novel. But as *The Magus* and *The Ebony Tower* both suggest, that sense of the intimate connection between power and violence which permeates *The Collector* returns repeatedly in later work.

Furthermore, although the book's generic borrowings do not add up to the radical formal revisionism of *The French Lieutenant's Woman*, the overall technique of *The Collector* expresses that interest in the relationship between narrative and power which preoccupies Fowles subsequently. The style and structure of the novel identify Clegg's strategies for controlling Miranda as not just physical but linguistic as well. In this way they point beyond themselves to that more pervasive methodology of authorial control which further restricts Miranda in the text.

The novel's shock value comes undoubtedly from its exploration of force as an irreducible physical fact, from its

concretization and literalization of violence.   If Fowles's work is
consistently fascinated, as we shall see, with the idea of the enclosed
space, the magical landscape modelled on the *domaine perdu* of
Alain-Fournier,[1] his first fictional expression of this idea is ironic.
Unlike Bourani, the Undercliff, or Coëtminais, for example,
Clegg's house, Fosters, is a savagely deromanticized *domaine.* The
apparent illogic of an author ironizing a central image before its
unironic presentation in his work is mitigated by the fact that
Bourani, Fowles's first romanticized *domaine,* actually predates
Fosters in imaginative conception.   Fowles began work on *The
Magus* in the early 1950s, well before he wrote *The Collector.*
Although insulated from time and mundane reality, Fosters generates its own mundanity by its lack of beauty and imaginative resonance, for the events which take place within it cannot and do not
partake of the magic, the experiential unpredictability, that usually
characterizes these reserves in Fowles's work.   Clegg's basement,
combining trendy furniture and art books with ten-inch bolts and a
reinforced door, is instead an anti-*domaine* which, lacking in mystery, is almost entirely without the imaginative possibilities that
mysteriousness evokes for Fowles.   Through the narrow creativity
of Clegg and the all-too-comprehensible enclosed space which he
produces, the novel emphasizes those negative aspects of the
domaine which later fictions suggest less directly: the unhealthiness
of its isolation, the irresponsible nature of relationships formed
within it, its capacity to entrap and stifle even as it protects.

    The Collector's engagement with power as physical force
and mere control is further seen in its portrayal of its heroine,
Miranda Grey.   She is Fowles's first fictional embodiment of the
princesse lointaine,[2] the idealized and erotically desirable woman
who inhabits the Edenic enclosure, and whose elusiveness usually

---

1   Robert Huffaker discusses Fowles's well-known indebtedness to
     Le Grand Meaulnes in the first chapter of his *John Fowles* (Boston:
     Twayne Publishers, 1980), pp. 25–27.

2   For a discussion of this concept in Fowles's work, and of an earlier fic-
     tional model for the *domaine,* see Ishrat Lindblad, " '*La bonne vaux,*'
     '*la princesse lointaine*' — Two Motifs in the Novels of John Fowles," in
     *Studies in English Philology, Linguistics and Literature Presented to Alarik
     Rynell,* ed. Mats Rydén and Lennart A. Björk (Stockholm, Sweden:
     Almquist & Wiksell International, 1978), pp. 87–101.

reflects its numinous mystery. But here Miranda is implicated in the bitter ironization of the environment which houses her. Designated by her mentor Paston as merely "'*une*' *princesse loin-taine*,"[3] Miranda is demystified partly through the obscene impulses of Clegg and partly through her narrative itself — which permits the reader to enter and know her mind as he/she cannot know the minds of Julie Holmes or Sarah Woodruff. As Clegg acts out his erotic fantasies by kidnapping Miranda and making her his "secret guest" (20), the novel depicts the systematic abuse of the heroine with an explicitness and consistency rare in Fowles's work. With the possible exception of "The Cloud," Fowles would not again present so directly such a competitive and brutal model of gender relations until twenty years later, in his first fiction of the 1980s, *Mantissa*.

Given its emphasis on physical violence, it is appropriate that *The Collector* should explore power specifically as tyranny and tyranny as a consequence of impoverishment. Clegg's fantasies about Miranda are basically possessive, and spring partly from his frustrations with a tedious job and a depleted emotional life. Moving between his ledgers at the Town Hall Annexe, his austere Nonconformist home, and meetings of the Bug Section, Clegg imagines Miranda "loving [him and his butterfly] collection, drawing and colouring them . . . [s]he all pretty with her pale blonde hair and grey eyes and of course the other men all green round the gills" (10). The novel's awareness of Clegg's economic poverty and the intellectual and social limitations which this imposes upon his life associates it generically with that fiction of the 1950s which depicted English working-class experience. *The Collector* dramatizes the clash between a socially entrenched, wealthy middle class and an underprivileged but upwardly mobile working or lower middle class, dubbed "the New People" in the book. Authors like Kingsley Amis and Alan Sillitoe saw this clash as characterizing English society in the post-war years. Thus Amis's *Lucky Jim* (1954) deals with the struggles of a dispossessed anti-hero for social power and control over his own life. Sillitoe's *Saturday Night and Sunday Morning* (1959) confronts a young worker's attempts to retain the

---

3   John Fowles, *The Collector* (London: Jonathan Cape, 1963), p. 177. All other page references appear in the text and are to this edition.

charismatic power of his animal energies in the face of societal pressures to produce and conform.

The Collector portrays the class conflict essential to this kind of fiction while also rebelling, in ways that the reader comes to expect of Fowles's work, against some of its premises. Thus it reformulates, in the direction of the sinister and obsessive, that 1950s fictional convention of the fruitless encounter between an educated, class-privileged woman and a resentful, socially deprived man. Fowles's interest in the flexibility of fictional form is further evidenced here in his reversal of the terms of class struggle as it usually appears in "proletarian" fiction. Instead of imitating Sillitoe and making Clegg into a kind of Arthur Seaton, who tries to liberate his heroic vigour from the environmental torpidity that imprisons it, Fowles constructs a wholly negative working-class protagonist. Clegg does not embody any displaced or inchoate heroism, but himself partakes spiritually and metaphorically of the insect life which preoccupies him. Fowles deliberately questions a fictional concept of the anti-hero and his rebelliousness as misunderstood nobility by revealing in Clegg a quiet and meticulous capacity for evil. He has described his own motive as a wish "to attack . . . the contemporary idea that there is something noble about the inarticulate hero. About James Dean and all his literary children and grandchildren."[4] Peter Conradi, tracing Clegg's origins back to the Bloomsbury novel in general and Howards End in particular, sums up the pathetic invertedness of the collector and the wider implications of the novel as a whole:

> Clegg is in a sense the charmless great-nephew of Bast or the talentless younger brother of the classic 1950s hero, too witless to benefit from the new educational opportunities [offered by the 1944 Education Act], too sensitive not to suffer his inadequacies ceaselessly. The Collector, in addressing itself to the politics of sexuality and social divisiveness, contrives to be a modest psychopathology of the age and its culture, as well as a sexual thriller.[5]

---

4   Newquist, p. 218.

5   Conradi, p. 33.

Working-class economic impoverishment is not, however, the only or even the principal kind of deprivation which the novel focuses upon. In its presentation of Clegg as imaginatively undernourished, the novel directs us to other generic influences upon it, mainly the Gothic novel and pornography, which present power relations in more or less aggressive, authoritarian ways. And here the book begins, through its central male characters, Clegg and Paston, to foreground its specific concern with creative incapacity and the nature of artistic might. Clegg's limited imagination is expressed partly through the clichés which shape his fantasies in both their sentimental and violent transmutations. Thus he relishes the thought of playing "popular host and hostess" (10) with Miranda, like "one of those adverts come to life" (82), and also of hitting her across the face "as [he] saw it done once by a chap in a telly play" (11). His literalization of his fantasies through abduction and confinement is an attempt to live out such hackneyed visions, which also reveals to the reader a morally anaesthetized pedantry: the precision with which Clegg plans the "collection" of his human specimen, Miranda, generates much deliberately tedious detail in his memoir. This presents Clegg as effectively an engineer of incarceration, a torturer absorbed only in the mechanics of his instruments and not their effects. Evidently relishing his own efficiency, Clegg describes the leaden routines of imprisonment:

> I fitted the room out very nicely, though I say so myself. After I got it dried out I put several layers of insulating felt and then a nice bright orange carpet (cheerful). . . . The door was two-inch seasoned wood with sheet metal on the inside so she couldn't get at the wood. . . . I could go on all night about the precautions. I used to go and sit in her room and work out what she could do to escape. I thought she might know about electricity, you never know with girls these days, so I always wore rubber heels. I never touched a switch without a good look first. (23–25)

This concentration on the minutiae of his task reveals Clegg's obsessiveness while placing it in the perspective of a stupefying monotony: one of Miranda's challenges in the novel is to deal with the boredom of life as Clegg's "guest." It is thus Clegg's literal-mindedness, another implied legacy of his socio-economic deprivation, which defines him as a quotidian villain, a representative in fiction of the banality of evil. And the ordinariness of Clegg in turn balances and re-orientates those colourful generic elements which the novel borrows from both Gothic fiction and its popular modern offshoots, the detective story and the thriller. While it would be wrong to see *The Collector* as some of its British reviewers saw it, as little more than a lurid crime novel,[6] the book's debt to such sub-genres is shown in its suspenseful handling of a criminal action and its delineation of the relationship between a persecutor and a victim.

The punitive, sexually coercive nature of this relationship in *The Collector* further associates Clegg as the novel's hero with that masculine wish to be both lover and captor which, for Leslie Fiedler, lies at the heart of sexual experience as Gothic fiction depicts it.[7] The incarcerated women and tormented jailer-lovers of Gothic novels suggest an equation between love, despotism, and the urge to violate which *The Collector* explores through a dero-manticized hero whose phallic energy, effectively transferred to his camera, expresses not innate virility but the mere functionality of the machine. Thus the novel relates Clegg to earlier fictional paradigms of masculine behaviour, and to other fictional expres-sions of sexual coercion, not only to highlight the brutality of a cer-tain kind of *machismo*, but also to demystify it by associating it with the collector's banal criminality. Here Fowles's refusal to accept the usual nobility of the hero in "proletarian" fiction meets his interro-gation of glamourized masculine violence in other novelistic forms.

Stylistically this implies that Clegg's unimaginative pedantry, while effectively domesticating his obsessionality, acts as a kind of narrative solvent throughout the book. By means of Clegg's fussy attention to detail and the tonal monotony which this lends to his memoir, Fowles undercuts and controls the potentially

---

6   Newquist, p. 221.

7   Fiedler has traced the genealogy of the Gothic novel back through such figures as the Brontës, Mrs. Radcliffe, and the Marquis de Sade to *Clarissa*, with its central emphasis on the seduction, imprisonment, per-secution, rape, and death of the woman whom he sees as the first fiction-al embodiment of the Persecuted Maiden. *Love and Death in the American Novel* (New York: Stein and Day, 1966), pp. 62–73, 217–90.

lurid Gothic aspects of the story. This process of generic demystification echoes the sexual demystification outlined above, and reinforces that equally demystifying irony of conception that dominates
Fowles's presentation of the *domaine* in this novel. Thus *The
Collector* combines certain melodramatic features of the Gothic
novel — the impregnable cellar, the Persecuted Maiden, the besotted tyrant — with an insistence on the tedium of Miranda's ordeal.[8]
Her experience at Fosters does not evoke the supernatural and it
completely lacks the suggestiveness or excitement of mystery. It is
instead a thoroughly mechanistic affair involving the routine
deployment of bolts, locks, gags, and ropes. These, as the novel
progresses, come to suggest less the imaginative excesses of the
Gothic and more the devastating literalness of pornography.

It is through an examination of the effects and techniques of pornography that *The Collector* develops its ideas about
the artist and the nature of his art. Fowles's approach to both form
and character strikes a keynote of demystification, and his first novel
is the only one in which the young hero — that quester after emotional experience who becomes so familiar in later works — is not
just ironized, but unambiguously presented as the devotee and creator of debased anti-art. Thus Clegg's refusal to engage with experience as potential growth is shown in the hobby which provides
the novel with its central metaphor: collecting.[9]

---

8   The book further reveals its formal elasticity by borrowing from such
     popular genres as fairy-stories, comic books, and the cinema. The rela-
     tionship between Miranda and Clegg evokes *Beauty and the Beast*, and
     she creates a strip-cartoon about Clegg, "The Awful Tale of a Harmless
     Boy," in which the protagonist "starts by being a nice little clerk and
     ends up as a drooling horror-film monster" (203).

9   The fact that Clegg is also Fowles's only working-class male protagonist
     perhaps establishes the conditions under which the hero can be treated
     with such an atypical lack of sympathy. Clegg is so different from his
     author in background, education, and imaginative vigour that he cannot
     function as authorial surrogate to quite the same spiritual and intellectual
     extent as Nick Urfe, Charles Smithson, and David Williams can. But, if
     Fowles does perhaps romanticize himself in his heroes, his refusal to do so
     here facilitates his self-condemnation as a reformed lepidopterist. Fowles
     discusses his erstwhile interest in collecting, and his sense of the hoarding
     of living things as "obviously evil," in an article on conservation, "Weeds,
     Bugs, Americans," in *Sports Illustrated*, 21 Dec. 1970, 84–102.

Miranda expresses Fowles's own sentiments when she says of Clegg: "He's a collector. That's the great dead thing in him" (161). As the figure of de Deukans, *The Magus*'s perverse and aetiolated collector of collections would later show, Fowles perceives this activity as expressing a death wish. The fact that his works regularly discover strategies for the re-imposition of those constraints and categorizations which they also abhor is a paradox which may reflect their author's lingering emotional attachment to a repudiated desire. But on the most accessible level of narrative utterance, *The Collector* both analyzes and condemns the hoarding mentality: the only kind of change to which Clegg can commit himself is progressive devitalization, for his collecting imposes stasis and a kind of living death on organic creatures. Unlike Nick Urfe and Charles Smithson, who engage (even if ambiguously) with motion and growth as possibilities, Clegg seeks only immobilization. His imprisonment of Miranda is an effort to animate, in a paradoxically de-energized way, a cold tableau of erotic possessiveness: "What she never understood [he says] was that with me it was having. Having her was enough. Nothing needed doing. I just wanted to have her, and safe at last" (95).

This suggests that the metaphor of collecting governs Clegg's sexual nature as well as his mentality in general. Observing Clegg's treasures, with their "little wings stretched out all at the same angle," Miranda identifies with them: "poor dead butterflies, my fellow-victims" (127). The sustained comparison between woman and butterfly, which parallels that between man and collector in the novel, provides the terms for Clegg's initial idealization of Miranda:

> Seeing her always made me feel like I was catching a rarity, going up to it very careful, heart-in-mouth as they say. A Pale Clouded Yellow, for instance. I always thought of her like that, I mean words like elusive and sporadic, and very refined — not like the other ones, even the pretty ones. More for the real connoisseur. (9)

The imagery of lepidoptery illuminates Clegg's worship of Miranda as a kind of reification — words like "it" and "connoisseur" imply his perception of her as an object — while also showing the double-edged nature of his reverence. Clegg's language here associates the adored woman with the humanly unattainable perfection suggested by the butterfly's beauty; it also arrogates sexual power exclusively to Clegg himself as collector. Thus when he presents Miranda in his narrative as a butterfly, Clegg is celebrating not only her beauty, but her vulnerability to capture as well. He is elevating her spirituality — the Greeks used the same word for "butterfly" and "soul" — even as he locates her firmly within the non-human world as a particularly fragile example of a lower form of life.

The pervasive metaphor of collecting and the specific imagery of lepidoptery thus effect the simultaneous elevation and debasement of Miranda in the novel. Her sinister admirer inscribes her as both goddess and insect, at once superhuman and subhuman. Both extremes ignore her human reality. In this way the novel develops a critique of male sexual idealization which reinforces and extends its questioning of masculine erotic violence, and which prepares us for Clegg's final degradation of Miranda by showing the contempt informing such worship. Just as Clegg's entomological activities provide him with the imagistic and linguistic means to idolize Miranda, so the aesthetic equivalent of collecting in the book, photography, provides him with the literal means to degrade her. Once Miranda, by attempting to seduce him, has crossed Clegg's psychic dividing line between the stereotypes "madonna" and "whore," he abandons his disproportionate chivalry and expresses his brute power through his camera.

The relationship between Miranda and Clegg culminates in a photographic "rape" where the sexual and possessive meanings of the word "take" (and, by association, of "have") operate interchangeably to reveal the hatred behind Clegg's "love": "I got her garments off and at first she wouldn't do as I said but in the end she lay and stood like I ordered (I refused to take if she did not co-operate). So I got my pictures. I took her till I had no more bulbs left" (110). With Clegg's personal ineffectuality obliterated by the mechanical potency of his camera, the imagery of photography identifies this movement from dubious veneration to violation as essentially one of exposure — not, as Clegg thinks, of Miranda's true nature as a whore, but of his own sexual reverence as a matter of raw power and the need to compel feminine submission to it.

The novel requires us to perceive collecting and photography as pornographic activities: both are seen systematically to dehumanize and objectify organic forms, and to facilitate their consumption by a passive, voyeuristic devotee. Appropriately, Clegg is happiest and most dazzled by Miranda on the night of their first formal dinner, when she looks "just like one of those model girls you see in magazines" (80). This reifying vision is expressed in Clegg's enjoyment of obscene pictures and fetishistic texts: his two favourite books are called *Shoes* and *Secrets of the Gestapo*. In relation to pornography, Clegg is both consumer and producer: his "main idea" in buying a camera is not only to "take butterflies living" but also to photograph "couples" in the fields (15). To pursue lepidoptery is thus by definition to further the cause of pornography, and the obscenity of collecting is two-fold: Clegg wants to possess butterflies not only as dead creatures but also as sets of frozen images, killed as effectively by the camera lens as by the killing-bottle. Miranda, an art student who often draws from life, echoes Paston's identification of photography with death when she looks at some of Clegg's pictures: "They're dead. . . . Not these particularly. All photos. When you draw something it lives and when you photograph it it dies" (55). Remembering the double meaning of the word "take" for Clegg, this suggests that in *The Collector* the urge to photograph is both sexual and aggressive, the desire to punish and kill through violation. Thus the static, debased images of Miranda created during her illness represent a spiritual death suffered before her physical death occurs. The camera becomes an erotic instrument for Clegg, and it is appropriate that his photographic activities should grow from his surreptitious absorption in "some of the books you can buy at shops in Soho, books of stark women and all that" (15).

If, as I have suggested, *The Collector* presents a critique of masculine sexual idealization, it does so by drawing together collecting and photography as twin obscenities in order to show that the erotic worshipper, with his puritanical hatred of the "crude animal thing" (13) and his belief in his own "higher aspirations" (15), is himself prey to the desires he tries to reject.[10] But he masks his

---

10   Woodcock discusses what he sees as "this classic schizophrenia of the male psyche" in his chapter on *The Collector*, pp. 27–43.

impulses with shopworn and sentimental notions of love that protect him from a confrontation with his own sadism: "In my dreams it was always we looked into each other's eyes one day and then we kissed and nothing was said until after" (37). The deflected cruelty of those impulses which dictate Clegg's behaviour makes his frigid chivalry positively menacing in the novel. As Miranda perceives, the role of Ferdinand, of romantic lover, is a mask which hides his reality as Caliban, the would-be violator.

The Collector is unique among Fowles's fictions, not so much because it shows the destructiveness of erotic idealization, but because it deals very explicitly with those processes of reification which tend to operate less obtrusively in later works. By identifying pornography as a product of the imagination which also manifests itself in photography, the novel effectively engages with those aesthetic issues that preoccupy Fowles in subsequent books. For if Clegg is presented, on the one hand, as both obsessional and insane, and his idealizations can be so anatomized because of the grotesque extremes to which he takes them, he is also portrayed as a kind of artist and is implicitly related throughout to the painter G.P. Thus Fosters itself, as well as Miranda's ordeal there and Clegg's pictorial record of her stay, can be seen as his "text," a viciously ironic prefiguration of Conchis's numinous and magical "text," Bourani, in *The Magus*. To express the relationship between these two novels in terms of those analogies with *The Tempest* that both books in different ways invite, Clegg as Caliban might be seen as an inverted forecasting of Conchis — and his lonely house as a parody of both Prospero's island and Conchis's *domaine* — while Paston as a kind of Prospero-figure foreshadows the magus with somewhat less sarcasm.[11]

Both Clegg and G.P. can be perceived as Fowles's earliest published attempts at creating magus-figures. In them he begins to express the contradictions involved in his conception of the artist as

---

11   One of the few interpretive controversies about the novel has centred on the implied relationship between G.P. and Prospero. Some critics and reviewers see G.P. as a father-magician who is nonetheless powerless to help Miranda through her ordeal. Others see the novel as an anti-romance which refuses to incorporate any equivalent of Prospero at all. Olshen (p. 26) and Conradi (pp. 37–38) provide examples of these opposing views.

both ambiguously wise and cruel, like G.P., and besotted at once
with beauty and its obscene inversions, like Clegg. Thus Clegg's
photography identifies the mind which has fashioned Miranda's
prison as pornographic. Confronting the living and vibrant
Miranda, Clegg's strongest impulse is to imagine her immobilized,
silenced, and made submissive, with her beauty reserved for him and
placed at his disposal: "I thought of her sitting on my knees, very
still, with me stroking her soft blonde hair, all out loose as I saw it
after" (36). The aim of pornography is to accomplish just such a
destruction of vitality by effecting a transformation from the specific
to the general — that is, from individual being to mere generic
form, from whole to depersonalized part, and from human subject
to thing. As Angela Carter observes in her analysis of de Sade,
pornography is the process whereby flesh becomes meat, inviting us
to consume what is dead rather than to experience what is alive.[12]
This is the transformation — diametrically opposite to the redemptive one which Miranda hopes throughout to work on Clegg — that
is achieved in his pictures of her as nothing more than a series of
anatomized female parts: "I got the pictures developed and printed
that night. The best ones were with her face cut off. She didn't look
much anyhow with the gag, of course. The best were when she
stood in her high heels, from the back. The tied hands to the bed
made what they call an interesting motif " (110). This suggests that
Clegg, like those male artists who appear in Fowles's later work,
looks upon Miranda as the very material of his art. He uses her
quite literally to construct his "text," and this process of textualizing
a woman gratifies the narcissism of the creator by focusing both her
beauty and her very selfhood on him alone.

      What *The Collector* presents explicitly as an aspect of
pornography — that is, the reification and effective transformation
of the woman into an artefact — Fowles's other fictions usually present as a part of legitimate artistic endeavour. His *œuvre*, as we will
see, seeks elsewhere to valorize or justify a conception of woman as
aesthetic instrument which it here recognizes as persecutory and
immoral, and which it can acknowledge as such because of the mad
extremity of the situation it depicts. Taking a different view of that
stylistic manoeuvre which I analyzed earlier, we might say that *The*

---

12   Angela Carter, *The Sadeian Woman: An Exercise in Cultural History*
      (London: Virago, 1979), pp. 137–50.

Collector's borrowing from grotesque fictional forms like the Gothic novel facilitates a frankness in the examination of such issues which later works seem to disallow. Perhaps the emotional melodrama of the Gothic — together with the portrayal of Clegg as a banal sort of madman — permits the novel clearly to identify as pornographic the kind of gender relations which become typical in Fowles's work. In *Mantissa* he would again create, with less generic specificity, a contrived and preternaturally isolated environment for a warring hero and heroine. Within the anti-*domaine* of another artist-pornographer's feverish and obsessive mind, a similar recognition of the obscenity of such relations becomes possible.

But Clegg and his somewhat more sane variant, Miles Green, are exceptions in the Fowles corpus. When the male protagonist loses Clegg's psychoses while retaining in less lethal forms his basic erotic and aesthetic drives, the sexually suspect machinations of the artist are treated more ambivalently and indirectly in Fowles's work. And this process of displacing the creative, predatory male in the direction of less anti-social behavioural options begins in some ways with the characterization of G.P.: presented as aggressive and controlling but not as insane, Miranda's mentor partakes of both the magus-figure's knowledge and the Fowlesian hero's erotic susceptibility. Through both G.P. and Clegg, then, Fowles's first novel postulates a link between art and anti-art which later fictions, notably *The Ebony Tower*, explore in more detail.

This contradictory sense of the textualization of women as at once erotically desirable, creatively necessary, and morally dubious, stalks Fowles's work in more or less subtle and disguised forms. *The Collector* deals with it ambiguously, by developing a distinction between Clegg and G.P., art and pornography, which it evidently does not intend to be fully convincing. Thus the novel equates the two men, and the modes of representation for which they stand, as much as it separates them. It also suggests that the only place where the attitudes of Clegg and Paston can be held in diametrical opposition is the immature, equally idealizing mind of Miranda. In this way the book communicates a radical ambivalence about the artist and his feminine material which, unable to resolve, it acknowledges as problematic. In order to appreciate this, we must consider in more detail both the processes of Clegg's anti-art and the presentation of Miranda, for it is she who stands in the novel between the collector and his close spiritual relative, the artist.

• • •

Clegg's pictures of Miranda as faceless female commodity elicit his strongest erotic reactions: "The photographs . . . I used to look at them sometimes. I could take my time with them. They didn't talk back at me" (103). This suggests the novel's conception of pornography as autoerotic, an expression of the collector's solipsism and his self-involved disengagement from experience. For Clegg is quintessentially a "masturbating worm" (109) in temperament as well as in practice, and this sexual narcissism is also a metaphor for that alienation implied in his solitary life, his voyeurism, and his remote house. In *The Collector*, onanism is not simply a physical activity, but a state of mind and being as well. The autoeroticism of pornography focalizes[13] its concern with power, particularly as a function of the consumer rather than the consumed.

That Clegg enjoys Miranda's powerlessness is shown in the disproportionate relationship between his elaborate security measures and her obvious vulnerability. This systematic application of strength to evident physical weakness evokes the pornography of torture, perhaps learnt from Clegg's books on Gestapo techniques. In representing the sensate being as an object to be used rather than a subject to be engaged with, the pornographic work safely insulates its consumer from experience, especially from responsibility and relationship. In so doing it offers the consumer a chance to experience himself, and by implication his own power, through a safely objectified agent. The novel suggests that, in its endorsement of alienated and solipsistic pleasure, pornography is similar to sexual idealization: both rely on distance and reification, the one to accomplish defilement, the other to promote a dubious and ruthless worship. In *The Collector*, pornography and idealization are revealed as part of a single continuum. Thus Clegg is effectively a kind of Pygmalion, for he attempts to assimilate a woman entirely

---

13   Throughout this study, I am using the word "focalize" not in Mieke Bal's sense, but more simply — in the sense specified by one of its definitions in *Webster's Dictionary*: "to bring to a focus." Bal's definition appears in her *Narratology: Introduction to the Theory of Narrative* (Toronto: University of Toronto Press, 1985).

to his fantasies and he loves not her, but his own self-flattering creation of her:

> She drew pictures and I looked after my collection (in my dreams). It was always she loving me and my collection, drawing and colouring them; working together in a beautiful modern house in a big room with one of those huge glass windows; meetings there of the Bug Section, where instead of saying almost nothing in case I made mistakes we were the popular host and hostess. (10)

If Clegg's photography defines him within the world of the novel as a pornographer, his memoir itself identifies him for the reader as also an author. And here the processes and mechanisms of the pornographic text as the novel depicts it become equated with those of the literary text as Clegg (via Fowles) produces it. Through Clegg's narrative, *The Collector* implicitly invites us to see the pornographer as also a figure of authorial power in a more literary and hence artistically legitimate sense. By association then, Clegg — even before the book permits any comparison between himself and Paston — communicates Fowles's vision of the author as a potential collector who expresses his reifying fantasies of women and immobilizes them for his own pleasure in narrative. Clegg's memoir abounds in stylistic mannerisms which enact linguistically those manipulations of Miranda that the narrative itself describes.

In the above extract, grammatical elisions reveal Clegg's deepest perceptions: his view of Miranda as a function of himself is shown here as a failure to discriminate between them in language. So the word "working," preceded by no explicit clarifying pronoun, draws together Clegg, Miranda, and the butterfly collection into a wilfully homogenized whole. Later in the passage he shifts illogically from the mistake-making "I" to the hostly "we," whose *joint* accomplishments compensate for *his* individual inadequacy. Clegg's language has a disconcerting tendency to consume or absorb Miranda's subjectivity, as if writing about her were yet another way of appropriating her being. Through such attempts to control and imaginatively possess Miranda, Clegg reinforces and communes with the self-gratifying structures of his own mind. Here the novel, by linguistically enacting a pornographic process, associates pornography with authorship and the production of texts generally. In this way *The Collector* prefigures Fowles's ongoing sense of authorial power as always potentially unethical, and the narrative artist as onanistically preoccupied with fantasies of coercion.

The novel embodies and questions various aspects of the ethos of pornography while implicitly extending its observations to narrative as a whole. Clegg's memoir further enacts his obsession with control stylistically by keeping monotonously to the simple present tense and so treating the experience it describes as concluded, contained, and effectively dead.[14] For Clegg, language not only facilitates appropriation; it acts as a kind of embalming fluid, artificially preserving a past incapable of touching or altering him. Through language Clegg reifies the past as efficiently as he reifies Miranda, and this disengagement from historical time precludes any awareness of futurity. Instead, his narrative denies progress and growth in favour of cyclical recurrence. *The Collector* ends with Clegg quietly preparing for his next "guest": "I have not made up my mind about Marian (another M! I heard the supervisor call her name). This time it won't be love, it would just be for the interest of the thing and to compare them[.] . . . Of course I would make it clear from the start who's boss and what I expect" (283).

These details locate Miranda retrospectively in a projected sequence of victims, as Clegg shifts effortlessly from the individual to the generic woman, from his one-and-only to her replacement. His "guests" have, like their names, become almost interchangeable.[15] At the end of the novel, then, Clegg is planning not action but re-enactment, the compulsive remaking of a situation and an erotic paradigm which he cannot escape. It is his love of stasis and his quest to discover and preserve it within time that finally imprison the jailer, while assimilating him into the realm of

---

14   A point made by Simon Loveday, *The Romances of John Fowles* (New York: St. Martin's Press, 1985), pp. 20–21.

15   For a reading of the repeated letter "M" as the sign of a mother-obsession which Clegg lives out through kidnapping, see Patricia V. Beatty, "John Fowles's Clegg: Captive Landlord of Eden," *Ariel* 13, No. 3 (1982), 73–81.

myth and folklore as the typological equivalent of Bluebeard.[16] In *The Collector*, narrative is thus at once mimetic and metaphoric: it creates the very closed circle which it describes and, as the story prepares to turn back on itself at the end, onanism becomes not just an image pattern but a structural principle in the novel as well. The idea of control is also centralized structurally through the placement of the novel's three chapters: Clegg's monologue literally contains and envelops Miranda's in a mimetic recapitulation of their situation.

Once again, Clegg's narrative strategies suggest an effort to appropriate and control Miranda which his memoir both depicts and enacts. The narrative technique further seeks to suppress her individuality, not only by incorporating her fragmented image into Clegg's obscene pictorial text, but by encoding her in his written text as a kind of imminently replaceable generic woman. This prepares us for the identical but less obtrusive use that Fowles's own fictions make of such strategies.

The rest of this chapter and the following ones will show how Fowles's works covertly entrap their heroines while overtly seeking to liberate them. They will trace the ways in which the heroine's uniqueness is suppressed through the generalization of her identity within a narrative that usually, like the collector's, relates ambiguously to change and evinces a nostalgia for the mythic and timeless. The similarities between the effects and processes of Clegg's narrative and Fowles's own texts suggest again the frankness with which he treats the hidden agendas of authorship in *The Collector*. Fowles has declared the close personal relationship between himself and his material here and has described the book, appropriately enough, as "really a casebook for me."[17]

It should be noted, however, that the implied acknowledgement of the author as almost inevitably a kind of collector is

---

16   The direct inspiration for the novel was a performance of Bartók's opera *Duke Bluebeard's Castle*, which Fowles saw in the 1950s. He was struck by "the symbolism of the man imprisoning women underground"; in Newquist, p. 219. Fowles's essay on Hardy considers the desire for absolute isolation with the beloved woman as an aspect of the male author's creative drive.

17   Campbell, 457.

partially offset by the novel's attempt to present Miranda as a narrator who pursues strategies other than Clegg's, and Paston as an
artist who at least grasps the need to respect human integrity. It
seems that, in Miranda's diary, Fowles tries to delineate narrative
principles different from Clegg's and, by implicitly aligning himself
with these (if not always with Miranda herself), to explore more
positive and vital creative possibilities. But here the ambiguous
depiction of G.P. acts indirectly to control Miranda and curtail her
creativity in ways which reaffirm that connection between artist and
collector which the diary seems designed to undermine. But
Miranda's narrative, while its embedding in Clegg's memoir suggests stylistically the triumph of the author-as-pornographer, does
repudiate the voicelessness which pornography attempts to impose
on women.[18] It also dominates the novel in terms of length, and
symbolically opens Clegg's closed, solitary world by functioning as
the vehicle for some of Fowles's own philosophical beliefs.[19] In
Miranda and Clegg, the extrovert clashes with the solipsist, and
although her hopes for a "brave new world" are overwhelmed by
her experience of a "sick" one (245), the expansiveness of her perspective is intended as life-enhancing: "This is the worst possible
time in history to die. Space-travel, science, the whole world wak-
ing up and stretching itself. A new age is beginning. I know it's
dangerous. But it's wonderful to be alive in it. I love, I adore, *my*
age" (234, emphasis in original).

　　　Miranda's vitality is expressed in literary terms by the
thematic eclecticism of her narrative and its fluidity of style. Unlike
Clegg, she does not seal off experience into compartments: she uses

---

18　　Susan Griffin, *Pornography and Silence: Culture's Revenge Against
　　　Nature* (New York: Harper & Row, 1981), p. 202.

19　　Miranda rather than Clegg introduces Fowles's own philosophical cate-
　　　gories of the Few and the Many: she feels herself one of a "band of peo-
　　　ple . . . [t]he Few," who must stand against the corrupting vulgarity of
　　　"all the rest" (208). She also expresses Fowles's liberal political beliefs in
　　　her anti-nuclear protesting, and his critical views on contemporary litera-
　　　ture in her negative comments on *Saturday Night and Sunday Morning*
　　　(230). See Fowles, "I Write Therefore I am," *Evergreen Review*, No. 33
　　　(1964), 16–17, 89–90; Campbell, 455–69. We should observe, howev-
　　　er, that certain critics, notably Huffaker (p. 76), emphatically reject the
　　　idea of Miranda as Fowles's mouthpiece.

both past and present tenses, thinks often about the future, and even switches genres within her chosen diary form. She sometimes renders conversation as drama (132–36, 182–84), writes a letter to her sister (124), tells Clegg fairy-stories (187), and in her last entries lapses into free verse (258–60). Miranda's diary thus prefigures the association, developed later in *The French Lieutenant's Woman*, of generic rigidity with imaginative and existential devitalization. Neither does Miranda share Clegg's obsession with closure; her narrative ends with death still only a possibility and it is left to Clegg to "finish off" Miranda both literally and linguistically. Thus her cry — "Oh God oh God do not let me die. / God do not let me die. / Do not let me die" (260) — is contrasted with the finality of Clegg's: "She is in the box I made, under the appletrees. It took me three days to dig the hole. . . . I don't think many could have done it. I did it scientific" (282). The link implied here between the drive towards closure and the urge to possess foreshadows the connection made in *The French Lieutenant's Woman* between narrative indeterminacy and the autonomy of both characters and author. From very early on in his *œuvre* Fowles seeks to identify closure, the formal enshrining of narrative stability, with arbitrary power or death.

• • •

The contrasting narrative approaches of Miranda and Clegg are meant to signal a dialogue in the novel between art and pornography: Miranda is associated with a vital and imaginative creativity which seems very different from that represented by Clegg. When she reviles him for preferring the most technically realistic of her drawings of a bowl of fruit — "That's the worst, . . . [t]hat's a clever little art student's picture" (60) — she is expressing what the novel on one level presents as the spiritual opposition between the literal or clinically explicit and the truly imaginative or mysterious, between pornography as a kind of persecution and art as a kind of liberation. Thus Clegg communicates his aggression verbally by appropriating the word "artistic" and applying it to his own pictures. In describing Miranda's bound hands as "an interesting motif" and equating "[a]rt-photographs" with "photos you wouldn't want to be published" (106), Clegg effectively imposes his will on Miranda through a violation of both her values and her vocabulary. Miranda draws the distinction between pornographer and artist when she says to Clegg: "I knew you didn't [know anything about art]. You wouldn't imprison an innocent person if you did" (43).

This appears to develop in the novel an association between art and femininity on the one hand, pornography and masculinity on the other. In terms of *The Tempest* analogy, the "magic" of art seems to be focused on Miranda, "she who ought to be admired," while Clegg embodies the "slave" (245) Caliban's artistic impoverishment, sexual violence, and confused yearning for beauty. But, the text's ambiguities prevent such a simple identification, just as they undermine the judgement of the book's first reviewers by precluding any view of the novel as a mere clash between monolithic forces of good and evil. We have already seen how Clegg's authorial function invites us to extend the novel's critique of pornography to narrative art in general; Clegg's use of the word "artistic" to describe his productions becomes ambiguously appropriate in context. Similarly, the apparent connection between femininity and creativity is by no means unproblematic in *The Collector*. It is essential to examine the ways in which Fowles complicates the premises of the novel and the extent to which the text itself reveals an allegiance to those values and processes which it rejects.

• • •

The novel's potential for moral over-simplification is undercut principally by its presentation of Miranda. Bruce Woodcock's comments on her ambiguities are worth quoting at length:

> Clegg embodies [the] rationalistic, possessive male principle, whereas Miranda herself embodies in part a Zen-like intuition of essences and interrelatedness. By implication, this is the antidote to Clegg's self-centred male egoism. Given Fowles's own predisposition, this suggests a privileging of Miranda's narrative, but the book does not fully endorse it. She is, as Fowles himself has pointed out, "arrogant in her ideas, a prig, a liberal-humanist snob." . . . While many of the values

> and ideas Miranda expresses are used critically to ana-
> lyse Clegg, the book's strategy is to intertwine this
> evaluation with Miranda's reflections on her friend
> and mentor George Paston in such a way as to broad-
> en the impact of the analysis. . . . Unwittingly,
> Miranda provides in G.P. a mirror image for Clegg,
> another man whom she admires but whom the reader
> can see as a version of Clegg.[20]

This suggests the central role which Paston plays in the novel, despite the fact that he reaches us entirely through Miranda's narrative. Her diary's intense preoccupation with him and its tendency to quote him repeatedly imply that it is not so much Miranda but her mentor who is associated with authoritative creativity in the book. Thus Miranda's views on photography are originally Paston's (159), and it is he who sees art as concerned with "essences" (131) and the transcending of personality in its exploration of "the furthest limits of . . . self" (159). In the first fictional expression of a pattern that becomes consistent in Fowles's work, the burgeoning creativity of a potential woman artist is placed under the indirect but potent control of a creatively mature male artist. Neither can Miranda's many references to Paston be seen as her effective textualization of him — a way of possessing him by appropriating his wisdom, in the same way as the narrator of *The French Lieutenant's Woman* textualizes and takes possession of the nineteenth century by appropriating (as we will see) the works of Victorian poets and thinkers within his own narrative frame. For Miranda never adopts a personal perspective of her own on Paston's opinions; she is basically unquestioning of his views on life and art, and her commitment to G.P. makes her more his passive mouth-

---

20   Woodcock, p. 34. The quotation from Fowles appears originally in his
      "Preface to a New Edition" of *The Aristos* (New York: New American
      Library, 1970), p. 10. Fowles's work seeks consistently to associate mas-
      culinity with an overtly denigrated scientific rationalism, and femininity
      with an apparently valorized imaginative and emotional susceptibility.
      But this study contends that, despite such categorization, truly creative
      imaginative power in Fowles's *œuvre* resides with men, while the non-
      analytical capacities of women come to guarantee their instrumentality
      rather than their artistic stature.

piece than a creative and independent reworker of his intellectual or artistic products.

Significantly, it is through Paston that the book sets up its most striking irony: in committing herself to the artist-mentor, Miranda is effectively choosing one collector over another, for both Clegg and G.P. exploit and try to control women — one through an icy celibacy and the other through an indifferent promiscuity. Paston tells Miranda: "I've met dozens of women and girls like you. Some I've known well, some I've seduced against their better nature and my better nature, two I've even married" (176). If G.P. can be seen as a forerunner of later, more developed magus-figures, he partakes fully of the sinister cruelty of his successors; his attempts to initiate the existential novice into life are often more threatening and suspect than even Conchis's. Thus Miranda imagines, with disconcerting relish, a life of violence and misery with G.P.: "[H]e deceives me, he leaves me, he is brutal and cynical with me, I am in despair" (235). Despite her proviso — "[b]ut there is the closeness of spirit" (235) — the sadistic nature of this fantasy and Miranda's enthralled perception of G.P.'s behaviour as life-enhancing bring an element of sado-masochistic sexuality to the relationship between magus and initiate which Fowles's later work avoids.

In fact, this crucial teacher-pupil configuration never again involves a female initiate. In *The Magus*, "The Ebony Tower," and *Daniel Martin* particularly, the Fowlesian heroine moves into a more or less asexual association with the hierophant, while the young male protagonist is directly involved with him as existential — and usually artistic — apprentice. This allows Fowles to deal in subsequent fictions with the magus-figure as a kind of creative father to the younger artist while marginalizing the potentially threatening creative woman more decisively. It is a way of guaranteeing the masculinity of the artist and the aesthetic materiality of the woman. In *The Collector*, however, Miranda's masochistic response to G.P. associates the two implicitly with the pornographic impulses they despise. Thus G.P. collects different women as assiduously as Clegg collects one, and he reminds Miranda of her generalized feminine function when, addressing her as *"une" princesse lointaine*, he underlines the *"une"* "very heavily" (177).

Paston is, furthermore, as adept at psychological violence as his apparent opposite, Clegg. He dallies with Miranda's friend

Antoinette, whom he evidently despises (167–68), and disregards the pain which this causes Miranda. His negative response to her work is like an assault: "It was as if he had turned and hit me with his fist, . . . [i]t hurt like a series of slaps across the face" (158). His passion too is condescending: "I like the way even the shallowest of women become beautiful when their clothes are off and they think they're taking a profound and wicked step" (176). Antoinette's comment on G.P. to Miranda — "Darling, he'll murder you" (168) — is thus a shrewd summary of the basic direction which his sexual impulses take, and this unnerving observation hovers over Miranda's assertion near the end of her ordeal: "His promiscuity is creative. Vital. Even though it hurts. He creates love and life and excitement around him" (246). This is not just the cry of a repentant puritan, and the irony here is that Miranda's narrative has itself failed to support her conviction. Instead it has revealed G.P. as truculent, pompous, and cruel, his seductiveness motivated by a wish to dominate and control. Even Miranda has a vague sense, when G.P. murmurs to her of Botticelli, Eve, and Anadyomene, that he is "drawing a net round" her (176). Like Clegg, G.P. has an ambiguous ability to be both lover and jailer.

Clearly Miranda is no more in control of all the implications of her narrative than Clegg is of his. As a narrator, she is not only intellectually and artistically dependent on G.P.; in her idealization of him, she too partakes in certain ways of the creative dubiety of Clegg himself. Some of the novel's darkness is thus generated by Miranda, both in her uncritical acceptance of G.P.'s sometimes "trite existential maxims"[21] and in her unintended presentation of him as a sort of death's head at the feast: "And the face is too broad. Battered, worn; battered and worn and pitted into a bit of a mask" (171). Through Paston as well as Clegg, then, Fowles begins to develop his sense of the artist as a morally suspect man, and of art as in many ways a sinister activity.

In her narrative Miranda refers to a picture on G.P.'s Chinese bowl of "two fiendishly excited horsemen chasing a timid little fallow-deer" (176). Not apparently grasping the implications of the image, she makes no comment on it, but it constitutes a *mise*

---

21   Karen M. Lever, "The Education of John Fowles," *Critique* 21, No. 2 (1978), 91.

en abyme[22] of one of the novel's themes: the destructive relationship between sex and power, and the inevitable involvement (as Fowles sees it) of a controlling and predatory male erotic dynamic in the production of art. This image makes clear that the difference between Paston and Clegg is more one of degree than of kind, for it draws together the two men whom Miranda perceives as so different[23] and reveals the level on which they are united. Intellectually irreconcilable, Paston and Clegg are identical in their male perception of the desired woman as actual or potential victim. Both enjoy the physical and emotional fragility of their shared quarry, for each seeks to bully Miranda out of her artistic ambitions and into a relationship that emphasizes only her sexuality. Thus Clegg fragments and objectifies Miranda in his pictures while also controlling her through his written text. Paston dismisses female creativity in general — "most women just want to be good at something, they've got good-at minds" (159) — while assuring Miranda that "the art of love's [her] line: not the love of art" (160).

Mainly through Paston, Fowles explores the erotic will-to-power as a function not only of the collector temperament but of the imaginatively powerful artistic temperament as well. Pornographer and artist, killer and painter, are by no means the opposites they seem. Rather, they represent two aspects and two

---

22   For a discussion of Fowles's first three novels in terms of the extensive use which each makes of various *mises en abyme*, see David Walker, "Subversion of Narrative in the Work of André Gide and John Fowles," *Comparative Criticism: A Yearbook*, ed. Elinor Shaffer (Cambridge: Cambridge University Press, 1980), II, pp. 187–212.

23   But Miranda's narrative does at times imply a possible unconscious sense of the similarities between them. This could be suggested in her eliding of pronouns when she shifts focus from Paston to Clegg. The best example is from two entries midway through the diary; she concludes one with: "And G.P. was *sweet*. That's just what he was. Even though he never apologized" (169, emphasis in original). Her next entry begins at once with: "I don't trust him. He's bought this house" (170). Nothing in the grammar here clarifies the movement from Paston to Clegg. This awareness evidently remains unconscious in Miranda, however, and the closest she gets to seriously questioning her mentor's behaviour is the poignant and unanswered: "But is G.P. Mr. Knightley?" (218).

manifestations of a single attitude, and to argue in this way for a link between obscenity and art is to take issue with the accepted critical belief in their simple opposition in Fowles's work.[24] Such an approach further illuminates the contradictions at work in the novel, itself the product of a male creative artist and reformed collector.

The critique of male sexual idealization offered by the novel, and the aggression which informs it, is rendered ambivalent by *The Collector*'s implied fascination with those forms of erotic coercion which it also condemns morally. Fowles's early commitment to credibility of character[25] means that the depiction of that sexual power-play which he seeks to reject is precise and convincing. The novel at once exposes and exploits such behaviour, attacking a certain kind of titillation while itself eliciting a similarly titillated response — at least from the male reader.[26] Barry Olshen has shown that the book's narrative technique itself reinforces this ambiguity by indirectly inviting the reader to that voyeurism of which the text disapproves:

> Because of the conventional assumption in the diary form that the writer is the only reader (or, as Miranda says, that she is "talking to herself"), we must assume that we are getting a very private glimpse into the innermost thoughts and feelings of the diarist. We are thus ironically required to imagine ourselves in an analogous role to Clegg's, the role of the voyeur,

---

24   The best summary of this view is in Palmer, pp. 29–47.

25   Loveday, p. 155; Newquist, p. 223: "For *me* the obligation is to present my characters realistically. They must be credible human beings even if the circumstances they are in are 'incredible'" (emphasis in original).

26   Woodcock, p. 39: "One imagines *The Collector* to be a quite different reading experience for a woman than it is for a man, partly because for the male reader . . . the book unlocks a male fantasy which has had general currency at least since de Sade, even while exposing its fundamental roots in a desire for power over women." In this way *The Collector* prepares us for that construction, in *The French Lieutenant's Woman*, of a novel's implied readership as exclusively male.

reading what was never intended for us to read, and gaining vicarious enjoyment from this experience.[27]

In condemning pornography, then, *The Collector* uses with some dexterity the pornographer's own tools, while identifying them implicitly as also the tools of the creative artist. It thus introduces that ambivalence in Fowles's work about art in general and narrative in particular: if the text cannot escape from what it also abhors, then art itself is potentially both corrupt and corrupting. When G.P. laments the loss of innocence in the female sex (176), he suggests why Miranda's narratorial efforts in the novel must end and her diary be contained by Clegg's memoir. For Fowles, the woman author/artist is not only aspiring to wield an inappropriate power, but is sullying that purity which — as G.P.'s efforts to imprison Miranda in the role of infatuated protégée imply — the artist himself relies on as material and inspiration. Paston is Fowles's first acknowledgement of the artist's implication in brutality and despotism, as well as his admission of the problematic relationship between the artist and women.

The Collector exposes not only the artist's desire for control, but his urge to gain that control by assimilating women into his art. Clegg's photographs of Miranda may parody artworks and contrast spiritually with G.P.'s drawing of a nude, but both men produce images of women. Clegg's pictures accomplish and record Miranda's emotional destruction while she clings to G.P.'s drawing as a consoling extension of himself: "I've been looking at some of the lines not as lines, but as things he has touched" (197). One type of picture is presented as morally repulsive and the other as aesthetically beautiful in its "simplicity of line, hatred of fussiness" (197). The ambiguity here is that these pictures, like their creators, are at once separate and joined. Opposite in spirit and intention perhaps, they are equal in that both creators have observed and, to differing extents, have objectified the women they depict. Throughout Fowles's work, this is the paradox of art and the double bind of the creative gift: in seeking to express and celebrate the individual, art objectifies and generalizes women; in signalling (as Fowles's fictions overtly do) the importance of freedom, art inaugurates other kinds of imprisonment. Clegg's concealed cellar thus

---

27   Olshen, p. 24.

becomes a metaphor for the darker and more destructive agendas of art itself.

The novel's ambiguities and tensions focus sharply in its portrayal of Miranda. Although Fowles envisaged her as "an existentialist heroine . . . groping for her own authenticity," and as "the kind of being humanity so desperately needs,"[28] Miranda never attains full maturity or completely realizes her selfhood in the book: "Her tragedy is that she will never live to achieve authenticity. Her triumph is that one day she would have done so."[29] Forced into being by confinement, Miranda's self-confrontation brings movement into a static situation while apparently constructing her as a symbolic counterpart to Clegg. Despite this, Miranda dies suspecting but not fully perceiving the dubious aspects of G.P.'s character. Something of an erotic worshipper herself, Miranda believes in Paston as the embodiment of right values and their symbolic equivalent, good aesthetic judgement. She is even committed to his disquieting vision of herself as a disturbance and a disease (214, 177). Thus Miranda's diary records not only growth but a Clegg-like capacity for idealization and fantasy which converts even the violence of Paston into beatitude: "G.P., I shall be hurt, lost, battered and buffeted. But it will be like being in a gale of light, after this black hole. It's simply that. He has the secret of life in him" (247).

If Miranda uses G.P. imaginatively in much the same way as Clegg uses her, then the novel is deliberately refusing to imitate the collector by idealizing its own heroine. The complexity of the book consists in its examination of the artist as not only a collector, but as a deviser of strategies for resisting the temptation to collect: G.P. sends Miranda away even though he desires her (216). But in this attempt to depict sexual idealization without succumbing to it, the novel insists upon Miranda's immaturity and incompleteness, and this inevitably influences our perception of her as an artist. Miranda's death may be appropriate, given the characterization of Clegg and the intentions of the novel, but it also invites us to see her not only as a person who never grows up, but as an aspiring artist who never becomes the true custodian of art's power. Despite her creative efforts, Miranda remains a *potential* artist as

---

28   Newquist, p. 225; Fowles, *Aristos*, p. 10.

29   Newquist, p. 225.

well as a *potential* existentialist — always learning without really achieving. Her death is thus a thoroughly ambiguous narrative move. For while on the one hand it is an escape, a symbolic victory of the will to freedom, on the other it suggests an act of authorial control akin to Clegg's — and Clegg is, after all, the one who effects Miranda's death on the level of plot, just as Fowles effects it on the level of ultimate narrative authority. If Miranda is dead, she can never move from the creatively immature position of art student to the creatively powerful one of artist; never coming of age, she remains a protégée without ever becoming a competitor. This means that Miranda is kept a novice and willing recipient of G.P.'s ideas on life and art: he advises her to give up her artistic vocation and adopt a sexual one — "you don't really stand a dog's chance anyhow. You're too pretty" (161) — and he wants less to teach her about art than to marry her (214). Similarly for Paston's double, Clegg, Miranda is safely confined in images of his devising and cannot herself become the authoritative creator of images. If we postulate a logic of authorial substitution at work here, as it is elsewhere in Fowles's fiction, we might say that Miranda functions in these ways with regard to Fowles himself. Death is thus a way of containing Miranda's talent and freeing the book's various artist-figures from any responsibility to present their heroine as a mature female artist with the ability to challenge male creative hegemony. By these means, Miranda's relationship with art is kept indirect and she is encoded as an essentially passive, erotically significant artefact in the novel.

Miranda's authorial power is further compromised by the fact that her diary, rather like Sarah Woodruff's oral "autobiographical" narrative in *The French Lieutenant's Woman*, is a feminine creation effectively controlled by men. Its placement within Clegg's memoir affirms this by proclaiming that very control which the novel's structure is also designed to question. Dominated thematically by Clegg and G.P., the diary, through its mediation of Paston, effectively makes Miranda into his interpreter, the priestess to his oracle, who conveys the artist's wisdom in the same way as Diana, the art student in "The Ebony Tower," interprets Breasley to his hearers, David Williams and ourselves. Through Miranda, art and anti-art conduct their dialogue, and a woman's writing — like her life — is implicitly dominated by men. *The Collector* initiates that pattern in Fowles's work whereby the creative heroine is strategically constrained by the text, and Fowles's unease with feminine artistic aspiration, somewhat de-emphasized in his second novel, *The Magus*, is crucial to his third, *The French Lieutenant's Woman*. Here Sarah's creativity is textually controlled in complex ways, while Fowles's second portrayal of a woman diarist is less sympathetic than his first: Ernestina Freeman's journal, as male-centred as Miranda's, is ridiculed by the narrator as creatively worthless. It seems that, in Fowles's fictions, women must *live* creatively as inspirations and examples to men, without ever *working* creatively in their own right.

• • •

Fowles's first novel also engages with those broader issues of (masculine) creativity that return in subsequent works — the artist's involvement with the creative productions of the past, and the relation between art and criticism. *The Collector*'s investigation of these issues is not especially complex, largely because the indirect, theoretical relationship between Clegg and G.P. does not permit that focusing on creative paternity which the relationship between Nick and Conchis facilitates in *The Magus*. Instead, the novel communicates through Paston a general unease at the artist's struggles to express himself in the presence of other artworks, a theme that later fictions delineate with more precision. Thus G.P. tells Miranda that the Rembrandt self-portrait in the Kenwood Gallery "has the supreme mastery" (155) which he will never attain, and the artist implicitly compensates for his limitations by asserting his own irreducible uniqueness: G.P. "once lived under the shadow of Braque and suddenly [he] woke up one morning to realize that all he had done for five years was a lie, because it was based on Braque's eyes and sensibilities and not his own" (162). Miranda evidently admires G.P.'s fierce determination to "paint in [his] own way, live in [his] own way, speak in [his] own way" (176).

But the vehemence with which G.P. declares his freedom from creative influence is itself suspect, for his own work is presented in the novel in terms of its predecessors: Miranda describes the woman in his drawing as having "a heavy Maillol body" (197) and her aunt Caroline regards G.P.'s painting as "second-rate Paul Nash" (153). Furthermore, the inevitable presence of such formidable creative authorities is foregrounded in the book by Miranda's efforts to teach Clegg about art, her copying from the work of other artists (137), and her formulating of her own ambitions in relation to their work: "I want to paint like Berthe Morisot, I don't mean with her colours or forms or anything physical, but with her simplicity and light" (131). Thus *The Collector* neither resolves nor fully thematizes the issue of the artist's creative ancestry, which hovers in the text as a vague *locus* of anxious speculation. The novel's implicit need to valorize the artist's individual vision as absolutely self-created is seen in G.P.'s dismissal of Miranda's derivative painting as a kind of photography: "You're saying something here about Nicholson or Passmore. Not about yourself. You're using a camera" (159). This reviling of the aesthetically unoriginal through a metaphor which the novel itself applies to debased art suggests the text's paradoxical wish to claim for the artist a degree of creative independence which it also indirectly acknowledges as impossible.

A similar contradiction informs the book's attitude towards criticism. G.P. derides critics for "spiel[ing] away about technical accomplishment. Absolutely meaningless, that sort of jargon" (159). But the novel consistently sidesteps the issue of G.P.'s own problematic involvement in critical activity; his explaining of the Rembrandt to Miranda and his brutal response to her work are effectively acts of criticism performed by a self-proclaimed hater of critics. *The Collector* deals with this paradox not by clearly recognizing the artist as a kind of critic and reader of other artists' texts, but by seeking to maintain an irresolute and unconvincing distinction between artist and critic. This distinction is treated as less central to the novel than the equally irresolute one between artist and pornographer, and is less strongly developed by its narrative techniques. Nevertheless, the book's tentative engagement with the relationship between art and criticism, as well as its overstated claims for the artist's creative independence, introduce a nexus of ideas which Fowles's later fictions explore more specifically and vigorously.

The Collector is both an interesting text in itself and an important initiation of the reader into Fowles's work. Although it presents certain features — notably the undereducated and psychologically disturbed male protagonist — to which Fowles has not yet returned, it also erects a skeleton of ideas around which other, more complex fictions are built. Fowles's first novel may not pursue the extreme structural instability and aesthetic experimentation of *The French Lieutenant's Woman*; it may lack the intellectual daring of *The Ebony Tower*, the sweep of *The Magus*, and the sheer solidity of *Daniel Martin*. But it achieves a focusing on crucial problems of creativity and gender which facilitates their later sophisticated exploration. Deliberately concentrated in its view and restricted in its scope, *The Collector* is an effective starting point for the dense elaborations of Fowles's more ambitious fictions.

2
THE MAGUS

The second of Fowles's published novels, *The Magus*, appeared in 1966. It was written much earlier, however. Fowles first drafted the novel in 1952–53, just as he was leaving Greece after teaching for two years at a private boarding school, the Anargyrios School, on the island of Spetsai.[1] He then worked sporadically on the book until 1964 when, after publishing both *The Collector* and *The Aristos*, he "collated and rewrote all the previous drafts" of *The Magus*.[2] Apart from the tantalizing (if inconclusive) possibilities which Fowles's spell as a schoolmaster in Greece raises for an autobiographical reading of the novel, the genesis of *The Magus* in the 1950s — more than a decade before the appearance of *The Collector* — raises certain textual issues which should be considered before any discussion of the novel itself is undertaken. As Fowles himself has stated, the imaginative conception of *The Magus* so early in his career means that "in every way except that of mere publishing date, it is a first novel."[3] In discussing the book, Fowles has emphasized the technical difficulties which he experienced as a first-time novelist — "my strongest memory is of constantly having

---

1   Fowles mentions his Greek experiences and their literary significance in his Forewords to *The Magus: A Revised Version* (London: Jonathan Cape, 1977) and *Poems* (New York: The Ecco Press, 1973). But he is well known for his reticence about this period in his life.

2   Fowles, Foreword to *The Magus: A Revised Version*, p. 5.

3   Fowles, Foreword to *The Magus: A Revised Version*, p. 5.

to abandon drafts because of an inability to describe what I wanted"[4]
— and he has declared the novel to be not only "haphazard," but
"essentially where a tyro taught himself to write novels — beneath
its narrative, a notebook of an exploration, often erring and miscon-
ceived, into an unknown land."[5]

In view of these facts of composition and Fowles's interpretation of them, it would seem logical in a study of his fiction to
place *The Magus* first: the story clearly began to engage Fowles's
imaginative energies long before *The Collector* appeared in print.
Some critics accept Fowles's view of *The Magus* as effectively a first
novel,[6] and by implication as a kind of *Ur*-novel for the corpus.
According to this reading, it is in *The Magus* rather than in *The
Collector* — and presumably in the early drafts of the former as well
as in the printed text — that Fowles first articulated those themes
and motifs which have continued to preoccupy him. Thus Bourani,
not Fosters, is technically the first of the lost *domaines*, Julie
Holmes rather than Miranda Grey becomes the first incarnation of
the *princesse lointaine*, and Conchis rather than Paston is the first
magician-figure in Fowles's work. In many ways this reading makes
sense. It allows us, for example, to account for the odd-seeming
portrait of G.P. in *The Collector*. Puzzlement as to why Fowles's
first presentation of the magus should have been so ironic is
resolved if we see behind Paston the much more awesome and vital
(although by no means unambiguous) figure of Maurice Conchis
emerging through the various drafts of *The Magus*.

This reading also implicitly acknowledges that *The Magus*
had deeply absorbed its author for a number of years. Not only
did he work on it for some thirteen years before its appearance in
1966, but he returned to it later in his career and issued a revised
version of the novel in 1977. Perhaps the words used by Fowles
in the Foreword to this revision to describe his sense of the novel
during the 1950s are equally applicable to his attitude in 1977: "a

---

4   Fowles, Foreword to *The Magus: A Revised Version*, p. 5.

5   Fowles, Foreword to *The Magus: A Revised Version*, p. 5.

6   For example, Huffaker, p. 44; Kerry McSweeney, *Four Contemporary
     Novelists* (Kingston and Montreal: McGill-Queen's University Press,
     1983), pp. 102–103.

subjective [side of him] could not abandon the myth it was trying, clumsily and laboriously, to bring into the world."[7] Clearly *The Magus* has persistently gripped Fowles's imagination and called powerfully upon his creative resources for most of his career. In effect he spent twenty-five years writing it.

Yet while it may be profitable in some ways to see the novel as a kind of quarry from which the raw material of other fictions has been dug, we should not overlook the date of *The Magus*'s public literary birth — its publication date — as opposed to that of its imaginative conception. Whatever his relationship with the developing embryo of the text, Fowles did choose to withhold and to rework the novel until 1966. As he explains: "Yet when the success of *The Collector* in 1963 gave me some literary confidence, it was this endlessly tortured and recast cripple [*The Magus*] that demanded precedence over various other novels I had attempted in the 1950s . . . ."[8] This suggests that he perceived *The Magus* as essentially unfinished until at least the early 1960s, and that its eventual release was in part made possible by the success of *The Collector*.

Historically, then, we are bound to view *The Magus* as a second novel despite Fowles's apparent dismissal of its "mere" publication date. The very existence of this date implies that Fowles was, to some extent at least,[9] content to have *The Magus* perceived as a second novel. It is worth noting in this regard that his most extensive comments on the book, in the Foreword to the revised version, date from the 1970s and might reflect a hindsight obviously unavailable to him in 1966. Furthermore, Fowles has not made the early drafts available for study and it is surely these early reworkings which (if one accepts this view) would make the book effectively a first novel. The data that would support the hypothesis are thus not entirely accessible, and the critic has to work with what is publicly within his/her reach, the published text(s). For these

---

7   Fowles, Foreword to *The Magus: A Revised Version*, p. 5.

8   Fowles, Foreword to *The Magus: A Revised Version*, p. 5.

9   We should remember here that Fowles has always regretted having published the book so soon. Even in 1966, he feels, it was not "truly ready." See Huffaker, p. 44.

reasons I have chosen to place *The Magus* second, in observation of
the letter of bibliographical law. (The spirit of literary law, the
novel's ability to haunt Fowles's work, I will consider later.)

This immediately raises the second textual problem
which must be tackled if one is to write on *The Magus*. Which of
the two versions of the novel is one to choose? And if the choice
falls to the later version, does one not then resurrect the problems
of chronology and placement? The revision appeared after *The
Ebony Tower* in 1974 but some months before *Daniel Martin* in
1977. Does this make it in effect neither a first nor a second novel
but a fourth — or even a fifth, if one decides to regard the 1966
version as a separate, earlier work? This problem is exacerbated by
the lack of critical consensus on the issue. Those critics of the late
1970s and 1980s for whom the problem has arisen do not always
articulate the principles behind their choice, although the revised
version seems generally to have supplanted the earlier one. In this
regard Bruce Woodcock's 1984 book is interesting, for his choice
of the 1966 text is based strictly on the necessities of his argument.[10] In general, the choice seems to be basically a personal one,
made chiefly in relation to the kind of discussion the critic is offering and the requirements of his/her thesis. I have decided to take
the 1977 version as a reliable statement of final authorial intentions
with regard to the text. (It has not so far been Fowles's practice to
revise a published text more than once.) I do not propose to dis-
cuss the overall effects of the revisions to *The Magus*, as this has
been done by Barry Olshen and Ronald Binns, among others,[11] but
I will refer at certain points in my notes to those textual modifications which bear on my own argument.

I have also decided to leave my chapter on *The Magus* in
second place in this study, despite the historical ambiguity created
by the revision and my own acceptance of the revised version as
the most authoritative text. The reason for this is simple: Fowles's

10   Woodcock, pp. 168–69.

11   Olshen, pp. 56–62; Ronald Binns, "A New Version of *The Magus*," *The
Critical Quarterly* 19, No. 4 (1977), 79–84. See also Richard Holmes,
"Crystallizing Powers," *London Times*, 9 June 1977, 12; Michael Boccia,
"'Visions and Revisions': John Fowles's New Version of *The Magus*,"
Journal of Modern Literature 8, No. 2 (1980/81), 235–46.

revisions, although at times extensive, do not constitute a new
novel. Although certain modifications of character — especially
with regard to Julie and June Holmes — do indeed suggest a revision which is "rather more than a stylistic one,"[12] Fowles has left
the structure of the book and its two main characters, Nicholas
Urfe and Maurice Conchis, substantially unaltered. His view of the
revised text as "not, in any major thematic or narrative sense, a
fresh version of *The Magus*"[13] seems quite reliable. It would thus
be unwise to see the revised novel as radically different from its predecessor and to treat it as anything other than what it seems: a
chronologically second novel updated and somewhat expanded by
a mature author looking back in mid-career to a youthful, explora-
tory work. This very process of revision has, I hope to show,
important consequences for our understanding of *The Magus* itself
and of its relationship to those works which postdate it in the
Fowles canon.

• • •

Although *The Collector* and *The Magus* appear at first
sight to be very different novels, they are in many ways engaged
with similar themes. *The Magus* also suggests, more strongly than
its predecessor, Fowles's deep interest in narrative itself and his
increasingly sophisticated awareness of its capacities. Thus *The
Magus* returns us to that symbolic location which is crucial to
Fowles's imagination and his novelistic creativity: the magical enclosure, the *domaine sans nom* of Alain-Fournier.[14] Here the young
man enjoys the exclusive attention of a romanticized woman and
from here he must eventually be expelled — returned to the tedium
of daily reality, and challenged with the task of forging an intelligible link between his experiences in the rarefied, timeless world of

---

12   Fowles, Foreword to *The Magus: A Revised Version*, p. 5.

13   Fowles, Foreword to *The Magus: A Revised Version*, p. 5. He also told
      Carol Barnum: "The second version is the one I want to see reprinted"
      (194).

14   Fowles discusses *Le Grand Meaulnes* as an influence specifically on *The
      Magus* in his Foreword to *The Magus: A Revised Version*, p. 6.

the *domaine* and his existence within the timebound flux of every-day life.

In *The Collector*, however, these elements of a recurring Fowlesian configuration are presented as discontinuous or frac-tured. As we have seen, Fosters is an enclosed but vicious private world, where exploitation and loathing characterize the relationship between the young man and the *princesse* — herself an ironic and contradictory figure, part prim suburbanite and part Perdita. Above all, the presence of the hierophant is truncated and there is no contact between the anti-hero Clegg and the ambiguously wise older man. Faced at the end of the novel with the exigencies of reality and the problem of the experiential status of the enclosed world vis-à-vis that reality, Clegg retreats from the challenge and prepares to live his life in endless re-creation of an obsessive "romantic" fantasy. *The Magus* rearranges these elements and gives them a new cohesion: Phraxos is literally an island, itself enclosing the magical world of Bourani where all borders are elastic and everyday reality seems a chimera. Here the hierophant is placed within the *domaine* as source and wielder of power, and it is in rela-tion to him primarily that the hero must confront or otherwise deal with his self and his desires. This magus is no scruffy bohemian painter but the mysterious orchestrator of ontological games. He works through an even more mysterious princess-figure whose ulti-mate inaccessibility is guaranteed by Fowles's refusal to identify or place her reliably within either the magical or the quotidian world — the latter typified in the novel by London, as well as Rome to a lesser extent, and by the character of Alison Kelly.

Most significantly perhaps, Nicholas Urfe represents an advance on Clegg. He is Fowles's first fully articulated presentation of that middle-class Everyman, the typically inauthentic young representative of his generation,[15] who reappears in *The French Lieutenant's Woman*, *The Ebony Tower*, and *Daniel Martin*. In *The Magus* Fowles develops this male protagonist by moving him away from the behavioural extreme of Frederick Clegg towards the more recognizable emotional immaturities and social maladjustments of

---

15   Fowles, Foreword to *The Magus: A Revised Version*, p. 9: "Gradually my protagonist, Nicholas, took on, if not the true representative face of a modern Everyman, at least that of a partial Everyman of my own class and background."

Nicholas Urfe. In Nick, Clegg's sick sexuality is modulated into the more "banal" disease of "congenital promiscuity,"[16] and his hostile anti-social impulses are transformed into a somewhat less aggressive melodramatic wish to project himself as the eternal solitary. It is as if, in order to discover the more ordinary imperfections of Nick, Fowles had to go through the grotesqueries of Clegg, to anatomize Caliban before finding a way to displace him — just a little and very ambiguously — in the direction of Ferdinand.[17]

These adaptations represent important shifts of emphasis in a typically Fowlesian fictional pattern. They reveal, much more clearly in the second novel than in the first, Fowles's debt to mediaeval romance, with its emphasis on ordeal, sexual temptation, and masculine *rite de passage*. This literary influence was to receive its fullest expression in *The Ebony Tower*, whose title story deliberately recapitulates the central situation of *The Magus*.[18] Reading Fowles's *œuvre* developmentally, one can see David Williams as a sort of older, more domesticated Urfe, who has fulfilled the psychiatric prophecy made at his trial: "Although previous attempts at an artistic resolution [of his sexual repetition-compulsion] have apparently failed, we may predict that further such attempts will be made" (510). Nick, the failed poet and inept teacher, transmutes into David, the successful painter and accomplished lecturer. Structurally and stylistically, however, *The Magus* prepares us less for *The Ebony Tower* than for the elaborate narrational experimentation of *The French Lieutenant's Woman*. In this sense, too, it represents a major advance on *The Collector* and can be seen as the first of Fowles's fictions decisively to foreground narrative, the act of

---

16   Fowles, *The Magus: A Revised Version*, p. 264. All other page references appear in the text and are to the Jonathan Cape edition.

17   In the revised version of the novel, Fowles increased the number of direct allusions to *The Tempest*, and in Chapter 33 he replaced the rhyme "A frog he would a-wooing go," which Julie recites to Nick, with one of Caliban's speeches from Act III, Scene II of Shakespeare's play. Clearly *The Tempest* is as important to *The Magus* as it is to *The Collector*.

18   Interviewed by Robert Robinson, Fowles commented on "The Ebony Tower": "In a way I wanted to demystify *The Magus*, which I think was altogether too full of mystery"; in "Giving the reader a choice — a conversation with John Fowles," *The Listener*, 31 Oct. 1974, 584.

narration, and language, making them as much the object of the artist's scrutiny as the content of the story itself. *The Collector*, through its discontinuous narrative, competing parallel voices, and careful mimicking of speech mannerisms based on class, suggests that Fowles was interested very early on in the resources of the novel. He was already preoccupied with the acts of writing and reading, the ontological and cognitive status of narrative, and the relationship between language, narration, and gender.

● ● ●

Despite the enormous surface complexity of *The Magus*,[19] it is not difficult to see that its central concern is with art in general and narrative art in particular. We have only to look at the persistence with which the text foregrounds individual works of art, and the sophisticated interweaving of art with both personality and moral conduct in the presentation of the characters. Thus Nicholas is a man with literary ambitions whose sensibility is conditioned and directed by art. He defines his posturing at Oxford as the uncomprehending misapplication to life of a specifically literary style and attitude, which he and his sherry-sipping cronies discovered in books: "[W]e didn't understand that the heroes, or anti-heroes, of the French existentialist novels we read were not supposed to be realistic. We tried to imitate them, mistaking metaphorical descriptions of complex modes of feeling for straightforward prescriptions of behaviour. We duly felt the right anguishes" (17). This is literally life as misreading.

Much later in the novel, on Parnassus, Nick experiences desire for Alison in literary terms, describing his apprehension of her appeal as "an intensely literary moment. I could place it exactly: *England's Helicon*" (268–69). When Alison "dies," he poeticizes the grief he cannot really feel by reading Marlowe's "The

---

19   Loveday believes that this complexity is based on "two very simple patterns": "The first is the love story — boy meets girl; boy leaves girl; boy returns to girl. And the second is the quest narrative, in which the hero undertakes a magical journey whose true but more or less sublimated goal is a fuller understanding of himself" (p. 30). Although his reading examines many of the novel's ironies and subversions, Loveday sees nothing in *The Magus* that seriously challenges these basic patterns.

Passionate Shepherd to his Love," and with cunning grace, in his capacity as narrator of the story, he concludes a chapter with the elegiac quoting of three stanzas (400). Given Nick's tendency to find in literature metaphors by which to structure and perceive his own experience, it seems appropriate that he should play the role of suicidal poet while working at the Lord Byron School in Greece. He goes on to see himself, at different times in the book, as Pip in *Great Expectations* (with Conchis doubling as Miss Havisham [347]), Ferdinand in *The Tempest* (383), Malvolio in *Twelfth Night* (406, 564), and Iago in *Othello* (530).[20] Well before the "mysteries" begin on Bourani — throughout the book in fact — we are thus encouraged to see Nick as less a poetic hack than a rather narcissistic reader of other people's texts. His quest for identity is deeply involved with the finding of literary role models, and he himself understands the potential moral evasiveness of this when he describes coming to terms with Alison's "death" as an "edg[ing] it out of the moral world into the aesthetic, where it was easier to live with." Nick sees this as a "sinister elision, [a] slipping from true remorse," which indirectly elevates the griever and flatters his self-pity (401).

It is as a reader of texts that Nick first enters the *domaine*: his initiation begins with the finding of some fragments of poetry on Moutsa. These extracts from works by Eliot, Auden, and Pound are all applicable to Nick's life, specifically to his present and future. The four lines from "Little Gidding" — "We shall not cease from exploration / And the end of all our exploring / Will be to arrive where we started / And know the place for the first time" (69) — anticipate the completed circle of the novel's structure, which returns Nick to London and Alison with (presumably) increased

---

20   He also identifies himself repeatedly with mythological characters like Theseus (157, 313) and Ulysses (157, 279), and with archetypal figures from Greek drama like Orestes (77) and Oedipus (157). In fact Nick's first (and periodically reiterated) response to Bourani is the uncanny feeling "of having entered a myth" (157). If the central section of the novel is implicitly dominated by Theseus and Ariadne, its last third refers indirectly to Orpheus and Eurydice; Nick's surname (Urfe) reinforces the connection here. Avrom Fleishmann discusses the novel's involvement with Greek myths and ancient religions in "*The Magus* of the Wizard of the West," in his *Fiction and the Ways of Knowing* (Austin and London: University of Texas Press, 1978), pp. 179–94.

wisdom and understanding. The two lines by Auden — "Each in his little bed conceived of islands . . . / Where love was innocent, being far from cities" (69) — prefigure the romantic, pastoral isolation of Bourani and the experience there of what seems to be ideal, almost pre-lapsarian love. The extract from the *Cantos* (lengthened in the revised version of the novel) stresses the need to explore mysterious, mythic landscapes: "First must thou go the road / to hell / And to the bower of Ceres' daughter Proserpine . . . . " The purpose of this journey is knowledge: ". . . the shade of a shade, / Yet must thou sail after knowledge / Knowing less than drugged beasts" (69–70). This sums up Nick's existential mission on the island while attesting to the power of and the need for knowledge — in this case both self-knowledge and the arcane, obscure wisdom of the magus.[21]

This is the first of the novel's imagistic *mises en abyme*. It not only prefigures Nick's experiences in the book but instructs us to perceive these as "intensely literary" and artistic in nature. In doing so it inevitably comments not just on Nick's experiences but on the structure and content *per se* of the novel we are in the process of reading. It directs us to perceive Bourani as a text while signalling the textuality of the book as a whole. This reinforces the identification, already accomplished by the first-person narrative, between the reader and Nick: he too is a reader, we too are initiates. Nick confronting the mystifying text of Bourani figuratively represents the reader confronting the mystifying text of *The Magus* — with these internal and external texts both functioning perhaps as metaphors for the impenetrable text of human existence. For both the reader and the character-as-reader, then, the initiation into existential wisdom is also the initiation into artistic wisdom, and specifically into knowledge of narrative. This is made especially clear in Nick's most critically celebrated moment of self-recognition,

---

21   Fowles has commented on the novel's imaginative genesis: "I only knew the basic idea of a secret world, whose penetration involved ordeal and whose final reward was self–knowledge, obsessed me" (Halpern, 35). The reference in the Pound extract to Ceres and Proserpine is especially important for the last part of the novel, where Lily de Seitas is associated with Demeter and Julie, by association, with Persephone. Fowles evidently finds this myth attractive: he also drew on it for the central situation of *The Collector*.

that moment when he comprehends his past in terms of a misapprehension both theological and textual:

> What was I after all? Near enough what Conchis had had me told: nothing but the net sum of countless wrong turnings. I dismissed most of the Freudian jargon of the trial; but all my life I had tried to turn life into fiction, to hold reality away; always I had acted as if a third person was watching and listening and giving me marks for good or bad behaviour — a god like a novelist, to whom I turned, like a character with the power to please[.] (539)

To be inauthentic in Fowles's terms is effectively to misunderstand art; in *The Magus* awareness of self and awareness of text are made inseparable.

On the level of internal narrative action, it is Conchis who encourages Nick to perceive Bourani as a text. He begins by asserting that the "novel is dead" and telling Nick how he "burnt every novel [he] possessed" years ago. He believes, he says, that "[w]ords are for truth. For facts. Not fiction" (96). In ostensible proof of this, he offers Nick apparently factual documents, like the pamphlet by Robert Foulkes and his own entitled *De la communication intermondiale*. But the latter proves to be a fiction, like the "original" paintings and sculptures at the villa, which all turn out to be fakes. Furthermore, Conchis structures Nick's experience at Bourani around four great narrative set-pieces: the "stories" of Neuve Chapelle, Givray-le-Duc, Seidevarre, and Phraxos *circa* 1943. Ostensibly autobiographical, these narratives cannot be verified specifically as fact by Nick. Their documentary status remains unconfirmed and this implicitly pressures both the reader and Nick-as-reader to view them as literary or fictional creations. Nicholas comes to think of Conchis as a sort of "novelist sans novel, creating with people, not words" (242), and when he notes the similarity between the old man's activities and what he "hate[s] so much — fiction," Conchis admits his desire to extend the principles of fiction beyond the physical boundaries of books: "I do not object to the principles of fiction. Simply that in print, in books, they remain mere principles" (231).

Such textual details direct us to perceive Conchis as an artist and, by extension, as a figure in the novel for the author himself, John Fowles. Bourani is Conchis's text just as *The Magus* is Fowles's. It is no accident that the old man refers to Leverrier's experience on the island as one of Bourani's "chapters," and that Nick registers Conchis's manipulation of suspense as "one of the oldest literary devices" (139). Also, the explicit association in the novel between Conchis and the drama reinforces our sense of him as an artist involved in a unique creative endeavour. Conchis himself suggests the word "masque" to describe his activities when he leaves in Nick's bedroom a sumptuous book, *Le Masque Français au Dix-huitième Siècle*, with appropriate passages marked. The artificial, highly orchestrated nature of the Bourani events is stressed in this implied analogy not only with a ritualized and archaic form of drama, but with a prose work which itself further textualizes that drama. Conchis then produces the mythological play of Apollo and Artemis (180–84) and later classes himself with Artaud, Pirandello, and Brecht as an experimenter in theatrical technique:

> During the war . . . I conceived a new kind of drama. One in which the conventional separation between actors and audience was abolished. In which the conventional scenic geography, the notions of proscenium, stage, auditorium, were completely discarded. In which continuity of performance, either in time or place, was ignored. And in which the action, the narrative was fluid, with only a point of departure and a fixed point of conclusion. (404)

All these factors combine to suggest that the mysterious, even supernatural power of the magus is, in fact, the power of creativity: Conchis at work on his boundaryless, numinous "dramatic novel" about the adventures of a caddish young schoolmaster in Greece mirrors Fowles at work on the same project. *The Magus* can therefore be seen as an allegory of the creative process; it investigates the way in which art is conceived, realized, and responded to, while itself constituting an accomplished work of art. It thereby enacts and embodies its own preceptorial

investigation.[22] This is the specifically metafictional nature of the
book: it is a text that examines textuality while consistently signposting its own.   Nick makes the textuality of Bourani and the
multiple textuality of *The Magus* perfectly explicit when he tells
Alison in the Athens hotel room, almost at the midpoint of the
novel: "This experience. It's like being halfway through a book. I
can't just throw it in the dustbin" (273).

If the maze of the text, Bourani, re-presents the maze of
the text, *The Magus*, and the author/impresario Conchis doubles
for the author/impresario Fowles (who would present the narrator
of his next novel as, among other things, a flashy producer of grand
opera), then *The Magus* and what it describes reflect mutually upon
one another. This forces the reader to be constantly aware of what
he/she is reading as a construct; the artificiality of Conchis's text,
Bourani, necessarily directs the reader back to the artificiality (or
fictionality) of Fowles's text, *The Magus*. The allegorical poise of
the novel is somewhat disturbed, however, by the ambivalent figure
of Nick; the book's self-reflexiveness places Nick in a structurally
unstable position with regard to the interlocking textualities which
comprise it.

On one level, as I have already indicated, Nick doubles
for the reader: his search for the meaning of Conchis's fiction represents ours for the meaning of Fowles's. As such, Nick is an effi-
cient vehicle for Fowles's examination of the act of reading and the
various ways in which the reader attempts to make sense of a text.
Thus we see him baffled and intrigued, trying to explain the
"magic" of Conchis's theatrical effects and, in so doing, to bring
the masque into line with verifiable fact and the quotidian world.
Back in England, he tries to investigate the masque in the
thorough, meticulous way of a detective working on a case or a

---

22   Earlier critics often overlooked the book's concern with art and read it as
      simply the depiction, with some phantasmagoric trappings, of an individ-
      ual's moral and existential growth. Examples are the monographs by
      Palmer, Wolfe, and Huffaker. Later critics like Loveday and McSweeney
      are more aware of the novel's self-conscious engagement with art as cru-
      cial to both its content and form. An exception here is Malcolm
      Bradbury, whose art-centred reading appeared in his *Possibilities* (1973),
      pp. 256–71. Bradbury is one of the few literary critics whom Fowles
      himself admires. See Campbell, 460.

researcher engaged in an academic task. He also at times projects himself into Conchis's text, seeing it at one point as an attempt to recover through narrative "some lost world of [Conchis's] own and . . . I was cast as the *jeune premier* in it, his younger self" (192). Faced with the masque as "an obscure poem" (192), Nick persists in his systematic efforts to render its obscurity into clarity, its mystery into revelation. In his implied insistence on meaning as intelligible, accessible to the intellect, and precisely locatable within the text, Nick offers the reader an image of him/herself vainly trying to penetrate the text and solve the mystery of art. The failure of Nick's attempts to understand rationally prefigures the comparable failure of Mike Jennings in Fowles's story "The Enigma." In *The Ebony Tower*, Fowles would go on to elevate the plight of the reader into a full-scale examination of the clash between writer and reader, creator and interpreter, artist and critic.

This examination does in fact begin in *The Magus*. The text of Bourani defies interpretation and Nick never finds out what the masque means in any logically definitive or quantifiable way. He is left with an apprehension of, rather than a solution to, mystery. As Conchis asserts: "[M]ystery has energy. It pours energy into whoever seeks an answer to it. If you disclose the solution to the mystery you are simply depriving the other seekers . . . of an important source of energy" (235). The meaning, it would seem, *is* the mystery; the meaning consists paradoxically in the very refusal of the text to render up its meaning in a discursive or intellectually intelligible form. Lily de Seitas confirms this when she tells Nick that "[a]n answer is always a form of death" (626).

In *The Magus*, then, it is the reader, and particularly the reader as interpreter and potential critic, who is thwarted and actively discouraged from imposing the reductive processes of analysis on the text. In wry reinforcement of this point, Fowles includes a brief but scathing portrait of a professional reader in *The Magus*. This nameless person is "a little middle-aged queer, a critic, who had come to do some lectures [in Athens]. There was a good deal of literary chit-chat [at dinner]. The queer waited like a small vulture for names to be produced" (559). The petty repulsiveness of this man is conveyed in "little" and "small," the contemptuous "vulture" and "chit-chat." Nick's designation of him as "queer" is the beginning of an association developed fully in *The Ebony Tower* between criticism and homosexuality, between the explaining of art and sterility. At this point in his work, then, Fowles uses his protagonist Nick to identify and map out an area of conflict which will deeply absorb his attention in later fictions: the difficult, ambiguous relationship between the creative and interpretive impulses. The indeterminacy of the novel — typified in Nick's inability to categorize his experience on the island and the reader's inability to grasp fully what he/she has read — preserves both the mystery of the text Bourani and that of the text *The Magus*. In this way Fowles shows himself a supporter of Conchis's view, a believer in mystery and hence in art.[23]

On another level, Nick functions to complicate this clash between writer and reader, and here various other paradoxes in *The Magus*, as well as its presentation of women, become important. Nick's ambiguous function is most obviously demonstrated in the implications of the book's first-person narrative form. Fowles's choice of a personalized and exclusive narrative perspective means that Nick is not only the reader of one text but the effective producer of another. Although we have already identified Fowles as author and as allegorical referent for the figure of Conchis, we cannot overlook another structural fact of the novel: *The Magus* is set up in such a way that it requires us to perceive Nick as the writer of the book we are reading.

In a more conventional novel, this need not be problematic. *David Copperfield*, for example, is in one sense an autobiography of David. Although we know that Dickens wrote the book, we have no difficulty in suspending disbelief, accepting the "I" of the narrative as an authorial mask, and perceiving David as both protagonist and narrator. But the metafictional concerns of *The Magus*, its self-conscious scrutinizing of art and creativity, mean that Nick must function as protagonist/narrator not only of *The Magus*, but also of the text which it contains, Bourani. He is a character in a

---

23   This reading counters Bernard Bergonzi's view of *The Magus* as a fundamentally useless piece of work: "[T]he novel is vitiated by its basic pointlessness, its inability to relate to anything except itself as a centripetal imaginative entity," in *The Situation of the Novel* (London and Basingstoke: The Macmillan Press, 1979), pp. 75–76. Rather, the book gives us one aesthetic and imaginative structure, itself, commenting on another larger and more abstract one, art. Its impenetrability is therefore its message, and not a sign of mere capriciousness.

multiple sense, inhabiting a text effectively presented as his own but actually produced by Fowles, and simultaneously playing his part in Conchis's eccentric "dramatic novel." The book thus centralizes Nick both structurally and thematically as reader and writer. Forced by his author, John Fowles, to read the text of the authorial surrogate, Maurice Conchis, Nick then makes his own text out of this act of reading, this attempt at interpretation, and produces the book which we hold in our hands — a book which we know is only an ostensible autobiography and only ostensibly written by Nick.

What this amounts to is a perfect mirroring, in terms of narrative technique and structure, of that solipsism of Nick's which the book so meticulously dissects. Nick is reading himself as protagonist of various stories while writing one in which *he* is narratorially and thematically "at web-centre" (511). And if we choose to see Nick as a sort of younger Conchis, we can even view him as the indirect and transposed protagonist of the old man's "autobiographical" narratives. This adroit interpenetration of form and content establishes a congruence between the apparent opposites of reader and writer, offering us Nick as another and very different implicit authorial surrogate in the novel, and affecting our perception of that allegory of art which I have designated as its main subject. A closer discussion of the novel's strategies for relating structure to theme will further illuminate this association of interpreter and author.

If Fowles creates a narratorial analogue for the psychosexual syndrome which the book is examining — male solipsism and narcissism — he also constructs a similar analogue for the philosophical and ethical principle which it apparently seeks to promote: *eleutheria* or freedom. While Nick may be considered on one level as a character in Conchis's "novel," he is also a character with a mind of his own and a certain freedom of action and choice. Conchis (whether we are inclined to believe him or not) emphasizes this when he tells Nick that, between its points of "departure" and "conclusion," the "new kind of drama" is shaped by the inventiveness of the participants (404). June Holmes has already expressed this idea of the character as influential in relation to the text by telling Nick that Conchis wants his "cast members" to be "mysteries to him as well" (404). This foregrounds an essential aspect of the allegory of reading and writing, and an issue of great importance in Fowles's work as a whole: the question of authorial control and the moral pressure, which for Fowles weighs upon the writer, to refuse the omniscient point of view as an exercise in tyranny. His own support of individual freedom is manifested in *The Magus* by the illusion, always effected by first-person narrative, that the wielder of authorial power is also a character. First-person narrative is thus intended as a model of creative power-sharing in *The Magus*: it has its corollary on the level of internal narrative action in the apparent absconding of Conchis and his "troupe" at the end of the novel. Looking up at the Olympian front of Cumberland Terrace, Nick realizes with a shock that the "windows were as blank as they looked. The theatre was empty. It was not a theatre" (654).

The withdrawal of those apparently omniscient "watching eyes" (654) is an image of the morally responsible author's need to desist from coercion and to set his characters free. It is principally in his vanishing, in the way he absents himself, rather than in his manner of making himself present, that Conchis communicates to Nick what seems to be an important moral lesson of both his text and Fowles's — the lesson, both metaphysically portentous and aesthetically apposite, that while God may perhaps be an artist, the artist cannot afford to be a god. Conchis deserting his text is thus a deliberate evocation of God absconding from the world, guaranteeing the freedom of its inhabitants by a self-conscious act of abandonment. This makes sense of that persistent equation in *The Magus* between creator and Creator, that identification of Conchis with both Picasso and Zeus, Prospero and Poseidon. The last trick of the artist/magician/god, who fulfills his obscure purposes through an apparently endless and inexplicable series of quick-change acts, is to make himself literally bodiless. Refusing, in his mysteriousness, to locate or even concretize himself, he leaves only the *memento mori* of his own gravestone and his wisdom inscribed as the smile of an ancient, faceless stone head (146–47). Fowles's sense of the artist's commitment to freedom is thus summed up in *The Magus* by this image of Conchis (and hence of Fowles himself) as a kind of synecdoche: the author is, at the last, absent in every feature but the one which encapsulates his essence; he is the artist as Cheshire Cat, "a smile fading into thin air" (559).[24]

---

24   *Alice in Wonderland* seems almost as fascinating to Fowles as *The Tempest*: *The Magus* refers to it, as do *The Collector* and *The Ebony Tower*. Although *The Magus*'s allusions are mostly casual and descriptive — for

But unfortunately for Fowles, the freedom which he seeks both to investigate and to enact in *The Magus* as an allegory of art is more smoothly expressed on the internal level of narrative realization than on the external. This is because Fowles's attempt to imitate Conchis (who is simultaneously Fowles's character and *his* imitator) by setting Nick free places the novel in a highly problematic relationship with certain aspects of first-person narration. Fowles tries to release Nick from authorial domination by allowing him, in the narrative which is being presented (if only ostensibly) as Nick's own, to leave the rest of his history undisclosed. We know nothing of what has happened to Nick subsequent to the events described in the book.

In one way, this is an act of authorial good will on Fowles's part: the "completion" of Nick's story would not only have dissipated that mystery that Fowles sees as crucial to art; it would also have betrayed the principle of freedom by the imposition of structural closure. Here the novel performs what it describes: as Nick refuses to violate the bodily integrity of Julie by lashing her at the trial, so Fowles will not violate Nick's narratorial integrity by intruding further into his life. Both the character, literally, and the author, metaphorically, refuse to bring down the whip. In this sense Nick's perception of a "god like a novelist" is also Fowles's: like a responsible god, the good author must strive to qualify and undermine his own power.

But in another way this act creates a structural instability in *The Magus*, which prepares us for the novel's tendency to undermine the very moral and aesthetic positions that it seeks to adopt. When the narrative voice is the voice of the "I," the reader should be able to locate that "I" not only as protagonist but also as writer — otherwise we have no clear way of understanding the relationship between the self who writes the story (of necessity an older self) and the self who appears within it (of necessity a younger self). First-person narrative, it seems, requires this kind of chronological continuity. It is only in terms of what comes later in the narrating

---

example, Lily de Seitas is described as "Alice-like" in her portrait (592) — they emphasize the phenomenological elasticity of the novel's world. It is worth noting that Fowles's revisions excised from Chapter 31 a brief comparison between Lily/Julie's smile and that of the Cheshire Cat — perhaps to lessen the inscrutability of Julie as a character.

persona's life — or, in the case of a narrator like Clegg, what we feel
sure *will* come later — that we can fully comprehend the significance of what has transpired earlier. This is particularly true if
the first-person narrative functions, as it does in *The Magus*, in conjunction with a format or general shape adapted from the
Bildungsroman — that is, if it is to some extent a novel of education in the first-person form.[25]

     Fowles's refusal to situate the *writing* Nick precisely in
time and space means that Nick's story comes to us out of an historical vacuum. There are one or two tantalizing references to an
unspecified lapse of time, which provide a glimpse of the older Nick
without defining his position. After his suicide attempt, he comments: "Years later I saw the *gabbia* at Piacenza. . . . And looking
up at it I remembered that winter in Greece, that *gabbia* I had constructed for myself out of light, solitude and self-delusions" (62).
Near the end of the book he says of Mitford: "Years later I discovered that he *had* been lying that day" (616, emphasis in original).
These throwaway allusions to a futurity withheld by the novel only
serve to enhance its temporal ambiguity. It becomes difficult to
assess the effect which the events described in the novel have had
upon Nick and his life, for the perspective in time which would

---

25   We must note that in many ways *The Magus* is not a true *Bildungsroman*:
    we learn very little, for example, about Nick's childhood and nothing
    about his later life. It is interesting to observe that, although Fowles is
    passionately concerned with issues of growth and identity, his work in
    general exhibits no interest in childhood (and very little in old age).
    This could be because, for him, identity is inseparable from sexuality;
    Fowles's questing heroes invariably make their self-discoveries in
    response to an erotically enticing woman. The frequent presence at this
    kind of encounter of an older man also signals Fowles's preference for
    dealing with parent/child relationships through surrogates rather than
    through the hero's biological parents. Olshen has noted in this regard
    Fowles's repeated attraction to the orphaned (and siblingless) protago-
    nist (p. 117). This supports my view that for Fowles "motherhood" is a
    sexual and aesthetic category, while "fatherhood" describes a specifically
    artistic relationship between two imaginations and two creative drives. It
    is thus significant that Fowles has described *The Magus* as "a young
    man's first novel . . . this sort of adolescent book" (Campbell, 457, 458).
    The stage of development which seems to interest him most is adoles-
    cence; Fowles's heroes are invariably what he felt himself to be at the
    time of writing the novel — retarded adolescents.

enable us to measure the extent and nature of his inner growth remains unspecified. This combines with the aesthetically and philosophically necessary presentation of the masque as radically ambiguous to leave the reader, as well as Nick, unlocated and unsure at the end of the novel. As Malcolm Bradbury has observed:

> The question remains . . . has [the masque] been a plot against [Nick], or a plot *for* him — a plot to lead him to wisdom? The final pages are ambiguous; we do not know whether Urfe has been saved or damned by his experiences, whether the mysterious powers have withdrawn or remain in his life, whether he accepts Alison or ends the novel in renewed isolation. Above all we are left doubtful about whether the masques and mysteries, which have been given such fictional density as an experience, are a diabolic trap or a species of recovery and revelation.[26]

I would suggest that this ambivalence stems directly from the lack of a clear relationship between the older Nick who narrates and the younger Nick who has experienced. It is a lack of clarity which emerges from an attempt by Fowles, in his second novel, at the kind of generic revisionism at which he would become so adept later, in *The French Lieutenant's Woman* and *The Ebony Tower*. In *The Magus* he tries to borrow from the *Bildungsroman* its basic shape — the educative journey to self-knowledge — while jettisoning its need for chronological intelligibility, that is, for closure.

One consequence of this is the reader's nagging sense at the end of the novel that Nick, in spite of frequent and rather obvious assertions to the contrary, has really learned nothing from

---

26   Bradbury, p. 267, emphasis in original. The revised ending is slightly less ambiguous than the original one — Bradbury of course was using the 1966 text. For example, in the later version Nicholas says to Alison: "You can't hate someone who's really on his knees. Who'll never be more than half a human being without you" (667). But this revision, like the lines from the "Pervigilium Veneris" which conclude both texts, does not constitute finality in any sense; Bradbury's comments apply equally to both versions.

his experiences.[27] This impression persists, even though the book
has set him up as an initiate and moral novice enrolled as a pupil at
the Maurice Conchis school of existential wisdom, Bourani.[28] It is
important to note in this regard that back in London Nick, who has
presumably "graduated" by means of trial and disintoxication,[29]

---

27   This aspect of *The Magus* has troubled a number of critics. See, for
     example, Woodcock's chapter on the book (pp. 45–79), and Loveday's
     (pp. 29–47).

28   *The Magus* is dominated, interestingly, not only by notions of education
     and enlightenment, but by the idea of school. The book sets up Bourani
     as a kind of school, a moral and spiritual alternative to its geographical
     opposite on the island, the Lord Byron. Bourani is a school for life as it
     were and, by implication, for artists; the Lord Byron is merely academic
     and canonical — a school for critics. Significantly, the Lord Byron
     is summed up in the figure of Demetriades who is, as Loveday notes,
     a travesty of the English public-school ideal of manhood (p. 40).
     Furthermore, the Bourani calendar depends on the timetable at the Lord
     Byron: Nick can only visit Conchis at weekends after prep.; Bourani goes
     into recess at the school's half-term, when Nick meets Alison in Athens;
     the end of the masque and Nick's expulsion from the *domaine* coincide
     with the end of the school year. Thus the trial and disintoxication are a
     sort of final exam for Nick — who ironically is marking final exams at the
     time — and we might expect, when he is back in London, some evidence
     of how his education has altered him. This centralizing of school brings
     The Magus very close in imagery and structure, as well as in spirit, to *Le
     Grand Meaulnes*, in which the boys' lives are conditioned by the routines
     of their village school, whose timetable limits their access to the romantic
     world of the ruined manor. It also makes any reference to the sadistic,
     punitive aspects of the masque as "discipline" doubly appropriate, for
     Conchis's punishments of Nick are at once sado-masochistic and prefec-
     torial. This orientation towards school obviously contributes to what
     Fowles has called the book's "adolescent" quality.

29   Strictly speaking, the term describes the part of the masque beginning
     immediately after Nick's mock trial and consisting of the invitation to
     flog Julie, the "blue" film, and the erotic performance featuring Julie and
     Joe (Chapters 61–62). But my reading of the novel centralizes the latter
     scene as the essential disintoxication, the principal focus of significance in
     this traumatic phase of Nick's experience. Collectively these episodes
     function as a kind of anti-seduction, or revulsion therapy, to weaken
     Nick's attachment not only to the Bourani world but particularly to Julie,
     as a preparation for Conchis's apparent withdrawal and Nick's return to
     daily reality and to Alison.

begins a relationship with a woman, Jojo, which essentially recapitulates the narcissistic and manipulative connections of his pre-
Phraxos days: "She slipped perfectly into the role I cast for her. . . .
She fulfilled her function very well; she put off every other girl who
looked at us and on my side I cultivated a sort of lunatic transferred
fidelity towards her" (636).   This echoes precisely Nick's earlier
self-pitying confession when Alison "dies": "My monstrous crime
was Adam's, the oldest and most vicious of all male selfishnesses: to
have imposed the role I needed from Alison on her real self" (400).

        Nick's recognition of such moral errors is overtly intend-
ed, it seems to me, to indicate increasing maturity. A similar intention seems to inform his assertion to Alison in Regent's Park that
he is finally coming to understand the nature of the affection
between them: "You've always been able to see this . . . whatever it
is . . . between us. Joining us. I haven't. That's all I can offer you.
The possibility that I'm beginning to see it" (665). But against this
we must set other textual details which suggest that the complacen-
cy and aggressiveness of Nick's earlier sexual attitudes remain
unchanged. His treatment of Jojo is shoddy not only in moral
terms but in narrative terms as well. He condescends to her without demonstrating any awareness that his condescension is a feature
of an earlier and less enlightened self, as opposed to a later and
wiser narrating one. Thus we have the completely unironized presentation of Jojo as not even a human being at all, but an amalgam
of various animals: she sits "puppy-slumped" and dejected, possesses a "froglike grin," and eats "like a wolf" (634–35). Her lack of
sexual attractiveness for Nick means a freedom to patronize her
warmly — "I grew full of kindness to dumb animals" (635) — and
he goes on to regret the fact that, in rejecting Jojo, he has "kicked a
starving mongrel in its poor, thin ribs" (643).

        Despite Kemp's strident rebuke of him for his treatment
of Jojo (644–45), there is something in Nick's self-satisfied tone
here which works together with the essentially reductive portrait of
her (and indeed of both women) to imply subtly that Nick has been
justified in using and discarding a creature so pathetically subhuman. For Fowles's male protagonists, the discovery of self is
meant to be inseparable from the discovery of honesty and authenticity in sexual relations. But *The Magus* develops an unnerving
split between what Nick can recognize and what he can act upon.
As a narrator inhabiting some unspecified point on the other side of

the experiences he describes, he cannot enact on a textual level that apprehension of Jojo's value which he tries so vehemently to assert: "Jojo was a strange creature, as douce as rain . . . and utterly without ambition or meanness. . . . She was always equable, grateful for the smallest bone, like an old mongrel; patient, unoffended, casual" (636). Whatever his disclaimers, Nick's very imagery betrays him. He cannot refrain from condescension nor bring himself to acknowledge or value narratorially either her sexuality or her humanity: "She amused me, she had character, with her husky voice and her grotesque lack of normal femininity" (635). For both the experiencing as well as the narrating Nick, Jojo remains, in every sense of the word, a dog.

In a similar way, Nick's aggressiveness towards Alison, which she often recognizes as an expression of contempt,[30] remains basically unaltered at the end of the novel. Although he purports to have gained an understanding of Alison's "word," love (655), and we are meant to regard the slap across her face[31] which he delivers as a sign of existential insight and hence as "no breaking of [Lily de Seitas's] commandment . . . *Thou shalt not inflict unnecessary pain*" (654, 641, emphasis in original),[32] it is the violence of

---

30   For example, in the Athens hotel room she observes shrewdly: "I think you're so blind you probably don't even know you don't love me" (274). At the very end of the novel, she is shocked by Nick's looking at her "as if [she were] a prostitute or something . . . " (652). In fact, Nick is apt to see Alison in this way: in the hut on Parnassus he thinks "it's like being with a prostitute" (263), and when she reappears in Athens after her "death," she emerges "from the shadows as a prostitute might have done" (562).

31   Woodcock, referring to Wolfe and Huffaker, questions the tendency of male critics to take the slapping of Alison's face as "a gesture of existential liberation." He views it as "a brutal action which a feminist critic would see on a quite different basis" (pp. 73–74). But he does believe that the revised ending ameliorates some of the violence of the action, reflecting Fowles's rethinking of sexual issues in the interim between the texts.

32   The phrase is altered from the earlier "Thou shalt not commit pain," *The Magus* (London: Pan Books, 1966), p. 556. Perhaps the change is meant to express the inevitability of Nick's inflicting pain on both Alison and Jojo — a reflection of the "necessary" pain which Conchis has inflicted on him. If so, it is only partially convincing.

this blow together with Nick's assertion that "Lily" will always be
for him an irresistible "type of encounter" (653) which lead us to
suspect that the problems between Nick and Alison remain unresolved and unchanged. Nick seems in fact to be bullying Alison
back into the very relationship which he tried earlier to escape. His
own newly learned sense of the importance of individual freedom
does not, it would appear, extend to the recognition of Alison's
right to free choice. This seems little different from his previous
self-confessed tendency to impose on Alison's "real self" a "role" he
needs from her. The nature of this role is revealed in his words to
her in Regent's Park: "You have my part now" (653). Far from
suggesting that Alison, who has been part of Conchis's masque for
an unspecified but substantial length of time, is now being launched
on her own journey to authenticity,[33] these words actually imply
that Nick is trying to force Alison into becoming yet another reflection of his own self-regard. He wants her to play the role that Julie
had played earlier on Phraxos and that Jojo plays later — the role of
personification of Nick's own selfishness, as Lily de Seitas puts it
(601). This seriously undermines any sense we may have had of
Nick as discoverer of sexual "wisdom." Even though he asserts a
growing comprehension of what "good" sexual relations are, his
inability to act on what he claims to know makes us at the very least
doubtful of his reliability.

The implications of this are multiple, the strands of significance deeply intertwined, and they bring us to the core of the
novel. First of all, our recognition of Nick's moral "progress" as in
fact a kind of psychological regression greatly affects our sense of
the structure and overall technique of *The Magus*. It casts an ironic
light on those fragments of poetry which were earlier identified as
the book's first complex *mise en abyme*. If the extract from Pound
prefigured knowledge, why does Nick still seem so ignorant at the
end of the novel? If the lines by Eliot suggested enlightened return
and new recognition, why does Nick's violence towards Alison at
the end recall so forcefully his striking of her in the Athens hotel
room — that is, why does a point in the narrative which we might
expect to emphasize Nick as chastened and wiser actually hark back

---

33   A fairly standard critical response. See Olshen, p. 54; Huffaker, p. 67;
     Wolfe, p. 116; Palmer, p. 108.

to an earlier point when he was shown at his most arrogant and dishonest? [34]

On the level of language, how are we to reconcile Nick's returning to Eliot's words — "[Alison] was mysterious, almost a new woman; one had to go back several steps, and start again; *and know the place for the first time*" (650, emphasis in original) — with his tendency in this third section of his narrative to reify Alison as persistently and unself-consciously as he dehumanizes Jojo? For while we are being asked here to perceive Alison as quotidian reality made mysterious through enlightened rediscovery, we are constantly aware of the novel's language implicitly presenting Alison as an object. Nick feels outraged at being "barred from [his] own *property*" (650, emphasis added) in the Regent's Park encounter; this recalls the slightly earlier association of Alison with the china plate, which Lily de Seitas gives to Nick with the injunction that he learn to handle "fragile *objects*" (624, emphasis added). Lily goes on to declare that Alison is not "a *present*. She must be *paid* for" (631, emphasis added), and she has also described Alison previously as a "little *piece* of pure womankind" (601, emphasis added).

The fact that these reifying "compliments" come from Lily de Seitas does not make them any less a legitimate aspect of Nick's narrative. Nick's evident admiration for this older Lily suggests in fact that her perception of Alison is the most morally desirable one in the book — the one which Conchis (and hence Fowles) implicitly sanctions. It might not be too facetious to add to this list of dubious expressions Nick's description of Alison as "a *countryside* one has loved" (604, emphasis added), the symbolic association of her with the flower "Sweet Alison" (566), and Eliot's word "place"

---

34   For example, Nick only goes to Athens because Bourani is "closed" at half-term and he waits until the last minute for a reprieving message from Conchis (244). He manipulates Alison through the letter he sends tentatively accepting her invitation; this letter, he feels, balances "regretful practicality" with "sufficient affection and desire for her still to want to climb into bed if I got half a chance" (159). He also deceives her by lying about his syphilis, and when he finally tells her about Julie, he coldly admits: "I overcalculated the sympathy a final being honest would bring" (269–70). Even after their quarrel, at the bar on the steamer, he melodramatizes his actions: "I drank a mouthful neat, and made a sort of bitter inner toast. I had chosen my own way; the difficult, hazardous, poetic way; all on one number" (278).

as the novel appropriates it and applies it to her. The book's very language, therefore, seems to suggest a certain undertow of doubt and contradiction with regard to Alison, even while the narrative overtly presents her as the essence of sanity (her name means "without madness") and the best possible mate for Nicholas.

The linguistic ambiguity which at once compliments and degrades the novel's moral heroine alerts us to the fact that *The Magus* is not entirely that novel of education and initiation, that chronicle of a rake's progress, which it purports to be. In fact it is highly questionable whether the book, despite its indebtedness to the quest motif of mediaeval romance and the educative principles of the *Bildungsroman*, describes growth or progress at all. The reason for this peculiar stasis is, as I have suggested, that uneasy splicing in the novel of education as a part of both plot and theme, and indeterminacy as an aspect of narrative form: if we do not know where Nick and Alison end up in time, we have no way of judging how, if at all, their relationship *ever* develops. The *process* of education is exactly that, and it seems to demand progression of some kind in the text. But indeterminacy seems less dependent on narrative movement. The elisions it requires work against the idea of progress or logical development, making it more of a narrative situation than a process. Thus the *state* of indeterminacy seems to need a corresponding state of narrative stasis, and hence the almost inevitable foregrounding of the constructedness or artificiality of the text.

The end of *The Magus* effectively sacrifices that progression which one narrative thrust in the book demands to the stasis which another such imperative requires. This suggests that, while *The Magus* achieves some of its intentions in the structural embodiment of its theme of individual freedom, it cannot fully articulate this theme on every level of narrative operation and must therefore fail consistently to achieve its formal ambitions. In his next novel, *The French Lieutenant's Woman*, Fowles would work out an ambivalent but more intelligible equation between narrative closure and the lack of individual freedom, on the one hand, and fictional indeterminacy and self-realization, on the other.

Fowles's apparent wish, in this early work, to revise generic conventions in the direction of indeterminacy inevitably leads to the rather awkward and late obtrusion into *The Magus* of a different, unidentified voice which points towards the ambiguous ending, while a veil is deliberately drawn over the issue of the novel's problematic positioning in time. It is as if the restrictions of first-person narrative finally prove too confining for the strategies of metafiction:

> The smallest hope, a bare continuing to exist, is enough for the anti-hero's future; leave him, says our age, leave him where mankind is in its history, at a cross-roads, in a dilemma, with all to lose and only more of the same to win; let him survive, but give him no direction, no reward; because we too are waiting, in our solitary rooms where the telephone never rings, waiting for this girl, this truth, this crystal of humanity, this reality lost through imagination, to return; and to say she returns is a lie.
>
> But the maze has no centre. An ending is no more than a point in sequence, a snip of the cutting shears. Benedick kissed Beatrice at last; but ten years later? And Elsinore, that following spring?
>
> So ten more days. But what happened in the following years shall be silence; another mystery. (645)

This passage explicitly identifies the maze, or Conchis's masque, with two of Shakespeare's plays, thus underlining the textuality both of Bourani and of *The Magus*. It therefore throws the reader back again to an awareness of text — and particularly of the fictiveness of the text, for the historical referents which would make *The Magus* intelligible as a chronologically complete whole are conspicuously missing.

When this voice returns, in the last paragraph of the novel, it is in deliberate imitation of the mood and subject of Keats's great odes, with their emphasis on that state of narrative or poetic stasis which promises fulfilment without ever enacting a commitment to its expression:

> [Alison] is silent, she will never speak, never forgive, never reach a hand, never leave this frozen present tense. All waits, suspended. Suspend the autumn trees, the autumn sky, anonymous people. A black-bird, poor fool, sings out of season from the willows

by the lake. A flight of pigeons over the houses; fragments of freedom, hazard, an anagram made flesh.
And somewhere the stinging smell of burning leaves.
                                                     (656)[35]

With narrative itself poised on that Keatsian brink between anticipa-
tion and certainty, between the promise of revelation and the
refusal to tell — with the meaning, in short, consisting still in the
mystery — Fowles effectively extends the preoccupations of this
novel beyond the literal covers of the book. Fully aware of the contradictory demands of the *Bildungsroman* features he has chosen
and the open-endedness in which morally and artistically he
believes, Fowles creates an ending to *The Magus* which opens the
way not only for Nick but for himself. In refusing to tell us about
Nick, this ending transforms itself from a rather unsatisfactory endpoint into a springboard from which Fowles could go on to launch
the complex metafictional explorations of *The French Lieutenant's
Woman*. And the various endings of this later novel represent an
even more intense involvement on Fowles's part with freedom of
choice as both a literary and an ethical principle.

        But the reader is left meanwhile with the paradoxes of
The Magus and the developing awareness that this novel is not quite
what it purports to be, or what it seems to be on its intricately
dense surface. Fowles's second work (rather like his first) has a
peculiar tendency to undermine certain of its own crucial principles;
it slides away from its own implications and enacts, in unexpected
and bewildering ways, its own dictum: "an answer is always a form
of death." For the text offers no satisfactory or reliable answers to
those questions raised earlier about Nick's effective regression and
the difficulties the reader has in knowing how to assess both Alison
and her relation to Nick in the novel. In order to attempt such an

---

35   Keats is strongly present in the imagery and atmosphere here: the repeat-
      ed references to autumn, the smell of burning leaves, and the flight of
      pigeons suggest the mood of the ode "To Autumn," with its "gathering
      swallows twitter[ing] in the skies" (l. 33). The blackbird in the willows
      could be an oblique reference to the "red-breast" (l. 32) of "To Autumn,"
      or to Keats's nightingale, while the suspension of action, the unresolved
      romantic situation and the silent, motionless woman all recall the frieze
      on the Grecian Urn.

assessment, it seems that we must move beyond the narrative frame of the book, but the book itself does not adequately provide the means for us to do so. Furthermore, if the novel first invites us to join Nick on a journey towards self-realization and then retracts that invitation by forcing us to question both the hero's ability to arrive at that destination and the very idea of destination itself, then we must also question what *The Magus* is saying about those large issues with which it engages: art, ethics, sexuality, and textuality. In the exploration of these issues, the novel discloses its subtle refusals to commit itself to its own premises.

One of these premises is, as we have seen, freedom of choice. In terms of certain structural manoeuvres already mentioned and of beliefs expressed by important characters, *The Magus* appears to valorize freedom of choice as a sort of Arnoldian "one thing needful." Thus Conchis, facing the tortured rebel in the square during the war, perceives that "[h]e was the final right to deny. To be free to choose. . . . He was every freedom, from the very worst to the very best. . . . He was something that passed beyond morality but sprang out of the very essence of things — that comprehended all, the freedom to do all, and stood against only one thing — the prohibition not to do all" (434). And Nick, whatever his ability to behave accordingly, perceives the need for the responsible individual to embody freedom of choice in his every-day actions: "Conchis had talked of points of fulcrum, moments when one met one's future. I also knew it was all bound up with Alison, with choosing Alison, and having to go on choosing her every day" (641).

This seems to be one of the novel's object lessons, one of those crucial moral principles that Conchis's masque is designed to communicate to Nick, and *The Magus* confronts directly its own concept of freedom as a brutal, primal, and amoral force. In his last meeting with Nick, Conchis tells his pupil to embrace the savagery of freedom and the freedom to be savage by learning, like the stone head and the Cheshire Cat, to smile: "[F]or him the smile was something essentially cruel, because freedom is cruel" and learning to be cruel is learning to survive (531). Yet the novel has a way of emphasizing the cruelty rather more than the freedom. Conchis's sadism is repeatedly shown, particularly at the trial scene, where Nick feels himself subjected to "a viciously cruel vivisection of the mind" and made to endure terrible punishment for no clear reason

(493). Furthermore, the fact that the epigraphs which introduce
the novel's three sections are from de Sade draws attention to the
book's violent and sado-masochistic elements at least as much as to
its engagement with questions of existential freedom.[36]

This emphasis on brutality and punishment implicitly
raises questions which, persistently unanswered, remain to stalk the
text and to vitiate its valorizing of personal freedom and integrity,
its moralizing about humanitarian respect for life. Is it possible to
tyrannize someone into an awareness of his/her own freedom, to
torture someone into understanding why he/she should not torture? Can insight and generosity (and this is implicitly a problem
in *The Collector* as well) be the products of such brutalization?[37]
Specifically, can Nick be persecuted and punished into loving
Alison, and can he — for this is the unstated premise of the disintoxication — be forced into loving her by learning to hate Julie?
The narratorial equivalent of this undermining or deconstructive
process at work in the novel is Fowles's rather grim awareness that,
whatever the author's high-minded determination to embrace the
principle of freedom in his work, the final choice about all aspects
of a text is his own. The Olympians, however wayward, had Zeus;
every school, however progressive, has its headmaster. In the final

---

36   Ted Billy sees de Sade as "the presiding spirit" of *The Magus*: "De Sade's
      fictional technique depends on a grotesque pattern of ironic reversals
      that totally inverts the reader's expectations of order and justice and
      Fowles seems to collaborate with this perverse artistic ploy when
      he cites de Sade's cynical commentary on man's bondage to the 'des-
      potic caprice' of 'those obscure paths' of Providence as the epigraph
      to the final part of the novel," in "Homo Solitarius: Isolation and
      Estrangement in *The Magus*," *Research Studies* 48, No. 3 (1980),
      130–31.

37   A point made vehemently in an early review by Bill Byrom: "That a
      group of individuals should conspire to baffle another person until he
      comes to an improved sense of himself, is to put ends before means in a
      totalitarian fashion which the author seems to condone and enjoy. . . .
      Pervading the book there is a brutality not wholly acknowledged by the
      author; and Nicholas emerges from his . . . trial so mutilated that any
      self-revelation is an experience which he shares uniquely with his creator;
      the reader is left only with the battered husk of a character," in "Puffing
      and Blowing," *Spectator*, 6 May 1966, 574.

analysis, the novelist/god who rules both Bourani and *The Magus* is John Fowles.[38]

Supplementing what I have called this undermining process in the novel is a singularly paradoxical irony, which we will later also see operating in and adapted to *The French Lieutenant's Woman.* It is the very indeterminacy of the book, designed specifically to express and embody the principle of freedom, that itself undercuts *The Magus*'s overt commitment to this principle by ensuring that *eleutheria*, liberty, is never given the status of an absolute and unquestioned truth in the text. In this regard it is quite possible to see the very relentlessness of the novel's ambiguities, its fanatical and anxious determination to preserve its own mystery by escaping definition, as ultimately self-defeating: the layers of ambivalence in *The Magus* mean that nothing can be accepted by the reader as finally and definitively true. This amounts to a kind of pervasive cognitive uncertainty, a paranoia about meaning and how we apprehend it, which is vividly experienced by both the reader and Nick-as-reader; we cannot help but share his periodic sense that the whole of life, like the book, is one black conspiracy (240–41, 492).

Thus *The Magus* seems intent on effecting one of those improbable escapes found so often in Fowles's work. Here the flight is not only from definition but from cognition as well — or at least from those modes of cognition which depend upon categorization, identification, and the explicative capacities of the mind. And perhaps this is the only kind of liberation, an essentially negative freedom to evade, which the novel really endorses. It is interesting to note in this regard that, of the three men we meet in the novel who have endured the masque, the only one who seems fundamentally changed is Leverrier, who has embraced mystery to the point of committing his life to a religious and theological version of it. And Leverrier is the only one who refuses to write or speak about his Bourani experience. Here then, in the endlessly deceptive

---

38   Fowles has himself admitted this, whatever the endeavours and implications of the fiction. He told James Campbell: "I do try to give [the characters] freedom, yes, but only as a game, because pretending your characters are free can only be a game. The reality of the situation is that you're sitting with a pencil and at any point you like you can strike out developments in the book" (456).

inner world of the masque, the unstable external world of the novel as ambiguously authored by both Nick and himself, Fowles begins the exploration, finally accomplished in "The Cloud," of the difficult relationship between cognition, meaning, and language itself. In Leverrier's silence, his refusal of language, we may perhaps read an understanding denied to both Nick and Mitford. In this, his second book, however, Fowles expresses philosophical, ethical, textual, and linguistic uncertainty by refusing a resting place in the novel to either content or form. By offering us no fact that cannot be disproved, no truth that cannot be exposed as sham, and no character or situation unreachable by doubt, *The Magus* forces us to question any and every conviction that its own pages seem to promote as valid.

This view of the novel as in many ways a self-deconstructing text can be extended to its investigation of sexuality and its preoccupation with what constitutes good sexual politics. Here the novel's apparent endorsement of Alison as Nick's true partner cannot be taken at face value. For if the only kind of freedom not implicitly undermined in the book is the freedom to evade, then *The Magus* develops a tension both textual and sexual between the wish to escape, to remain unknown and impenetrable, on the one hand, and the need to be responsible, to embrace commitment, on the other. What this means is that, on one level, it is the novel which seeks to remove itself from our analytical reach and to evade the reader's cognitive powers — without, however, becoming itself incomprehensible. This tension between the unknowable and the communicable reformulates in linguistic terms that tension mentioned earlier between the book's two contradictory narrative drives: one towards indeterminacy and mystery, the other towards destination and closure. This tension of language or narrative is also a moral tension between the desire for withdrawal into fantasy and the need for commitment to reality. It returns us implicitly to the precarious poise of Keats's odes and makes clear why Fowles strengthened the Keatsian overtones of the ending when he revised the novel.

But, on another level, the tension between evasiveness and responsibility is essentially a sexual configuration in Fowles's work, which continually restates issues of art, and especially of narrative art, in sexual terms. Thus this tension describes the precarious oscillation of Fowles's male protagonists between an unattainable woman and an available one, between an endlessly receding and indeterminate feminine mystery and an all-too-knowable, physically much more palpable, female destination. In *The Magus* this provides the model for Fowles's psychosexual investigation of Nick: Julie Holmes embodies the fantasy of unattainable femininity while Alison Kelly persistently recalls her lover to the less glamorous and more carnal imperatives of the quotidian world. If we examine this mode of arrangement in a little more detail, focusing on the book's apparent endorsement of Alison and what she represents, we find that it is this configuration, and the book's involvement with sexuality and gender, which returns us to the central subject designated earlier: art and the workings of the creative imagination.

The Magus presents itself as a critique of male narcissism, self-interest, and manipulativeness in sexual relations. Nick is quite frank in the early stages of the novel about his exploitation of women: "I had my loneliness, which, as every cad knows, is a deadly weapon with women. My 'technique' was to make a show of unpredictability, cynicism and indifference. Then, like a conjuror with his white rabbit, I produced the solitary heart. . . . It was like being good at golf, but despising the game" (21). When he meets Alison, his inability to appreciate her fully is based on a snobbish perception of her as coarse, despite her vitality, and altogether too sexually available to arouse his deepest passions. He describes Alison as "crude, but alive" on their first evening together; later, at supper with his Magdalen friend, Billy Whyte, Nick feels "embarrassed by [Alison], by her accent, by the difference between her and one or two debs who were sitting near us." He then describes Alison to his friend as "cheaper than central heating" (36), and is hyper-aware of her sexuality as somehow constituting a signal to all men, not just to himself: "Men were always aware of her, in the street, in restaurants, in pubs; and she knew it. I used to watch them sliding their eyes at her as she passed" (31–32). It is interesting that these words, with their slight air of a proprietorial sense under threat, come immediately after Nick has noted Alison's "characteristic bruised look; a look that subtly made one want to bruise her more" (31). In his relations with Alison, it seems, violence is never very far beneath the surface.

Nick's fundamental contempt for Alison is based on an erotic sensibility which is both puritanical and xenophobic: it is

Julie's relative lack of sexual experience, her aura of enigmatic innocence, that arouses him, while he is both drawn to and flattered by
her genteel middle-class Englishness. For example, on the beach
soon after they meet, Nick is entranced by the "sort of innocent
sideways slyness of her smile" and her ability to look "so young, so
timidly naughty" (193–94). The image which Julie evokes of "a
pretty, rather skittish schoolgirl in a gay striped dress" leaves him
"hopelessly attracted" (198) and "transparently excited" (193). He
is also impressed by her Cambridge degree and her "completely
English" voice (168). Narcissistically exultant at finding a woman
whose background is apparently so like his own in national and class
terms — her accent "was my own; product of boarding school, university, the accent of what a sociologist once called the Dominant
Hundred Thousand" (168) — Nick dismisses Alison as a mere
colonial, unable to appreciate the subtleties of English middle-class
life. He tells Julie that he and Alison are "just friends now. . . . You
know what Australians are like. . . . They're terribly half-baked culturally. They don't really know who they are, where they belong.
Part of her was very . . . gauche. Anti-British. Another side . . . I
suppose I felt sorry for her, basically" (207).

        Given Nick's prejudices and his attitude to Alison, it is
not surprising that she should be almost completely replaced in his
emotional life by Julie, who is presented as her diametrical opposite,
in the Phraxos-Bourani section of the novel. This internal text, the
masque, is dominated by Julie, just as the larger text which contains
it is dominated by Alison. The London flat, like the hut on
Parnassus, becomes a kind of anti-*domaine* by virtue of Alison's
association with it, a place secluded but emphatically not idyllic.
Before the closing section of the novel, then, Fowles uses the contrast between Alison and Julie to illustrate both the nature and the
direction of Nick's tendency to idealize women sexually. The only
time in the novel when he explicitly admits to feeling any love for
Alison at all is on Parnassus. Here she assumes for a moment that
air of childlike innocence which arouses him, and the unspoiled pastoral landscape (itself an implied analogue for that state of sexual
purity which he seeks)[39] allows him to assimilate her into the
English literary canon by invoking Marlowe's shepherdess:

---

39   This is suggested in the comparisons of both the Greek landscape and
      Bourani to the Garden of Eden, and in the early identification of Greece

> She had woven a rough crown out of the oxeyes and wild pinks that grew in the grass around us. It sat lopsidedly on her uncombed hair; and she wore a smile of touching innocence. She did not know it, but it was at first for me an intensely literary moment. I could place it exactly: *England's Helicon.* . . . Suddenly she was like such a poem and I felt a passionate wave of desire for her. . . . [She looked like] a child of sixteen, not a girl of twenty-four; . . . [i]t rushed on me, it was quite simple, I did love her[.] (269)

He seems to love Alison in direct proportion to both her ability to approximate "a poem" and his ability to suppress her reality as an uneducated, promiscuous Australian air-stewardess.

Nick accomplishes this elision of Alison's identity through the deployment of a literary reference which exactly reflects his xenophobia; the allusion also functions as a metaphor by means of which Alison can be re-identified in terms specifically tailored to Nick's erotic desires, and effectively placed within the world of art. This world, as we have observed, is regarded by Nick as a sort of purely aesthetic and more abstract version of the *domaine*: it is infinitely available to him as a source of more or less self-flattering images for himself and his experience. This suggests that the most sophisticated kind of reification accomplished by Nick's idealizing imagination involves either an excited apprehension or a redefinition of the way in which a woman makes herself available to him and, by association, to men in general. In the case of Julie, her sexual unavailability to Nick is, for most of the narrative, counterpointed by the promiscuous use which Conchis makes of her in the masque; she is a versatile actress whom he requires to play many different parts. Julie is available therefore to the text, the work of art which is Bourani, but not, at least not until just before the trial, to its hero, Nick. With Alison, by contrast, Nick's affection and desire are only aroused simultaneously when he can suppress the reality of

---

with femininity — especially with the kind of "pure . . . noble" (49) femininity that Nick admires. He compares Greece to "a woman so sensually provocative that I must fall physically and desperately in love with her, and at the same time so calmly aristocratic that I should never be able to approach her" (49).

her sexual promiscuity and, as it were, transfer that availability to an aesthetic realm which has already proved itself capable of exploitation in the service of his ego. With both Julie and Alison, then, a crucial part of Nick's erotic response is imaginative access to the woman either as artefact or as part of an artefact, together with a show of sexual reluctance on her part which seems to compliment and invite his predatory impulse.[40]

This process, a complex variation on the darker and more sinister manipulations of Frederick Clegg, reveals once more how adept Fowles is as an analyst of masculine sexual idealization. By assimilating Alison into art, Nick is transforming her into the sort of iconographic female whom he finds he can love. Clegg, a much more twisted man than Nick, sought a similar kind of transformation for Miranda. Finding the degraded icon finally more arousing than the elevated one, he fulfilled his wish simultaneously to love and to punish by reducing her to the anatomical components of his pornographic anti-art. Nick's reifications are more subtle. He tries to change Alison into the kind of woman that Julie is, or that she appears to be: a living work of art possessed of the convenient ability to function as a sexual tease.

In the Parnassus episode, the metaphorical conversion of Alison into a static and aesthetically located image is further accomplished through deliberately mythologizing her by means of a comparison to Eve. Seeing Alison as "a child of sixteen," Nick convinces himself that he is "seeing through all the ugly, the unpoetic accretions of modern life to the naked real self of her — a vision of her as naked in that way as she was in body; Eve glimpsed again through ten thousand generations" (269). This second re-identification of Alison, this time with Eve, allows Nick to mask something else about her which he finds unattractive: her

---

40   Acceptance of this point illuminates an earlier moment in the novel when Nick experiences some mixed feelings for Alison in, significantly enough, the Tate Gallery. Standing before a Renoir, he has "a terrible deathlike feeling" that he thinks is desire but which he later identifies as love (35). In light of the subsequent comparison of Julie to a Renoir (194), this incident illustrates what happens to Nick when he tries to love the woman who is outside the frame, as it were. With Alison occupying here the position of observer, and hence of potential artist, rather than that of the artist's contemplated object, he can experience their connection only as a "terrible" and "deathlike" inverted affection.

contemporaneity. Julie, with her elaborate period costumes and quaint 1915 expressions, attracts Nick partly because she evokes the past. Her erotic appeal for him is largely retrograde, and it is as Lily Montgomery that he first falls in love with her.[41] On Parnassus he tells Alison that Julie is "totally unlike you. Unlike any modern girl" (271). This suggests that for Nick the erotic is also the historically regressive; he seeks the titillating sexual restraints of an earlier era and finds these embodied in women who are, or can appear to be, childlike and innocent. That this process of mythological transformation is effectively a method of self-deceptive masking is further shown here in Nick's insistence that he is reinstating Alison's "naked real self" — a concept of identity which the radical ambivalences of the novel are constantly calling into question.

The mythologizing of Alison is, like the aestheticizing of her, an ambiguous process which serves once more to elevate and to control her simultaneously. It facilitates her assimilation into art by suppressing her individuality through submergence in an archetype. This again brings her metaphorically close to Julie, who, partly through her sister and symbolic extension, June, can "become" any woman from literature, art, or myth. At various stages of the novel she plays Astarte, Ariadne, and Artemis, as well as Miranda from *The Tempest*, Estella, and Desdemona. She also plays Eve in her capacity as betrayer of sexual faith, and Nick, in his disintoxicated fury, sees this identity as her true one: "I suddenly knew her real name, behind the masks. . . . I did not forgive, if anything I felt more rage. But I knew her real name" (530–31). Clearly, then, Nick must entirely renegotiate Alison's reality in terms of those metaphors which attract him before he can feel any love for her at all. He must, in fact, displace a real woman in the

---

41   Fowles's revisions did "modernize" Julie a little: she abandons the Lily Montgomery persona sooner in the 1977 version, along with Lily's first name; she begins wearing contemporary clothes sooner, sports a suntan, and has fewer sexual inhibitions. These changes make Julie more credible, but they do not vitiate her essentially old-fashioned appeal. Nick is, significantly, disintoxicated from Julie when her love-making with Joe suggests to him, among other things, an unacceptable level of "emancipation": "Lily now seemed to me as far ahead of me in time as she had first started behind" (529). In her ability to evoke the sexual behaviour of both past and future, Julie foreshadows Fowles's next *princesse lointaine*, Sarah Woodruff.

direction of a fantasy one, for he loves Alison only insofar as he can turn her into Julie. And Julie is the quintessential cipher — psychologically a mere projection of Nick's ubiquitous narcissism, morally a personification of his selfishness.

This suggests a reformulation in Fowles's second novel of the ambivalent relationship between women, sexuality, and art that he began to explore in *The Collector*. In a very direct way, Nick perceives Julie as a living artefact, and the novel directs us to view this kind of sexual idealization as at once morally pernicious and artistically necessary — even inevitable. Julie exists within Conchis's text as a part of the larger artwork which contains her. Although living, she is authorially controlled by him (as far as we can tell) for she has no definable presence or significance beyond his text, as well as no precise identity within it. Although her mother, Lily de Seitas, could be seen as another symbolic extension of Julie, neither woman inhabits a world beyond the reach of Conchis's power,[42] and Julie herself seems to exist only on Phraxos. This makes her very different from Nick, who frequently rebels against his status as "character" in Conchis's "novel" and tries to escape the old man's authorial control. Julie is entirely constituted by the text which contains her and she never asserts herself through an artistically creative act of her own — as Nick does when he writes the story of his Greek experiences. She is thus much more Conchis's creature than Nick can ever be, for while both are "written" by Conchis, only Nick becomes a writer himself.

It is no accident, then, that both Nick as sexual idealizer and Conchis as artist compare Julie often to works of art. Fowles is once again aware, as he was in *The Collector*, of idealization and creativity as not only essentially masculine but in many ways interdependent. Thus Nick first encounters Julie through Conchis's photos of her as Lily Montgomery. When he meets her, he observes her "beautiful neck; the throat of a Nefertiti" (173), and

---

42   Julie seems at times to be nothing more than a manifestation of Conchis's power: a personification of his irony (294) and an embodiment of his "truth" (646). But one of the questions which the book leaves unanswered is, as Bradbury points out, whether any aspect of the world it describes can be seen as beyond Conchis's reach — presuming of course that Conchis *is* what he seems to be: prime mover of the godgame and symbolic equivalent of Fowles.

later on the beach she reminds him of "a Renoir" (194). Conchis compares Julie to Shakespeare's Olivia (406), and indirectly to Miranda when he identifies himself with Prospero (83). It is Conchis, furthermore, who presents Julie to Nick at the disintoxication as the living embodiment of Goya's *Maja desnuda* (527–28): "The slender form lay in its greenish-tawny lake of light, without movement; and she stared at me as from a canvas. The tableau pose was held so long that I began to think this was the great finale; this living painting, this naked enigma, this forever unattainable. . . . For a few moments I was looking at a magnificently lifelike wax effigy" (528). While he watches Julie and Joe, Nick also comprehends Conchis's literary allusion here, and he designates Joe as "the Negro, the Moor" (529) and Julie as Desdemona looking back dispassionately on Venice (530).

In this novel, then, women and female sexuality are presented once more as the material of art and as a kind of natural resource available to the artist. Although Nick shares in Julie's materiality to some extent, *The Magus* suggests that feminine material is more pliable and less rebellious than masculine, for the individual man, unlike the individual woman, has the ability to be an authoritative creator as well as an instrument.[43] Thus, while Conchis's living reference to Goya implicitly sets Nick in the place

---

43   Obviously the disintoxication would be radically incomplete without Joe. He joins Julie within the canvas frame and is as much a part of Conchis's text as she is. But Joe is not deployed in the same way as Julie: he has very little contact with Nick, the protagonist, and this makes him more a part of the Bourani decor than anything else. Also, his sexuality does not mean what Julie's means in relation to art and the artist. His body is never exhibited in the same way; his physicality is not observed by either the reader or Nick as an invitation to erotic fantasy or aesthetic appropriation. This is true even in the masque of Apollo and Artemis, where Joe appears as the naked "statue" (181). In both this miniature drama and the metatheatre, Joe is more a stage prop than an actor. Fowles treats Joe's sexuality in much the same way as he treats David Williams's in "The Ebony Tower": the naked man has none of the sexual and artistic significance of the naked woman. Similarly, Nick's mythologizing of himself via comparisons to Theseus, Ulysses, and others is very different in cause and effect from his mythologizing of women: Nick does not try to transpose himself metaphorically into these figures and, as narrator, *he* is in charge of the mythic comparisons which he invents for himself.

of the artist/observer/voyeur, Julie's place remains securely that of the *objet d'art*, the subject of Nick's fascinated, tortured gaze. Here the situating of Nick within the flogging frame suggests a position of creative power as well as one of entrapment and torment. The situating of Julie within the frame around a "canvas" implies a position with no such flexibility. She is the object of contemplation awaiting the artist's powers of inscription, and her identity as *objet d'art* is in fact the only one left unambiguous or unquestioned in the novel.

Julie as the *Maja* represents a kind of ultimate assimilation of the woman into art, the ultimate expression of that compliment which at once elevates and degrades. In moral terms, this re-presentation of an already represented woman is designed to offer Nick a purgatorial image of his own exploitative reifications, for what he sees is a woman immobilized by an aesthetic transformation no longer metaphorical but literal. Here is Nick's sexual methodology summed up for him in an image of vitality made static and individuality suppressed in favour of iconographic perfection. This *Maja* is life become art, a metaphor made flesh, and in this literalization the metaphor is lost and the flesh dehumanized. In *The Magus*, to grasp a literary allusion is to experience a moment of self-insight: this high-minded exposé of a rake to himself is also inevitably the self-exposure of an artist. Here the artist is implicitly not only Conchis but Nick, for one of the unstated purposes of the trial and disintoxication is to show Nick that the reader and interpreter of texts is also paradoxically his opposite, the creator of them. The aesthetically remodelled and displaced female body, located and categorized by an almost grotesquely immediate reference to art, confirms this by offering itself so passively to the eyes of the spectator. Nick is the spectator here, but he also fills the space reserved for Goya and, by association, for both Conchis and Fowles.

This re-creation of a famous painting — a technique which Fowles would return to in "The Ebony Tower" — functions therefore as another *mise en abyme* in relation to the allegory of art in the novel. By identifying Nick with the artist and the artist with the exploitative methods of the sexual imperialist, the re-created *Maja desnuda* presents the artist as an ethically dubious man and the rake as a creative force. That this constitutes a critique of masculine sexual behaviour and of the artist as exploiter of women is conveyed by the sadistic trappings of the trial and disintoxication. Their Gothic, pornographic apparatus of drugs, blindfolds, gags, and whips deliberately recalls *The Collector* and associates Nick with Clegg. The image of Nick forced into Goya's place while tied to a flogging frame is a punitive and disturbing one; it conveys the dubiety of the artist, while suggesting that punishment and suffering are not only his ontological condition but his due.[44] In this way *The Magus* communicates a peculiar distrust of the artist and of creativity even as it presents them as numinous, transformative, and almost magical.

It is in the context of the last disintoxication scene and what it says about sex and art that we finally understand the reference earlier in the novel to de Deukans' sinister female puppet, Mirabelle, *la Maîtresse-Machine*. This creature, mechanical but offering the consolations of the flesh, is another variation on the self-deconstructive process at work in the novel. Mirabelle, whose essence and sole function is a sexuality not only devitalized but fatal, reflects retrospectively on the Goya tableau to reveal explicitly the corruption and death that the beautiful image of Julie as the *Maja* only implies: "A naked woman, painted and silk-skinned," Mirabelle possesses "a stiletto on a strong spring" which stabs her lover during coition (177–78).

The mutually reflexive relationship here between Mirabelle and Julie parallels that between de Deukans and Conchis. The count is an anti-magus, a collector of collections (175), who is at the same time a motive force behind the masque — it is his money, according to Conchis, which has made the metatheatre possible. Conchis is also de Deukans' protégé, if only in a spiritual sense, for Nick never finds any trace of him as an historical personage.

---

44   This anxiety about the artist as morally questionable is somewhat ameliorated in "The Ebony Tower." Here the artist Breasley is tolerantly presented as a man whose spiritual largesse, like his creativity, rests to some extent on his unorthodox morality. In Fowles's later work, his attitude towards the artist as incorrigible rake softens slightly as his vision of the artist as creator becomes less awestruck. Woodcock sees *The Magus* as an attempt to exorcise personal guilt; he notes that Fowles met his wife on Spetsai while she was married to another teacher. Whatever the validity of this kind of reading, it might account for the emotional intensity with which the philandering of an incipient male artist is chastened in *The Magus.*

This means that, like Clegg and G.P., these two men, one an embalmer and the other a creator, are inseparably linked. The grotesque misogyny of de Deukans points indirectly to the darker forces which seem to lurk beneath Conchis's devotion to women and his secular humanism in general. Similarly, it is through Mirabelle as a kind of opposite but identical image of Julie that we perceive the aesthetically controlled and defined erotic fantasy of a woman as actually a monstrous and lethal machine, debased more than elevated by the idealizations of those who wish to love and to use her. Having desired a woman made to his specifications and in his own image as little more than an instrument of his onanism,[45] Nick must watch the encounter between Julie and Joe which signals his loss of her. Having played the "unscrupulous collector . . . in love with a painting he wants" (601), Nick is stabbed symbolically by Mirabelle's stiletto, and is in a sense destroyed by his own solipsistic fantasy.

But while the novel insists graphically on the punishment of Nick and on the suffering of the artist, it once more undermines its own insistence through the relentlessness of its ambiguities. Just as we cannot wholly accept the valorization of freedom of choice in the book, so we cannot fully commit ourselves to the critique of sex and art which it communicates. In a narrative which so consistently undercuts and undermines what we think is the truth, how can we take on trust what seems to be Conchis's criticism of himself as artist embedded in his criticism of Nick as man? Both the artist as rake and the rake as artist seem to be dubious figures, but we cannot know this for certain. Neither can we ignore the power of the creativity that they possess, which the novel implies is impressive even if repugnant.

Furthermore, Fowles makes no attempt in *The Magus* to follow up the logic of his own exploration of this issue. If the male artist is not to be trusted, why does the novel not offer us his alternative, a female artist? Conchis is lavish in his praise of women and

---

45   Significantly, Fowles's revision added a love scene in which Julie masturbates Nick during a midnight swim (Chapter 49). This emphasizes not only Nick's autoerotic sexuality but the masturbatory quality of Bourani and of the *domaine sans nom* in general. Such imagery identifies the *domaine* as a world of immaturity — prolonged adolescence perhaps — in which the hero should not linger too long.

seems convinced of their superiority to men. He tells Nick that neither of them "has the intuitive humanity of womankind" (296), and that the atrocities of the Occupation could not have occurred in a world in which men and women were truly equal (413). Despite these sentiments, and their correspondence to some of Fowles's own opinions,[46] no woman artist appears in the book — even though Fowles himself has stated that he "long toyed with the notion of making Conchis a woman," but found that the "technical problems" were too "great." He has not further specified what those problems were.[47] One cannot help wondering whether Fowles, after writing *The Collector*, felt that art and its interdependent "opposites" — collecting and pornography — were altogether so closely linked and so disreputable that only men could debase themselves by meddling with such things! But as *The Magus* implies, and as both *The French Lieutenant's Woman* and *The Ebony Tower* go on to declare, creativity is a formidable power, essentially masculine, and desirable for its ability to rearrange reality (219) while affecting lives. In his second novel, it seems that Fowles is once more expressing his implied conviction that the woman artist is for him a contradiction in terms. In his third, as the following chapter will show, he would experiment boldly with the possibility of authoritative female creativity before returning to this belief.

The relation between women and art is fundamentally passive in Fowles's work. Although he perceives the negative aspects of the artist's tendency to exploit women sexually and aesthetically,

---

46   His views were expressed in several interviews. Fowles told Lorna Sage: "I think I'm under a feminine star, quite definitely — mother-dominated and so on," in "John Fowles — A Profile," *The New Review* 1, No. 7 (1974), 37. He commented to James Campbell: "I feel that the universe is female in some deep way. I think one of the things that is lacking in our society is equality of male and female ways of looking at life" (465). See also Singh, 189, 190; and Fowles's "Notes on an Unfinished Novel," in *Afterwords: Novelists on their Novels*, ed. Thomas McCormack (New York: Harper & Row, 1969), p. 172.

47   Fowles, "Notes," p. 172. Out of justice to Fowles, I quote here his own opinion on Lily de Seitas and her daughter — an opinion from which my argument implicitly dissents: "The character of Mrs. de Seitas at the end of the book was simply an aspect of [Conchis's] character, as was Lily."

Fowles cannot quite envisage femininity in active and effectual conjunction with artistic power. Feminine power remains for him mysterious and unquantifiable. Without definition in and of itself, it receives shape and direction at the hands of the male artist. *The Magus* is consistent with Fowles's later work in its suggestion that the power of women is obscure and contradictory: dissociated from control and lacking either assertion or independent utility, it is still implicitly identified as power. Lily de Seitas is in one sense an aspect of Conchis's creative godhead, but she nevertheless tells Nick that her role in the masque used to be "somewhat similar to Lily's" (603) and she is now muse and helpmeet to Conchis. A middle-aged handmaid to a polysemantic artist, she shows Nick her portrait, for she too has been painted: "[A] little Alice-like girl with long hair, in a sailor-dress . . . *Mischief,* by Sir William Blunt, R.A." (592).

The reticence that lies behind the vehemence of the novel's critique of both Nick and Conchis is further suggested in the book's problematic third section. Fowles's dissection of Nick's manipulative narcissism is so frank and so vivid, it culminates so graphically in the cruelly self-revealing lessons of the disintoxication, that the reader comes to expect some sign that Nick is at least starting to change his reprehensible ways. But this expectation is, as we have seen, frustrated, despite the fact that Nick's awareness of what he should be doing remains unimpaired. Thinking about Jojo, he observes: "Adulthood was like a mountain, and I stood at the foot of this cliff of ice, this impossible and unclimbable: *Thou shalt not inflict unnecessary pain*" (641). But that chasm between what Nick knows and how he behaves cannot be bridged in the novel, and he goes on to reify both Jojo and Alison while perceiving Kemp wholly in terms of his own need for perfunctory and indirect mothering: "[S]he was what I wanted and what I needed: a warm heart . . . [she] stopped me from being, whenever I felt it, too morbidly abandoned and alone" (576). It seems that the only way in which Nick's reifying sensibility has changed is in the addition of sentimentality to its more or less blatant and brutal techniques of imaginatively recasting women.

Appropriately enough, Nick makes no attempt to abandon those artistic and mythological metaphors which have accomplished his reifications: Alison is now associated with china plates rather than with pastoral poems, and implicitly compared to Persephone and Eurydice rather than to Eve; Jojo is seen as a

"Beckett-like thing" (634) and an animated "Munch lithograph" (638). Furthermore, Alison has been colonized by the Bourani world; she has entered Conchis's text and become an instrument of his art. In a similar way, she is also an instrument of Nick's art, insofar as Nick is writer of the text we are reading, and it is his art also which contains and constitutes her. In terms of the larger framework of the novel, therefore, Alison is to Nick what Julie is to Conchis. Here we must consider the novel's treatment of sexuality in conjunction with its presentation of Nick as himself a sort of Conchis-figure, an author/artist in his own right. If we bear in mind the book's tendency to question and undermine its own explicit premises, it is possible to see Nick's failure in his narrative to fully acknowledge Alison's humanity and to act upon what he can perceive as her human worth as a direct reflection upon that psychological regressiveness of his which we observed earlier. We can see Nick's behavioural and authorial incapacity not as incapacity at all, but as refusal — an emotional, psychological, and moral rebellion expressed as an act of narratorial defiance.

This view of Nick's regressiveness as a deliberate narratorial stance — as an act of artistic choice rather than an exhibition of emotional failure — is based on the fact (implied but not directly stated in the novel) that he does not and cannot love Alison, no matter how much his externally coercive author, John Fowles, and his internally effectual author, Maurice Conchis, feel that he should. To this end it is Conchis who states what seems to be the basic (and very conventional) sexual lesson of the book when he tells Nick to take his advice: "Go back to England and make it up with this girl you spoke of. Marry her and have a family and learn to be what you are" (406–407). But the endless ambiguities and contradictions of *The Magus* are also the source of its peculiar puritanism: although the novel *asserts* a positive if indefinable connection between Nick and Alison, a connection which Nick must learn to recognize as he sloughs off his xenophobic snobbery, it cannot make us *feel* this repeatedly declared emotional link with any real conviction. This is because, for Nick, the warm intensity of the connection remains fundamentally unfelt throughout the novel. He cannot act on his insights, either as man or as narrator, because they have no meaning in terms of his emotional life.

Even when he draws together the overt existential and sexual lessons of the book in the last third, the language of coercion and conscious determination which he uses betrays his true feelings: "I knew [authenticity] was all bound up with Alison, with choosing Alison, and *having to go on choosing her every day*" (641, emphasis added). There is a revulsion here which pulls against the high-mindedness, for it is Julie who commands Nick's deepest passion, and the intensity of his desire for her radically undermines the moral and sexual rectitude of his choosing Alison. In this split between emotion and will, the reader begins to sense, beneath the lush surface of *The Magus*, informing this novel of imaginative and erotic excess, the strict spirit of a schoolmaster in confrontation with a recalcitrant boy.[48] The punishments of the masque resemble retrospectively a sustained effort to make Nicholas Urfe accept Alison Kelly, not just as his apparent destiny, but as his medicine.

It is not too facetious to identify Fowles with Conchis in this role of heuristic schoolmaster; in *Daniel Martin* he would go on to attempt once more the suppression of the ideal, fantasized woman in favour of the accessible one. But in narrative terms, this effort to equate the desirable with the available is more morally righteous than emotionally or psychologically credible. Thus in *The Magus*, it seems to me, Fowles expresses, along with Nick, an ambivalence towards his own sexual and moral lessons by means of that remarkably multifunctional ending. By refusing to bring Nick and Alison unambiguously together, this ending achieves a kind of doubly deconstructive effect: it implicitly supports those fantasies of erotic innocence and possession, those controlling processes of reification and transformation, which it seems to repudiate; and it allows the book to be read as a statement of Nick's rebellion against Conchis's sexual and ethical catechizing. If both Conchis and Nick are in effect artists, then it is quite possible to see *The Magus* as a psychomachia, a dramatic externalization of one individual's inner conflicts. The novel becomes an allegory not only of art but of the artist's psyche, in which his more responsible and mature

---

48   It is no accident that, when talking about fiction, Fowles has referred to "the character-building novel" and to his own didactic tendency "to be the schoolmaster." See Sage, 32, 33. His language often reveals the indebtedness of his sensibility to that public-school education system which he also abhors. Noting this about Fowles's rhetoric, Conradi dubs this former headboy at Bedford School "a reformed practitioner of the pleasures of petty school power" (p. 24).

recognitions meet and do battle with his anarchic and youthful, but still strongly creative, energies. In fact, the novel almost seems to imply that true creativity resides with these subversive energies, with those aspects of an artist's inner life that belligerently refuse maturity.

Thus Nick's narrative becomes a study in recalcitrance rather than incapacity, more an attempt to defy the magus than to imitate him. That split between perception and action becomes a deliberate strategy expressing in narrative terms Nick's refusal to be bullied into anything. This prefigures an idea about narrative which Fowles would return to in his story "Poor Koko": the act of narration can be an act of revenge, an exorcism of violent and angry feelings through the exploitation of language and its transformative power. By writing his own novel — and by choosing, unlike Conchis, to create it with words — Nick uses his own creative resources to attack symbolically those of his philosophical and artistic "progenitor," Conchis. In the same way Bourani, with its collections of fake curios, photographs, and artworks, is Conchis's challenge to his own aesthetic and moral "father," de Deukans. Through narrative, furthermore, Nick not only expresses his own refusal but effectively traps his mentor by that very process of literalization which Conchis has used to torment him. By writing what is literally a novel (on one level at least, and here Nick's unreliability as a narrator helps to make "novel" arguably more appropriate than "autobiography"), Nick undoes Conchis's effort to liberate the novel from language, the principles of fiction from books, and to write without words. By turning the masque itself into a novel, by aligning it finally with fiction if not with life, Nick confines the magus and his notions between the covers of a book.

In this sense, the novel describes a multifaceted power struggle — not only between a character and an author or between different aspects of an author's psyche, but between an aspiring, potential author and the mature artist who has fathered his creativity. This further illuminates the complex textuality of *The Magus* by revealing its concern with the text as a place of competition where the fledgling creator must confront not only the controlling powers of his forebears, but the ineradicable presence of other texts and the problem of their status in relation to his own. Both Nick and Conchis can thus be seen as manifestations of Fowles's own imaginative conflict as an artist working inevitably in the authoritative presence of other artists and their productions. And here the many references in *The Magus* to other works of art take on a specifically textual significance which supplements and counterpoints their function in relation to the novel's treatment of sexuality. Just as Nick looks to art for models of his own experience, so the novel is written — by Nick on one level of production, and by Fowles on another — in the acknowledged presence of other texts and other works of art.

This sense of art as inevitably intertextual and dependent on other art is emphasized in the re-creation of the *Maja desnuda* and in the extended reference to *Othello* which Conchis makes during the disintoxication. Julie's copulation before Nick's eyes with the "Negro" Joe is a crystallized metaphor for the artist — Goya/Conchis/Nick/Fowles — forced to create in the formidable shadow of masterpieces, for it effectively projects a scene from *Othello* that Shakespeare did not write: the consummation of the love between Desdemona and the Moor. Nick makes this explicit when he identifies himself with "the traitor Iago punished, in an unwritten sixth act. Chained in hell" (530). This crucial scene, a network of allusions and re-creations, throws into focus many of Fowles's deepest preoccupations with art and creativity. By identifying Nick as both spectator and creator, the disintoxication draws together the artist, his artwork, and its interpreter in ways which suggest the inevitable functioning of all artists as the readers of other artists' texts.

If Fowles's first novel established a subversive equation between the apparent opposites of collector and creator, *The Magus* begins an exploration, extended in *The Ebony Tower*, of the contradictory but necessary identification between critic and artist. It is, after all, from Nick's attempted reading of Conchis's text, Bourani, that his own text, *The Magus*, springs. The Oedipal conflict with the creative progenitor can only take place once the younger artist has steeped himself in the work of his threatening, inspiring forebear. Enriching in this way the significance of those references to Oedipus in the novel (157, 254) and of Fowles's interest in the orphaned protagonist, *The Magus* suggests that all art is effectively criticism and all writing is rewriting. Nick expresses this clearly when he describes his effort to explain the masque as an act of criticism designed to rewrite a great work of art in terms of the conventions of a minor genre. Glossing the fable of the prince and the magician, Nick comes to realize that,

[b]y searching so fanatically I was making a detective story out of the summer's events, and to view life as a detective story, as something that could be deduced, hunted, and arrested, was no more realistic (let alone poetic) than to view the detective story as the most important literary genre, instead of what it really was, one of the least. (552)

The disintoxication can be seen, then, as a layering of rewritten texts enacting a process of creative usurpation on several levels, and functioning perhaps as a metaphor for the novel itself. Conchis changes Goya's *Maja* by arranging a kind of extension — the literal depiction of that erotic act which the painted woman invites and suggests but does not perform. He thus modifies the art of a progenitor by making manifest in his text what the earlier work left implicit. In the same way he rewrites *Othello* by showing the consummation implied but not depicted in the play. Nick then, in an act of literary interpretation, identifies Julie with Desdemona and, prefiguring Fowles's manipulation of narrative personae in *The French Lieutenant's Woman*, writes himself into this text as Iago. Through reading, interpreting, and expressing his interpretation in narrative, Nick implicitly asserts himself over Conchis and Goya, as well as over Shakespeare, whose place as author/artist he is also made to occupy.

By extension, and by virtue of authorial doubling within the novel, Fowles himself incorporates these multiple acts of rewriting into *his* text, and thus alters our perception of pre-existent artworks by reformulating them in his own terms and appropriating them for his own reasons. He also, true to the metafictional endeavours of the novel, draws attention to the very act of rewriting which he performs through his deployment of both Nick and Conchis as readers and writers. Through them Fowles answers indirectly, and in relation to another of Shakespeare's plays, his own question: "And Elsinore, that following spring?" To write is to rewrite, literally to fill in and flesh out the gaps of other texts and in so doing to discover and occupy a literary space of one's own. The artist is not only a sexual imperialist but inevitably a textual one as well, and this enables him to assert himself, with varying degrees of aggressiveness, in relation to other works and other artists. It may enable him also to write himself into other texts and so to disturb the authority conferred upon them by historical priority. This is the situation which Fowles would return to in both *The French Lieutenant's Woman* and *The Ebony Tower*: an awareness of the anxiety of influence and the power struggle which it can precipitate. In the latter book especially he explores, with more sophistication than he could command in *The Magus*, his own problematic relationships with forebears like Edouard Manet and Marie de France. Here, too, he links the problems and implications of textuality very closely to complex issues of language and gender, for in *The Ebony Tower* he confronts not a literary father but a mother, Marie de France.

It is tempting to extend the correspondences and analogies worked out in this discussion of *The Magus* to *The Ebony Tower*, and to see the latter as a kind of reworking of an earlier novel by the same author, a reworking designed to draw out and explore in more detail issues left implicit in the prior work. This allows me to conclude my chapter where I began it, with the ambiguous status of *The Magus* as a revised text — a text released, significantly, three years after the appearance of *The Ebony Tower*. While it would be far-fetched to see "The Ebony Tower" as providing exactly those historical referents omitted in *The Magus* and offering us David Williams as literally an older version of Nick, still playing *jeune premier* to an eccentric genius, we can perhaps see Fowles's revision of the novel as a confrontation not only with his younger creative self, but with that (historically prior) self as a *bona fide* literary influence. In modifying the text created by the earlier self and simultaneously drawing attention in his Foreword to that text as a layering of many drafts, Fowles himself enacts the paradigm of creativity which his novel in both its versions asserts and explores.[49]

Like Conchis reworking Goya and Shakespeare, like Nick rewriting Bourani, Fowles seeks in the rewriting of his own book to weaken or even eradicate the authority of an earlier text through

49   Interestingly, Fowles modifies his own work in the same way that Conchis reformulates works by Goya and Shakespeare: he draws out erotic details left implicit or unstated in the earlier piece. Thus Nick's love scenes with Julie are franker and more numerous in the revised text, and the relationship is consummated in Chapter 58. But this does not make Julie any less the unattainable woman, just as Charles Smithson's single encounter with Sarah does nothing to dissipate her mystery or render her more accessible to him.

the creation of a superseding one, and at the same time to possess it by stamping it even more thoroughly with his own mark.[50] As he would do later with Marie de France's *Eliduc*, Fowles disrupts the historical relationship between two texts in order to enhance and re-emphasize his own artistic authority. It is here, perhaps, in Fowles's own life as a man and an artist, that we might find those missing co-ordinates of the *Bildungsroman* which I alluded to earlier. But any critical attempt to look into his personal history in this way would be inappropriate and intrusive — the task perhaps of that biographer whom the text of Fowles's life still awaits. The reader, in accomplishing for him/herself those acts of criticism which for Fowles are always disreputable and sometimes impossible, is left with the vertiginous ambivalences of *The Magus*. These, in their complexity and elusiveness, are suggestive without ever being reassuring.

---

50   Fowles's own comments suggest the potentially aggressive nature of the act of revision, the tendency of modification to become destruction: "A lot of revision is really a form of masochism — what you are today savaging what you were a year ago," in Halpern, 40. His opinion further reflects the concern of *The Magus* — which Fowles refers to in his Foreword as "this endlessly tortured and recast cripple" — with art and its processes as a kind of violence. For a discussion of the theoretical relationship between the two versions, see J. A. Wainwright, "The Illusion of 'Things as they are': *The Magus* versus *The Magus: A Revised Version*," *Dalhousie Review* 63, No. 1 (1983), 107–19.

3

THE FRENCH LIEUTENANT'S WOMAN

In *The French Lieutenant's Woman* (1969), Fowles extends his investigation into the nature and capacities of narrative by self-consciously evoking the generic past of the novel and problematizing both the aesthetic and moral obligations of prose fiction in the twentieth century. In the famous Chapter 13, which deliberately breaks the illusion of the fictional world as self-consistent and enclosed, the Fowlesian narrator declares:

> If I have pretended until now to know my characters' minds and innermost thoughts, it is because I am writing in . . . a convention universally accepted at the time of my story that the novelist stands next to God. He may not know all, yet he tries to pretend that he does. But I live in the age of Alain Robbe-Grillet and Roland Barthes; if this is a novel, it cannot be a novel in the modern sense of the word.[1]

This indicates the ways in which Fowles's third novel further considers the textual and, specifically, metafictional issues under scrutiny in his second. Abandoning first-person narrative, and what I presented in the last chapter as its uneasy relationship with fictional self-awareness, Fowles clearly emphasizes the author's access to absolute power in relation to the fictional world. Then, by means

---

1   John Fowles, *The French Lieutenant's Woman* (London: Jonathan Cape, 1969), p. 97. All other page references appear in the text and are to this edition.

of a narrator who periodically enters his own narrative to comment upon (among other things) the processes of story-telling itself, Fowles explores ways in which authorial omniscience might be rejected as formally and ethically presumptuous, and considers how the potentially despotic power of the writer might be responsibly deployed.

Lacking the solipsism of Clegg and Urfe but also undeniably powerful by virtue of his creative function, this authorial persona allows *The French Lieutenant's Woman* to foreground, more openly and explicitly than *The Magus*, Fowles's sense of the postmodernist text as obliged to exhibit its textuality, to signal and display its fictional nature: "If *The Collector* is crystallized and unself-conscious ideation, a fiction pretending to autonomous existence, then the next two novels represent a progressive iconoclasm that proclaims the fictiveness of their own enterprises."[2] The insertion of a self-questioning narrator between Fowles as a twentieth-century author and his Victorian characters effectively generates what Linda Hutcheon calls "a number of worlds within worlds. The core or most traditional novelistic universe is that of the characters. Outside and including that is a world in which exist the man in the train, the impresario — in other words, the narrator's personae who enter at times the core world." Beyond these worlds stands Fowles himself, "who masterminds both the creation of the Chinese-box structure *and* the tensions which exist between these worlds and which are functional within the novel as a whole."[3] Through a narratorial sensibility which both masks[4] and mediates Fowles's own is diffused all that the reader receives of the "core . . . universe" and

---

2   Dwight Eddins, "John Fowles: Existence as Authorship," *Contemporary Literature* 17, No. 2 (1976), 208.

3   Linda Hutcheon, *Narcissistic Narrative: The Metafictional Paradox* (Waterloo, Ontario: Wilfrid Laurier University Press, 1980), pp. 57–58, emphasis in original.

4   In "Notes," p. 167, Fowles has commented: "[T]he 'I' who will make first-person commentaries here and there in my story, and who will finally even enter it, will not be my real 'I' in 1967; but much more just another character, though in a different category from the purely fictional ones." In this sense, the breaking of one fictional illusion in the novel is also the establishing of another.

all that he/she must grasp of the contemporary world inhabited by the author. It is therefore in terms of the narrator's precise situation that the reader perceives the novel's particular historical poise: the narrator says of Ernestina's clothes that their colours "would strike us today as distinctly strident, but the world was then in the first fine throes of the discovery of aniline dyes. And what the feminine, by way of compensation for so much else in her expected behaviour, demanded of a colour was brilliance, not discretion" (11). This historically Janus-faced sartorial analysis immediately identifies the narrator as that centre of consciousness which holds the balance between the two centuries, nineteenth and twentieth, upon which the novel simultaneously focuses.

The narrator stands therefore as a *mise en abyme* for Fowles's stylistic treatment of time in *The French Lieutenant's Woman*. By offering a contemporary perspective on nineteenth-century experience, the narrator represents the hindsight made possible by history, and in this way facilitates the illumination of the past in the optic of the present. Furthermore, in an opposite but equal way, his historical double vision also allows the present to function as a mirror for the past, and the reader may contemplate the Victorian age from the paradoxical perspective of futurity — a futurity uninaugurated in the central story, but informing and directing the narratorial mediation of that story. This, then, is the interpenetrating or telescoping of past and present which establishes the historical framework of *The French Lieutenant's Woman*; it is personified in a narrator who ranges knowledgeably over the intellectual landscapes of the twentieth century while appearing, with disconcerting physical specificity, in the geographical landscapes of the nineteenth.

If the novel's double or telescoped temporal perspective is held in a kind of synthesis by the narrator, his capacity to operate within and without the "core world" gives to this synthetic function its vital aesthetic and moral dimensions. For it is quite possible to argue that the evident aim of the novel — to view the past under the auspices of the present and to go, as it were, back to the future — might have been achieved without objectifying the narrative voice in so concrete and flamboyant a way. In *A Maggot*, for example, Fowles would go on to create a similar sense of interpenetrating eras through a generic revisionism which is compatible with a more traditional authorial projection of the narrator as historian.

But Fowles's choice here of a narrator who can deploy the hindsight of history while writing himself at will into his own narrative allows the novel to highlight with particular immediacy the issue of authorial control, and to examine this in relation to the specific past of the novel as genre.

The self-aware and self-exhibiting narrator foregrounds this issue of the writer's power in the perspective of history when, after twelve chapters of acting the "local spy" (10) in not especially unusual ways, he draws explicit attention to the illusory or fictional nature of his text — "This story I am telling is all imagination. These characters I create never existed outside my own mind" (97) — and declares himself a mere reporter of his characters' actions. Morally obliged to "respect" their free will, he must "disrespect all [his] quasi-divine plans" for them (98) in the interests of philosophical credibility and verisimilitude. He then presents this reading of the author's role in terms of its limitations rather than its capacities, as indicating *the* crucial shift in the generic development of the novel over the last one hundred years: "The novelist is still a god, since he creates (and not even the most aleatory avant-garde novel has managed to extirpate its author completely); what has changed is that we are no longer the gods of the Victorian image, omniscient and decreeing, but in the new theological image, with freedom our first principle, not authority" (99). These declarations render the narrator's function as index of the novel's historical poise inseparable from his role as index of its generic poise, for *The French Lieutenant's Woman* looks forwards and backwards in relation both to history generally and to the novel's history in particular. Thus the book's temporal framework of interpenetrating centuries has its equivalent on the level of structure as well: *The French Lieutenant's Woman* situates the contemporary novel in a relationship with its Victorian ancestor that acknowledges historical development while effecting a more ambiguous — and vitally important — disruption of chronology.

Clearly the function of Chapter 13 is to rearrange radically the premises of the text on different levels. Most obviously, this first blatant intervention of the narrator challenges conventional notions of "theme" and "structure" by obtrusively focalizing those processes of fictionality which the reader might expect to operate more discreetly or implicitly in the text. The constructedness of narrative thus becomes as much a thematic concern in the

novel as the nature of love or moral choice. This manifest destabilization of descriptive literary categories functions, together with the
narrator's other two dramatic appearances, to interrogate fictional
conventions as deployed in the nineteenth-century novel through a
literal invasion of the Victorian "core" by what Fowles sees as the
metafictional responsibilities of postmodernism. Obliged to reject
the omniscience so frequently favoured by Victorian novelists, the
narrator observes that "a genuinely created world must be independent of its creator. . . . It is only when our characters and events begin
to disobey us that they begin to live" (98). So, by means of a
repudiation of authorial might and a thematized insistence on the
unpredictability of the fictional world, *The French Lieutenant's
Woman* revises Victorian novelistic conventions in the light of
twentieth-century experience. It is the clearly signposted self-
referentiality of this novel that chiefly distinguishes it stylistically
from *The Magus*, and also indicates the depth and urgency of
Fowles's interest in metafiction at this point in his career. In relation
specifically to this interest, Fowles confronts the issue of artistic
power and the relationship of women to that power in *The French
Lieutenant's Woman*.

But it is important to remember that, despite its disclaimers, Chapter 13 also acknowledges that the author, however
great his respect for freedom as a "first principle," is still a powerful
figure. He cannot fully dismantle his own power without destroying
his identity as an author.[5] The novelist, "since he creates," is indu-
bitably "still a god." If the novel's obtrusive narrator facilitates its
self-conscious investigation into the nature of authorial power — and
if he regularly stresses the need for that power to be limited — it is
also through him that the book implicitly suggests those ways in
which it *cannot* be limited. For the narrator himself must choose his
endings from among infinite possibilities, and the fact that he offers
more than one ending does not, strictly speaking, make this act of
choosing any less arbitrary and controlling. The indeterminacy which
is designed to express the idea of liberty in the text is inevitably the

---

5   Fowles himself expressed this more crudely in an unpublished interview
     with Melvyn Bragg: "What I say on that subject [whether the author
     controls the characters] . . . is really a little bit of eye-wash. And I'm
     afraid I'm playing a sort of double trick on the reader. Of course I con-
     trol the text[,] we all do"; quoted in Woodcock, p. 98.

decision of both the narrator on one level of textual operation and Fowles on another, absolute one. In *The French Lieutenant's Woman*, the structural enacting of freedom is necessarily incomplete, for neither the novelist-god nor his representative will fully commit himself to strategies that would destroy his own function.

To a certain extent, then, the narrator's signposted attempts to relinquish control are merely gestures towards an ultimate freedom which the very nature of the authorial task makes impossible. In fact, neither Fowles nor his narrating surrogate ever gives up entirely the power which he undertakes to repudiate. But the novel invites us to suspend disbelief on this issue by not explicitly identifying any creative source beyond the narrator. In other words, he, unlike the characters in the "core world," is not openly and specifically foregrounded as a fictional construct. This means that, in relation to the narrator, Fowles himself is no more nor less present than the author of any more conventional, less self-conscious fiction. Thus the reader's experience of the novel's narrator is very different, as we will see, from his/her experience of Sarah — who is also a story-teller — for he/she can perceive the narrator without automatically becoming aware of the creative power which is authoring *him*.

In view of this, the narrator's gestures in the direction of abdicated creative control gain a kind of theoretical credibility in the novel that effectively de-emphasizes, for the reader, that impossibility which they also suggest. We respond positively, therefore, to what these gestures symbolize rather than to what they literally effect. We also accept them as moral indices of the good faith of both narrator and author: when the former admits that the novelist is by definition a god, he also implies that the best an author or narrator can do is try to avoid any tyrannical wielding of his power in (and over) the text. The reader accepts the ultimate limitation of the principle of freedom as it operates with regard to both Fowles and his narrator; and he/she does so as part of an unspoken contract between author and reader which allows the book to exist in the first place. But *The French Lieutenant's Woman* finds other ways to problematize the issue of authorial control and to render its overt stand on the dubiety of omniscience deeply ambivalent — for Sarah's story-telling is treated very differently from the narrator's, and the century which she inhabits can be seen as a kind of text which Fowles, through his narrator, is attempting to influence.

Appropriately enough, the sense of fictional self-consciousness as involving (whatever its limitations and difficulties) a creator's rejection of power and his acknowledgement of the fictional world(s) as artificial and unpredictable is formulated in moral terms by the novel's pervasive emphasis on individual freedom. On the level of the narrative "core," this means that Charles's quest for romantic love becomes an initiation into the loneliness of personal liberty, a perception of human isolation on the "unplumb'd, salt, estranging sea" of life (445). On the narrator's mediating level, the idea of freedom is worked out overtly in terms of both form and content,[6] as the narrator attempts to enact his repudiation of authorial despotism by means of an indeterminacy not usually found in Victorian novels. The alternate endings refuse closure in an effort (not entirely successful) to respect the free will of characters and reader alike. This open-endedness, like that of *The Magus*, is designed to force the reader into a position equivalent to that occupied by the male protagonist in each book: Nick and Charles both find themselves deserted by an authorial surrogate, a narrator-cum-*Deus absconditus*, who will not locate them textually in a definitive ending or temporally in a narratively comprehensible future.[7] The reader too is left in the lurch by his/her narrator, and

---

6   Hutcheon argues for the congruence of these in the novel, the impossibility of perceiving content except in relation to those forms which embody it: "[T]his parodic rehandling functions thematically and structurally on a purely introverted level in [the book]. However, it also has an extramural role, directing the reader to the moral and social concerns of the novel. . . . [T]he *reader* . . . is never allowed to abstain from judging and questioning himself by condemning or writing off the novel's world as 'just' Victorian (as well as 'just' fiction)" (p. 18, emphasis in original). Hutcheon here counters many of the first reviewers, who dismissed the literary parody as a contrived obtrusion into a work of historical fiction. See, for example, Walter Allen, "The Achievement of John Fowles," *Encounter* 35, No. 2 (1970), 67; and Elizabeth D. Rankin's more academic expression of this view in "Cryptic Coloration in *The French Lieutenant's Woman*," *Journal of Narrative Technique* 3, No. 3 (1973), 196.

7   Charles is also marooned at the end in a philosophical sense, for he has developed an existentialist awareness at an historically inappropriate moment. This corresponds to Fowles's original conception of him as "an existentialist before his time," in "Notes," p. 166.

forced to participate actively in the shaping of his/her readerly destiny by an act of choice.

On the less accessible level of Fowles's own intentionality — and here we engage with the differences as well as the similarities between author and narrator — it seems safe to assume that, for him, narrative indeterminacy and rejection of closure constitute the greatest challenge which postmodernism can offer to more traditional novelistic forms. Thus the idea of freedom, and Fowles's sense of the contemporary novelist as obliged to explore ways of respecting it, is embedded in the text on multiple levels of narrative utterance. Operating both ethically and structurally, it manifests itself through the alternate endings as effectively an aesthetic of fiction which highlights instability — a theory of narrative based on the refusal of the creator, as either author or narrator, to impose upon his created world the intelligibility of termination. The concluding reference to Arnold's "estranging sea" describes not only Charles's existential freedom, but the liberating directionlessness of the novel itself and its passage into the disconcerting spaces of indeterminacy. In identifying its own ending — and by extension the endings of all stories — as a place of radical uncertainty rather than a point of comfortable definition, *The French Lieutenant's Woman* insists, even more fervently than *The Magus*, on the kind of textual ambiguity and instability which thwarts criticism and thus preserves (in Fowles's terms) the primacy of the artwork by preserving its mystery.

• • •

This analysis of the book's general narrative approach provides a context within which to perceive Fowles's vision of artistic power in the novel. And the assumptions about freedom and dominance which inform this technique crucially affect — in some unexpected ways — our perception of the heroine, Sarah. For while the narrator is an authorially powerful figure, the generator of both a text and a theory of textuality that challenge his readers, Sarah too is overtly presented as creatively capable. The text which she generates is, like Conchis's, partly her own fictionalized life-story; in relation to Sarah, it is Charles who doubles for Nick in the role of interpreter. Like his predecessor, Charles strives to grasp the meaning of an ontologically ambiguous text which implicates him both as reader and as character, for Sarah's apparent determination to fictionalize herself involves the manufacture (in narrative terms, the plotting) of a love-affair between them.

In this sense *The French Lieutenant's Woman* seems to represent an attempt by Fowles to approach in a new way some of those problematic questions about creativity and femininity which, as we have seen, preoccupied him in *The Magus*. His perception in the latter novel of the artist as trickster and torturer, as well as redemptive creator, did not result there in the extension of creative power to women, despite the book's attempt to present women as morally and humanely more admirable than men. So, having previously toyed with and rejected the idea of a female magus, Fowles seems to confront this possibility seriously in *The French Lieutenant's Woman*. Sarah Woodruff can be seen as his first effort to empower his heroine by endowing her with a mature creativity, and by so doing to feminize the artist. While Sarah does in some ways function as the magus-figure which the novel on one level wishes her to be, on another level the strategies of that novel, like those of the text which she herself generates, effect her limitation and confinement. It is one of the profound ironies of the novel that this process of containment operates through, rather than in spite of, a metafictional machinery designed both to valorize and enact the principle of freedom in the book.

The apparent presentation of Sarah as not just incipiently but effectively a narrative artist is inseparably linked to the nature of the book's involvement with art; even more than *The Magus*, *The French Lieutenant's Woman* is passionately concerned with creativity and its products. The novel's very narrative technique, as I have suggested, is predicated upon an investigation into the power of the artist as author, while its self-reflexivity foregrounds textuality *per se*, or the artefact specifically as text. Furthermore, the novel recapitulates, albeit with some complex variations, the basic narrative situation of *The Magus*. The narrator at work on the story of Charles and Sarah mirrors Fowles engaged in the same task; and within that "core world," both the author and his surrogate find their *mise en abyme* in Sarah, who generates her own story — first about Sarah and Varguennes, and then about Sarah and Varguennes' double, Charles. From this point of view, Sarah's text corresponds to Conchis's "internal" text Bourani, while the narrator's is equivalent to that produced by Nick: both men, while created ultimately by

Fowles's imagination, must also be perceived as writers of their own texts.[8] What *The French Lieutenant's Woman* seems to add to this structural formula is a woman focalized specifically in terms of textual, that is artistic, control. It is Sarah who invents the story of Varguennes and she who, improvising as adroitly with her text as the narrator does with his, displays some of the impresario's flair by casting Charles in the role of the French lieutenant when he comes to Lyme Regis. Extending and developing her text through Charles and plotting her own seduction with the care of an author marshalling facts, she arranges her dismissal from Mrs. Poulteney's employ and lures Charles first to Carslake's Barn by means of a note (in French!), and then to Exeter by means of an address.

With a non-existent sprained ankle to support her ruse and a richly coloured shawl to provide personal decor, Sarah receives Charles in Endicott's Family Hotel, where the consummation of their love and the climax of her story coincide. It seems as if Fowles has reversed those premises supporting his model of creativity and gender by showing us male sexuality (Charles's) colonized by a female artist (Sarah) for inclusion in a text of *her* own devising. By the time Sarah, apparently in full possession of an independence guaranteed by creative triumph, tells Charles frankly, "You cannot

---

8   Fowles's third fiction is unique among his novels in its portrayal of a male protagonist who has, apart from some dabbling in poetry, no artistic role of his own. Instead, the book displaces the creativity of the Fowlesian hero onto the narrator, who thus partakes in a sense of both Charles's nature and his experiences. This effective splitting of the hero avoids the awkward alliance of metafiction with first-person narrative and, apart from "Poor Koko," Fowles would not return to the first-person until his most traditional novel, *Daniel Martin*. It accounts also for the close sympathy between the narrator and Charles: "[D]espite the ironic distance at which Charles is held . . . we are persuaded into sympathetic identification with [him] as narrative voice merges with Charles's point of view"; Terry Lovell, "Feminism and Form in the Literary Adaptation: *The French Lieutenant's Woman*," in *Criticism and Critical Theory*, ed. Jeremy Hawthorn (London: Edward Arnold, 1984), p. 118. In very different ways from Sarah, then, Charles also functions as a surrogate for both narrator and author; Fowles refers to Charles as his "surrogate" in "Hardy," p. 35. Conradi confirms the close links between this trio of men when he describes Sarah as "the object of a quest which is as explicitly that of the narrative voice as it is that of Charles" (p. 71).

marry me, Mr. Smithson" (343), it seems as if Fowles has accomplished in this book the resolution of his own contradiction in terms. In the context of a novel which scrutinizes the nature and extent of the artist's power over his artefact, he has apparently broken the link between creativity and masculinity by an elaborate reworking of *The Magus* that effectively transposes Maurice Conchis into Sarah Woodruff. To this end we see Sarah exhibiting some of the contradictory characteristics of Conchis;[9] manipulative and selfish as well as compelling, she generates an indecipherable text which transforms Charles's life while thwarting his powers of rational comprehension. When she abandons her besotted and despairing lover, in the novel's third ending, she acts out the savagery of freedom in the same way that Conchis does at the end of *The Magus*. Thus the metatheatricality of Conchis's masque seems to become the metatheatricality, or layered fictionality, of Sarah's text. It is no accident that self-dramatization should be her forte, or that Charles should finally come to see her as a ruthless and "accomplished actress," exploiting him to the last (433).

These aspects of the novel seem to suggest that the artist can be feminized by a mere transposing of gender, which allows the woman magus to exhibit even the negative qualities of her male equivalent. If this is true, the reader must ask him/herself why the prospect of such a feminization struck Fowles as so problematic at the time of *The Magus*, and why his work since 1969 has, as we will observe, repudiated the conjunction of woman and creativity apparently inaugurated here. Would it be correct, in short, to see *The French Lieutenant's Woman* as an aberrant book relative to the ideas of gender and art under examination in this study? To answer these questions, we must look more closely at the different narrative contexts in which this apparently empowered heroine is embedded,

---

9   Chapter 21 also links the two by casting Sarah as a version of Conchis's admired antiquity, the stone head: her "complex" smile reveals an "irony" that undercuts Charles's "pretensions"; disarming and profound, "it excuse[s] all" (180–81). The titles of the two novels further associate Sarah with Conchis by naming, apparently, a centre of artistic potency in each book. Loveday has averred that Fowles's titles often refer not to the focus of attention, but to the source of power in a novel (p. 70). My reading of Sarah's reveals the partiality and spuriousness of her comparison with Conchis, and implicitly contradicts Loveday's point.

and return to some of the technical procedures of the novel outlined in the opening pages of this chapter.

● ● ●

It is, significantly, with specific regard to Sarah that the
book first directly signals its own textuality. Objectifying himself as
an observer beneath her window, the narrator apprehends Sarah as
mysterious and inquires: "Who is Sarah? Out of what shadows does
she come?" (96). These are the closing lines of Chapter 12 and his
answer, "I do not know" (97), is the first sentence of the chapter in
which he thematizes the self-reflexivity of his text. In relation to
these opening words about her, his following comment on his narrative — "This story I am telling is all imagination" (97) — establishes an implicit connection between Sarah and "story" which
identifies both as essentially unknowable and fictitious, the indefinable products of the creative mind. Despite the overt acknowledgement of fictionality here, we are actually on quite familiar Fowlesian
ground: the heroine is presented more or less directly as a text or as
part of a text, and her romantic mysteriousness is an analogue for
the mystery (hence, for Fowles, the vitality) of the text as creative
artefact. The narrator makes the artistic or aesthetic dimension of
the heroine's mysteriousness clear when he uses it to invoke implicitly the limits of metafictional inquiry: the "world" created by the
author/artist becomes "a dead world" once it "fully reveals its planning" (98). His own intention, it seems, is not to push textual self-
exhibition too far, and this operates in relation to Sarah through the
narrator's simultaneous insistence on her mysteriousness and her
fictionality. These stand respectively in the novel for the numinous
indefinability of the artefact and its demystifying investigation into
its own processes.

Thus the novel's metafictional strategies, as expressed
and highlighted by the narrator, repeatedly emphasize the textuality
of Sarah and her participation in the fictionality of the text. She is
not only written by the narrator in a way similar to that in which
Conchis is written by Nick-as-narrator; she is written with the kind
of narratorial and narrational awareness that makes her part of a text
in the process of revealing its own artificial and illusory nature. The
reader is therefore inevitably directed to perceive Sarah in terms of
artificiality and illusion.

Furthermore, by instructing the reader to see Sarah as fictional text *before* he/she has enough information to see her as a creator- or narrator-figure, the novel prevents a simple equation between her manipulations of Charles and authorial directing of a character. This is more than a refusal to allow Sarah access to that omniscient authorial power which the novel repudiates; it is a way of undercutting Sarah as creat*or* by placing her in the compromising perspective of Sarah as creat*ed*. The accruing to her of the controlling power of authorship is thus made problematic by her chronologically prior presentation — despite the book's moral commitment to freedom — as herself the object of such control, and by her status as an exposed illusion. The reader cannot experience Sarah as author without being aware of her as authored, and her role as artificer is clearly conditioned by her function as artefact.

Like *Daniel Martin*, *The French Lieutenant's Woman* sets up its female narrator-figure in a narrative context, or in terms of a narrative methodology, which directs the reader to doubt the veracity of her utterance by questioning the relationship between fiction and truth. This kind of doubt does not, of course, necessarily vitiate the artist's power. Conchis tells many literal lies in the service of what *The Magus* seeks to present as the higher truth of existential freedom; and we have observed, in both *The Magus* and *The Collector*, how Fowles's work regularly combines an admiration for the artist with a suspicion of both his behaviour and the nature of his creative "magic." It might be argued that Sarah's mendacity is simply one aspect of a full-blown creativity, for the female artist evidently partakes of the moral dubiety and incipient charlatanism that help to define her male counterparts. To this end, we might say, she is presented at times in the novel as a cruel seductress who delights to twist the dagger in Charles's heart (433), and as a witch-like figure whose dangling bonnet, in Carslake's Barn, suggests to Charles's mind powers both sadistic and supernatural: "[H]e had an icy premonition that some ghastly sight lay below the partition of worm-eaten planks beyond the bonnet, which hung like an ominously slaked vampire over what he could not see" (235).[10]

---

10   The frequent association of Sarah with sinister or brutal imagery suggests, among other things, an anxiety about female authorship to which this discussion of the novel later returns.

But, again, it is the novel's very self-reflexivity that prevents us from unproblematically assimilating Sarah to the Fowlesian vision of artistic temperament. Her illusoriness, or evident fictionality, acts as a kind of springboard in the text, deliberately throwing the reader back to the actual narrator (and by extension to Fowles himself) as her creator: the narrator's exposure of his own role means that the responsibility for any spiritual or moral truth made manifest by Sarah's lies — the truth, once more, of existential freedom — must rest with him rather than with her. By showing that the female narrator, even as she herself "writes," is written, the novel implicitly focalizes her narrator and author as *de facto* generators of any narrative truth which might seem to originate with her.

This technique of effectively displacing the narratorial wisdom of the heroine onto her creator as its source and custodian denies her artistic power by rooting it in a creative imagination beyond her own. In this way the narrating heroine is indirectly presented as less of a truth-teller herself and more of a conduit for the truths of those who create and "tell" her. This complex textual manoeuvre is one to which Fowles would return in his next work, *The Ebony Tower*. There, his ongoing confrontation with the possibility of achieved feminine creativity leads him, in both "The Enigma" and "The Cloud," to undermine the power of a narrating heroine by explicitly placing her creativity under the auspices of a controlling force which authors *her*. It seems that, in Fowles's work, any emphatic empowering of the heroine as story-teller is countered by an unambiguous encoding of her as a story herself, a figment of authorial imagination.

In *The French Lieutenant's Woman*, then, the self-conscious foregrounding of fictionality also effects the crucial foregrounding of the heroine's fictionality. Charles's efforts to comprehend Sarah's motives and actions — like Nick's attempts to understand Conchis's — are both an analogue for the reader's efforts to grasp the meaning of an impenetrable text, and a re-emphasis of Sarah's status as herself a text, not entirely available to the rational analysis of the reader-as-critic. Like Conchis and Bourani, Sarah and her story are not to be fully deciphered. In Exeter she tells Charles: "Do not ask me to explain what I have done. I cannot explain it. It is not to be explained" (342); and in Chelsea she declares: "I am not to be understood even by myself" (431). But Sarah's unavailability to readerly comprehension is essentially different from Conchis's, for this very inaccessibility — a vital part of her apparent power — has already been to a great extent demystified by the signposting of her fictionality. If the novel demystifies Sarah by exposing her fictionality along with its own, it also demystifies her story in a similar way — by discovering in Sarah's text a fictionality equivalent to its own which reflects back on the constructedness of the novel as a whole. *The Magus* will not limit the indecipherability of Conchis or Bourani by clearly identifying either as ultimately fictional; but *The French Lieutenant's Woman*, by exercising in relation to Sarah that power of definition which it elsewhere repudiates through indeterminacy, explicitly asserts that ultimate fictionality which compromises her as a creator.

To shift attention from Sarah to her story is thus to shift the focus of this discussion from the processes of the novel-at-large to those of the "core world," the Victorian saga of Charles and Sarah. On this level, Sarah's narratorial power seems unchecked: she re-identifies herself through an invented "autobiography," extends this text by writing both Charles and herself into it, and generally seems to function as an unproblematic *mise en abyme* for the novel's narrator. Redirecting my analysis in this way entails a return to those questions posed earlier about Fowles's averred technical difficulties in conceiving of Conchis as female, his apparent resolution of those difficulties here, and the renewed insistence in his subsequent fiction on the quintessential masculinity of the artist.

The above discussion has implicitly answered these questions by revealing the deployment of the text's metafictional strategies to constrain, vitiate, and variously devalue the power of a creative woman. This suggests that Fowles's third novel, rather than expressing a radical change in his conception of artistic creativity, goes to complicated lengths to disguise the fact that this conception remains fundamentally *un*changed: Sarah-as-narrator can only be viewed in relation to self-conscious narrative manoeuvres which restrict her power even as they seek overtly to affirm and respect it.[11] Sarah's emergence in the novel as effectively a woman of limited,

---

11   This illuminates another possible reason for Charles's lack of artistic function, for if Sarah's fictionality is openly exhibited, then obviously his own is as well. Had the hero been an artist, *he* would have been subject to the same devaluations and restraints as Sarah is; the novel would have undermined Charles as neither Nick nor Conchis is undermined in *The*

authorially deflected creativity makes *The French Lieutenant's Woman*, all appearances to the contrary, basically consistent in its treatment of art and gender with Fowles's other fictions.

Furthermore, we can now grasp the impossibility, within the context of *The Magus* as a whole, of Fowles portraying Conchis as female. As I observed in the previous chapter, Conchis's creative power is never categorically delimited; the novel's refusal to define anything within its world as bedrock truth or reality means that nothing can be identified as clearly beyond Conchis's control. Nick's only recourse is to attempt the confinement of this conspiratorial creative intelligence by means of narrative: he writes a book about the magus (just as the narrator of *The French Lieutenant's Woman* writes a book about Sarah). To show Conchis as a woman would have meant the bringing together of femininity and a creative power which could not, given the premises of the novel, be logically or certainly depicted as limited. The magus, as *The Magus* presents him, is not entirely available to epistemology, and he therefore resists any absolute definition or delimitation of himself and his power. It is perhaps the potential suggested here for a conjunction between woman and a possibly boundaryless creative might that deterred Fowles in *The Magus*. In *The French Lieutenant's Woman*, the female artist is conceived in terms of a much more explicitly metafictional narrative structure, which builds into the novel an apparatus for the strategic containment of her creativity.

Also, the foregrounding of textuality and the inevitable questioning of authorial power that it provokes place the efforts of the female artist in a context which rejects on moral grounds the very power she seems to wield. Within its own manifest frame of reference, then, the novel provides us with the means to devalue the power of the feminized magus; Fowles presents the artist-as-woman only within a structure which re-incorporates her into the creative project (in this case, a narrative) of a male artist (in this case, the narrator). *The French Lieutenant's Woman* thus enacts a process

---

Magus. But with the hero's creative energies in the possession of a narrator whose ultimate fictionality is *not* so exposed — who exists, to quote Fowles again, "in a different category from the purely fictional [characters]" — the association between masculinity and uncompromised artistic authority is maintained. The reader once again willingly suspends, with regard to the narrator, the disbelief that the novel prevents him/her from suspending with regard to Sarah.

which "The Ebony Tower" later re-presents in the image of Diana finding her artistic vocation as a co-worker on Henry Breasley's paintings: the domestication of female creativity in the interests of the male artist. For Fowles, the woman may usurp the artist's creative function only if the text which constitutes and contains her can reveal her usurpation as incomplete and ineffectual; the categories of artefact and artist remain in crucial ways for him both gender-based and mutually exclusive.

Ironically, those very self-reflexive processes that express existential freedom morally and embody it aesthetically in the novel work also to limit and control Sarah. Even as she seems to stand in the "core world" for personal liberty and independence, she is constructed in and by the text in terms of restricted power and feminine instrumentality. In this way, the book develops a split between Sarah's emblematic function and the reader's experience of her, between what she *symbolizes* and what, textually speaking, she *is*. The reader, moreover, cannot accept this split in relation to Sarah in the same way as he/she can accept it in relation to the narrator's symbolically meaningful renunciations of power, which I mentioned earlier. This is because Sarah's fictionality is exposed by those metafictional procedures which the narrator in one sense generates, but to which *his* fictionality is not actually subject. Thus the narrator deploys Sarah to suggest for Charles a freedom not fully available to herself, and to symbolize for him an unleashed desire — "a whole ungovernable torrent of things banned" (336) — in which she herself does not appear to participate; in the love scene at Exeter particularly, Sarah's physical timidity, weakness, and delicacy are oddly at variance with the passion suggested by her intense dark eyes and the "sensuality of her mouth" (119). This brings us to a consideration of Sarah's narratorial role within the "core world," where the novel also depicts, in less abstract ways than those analyzed above, the domestication of the heroine and her movement into creative ineffectuality.[12]

---

12   For an opposite view of Sarah as liberated and self-determining feminist heroine, see Deborah Byrd, "The Evolution and Emancipation of Sarah Woodruff: *The French Lieutenant's Woman* as a Feminist Novel," *International Journal of Women's Studies* 7, No. 4 (1984), 306–21. Lovell's view of Sarah as a working-class woman whose exploitation by an upper-class man is masked by the novel's romantic mystifications questions, from a standpoint different from mine, both Fowles's apparent feminism here and the readings of critics like Byrd.

• • •

     Sarah tells Charles the ostensibly true story of her seduction in Chapter 20. Here she is presented for the first time as controlling narrator — although the reader at this stage perceives her as autobiographer rather than as fictionalizer — for up to now her story has reached us only through the fragmented versions of the vicar, Dr. Grogan, and the book's narrator. The apparent accruing to Sarah of narratorial or authorial power here also seems to be confirmed by the narrator's use of theatrical imagery to describe the setting: Sarah has chosen a "minute green amphitheatre" (163) in the Undercliff for the staging of what is evidently a *tour de force* performance. But the encounter between Sarah and Charles is not delineated exclusively by means of this imagery of implied feminine control. Sarah's indifference to fashion makes her like one of "the simple primroses at Charles's feet" (164). The simile recalls earlier comparisons of her to wild animals and plants, which suggest not only the "naturalness" that distinguishes Sarah from Ernestina, but a vulnerability inhering particularly in a certain ineptitude with words.[13] Sarah, on the very brink of articulation, is presented through images that help to dissipate the threat of her incipient creativity by confirming a kind of powerlessness. This vulnerability, by contradicting the implications of the theatrical imagery, helps to problematize Sarah's control of the situation, and to prevent an untroubled association in the reader's mind between Sarah and the artist's ability to shape words. By placing her creative act within the immediate context of a non-verbal simplicity, the narrator suggests

---

13   It is, in fact, Sarah's intense wordlessness which Charles finds so appealing, and he often responds to her as if she were a pre- or non-verbal organism. When he stops her from slipping in the Undercliff, he observes "the wild shyness of her demeanour[:] . . . she was now totally like a wild animal, unable to look at him, trembling, dumb" (118). Later her eyes remind Charles of some tortured "animal at bay" (121), and with Dr. Grogan he refers to Sarah playfully as "a specimen of the local flora" (150). On another occasion in the Undercliff, she is "like a child" (178), and later he finds her in Carslake's Barn, sleeping "curled up like a small girl" (239). The attempt, through such images, to present Sarah as "natural" is complicated of course by the admitted artificiality of both character and novel; the impression of immaturity which they create allies her indirectly to the powerlessness of extreme youth.

that Sarah undertakes this act only reluctantly: Charles observes repeatedly that she will not speak (163–64) and that his role is "to coax the mystery out of her" (164).

We are thus invited to see Sarah's narratorial function as at odds with her nature, a necessary artifice sullying her innate simplicity; it seems that to be an artist is not Sarah's vocation. The end of the novel confirms this by showing her as the contented assistant to an artist, and she is specifically characterized throughout as a woman whose verbal capacity is exceeded by the expressiveness of her physical features, especially her eloquent eyes. Thus Sarah frequently declares not a refusal, but an inability to express herself — "I do not know how to say it" (142); "I cannot explain it" (342); "I am at a loss for words" (427) — while Charles often interprets not her words but her looks: "Though direct, it was a timid look. Yet behind it lay a very modern phrase: Come clean, Charles, come clean" (143).

This suggests that Sarah's inarticulacy is intended in the novel as a kind of alternate language of female intuition. In Rossetti's house, Charles perceives the dissonance between himself and Sarah as linguistic: "Two languages, betraying on the one side a hollowness, a foolish constraint . . . and on the other a substance and purity of thought and judgment" (428). Given Sarah's verbal reluctance in the novel, the reader has been able to perceive this pristine language only as a virtual languagelessness; during the same encounter with Charles at the end, Sarah struggles to communicate her feelings and twice admits that she does "not know what to say" (427). Once again, what Sarah stands for diverges in the novel from what she is: if her inarticulacy symbolizes a higher and freer language, she herself has no access to her own meanings, and these reach us through the enthusiastic interpretive responses of Charles and the narrator. In this way Sarah prefigures Fowles's latest heroine, *A Maggot*'s Rebecca Hocknell, the meaning of whose experiences resides not in her own comprehension, but in that of a man, His Lordship.

The superior vision which Sarah's inarticulacy is meant to indicate remains essentially unutterable, and the task of expressing this feminine inexpressible falls to those men — the hero and his creative double — who invent, edit, and/or decode Sarah-as-text in the novel. Even if Sarah's narratorial actions link her to the articulating power of the artist, she remains associated in her

essence with the inarticulacy of the Fowlesian heroine. This prepares us for that concluding moment in the novel where her physicality, her sexuality, supersede in valorized significance her creative
power. And it is in order to preserve the inarticulate essence of
Sarah, which her pictorially transfigured sexuality comes to symbolize, that the novel deprives her of her narratorial role and recasts
her as muse and model to artists. Thus the inarticulacy which identifies the shapeless enigma of Sarah's vision radically complicates her
portrayal as a narrator-figure, while illuminating the reasons why
her creative efforts in the novel must end.

     Furthermore, the narrator's language in Chapter 20
emphasizes Charles as the recipient of Sarah's story about Varguennes quite as much as it does Sarah in the role of story-teller.
Described as a "strange supplicant" (164), she hesitates to speak
until Charles, with his promise "not to be too severe a judge" (164),
invites her to do so. Clearly Charles, the initiator of her narrative, is
by no means the passive auditor here. He is indirectly placed in the
position of a benefactor and confessor, identified with authority-
figures able to grant favour or absolution to a sinner. This imagery
of the confessional and the courtroom also resonates with that of the
theatre to reveal the ambiguity of the latter: like a confession or a
court case, a play depends for its full significance on both audience
and performer. Sarah as narrator-actor is thus dependent on Charles
as listener-observer, and control over her narrative rests at least partially with him.

     This empowering of a reader is not new in Fowles's
work. *The Magus* is consistently preoccupied with the relationship
between reader and text, and Conchis's masque requires the participation of Nick for its full execution. But the power-sharing
between Sarah and Charles, while in a sense reformulating that relation of narrator/author and reader designed to govern the book as
a whole, is also crucially different from that between Conchis and
Nick. The masque is an ongoing metatheatrical event which has
involved other readers besides Nick and will engage at least one
more, his successor, Briggs; Sarah's narrative is not intended for
such open-ended repetition. While she did originally, we must pre-
sume, conceive the Varguennes story with the larger readership of
Lyme Regis and Victorian society in mind, the individual reader
whom the novel specifically identifies is Charles. Sarah distinguishes
him from her other recipients by declaring: "[Y]ou understand

what is beyond the understanding of any in Lyme" (142), and she also makes clear that she has revealed the whole story to no one but himself (175).

It is in relation to Charles, therefore, that Sarah (at least within the framework of the book) assumes her full narratorial function — a function that defines him by association as a reader much more uniquely important than Nick. The effective irreplaceability of Charles limits the scope of Sarah's narratorial efforts, as Conchis's are not limited, by suggesting a certain finiteness of intention and direction, and this returns us implicitly to the centrality of gender in Fowles's conception of the artist. It seems that for him femininity and sexual potential are inseparable, and the feminized magus cannot but partake of the eroticism of the Fowlesian heroine, the *princesse lointaine*. This means that the male reader of a female narrator's text — and *The French Lieutenant's Woman*, by insisting on both the patriarchal nature of Victorian society and the youthful eligibility of Charles, encodes *all* Sarah's implied readers as effectively male — must inevitably become her lover.[14] So Charles becomes Sarah's, and so Mike Jennings, in "The Enigma," becomes the lover of incipient novelist Isobel Dodgson.[15]

---

14   For Woodcock, the masculinity of Sarah's readers within the novel implies the understood masculinity of those readers outside its frame, who consume both Sarah and the book with which she is equated. Commenting on the narrator's tendency to condemn Victorian sexism while himself assessing the "physical charms" of Mary (77) and berating Ernestina's shallow-mindedness (256), Woodcock observes: "The tone invokes a knowing male complicity between narrator and reader, which can be unfortunate if the reader is not male" (p. 91). This implicit construction in and by the text of the reader-at-large as male is supported by Huffaker's interesting admission that he too fell in love with Sarah: "In autumn of 1970, I was fortunate enough to be seduced by John Fowles's most famous heroine. The affair, of course, was purely literary[.]" Like Charles, Huffaker fell for "her mysterious aloofness, a reserve I admire in her still" (p. 9). In this novel, the textualizing of the heroine evidently sexualizes the act of reading along gender-specific lines.

15   Sarah's macroscopic male reader within the novel, Victorian society, is also effectively presented as her lover by her re-embodiment in an impure alter ego, the prostitute Sarah. The simultaneous degradation and elevation of the heroine which this bifurcation achieves recalls the erotic polarization of *The Collector* and implies a similar process of idealization at work here.

It is significant in this regard that Sarah's telling of her story to Charles constitutes a loss of narratorial virginity corresponding to and literalized by her loss of physical virginity to him in Exeter. This enactment of the central event in her original story initially confirms our sense of Sarah's ongoing authorship, as the text about Varguennes transmutes into the text about Charles. It also clarifies the intention of her narratorial act in Chapter 20 as seduction. Like the earlier encounter, the meeting at Endicott's problematizes Sarah's control of the situation by effecting the same kind of counterpoint. Within the framework of an event that she has arranged, Sarah as lover is presented in terms of a vulnerability similar to that which conditioned our view of her as narrator-figure. Thus Charles is stirred by her smallness and agonizing shyness (332), her "defenceless weeping" (334), and "invalid" helplessness (333); the narrator's description of the encounter emphasizes its violence and Charles's dominance of Sarah, as he "conquer[s]" her reluctance with "a frantic brutality" (337).[16] The relationship between Sarah's story about Varguennes and its extension as, or transformation into, her story about Charles elucidates the process whereby the heroine as fictionalizer becomes — at the level this time of the "core world" — the heroine as fiction. The very nature and motive of Sarah's narrative as framed in Chapter 20 prepare us for her effective redefinition by empowering Charles as both reader and lover: he is implicitly encouraged to write himself into Sarah's story as Varguennes.

The culminating point in her narrative here is a sexually charged moment. Meeting Charles's eyes for the first time, the flushed Sarah declares: "I gave myself to [Varguennes]" (170). But she does not here describe the love scene to which she has alluded. Instead, she elaborates on the social and emotional implications of the deed, explaining her need for a public identity commensurate

---

16   Sarah's vulnerability and Charles's response may, of course, be part of her plan, but the narrator's contradictory language refuses to clarify this: Sarah touches Charles's hand with "an instinctive gesture, yet one she half dared to calculate"; she only *seems* "self-surprised, as lost as [Charles]," and yet when they kiss, it is Sarah who is shocked into averting her lips (335). This chapter's favoured linguistic mode seems to be oxymoron: by describing Sarah as "proud and submissive, bound and unbound, [Charles's] slave and his equal" (334), the narrator obfuscates the issue of control.

with her inner sense of alienation: "I did it so that people *should* point at me . . . [s]o that they should know I have suffered, and suffer, as others suffer in every town and village in this land" (171, emphasis in original). This story then ends with the ritual renaming of herself: "No insult, no blame can touch me. Because I have set myself beyond the pale. I am nothing, I am hardly human anymore. I am the French Lieutenant's Whore" (171). While on the one hand Sarah seeks to re-create herself here by means of a fiction,[17] on the other her designation of herself as "nothing" focalizes Charles disproportionately, in context. For the nothingness which is Sarah resonates here with the gap in her text where the sexual act has been omitted; the dynamics of her narrative therefore suggest an invitation extended to Charles to project himself into her story and play the role of Varguennes.[18] Aiming to seduce, and employing one of the techniques of pornography, Sarah suppresses her own personality while allowing her auditor to participate in the scenario by identifying with her lover. He can thus accomplish the seduction to his own satisfaction through fantasy:

> He saw the scene she had not detailed: her giving herself. He was at one and the same time Varguennes enjoying her and the man who sprang forward and struck him down; just as Sarah was to him both an innocent victim and a wild, abandoned woman. Deep in himself he forgave her her unchastity; and glimpsed the dark shadows where he might have enjoyed it himself. (172)

Already empowered as judge-confessor forgiving Sarah her "unchastity," Charles is here also empowered as seducer, "enjoying her" through mental projection. The elision in Sarah's narrative thus constitutes a space which Charles is invited to occupy; his imagination, propelled by his desire, is required to effect the undescribed consummation and in so doing to conclude the story. He therefore becomes a kind of author in relation to Sarah's text,

---

17   Hutcheon, p. 63.

18   Huffaker's comments, quoted above, clearly indicate the efficiency with which the novel extends this invitation to its male reader as well.

and it is this authorial role which he resumes later in Exeter. Here the space reserved for Charles becomes a literal one, as his corporeal presence replaces the imaginary presence of Varguennes, his physical participation replaces sexual fantasy, and he again completes Sarah's text by converting her from an imaginary fallen woman, whose loss of virginity is only a metaphor, to a real one, whose sexual initiation has crucial consequences for her subsequent portrayal in the book.

This enacting of an unwritten love scene echoes Nick's trial in *The Magus*, where Conchis's reworking of *Othello* requires Nick to participate as a voyeuristic Iago in a scene of consummation omitted from the original play. In both books, and to an extent in *The Collector* as well, a fantasy of sexual possession is actualized through its concretization; each hero finds himself dissatisfied in different ways, while Nick and Charles both lose the women of their choice after a peculiarly literary disintoxication. In *The French Lieutenant's Woman*, the process of enactment is a way of exposing the fictionality of Sarah's original story by changing it from fiction to fact: her defloration in the flesh reveals the defloration in her text as false, and it thus converts her ostensible autobiography into her real one. As Sarah's textualizing and her sexuality are momentarily blurred together, the novel accomplishes at once the confirmation and denial of Sarah's creative power. The reader, like Charles, apprehends her story as fiction only at the point where it becomes fact, and he/she clearly perceives Sarah herself as a fictionalizer only at the moment when she ceases to be one.

Thus the very act which finally identifies Sarah as an artist is also the act which re-identifies her in terms of her sexuality; she becomes, if only for a moment, Charles's mistress and incipient wife, and later offers her radiantly mature beauty for incorporation into the art of the Pre-Raphaelites. Having arranged her own creative redundancy by the literalization of a fantasy, Sarah goes on to destroy her extended text, the story about Charles, by deserting him. But unlike Conchis, who in a similar way exposes his own fakery at Nick's trial and then absconds, Sarah reappears in the novel stripped of creative function, as Rossetti's helpmeet. In Chapter 60, she herself signals her repudiation of authorship and the end of her narratorial efforts by defining her true vocation as the handmaid of genius: "I am his amanuensis. His assistant. . . . I am at last

arrived, or so it seems to me, where I belong. I say that most
humbly. I have no genius myself. I have no more than the capacity
to aid genius in very small and humble ways" (430). She also presents her affair with Charles as an abandoned artefact, the equivalent of Miranda's juvenile and appropriately discarded still lifes: "I
have since seen artists destroy work that might to the amateur seem
perfectly good. I remonstrated once. I was told that if an artist is
not his own sternest judge he is not fit to be an artist. I believe that
is right. I believe I was right to destroy what had begun between
us" (428).

The end of the novel thus effectively displaces Sarah
away from the model of artistic power represented by Conchis and
towards the paradigmatic feminine instrumentality of Julie Holmes.
And like Julie, she combines an availability for assimilation into art
with a physical inaccessibility that signals not so much an independent spirit, but an aesthetically defined and pictorially significant sexuality at the service of the artist as his material.[19] And it is in the
context of Sarah's presentation as reified *objet d'art* that we must
set her refusal to marry. She tells Charles: "I do not want to share
my life. I wish to be what I am, not what a husband, however kind,
however indulgent, must expect me to become in marriage" (430).
The potent irony of this lies in our final perception of Sarah's identity: what she is is the very stuff of art, and this gives her allegiance
to Rossetti primacy over her attachment to Charles. In a sense
made valid by her relationship with the Pre-Raphaelites, Sarah cannot marry for she now has no life to give. When Charles converts
Sarah's art into her life at Exeter, he confirms a process in the novel
whereby that very life — imaged in Chapter 60 as an energized and

---

19   We should remember here that the version of *The Magus* which precedes
     The French Lieutenant's Woman is the 1966 one, in which the uncon-
     summated affair between Julie and Nick leaves the *princesse lointaine*
     absolutely chaste in relation to the hero. Even her availability to her
     semi-aestheticized lover, Joe, seems to be under the control of the artist,
     Conchis. Sarah, like the 1977 Julie, is no less unavailable to Charles
     despite her single encounter with him; it is the prostitute Sarah who
     embodies momentarily the possibility of the heroine as promiscuous. She
     then vanishes from the novel, while Sarah's chastity is guaranteed by the
     celibacy of her life in Chelsea.

flamboyant sensuality — itself becomes art. Thus Sarah, an "electric and bohemian apparition" in pink and blue, stands before Charles like a living work of art, and, in an image which again links her to Miranda by evoking butterflies, he sees her as a "creature . . . blossomed, realized, winged from the black pupa" (423–24).

In the opening pages of this chapter, I discussed various ways in which *The French Lieutenant's Woman* rejects structural and thematic closure and commits itself to indeterminacy. Paradoxically, however, the novel revokes its own principles in relation to Sarah. The explicit encoding of her as a fiction, which the book's narrator accomplishes at the intermediate narrative level, has its equivalent in the "core world" in the removal of Sarah's creative function and her redefinition as *objet d'art*. This effective shutting down of Sarah's options means that she cannot be consistently perceived as a *mise en abyme* for either the narrator or the author. The former, like Nick, continues to write even as he is written; the latter arranges the confinement of her creativity by means of his surrogate, the narrator. Through Sarah, then, the moral and aesthetic commitment of the novel to freedom is again perceived as partial and contradictory, for the narrative restricts her even as it insists upon liberating both Charles and the reader; it imposes closure on her while directing both itself and others outward, into the intoxicating spaces of indeterminacy.

This is confirmed by the fact that Sarah can be defined as the material of art with regard to both possible endings.[20] Even if she should leave Rossetti's house to marry Charles, she retains her place within the text generated by the narrator; the last possible ending finalizes Sarah's destination, her categorization as artefact, by situating her not only in Rossetti's house but in his art — just as she is situated, by a series of extensions, in the work of those other artists, John Fowles and his narrator. Clearly, the radical uncertainty, which I earlier declared valorized by the novel's open-endedness, in fact operates only selectively: Fowles will not unambiguously ally his heroine with the freedoms discovered by, and in certain ways granted to, his hero, his reader, and even the novel which brings them together.

---

20   The book's first putative ending, outlined in Chapters 43 and 44, is not a possibility, because the narrator openly dismisses it at the start of Chapter 45.

It is important to observe, however, that even though the textual strategies of *The French Lieutenant's Woman* undermine its apparent presentation of a female artist, Sarah does seem to have one moment of unqualified triumph in the novel: when she informs Charles at Exeter that he cannot marry her, she seems to have effectively changed her life through narrative and accrued to herself the transformative power of the word. But even here, Sarah is not allowed to retain either her creativity or her apparent independence. In the end she is almost as effectively imprisoned in Rossetti's house as she was in Mrs. Poulteney's, and her role as secretary-companion and general household functionary is in many ways the same. Having manipulated Charles and colonized his sexuality (albeit in terms of an ambiguously shared control) in the service of her own textualizing, Sarah is subjected to the same imperialistic drive and becomes herself a text. Having sought independently the transformative capacity of language, she now, as an amanuensis, transmits the words of her mentor and acts as a vehicle for his truth. In the "core world," therefore, it is Rossetti rather than Sarah who becomes the representative of both the narrator and author, for he is the man who paints her; and by at once celebrating her beauty and trapping her self in his art, he uses Sarah as they do, to express and embody his own vision.

This implied comparison between Fowles and Rossetti illuminates the consistent mythologizing of Sarah in the novel, and enables us to move beyond her to a consideration of the book's engagement with the problem of the artist's creative predecessors. Sarah's presence in Rossetti's house and his art effectively assimilates her into the iconographic feminine ideal evolved and represented in Pre-Raphaelite painting. The reader is thus invited to confirm the aesthetic materiality of Sarah by re-arranging retrospectively his/her impressions of Sarah's features — the heavy brows, ruddy skin, wide mouth, and abundant hair — in accordance with Pre-Raphaelite imagery. The evoking of such a specific pictorial blueprint of femininity in relation to Sarah encourages the textualization of the heroine while also associating her in the reader's mind with legendary Pre-Raphaelite models like Elizabeth Siddall, Fanny Cornforth, and Jane Burden. Thus the end of the novel casts Sarah retrospectively in terms of an idealized beauty, an aesthetically formulated sexuality, which might be called archetypal. This illuminates a contradictory tendency in the book to identify Sarah with the Pre-Raphaelite ideal of womanhood — the *princesse lointaine* as Blessed Damozel — while also emphasizing an individuality in her that defies Victorian stereotyping of women.[21] Charles's perception of Sarah's honesty as a sign of her audacious uniqueness — "[She] seemed almost to assume some sort of equality of intellect with him; and in precisely the circumstances where she should have been most deferential if she wished to encompass her end" (140) — is counterpointed by the reader's sense of Sarah as an aestheticized myth of female beauty and desirability.

     Furthermore, Sarah is accorded mythic status in the novel from the outset. The narrator, on first observing her in Chapter 1, describes her as "a figure from myth" (11), and he later equates her with Eve through her association with that "English Garden of Eden," the Undercliff (71). Our impression of Sarah as, amongst other things, a proto-existentialist and early model for female emancipation[22] is compromised by an even more pervasive apprehension of her as a timeless archetype of femininity. Charles expresses this mythologizing of Sarah in explicitly Freudian terms when he identifies her with his dead sister, and by association with the lost mother of his childhood:[23] feeling that Sarah's "confession"

---

21   Fowles presumably has this kind of stereotyping in mind when he makes the narrator remark: "Ernestina had exactly the right face for her age; that is, small-chinned, oval, delicate as a violet. You may see it still in the drawings of the great illustrators of the time — in Phiz's work, in John Leech's" (31). But it can be argued that Pre-Raphaelite art, especially from the twentieth-century reader's perspective, accomplished a similar kind of stereotyping in the uniformity of feature it imposed on its models. Given the novel's apparent insistence on Sarah's individuality, this irony is striking.

22   In "Notes," Fowles identifies Sarah as "also existentialist," along with Charles (p. 166). In the interview with Bragg which Woodcock quotes, Fowles explains that his "heroine of course represents at one level women's liberation[,] the beginning of the movement" (p. 82). A number of critics have either accepted Sarah's "modernity" at face value or related it unproblematically to her portrayal as an archetype. See, for example, Ronald Binns, "John Fowles: Radical Romancer," *The Critical Quarterly* 15, No. 4 (1973), 332; Eddins, 220.

23   For a Freudian reading of the novel, and one much respected by Fowles himself, see Gilbert J. Rose, "*The French Lieutenant's Woman*: The

offers "a glimpse of an ideal . . . mythical world" (172), he imagines "even then a figure, a dark shadow, his dead sister, mov[ing] ahead of him, lightly, luringly up the ashlar steps and into the broken columns' mystery" (173).

The various archetypal images used to characterize Sarah work against her proclaimed individuality to effect the suppression of her uniqueness and the generalization of her womanhood. Sarah's identity is, like Alison Kelly's, effectively submerged through the idealizing imagination of a male narrator, in a mythic femininity which further entraps her even as it confers upon her a kind of secular deification. It seems that *The French Lieutenant's Woman*, like the Pre-Raphaelite art whose pictorial conventions it appropriates, further enacts a covert desire to constrain its heroine by implicitly developing its own image of the idealized feminine, even as it seeks to expose as false the sexual idealizations of the Victorians. Sarah's apparent emotional strength, her bold features, and indifference to fashion might call into question conventional nineteenth-century notions of women as weak, demure, and trivial, but her simultaneous construction as an archetype generates a myth of essential femininity as potent in the novel as those myths of female dependence and ineptitude were potent in the Victorian age. Thus the undermining of Sarah's uniqueness is accomplished by a series of allusions which present her as a myth while also assimilating her to a model of femininity that is emerging as typically Fowlesian: elusive and tantalizing, enigmatic and contradictory, resonant with loss and desire, the Fowlesian heroine is woman as romantic ideal. And in this novel the myth that is Sarah finds its explicit iconography in the historically specific art of the Pre-Raphaelite Brotherhood.

The end of *The French Lieutenant's Woman* refers us back to the endeavours of the novel as a whole by inviting a comparison between Fowles and Rossetti and an identification of the novel itself with Pre-Raphaelite art. Just as the book's self-reflexive strategies implicate Sarah in the fictionality of the text, so the construction of Sarah as a Pre-Raphaelite artefact points back to the

---

Unconscious Significance of a Novel to its Author," *American Imago* 29 (1972), 41–57. It was under the influence of this article that Fowles wrote "Hardy and the Hag," associating the idealized woman — Hardy's "Well-Beloved" — with the absent mother, pursued through successive re-creations by her lover/son, the artist.

novel itself as essentially the same thing. Here we perceive another reason for that duality of temporal perspective which I commented upon earlier as part of the novel's narrative technique. For if *The French Lieutenant's Woman* is concerned on the one hand with an historical progression whereby the nineteenth century became the twentieth and the fictional conventions of the Victorian novel transmuted into those of the postmodernist narrative, it is equally concerned with disrupting chronology by holding two centuries within a single fictional frame. And it does so through the narrator's temporally and generically free-ranging sensibility.

This previously mentioned telescoping effect generates a kind of optical illusion in the novel whereby the past and present seem to become interchangeable, and notions of futurity are radically destabilized. It is, for example, in terms of a future literally unavailable to Charles himself, and already experienced by the reader as part of the twentieth century's philosophic past, that we recognize his emerging identity as existentialist. In this novel, certain categories of experience, and the names by which a contemporary reader knows them, remain ambiguously absent and present in the text — temporally uninaugurated in the "core world," but crucial to our understanding of events in that world. It is not Charles but the reader who can relate Sarah's beauty to the aesthetic codes of Pre-Raphaelite art, for the hindsight of history has both articulated those codes coherently and made him/her familiar with them. Sarah's relationship with her male readers can be seen, then, as an analogue for the novel's relationship with time: in the comprehension of the twentieth century resides the meaning of nineteenth-century experience.

With futurity at once missing from and operating in (as well as on) the novel and the narrator set up as a temporal two-way mirror, it becomes difficult to distinguish reality from reflection, as it were, and to tell which century is occupying which side of the glass.[24] This creates a confusion about cause and effect, origin and

---

24   This may be one of the reasons why the motif of evolution does not always operate coherently in the book: the true exemplar of evolutionary adaptability is also the novel's moral villain, Mr. Freeman. Throughout his work, in fact, Fowles's involvement with notions of change, adaptation, and progress is far too ambivalent to allow a wholehearted commitment to any Darwinian point of view.

result, that reveals Fowles's approach to the problem of the artist's relationship with his creative forebears. Essentially, the disruption of historical chronology in *The French Lieutenant's Woman* is also a disruption of the chronology of literary ancestry: the structural and technical premises of the novel make it difficult to effectively establish an order of historical priority in the production of works of art. As he was to do later in *The Ebony Tower* with Marie de France's *Eliduc*, Fowles here deliberately re-arranges a chronologically simple relationship between a creative ancestor (Rossetti) and his progeny (Fowles) to create the impression that the work of the former has actually been produced by the latter. By disrupting in this way the logic of temporal succession and then inviting the reader to perceive the novel as a work of Pre-Raphaelite art, *The French Lieutenant's Woman* generates its own *bona fides* on its own terms and effectively repudiates the stigma of imitation: it *becomes* that very work and thus it usurps, for itself and for its creator, the authority of pre-existence which history has obviously conferred on the art of Rossetti.

It is significant in this regard that the narrator's comments on Pre-Raphaelite art in general are equally applicable to the novel itself:

> The revolutionary art movement of Charles's day was of course the Pre-Raphaelite: they at least were making an attempt to admit nature and sexuality, but we have only to compare the pastoral background of a Millais or a Ford Madox Brown with that in a Constable or a Palmer to see how idealized, how decor-conscious the former were in their approach to external reality. (172)

Like the art to which it here alludes, *The French Lieutenant's Woman* aspires to be revolutionary in its challenging textual strategies. It also attempts "to admit nature and sexuality" by associating the (ambiguously) passionate Sarah with the rich natural landscape of the Undercliff, and contrasting her with the proper Ernestina, who is linked to conservatories and the stuffy interiors of bourgeois houses. In observing the artificial and decorative effects produced by Pre-Raphaelite efforts at naturalism, the narrator is commenting ironically on the book's similar inability to escape either its own or

Sarah's constructedness, even as it seeks to highlight her "natural-ness." By thus appropriating the Pre-Raphaelite agenda within a context of disrupted historical priority, the novel does more than locate itself in the tradition of general aesthetic radicalism represent-ed by the Brotherhood — it portrays itself as implicitly a work of Pre-Raphaelite art.

This act of artistic usurpation, which allows a creative "son" to supersede a "father" by seizing retrospective responsibility for his ancestor's work and so aggrandizing his own power, further involves a process of appropriation and reworking that operates clearly in *The French Lieutenant's Woman*. With regard to Rossetti as principal example, the novel makes use of Pre-Raphaelite con-ventions while effectively re-writing a portion of the Brotherhood's history to include Sarah Woodruff. It approaches the generic past of the novel in a similar way, for it utilizes certain conventions of Victorian fiction — the motif of the lost inheritance, for exam-ple[25] — while writing itself into the history of that fiction and so revising it.

Furthermore, the novel does not place the history of either the Brotherhood or the Victorian novel entirely in the hands of a providence which has already worked itself out in time — that is, of a retrospectively perceived literary tradition. Instead, the Pre-Raphaelites and the nineteenth-century novel come largely under the control here of an authorial presence which can alter the destiny of both merely by the resetting of a watch (441). Once again, nar-ratorial (and authorial) eschewing of omniscience becomes prob-lematic, as the observer of the nineteenth century becomes in effect its author. And this discloses the rationale behind the dense allu-siveness of *The French Lieutenant's Woman*: the plethora of epigraphs in the novel, the detailed references to Hardy, Tennyson, Arnold, and many others, combine to suggest the appropriation and re-working not only of Pre-Raphaelite art, but of other Victorian art as well. Within a novelistic structure that destabilizes

---

25   In his review, Christopher Ricks also noticed Fowles's adoption of the vocabulary of the Victorian novel, and he praises the book's combination "of the Victorian novelistic conventions with the hard-earned knowledge of what those conventions fended off, and what glittered through their interstices," in "The Unignorable Real," *New York Review of Books*, 12 Feb. 1970, 24.

notions of historical priority, abundant quoting from Victorian works implies an attempted re-possession of these by an author who has put them to his own textual uses, and deployed them indirectly to illuminate his own creative power.

In the same way, the novel's telescoping of two centuries may be understood as Fowles's effort to textualize, appropriate, and rewrite the nineteenth century itself. Under the auspices of that historical destabilization which the book effects, allusions to Victorian thinkers and scientists like Mayhew, Mill, Darwin, and Marx abound. The narrator as authorial surrogate chooses, edits, and situates these quotations for his own purposes, and in so doing he constructs his own version of nineteenth-century social and intellectual history. Thus those critics like Karen Lever, who have criticized Fowles for oversimplifying the Victorian age,[26] have misunderstood the novel's historical agenda; through his narrator, Fowles re-presents the nineteenth century as his own re-worked text, and the idiosyncrasies of this text signal the attempt to possess an era through an act of creative re-writing. For this reason the novel objectifies the author's creative ancestry not only in D. G. Rossetti, but also in other masters of Victorian art and thought.[27] Given the Oedipal terms which the artist's battle for creative primacy usually implies in Fowles's work, it is significant that the century to be so textualized and rewritten should be presented as powerfully masculine, and that almost all the works alluded to in the novel

---

26   Lever finds the book's "insights and details about the Victorian age to be commonplace . . . [and] trite" (96). Ricks feels that, despite its strengths, the novel crudely stereotypes "the Victorians."

27   One of the strongest presences in the novel is Thomas Hardy, whom the narrator presents (in Chapter 35) as a figure of rather threatening paternal authority: "I have now come under the shadow, the very relevant shadow, of the great novelist who towers over this part of England of which I write" (262). The narrator also shows Sarah as resembling Eustacia Vye — in her dark and witch–like aspects — and Tess Durbeyfield: Sarah's "rustic throne . . . [a] flint seat" (163) in the Undercliff, recalls Tess's resting-place at Stonehenge. Like Tess, Sarah comes of a now defunct aristocratic line: "The family had certainly once owned a manor of sorts in that cold green no-man's-land between Dartmoor and Exmoor. . . . There was even a remote relationship with the Drake family" (58).

are authored by men.[28] In *The French Lieutenant's Woman*, what Fowles sees as the patriarchal edifice of Victorian artistic and intellectual life comes to stand for that "father" whose power the "son" must displace onto himself in order to proclaim his own creative hegemony.

• • •

The narrative strategies and structures of *The French Lieutenant's Woman* reveal the various ways in which the book seeks to enact complex principles of destabilization and interrogation. By so doing, it searches after structural co-ordinates for its theme of freedom and presents the contemporary artist's struggle with his own and his age's monumentally embodied ancestor, the nineteenth century. The novel, like its creator, thus strives to confront the traditions within which it exists by reformulating them into a personal vision. But we have also seen that, in relation to Sarah, the novel compromises its technical and moral commitment to the freedom of indeterminacy, and strategically re-imprisons its heroine. In this respect, the text invokes the kind of fictional assumptions which it also views as conservative and traditional:

---

28   This is one way of accounting for the book's approach to the women writers of the age, whose work, despite the rich intertextuality of the novel, is omitted from or otherwise devalued in the text. Thus George Eliot, whose life might have suggested to Fowles a pattern for female sexual emancipation, is almost entirely missing; her "famous epigram" about duty appears in a footnote on page 52, while the work of an inferior writer, Caroline Norton, is referred to in some detail in Chapter 16. But even here, the narrator seems to mention Norton only in order to scoff at her as an "insipid poetastrix" (114), whose verse is used to indicate Ernestina's naive literary taste. Considering that the novel is set in Lyme Regis, *Persuasion* is mentioned infrequently and briefly (14, 31, 70, 101), and Hardy is a much more potent figure in the narrative than Austen. Charles's view of Christina Rossetti's mind as "absurdly muddled" and "femininely involute" (435), while not explicitly endorsed by the narrator, is nowhere countered in the text. These examples reinforce that discomfort with the female writer which the portrayal of Sarah evinces: by presenting Victorian artistic might as overwhelmingly male, the novel is also trying to avoid the female creativity of an era. Not until *The Ebony Tower*, where he negotiates the literary achievements of Marie de France, would Fowles confront the prospect of the literary forebear as specifically and authoritatively female.

these are the principles of definition and closure which are associated here with the Victorian rather than the postmodernist novel. This indirect re-situating of Sarah within the structural confines of the Victorian novel both reinforces and modifies the equally reifying, but more obtrusive, placement of her within the aesthetic confines of Pre-Raphaelite art. Not only does it suggest Fowles's vision of the nineteenth-century novel as in some ways monolithic, but it also offers a way for the text to retreat from its own palpable anxiety about female authorship.

I observed earlier those images of destruction, sadism, and violence which are used at times to characterize Sarah: Mrs. Talbot's mental picture of her plunging from a cliff, her cloak "a falling raven's wing of terrible death" (56), is echoed in Charles's repeated sense of himself, during or after his meetings with Sarah, as a man on the brink of some disaster (172, 180, 335). After they make love in Exeter, Charles's guilt is imaged as a sort of internal Hiroshima: "[N]o gentle postcoital sadness for him, but an immediate and universal horror . . . like a city struck out of a quiet sky by an atom bomb" (338). This disturbing imagery culminates in Dr. Grogan's medical textbooks, with their case histories of female sado-masochism and brutality. On one level, Fowles uses these images to expose Victorian sexual typecasting; unable to cope with Sarah, her society (represented at times by Charles himself) forces her into pre-existent categories of feminine non-conformity. But the imagery is also a reflection of the book's unease with its own apparent conferring of creative power on Sarah. This manifests itself in the novel's ignoring of Victorian women writers and in the portrayal of those female writers who appear in the "core world" — Ernestina and Marie de Morell — as either puerile or murderous. The narrator is condescending towards Ernestina's banal diary entries while implicitly associating Marie, the author of poison-pen letters, with Sarah through the incorporation into his narrative of another French lieutenant, Émile de La Roncière. This anxiety about the narratorially empowered woman suggests Fowles's reluctance to sully the muse-figure with the debased manipulations of authorship. That paradoxical mistrust of art, his simultaneous involvement with and repulsion from his own stock-in-trade, words, is expressed in *The French Lieutenant's Woman* with an intensity that almost approaches hatred.

The re-assimilation of Sarah to Victorian notions of fiction not only guarantees her reassuring loss of creative function, but
also implicitly identifies the nineteenth-century novel as itself a kind
of Edenic *domaine* — the generic or formal equivalent of the
Undercliff — where Sarah can unproblematically embody a regressive fantasy of the eternal feminine, and where the text which she
personifies can exist in a state of pre-lapsarian innocence. In this
respect, woman-as-artefact seems to stand as an emblem for the
redemption of art — and particularly the art of fiction — through a
continued association with those traditions which at once inhibit
and direct it. An ambiguously conservative ethic seems to haunt
the radicalism of *The French Lieutenant's Woman* — an ethic to
which Fowles would return in his next fiction; the title story of *The
Ebony Tower* suggests that Breasley's greatness depends on his ability to pay homage to old traditions while also thumbing his nose at
them.

Furthermore, the relocation of Sarah within the magical
enclosure of the Victorian novel implies a vision of fictional self-
consciousness as a kind of Fall from generic wholeness into the
fragmented world of postmodernism. For Fowles, the novel, having gained knowledge of its fictionality, must henceforth atone for
its loss of formal innocence by admitting and displaying the mechanisms of its own artificiality. This suggests another reason why the
heroine-as-text must be denied access to her own meanings — why,
as Sarah puts it, "I am not to be understood even by myself" (431).
Such self-comprehension would destroy that innocence which
stands for the purity of the text. It would categorically ally her, as
Catherine in "The Cloud" is allied, to the destructive fragmenta-
tions — the sheer *knowingness* — of postmodernism, and commit
her to an extreme of demystification which Fowles's work, even in
The Ebony Tower, is reluctant to enact. In *The French Lieutenant's
Woman*, then, a generic nostalgia for what Fowles sees as the innocent past of prose narrative informs his engagement with the
metafictional imperatives of the postmodern novel.

The reworked appearance in this novel of the Fowlesian
domaine perdu and the placing of Sarah within it prefigure *Daniel
Martin*'s revision of the myth of the Fall by narrative means. In
these two works, Fowles seeks the symbolic return of the text and
the textualized woman, or art and the female artefact, to a pristine
state wherein the similarly returned — or regressed — male artist/

author/narrator may enjoy the unlimited possession of both. This idea of redemption through an aesthetically relevant fantasy of maternal reunion associates both *The French Lieutenant's Woman* and *Daniel Martin* with the Freudian paradigm of creativity developed in Fowles's essay on Hardy. Both books illuminate the regressive tendencies of Fowles's creative imagination, its desire to colonize the past as a playground of authorial narcissism while striving to negotiate, in different ways, historical process and change.

The re-situating of Sarah within a novelistic *domaine* and her effective portrayal as an icon of textual purity return us to the novel's covert entrapment of her, which we may now view from another perspective as a kind of rescue. The novel undertakes to save Sarah, and by association fiction itself, from those darker, more threatening aspects of narrative indeterminacy and destabilization that are hinted at here and further developed in *The Ebony Tower*: disintegration, meaninglessness, and chaos. Along with its unease about female authorship, *The French Lieutenant's Woman* reveals a certain understated anxiety, as well as an exhilaration, at the problem of identifying and comprehending the nature of the text.[29] In Chapter 13, the narrator disrupts our sense of the novel's generic stability by openly wondering what kind of book he is writing:

> So perhaps I am writing a transposed auto-biography; perhaps I now live in one of the houses I have brought into the fiction; perhaps Charles is myself disguised. Perhaps it is only a game. Modern women

---

29   In the inseparability of the text and the woman we find a reason for the narrator's refusal (much discussed among critics) to enter Sarah's mind and portray her as psychologically three-dimensional. This symbolic reformulation of Sarah's virginity in specific relation to the book's narrator suggests that, while the incomprehensibility of the text is disconcerting, it is also crucial for Fowles to that numinous "magic" which defines the text as art. The novel thus insists paradoxically upon exposing and preserving, contemplating and fleeing from, both the text and the woman-as-text. This renders irrelevant the objection of critics like David Lodge and Ian Adam that the characterization of Sarah is too incomplete. See Lodge, *Working with Structuralism* (Boston: Routledge & Kegan Paul, 1981), p. 155; Adam, Patrick Brantlinger, and Sheldon Rothblatt, "*The French Lieutenant's Woman*: A Discussion," *Victorian Studies* 15, No. 3 (1972), 347.

> like Sarah exist, and I have never understood them.
> Or perhaps I am trying to pass off a concealed book
> of essays on you. Instead of chapter headings, perhaps
> I should have written "On the Horizontality of
> Existence," "The Illusions of Progress," "The History
> of the Novel Form," "The Aetiology of Freedom,"
> "Some Forgotten Aspects of the Victorian Age" . . .
> what you will. (97)

Like *The Magus*, *The French Lieutenant's Woman* formulates in terms
of a creatively engaged (male) narrator the issue of readerly comprehension and the search for meaning; both novels thus declare their
sense of the artist as inevitably a reader of others' texts. By means of
her participation in the fictionality of the novel, Sarah is deeply
implicated in the kind of formal anxiety expressed here. By realign-
ing her at the end of the book with what Fowles sees as the generic
coherence of Victorian fiction, the novel itself can partake of that
very coherence which it also repudiates, and the heroine cannot
form a committed alliance with what "The Cloud" would later identify as the centrifugal force of postmodernism, the drive towards disintegration. It is, then, the strategically complex presentation of
Sarah that chiefly enables us to perceive *The French Lieutenant's
Woman* as a contradictory and ambiguous document. The novel is
selective in its enactment and conferring of freedom, ambivalent
about the prospect of feminine creativity, and anxious — not just
about authorship and its own relation to time, but about the status
and integrity of narrative in an era of textual self-reflexivity.

     The underlying sense in this novel of the text as not just
energetically unstable but hovering on the edge of collapse links
The French Lieutenant's Woman to *The Magus*'s apprehensive
engagement with the elusiveness of meaning, while prefiguring
Fowles's sophisticated analysis of the limits of narrative art in "The
Cloud." The latter story, as the next chapter will show, similarly
associates radical and unnerving textual instability with a female
narrator capable, by virtue of her foregrounded fictionality, of
embodying the possible dissolution of narrative form and conse-
quent loss of meaning in the text. The effective rescue of Sarah
suggests that, by the time of *The Ebony Tower*, Fowles was ready to
push his exploration of the processes and capacities of narrative to
greater lengths. Sarah's recuperation within the *domaine* is an

inverted forecast of Catherine's fate in "The Cloud": locating her in an anti-paradise crawling with snakes, the author/narrator abandons Catherine to the meaninglessness of disintegrated form by ejecting her from the story and re-embodying her as a cloud. This repudiation occurs after Catherine has herself expressed and centralized, in her own narratorial efforts, what she calls "the death of fiction."

By the end of his third novel, then, Fowles's involvement with the nature of art is clearly becoming a contemplation of the extremes of narrative art in a postmodernist age. *The Ebony Tower*, although it does not offer us a creative woman as compelling and apparently audacious as Sarah Woodruff, shows Fowles's sense of the relationship between gender and artistic power developing along lines laid down in *The French Lieutenant's Woman*.

4
THE EBONY TOWER

Fowles has made clear that *The Ebony Tower* was written under the influence of mediaeval romance in general and Marie de France in particular. In the "Personal Note," which prefaces his translation of her *lai Eliduc*, he declares the book to be a series of

> variations both on certain themes in previous books of mine and on methods of narrative presentation. . . . However, *The Ebony Tower* is also a variation of a more straightforward kind, and the source of its mood, as also partly of its theme and setting, is so remote and forgotten — though I believe seminal in the history of fiction — that I should like to resurrect a fragment of it. . . . One may smile condescendingly at the naiveties and primitive technique of stories such as *Eliduc*, but I do not think any writer of fiction can do so with decency — and for a very simple reason. He is watching his own birth.[1]

These comments emphasize certain important aspects of the volume. They suggest, firstly, that Fowles sees *The Ebony Tower* as integral to his *œuvre* and not as the aberrant and rather peculiar experiment with the short story form which some critics have taken it to

---

1   John Fowles, *The Ebony Tower* (Toronto: Little, Brown and Company, 1974), pp. 117–19. All other page references appear in the text and are to this edition.

be.[2] Fowles himself ironically signals this fact in a self-referential detail in the title story: Anne, "the Freak," is reading *The Magus*, which David Williams dismisses as about "astrology" and "all that nonsense" (61). The informed reader is implicitly invited to associate the story, and even the volume which contains it, with Fowles's second novel. *The Ebony Tower* is thus consciously placed in line with a major work of the author's corpus.

Secondly, Fowles's remarks suggest that the similarities which the reader is instructed to find between his own books and Marie's *lais* are not structural but thematic and atmospheric; elsewhere in the "Personal Note" he derides "academic criticism" for being "blind to relationships that are far more emotional than structural" (118). Thirdly, Fowles makes clear here his belief in the mediaeval romance as the bedrock from which fiction itself emerged, that is, the very source of prose narrative as a form. As usual with Fowles's comments on his own work and on literature, these reveal his personal and sometimes idiosyncratic responses to literary history. The author does not make clear, for example, that the mediaeval romance is "remote and forgotten" only for a popular audience. The genre lives and thrives in the academic community, and mediaevalists have even been numbered among the critics of *The Ebony Tower*.[3] Fowles reveals, furthermore, his own implied placement of Marie de France on the scale of literary greatness when he talks about her "naiveties" and "primitive technique." His condescension to Marie, despite the admiration he avers, has been implicitly challenged both by Constance Hieatt, who argues for the

---

2   Critical reaction to *The Ebony Tower* has itself been rather peculiar. While critics like Conradi and Huffaker devote chapters to it in their books and treat it as part of the Fowles canon, others, like Woodcock and Fawkner, mention it only in passing. See H. W. Fawkner, *The Timescapes of John Fowles* (Toronto: Associated University Presses, 1984). Journal articles focus mainly on individual stories, avoiding the issue of the volume's overall unity. This irregular response implies some critical bewilderment: Olshen, an acute Fowles scholar, sees "The Cloud" as his "most difficult work to penetrate" (p. 103).

3   Most notably, Constance B. Hieatt, "*Eliduc* Revisited: John Fowles and Marie de France," *English Studies in Canada* 3, No. 3 (1977), 351–58; Ruth Morse, "John Fowles, Marie de France and the Man with Two Wives," *Philological Quarterly* 63, No. 1 (1984), 17–30.

complexity of Marie's delineation of Eliduc's situation, and by writers on Marie herself, who emphasize her "sophisticated and subtle
style, narrative sense and delicate sensitivity."[4] It is only in terms of
a rather facile, insinuated comparison with later, more "modern"
technical form that Fowles's view of Marie's apparent shortcomings
can be sustained.

      Also, Fowles's vision of the mediaeval romance as the
root of *all* fiction is questionable relative to comments he has made
elsewhere about the "great tradition of the English novel" being
"realism."[5] Commentators like Auerbach and Frye have stressed
the peculiar refusal of the mediaeval romance to compromise with
reality, particularly in its handling of its two great themes, love and
adventure. It is those very elements of myth and folktale, undis-
placed[6] in the direction of realism, that allow the romance, according to Auerbach,[7] to depict the values of a twelfth-century ruling
class in terms of that class's own *ideal* of moral virtue. Through its

---

4   Hieatt, 353–54; Emanuel J. Mickel, Jr., *Marie de France* (New York:
      Twayne Publishers, 1974), p. 141.

5   Newquist, p. 220.

6   In his *Anatomy of Criticism* (Princeton, New Jersey: Princeton University
      Press, 1957), Northrop Frye uses the word "displacement" to describe
      the various ways in which the world of myth, "an abstract or purely liter-
      ary world of fictional and thematic design," is moved in the direction of
      plausibility and hence of realism. For him the romance falls between two
      extremes of "literary design," myth and naturalism, for it tends to displace
      myth in a human direction while still conventionalizing and idealizing
      content (pp. 136–37).

7   Erich Auerbach, *Mimesis* (Princeton, New Jersey: Princeton University
      Press, 1953), p. 133. Auerbach sees the "fairy-tale atmosphere" as "the
      true element of romance" which, if it does portray "external living con-
      ditions" in the twelfth century, does so in an apolitical way that empha-
      sizes the ideals of a feudal society rather than its actuality. See too Frye,
      pp. 186–206. It is worth noting — perhaps as a comment on Fowles's
      tendency creatively to misread literary history — that Mickel sees Marie
      de France as embedded in the vernacular literature of her time, and he
      questions the theory that she herself was the originator of the narrative
      lai (pp. 31–33, 57–61). Auerbach's brief mention of Marie implies that
      he does not see her *lais* as courtly romances at all (p. 135).

very refusal of realism, then, the romance fulfills its own generic purpose. Yet Fowles has repeatedly declared himself principally loyal to the tenets of literary realism,[8] and his claims for the mediaeval romance make no attempt to deal with its relentless ethereality, its evasion of the quotidian world. This particular kind of evasiveness is not often associated with the traditions of the novel, especially not as they manifested themselves in the nineteenth century, a period in the history of fiction with which Fowles is deeply involved.

The contradictions suggested here place us on what is by now the familiar Fowlesian terrain of paradox and divided allegiance. Such contraries locate *The Ebony Tower* at the centre of the author's recurring and ambiguous infatuation both with realism and with those genres and styles which aetiolate it or alter its premises. By communicating the ambivalent nature of his admiration for Marie de France, these comments render Fowles's translation of *Eliduc* and his inclusion of it in his own volume highly problematic. His treatment of her *lai* constitutes a further exploration of the relationship between women and artistic creativity, while providing an explicit example in Fowles's work of the artist in confrontation with a creatively mature female forebear. Finally, the anti-academic emphasis in these comments reinforces one of the *œuvre*'s ongoing thematic concerns — the clash between the supposed imaginative aridity of the critic and what Fowles's fiction seeks to present as the almost magical imaginative efficacy of the artist.

Despite the fact, moreover, that the parallels between these tales and the romances of Chrétien and Marie are frequently structural as well as thematic and atmospheric, Fowles's observations in his "Personal Note" can still be used effectively as a model for discussing the individual stories. This is because these pieces, together with the translation from Old French, are indeed variations on Fowles's work as well as on Marie's. They thus constitute, as the "Personal Note" implies, a meditation on artistic creation generally and literary creation in particular which is even more anxious and profound than that evidenced in Fowles's previous fictions. Both similar to and crucially different from the novels that precede it, *The Ebony Tower* is Fowles's most daring investigation of

---

8   See also "Notes," pp. 166–67.

the artist's power. Here he confronts not only the possible demise of narrative itself, but the dissolution of language as the basic constituent of narrative. Here too Fowles reformulates, in the light of the literary artefact's potential for disintegration, the relation between gender and language, women and articulation. And the multifaceted exploration of aesthetics and sexuality undertaken in this work is placed in the controlling perspective of the artist's involvement with the literally vanished, but in a literary sense unvanquishable, power of previous artists.

• • •

The title story, "The Ebony Tower," makes use of a number of elements from *Eliduc*. Most obviously, there is the identity of setting: Fowles's story, like Marie's *lai*, is set in Brittany,[9] or more specifically in the forest of Paimpont, which also appears in Chrétien de Troyes' poems as Broceliande. Mediaeval romance thus tends to draw on the folklore of Brittany, the *matière de Bretagne*,[10] and Fowles seems to find this especially appealing. He has David Williams identify the world of romance and the isolated, "faintly mythic and timeless" (59) world of Henry Breasley under the rubric of "the old man's real stroke of genius, to take an old need to escape from the city, for a mysterious remoteness, and to see its ancient solution, the Celtic green source, was still viable" (74). For Fowles the essential mysteriousness of the romance — its evocation of magical realms removed from time and the circumstances of everyday living — makes it generically attractive to a creative imagination haunted, as we have seen, by the idea of the *domaine perdu*. Like *The French Lieutenant's Woman*, *The Ebony Tower* implicitly presents an historically superseded form of prose narrative as a kind of literary or aesthetic *domaine*.

Furthermore, this mysteriousness comes from the immersion of the romance in the *matière de Bretagne*, which itself evokes a world of Celtic myth and which manifests itself in stories

---

9   Mickel does point out, however, that for Marie the word *bretun* did not always describe only one individual geographical location; it could refer to Cornish and Welsh settings as well as French (pp. 54–56).

10   Auerbach, p. 131; Fowles, *Ebony*, p. 120.

like *Eliduc*. It is these stories, based upon and reflecting a body of myth and folklore much older than themselves, that nourish the art of the volume's presiding genius and magus-figure, Henry Breasley. As Auerbach observes:

> It is from Breton folklore that the courtly romance took its elements of mystery, of something sprung from the soil, concealing its roots, and inaccessible to rational explanation; it incorporated them and made use of them in its elaboration of the knightly ideal; the *matière de Bretagne* apparently proved to be the most suitable medium for the cultivation of that ideal.[11]

In the story, David observes in this connection that Breasley's "subject-matter [is] far less explicit [than Nolan's], more mysterious and archetypal. . . . 'Celtic' had been a word frequently used, with the recurrence of the forest motif, the enigmatic figures and confrontations" (13).

Thus Fowles takes from Marie de France a physical setting that is resonant with historical, literary, and mythic association. He uses it to embody the idea that art, like the imagination which shapes it, is nourished by and rooted in the kind of folk material that predates not only written history but perhaps even writing itself. This is what Fowles seems to mean when he locates the origin of fiction in the mediaeval romance, and his implied vision of the *matière de Bretagne* as not only seminal but unwritten invites us to see Breasley as a creator whose power has little to do with the written word, and as a master-artist whose lack of linguistic skill is almost a joke: Diana remarks on Breasley's almost complete inadequacy with words (50), and David observes that the old man "certainly misrepresented everything he talked about" (55).

Breasley is Fowles's only artist-magician who is clearly presented as verbally inept. Conchis, whose desire to escape from both language and narrative is shown in his burning of his novels, nonetheless relies on language to help accomplish the diverse ends of the "metatheatre." In the figure of the old painter, Fowles tries to deal with his mistrust of words by exploring a creativity which is, even more than G.P.'s, strong and efficacious despite its separation

---

11   Auerbach, p. 131.

from the verbal. But as we will see, this dissociation of the artist from language is not maintained throughout *The Ebony Tower*; as a writer himself, Fowles seems bound to return in his work to the ambiguous relationship between the artist and the word, and to negotiate the involvement of language in those ratiocinative processes that his fictions seek so often to condemn.

Nonetheless, the portrayal of Breasley as an instinctive creator and a painter uncomfortable with words suggests an identification here of the artist with those intuitions and emotional susceptibilities, as well as that avoidance of language, that other fictions associate with the artist's material, the woman. Breasley is not only nourished by the subrational in what Fowles here sees as its literary manifestation, the mediaeval romance; he himself is almost without reason, and is immersed in the archetypal, the subconscious, and the mythic. David, the critic, lecturer, and explainer of art, is smooth-talking and produces only tame, decorative, abstract works. By contrast Breasley, who calls David a "gutless bloody word-twister" (44), seems to depend for his creative potency on a deliberate anti-intellectualism. He says to David: "My dear boy. Painted to paint. All my life. Not to give clever young buggers like you a chance to show off. . . . Don't care a fart in hell where my ideas come from. Never have. Let it happen. That's all. Couldn't even tell you how it starts. What half it means. Don't want to know" (78).

This suggests a parallel between Breasley and Sarah Woodruff. The analytical cast of mind of which Fowles is suspicious, and which he connects so specifically in this story with verbalization, is here designated as foreign to the creative impulse, and we are reminded of Sarah's total lack of analytical capacity. Breasley's inarticulacy also echoes Sarah's in terms of verbal reluctance and an alternative, instinctive, and wordless "language." But the crucial distinction between these two characters is clear: in *The French Lieutenant's Woman*, Sarah's estrangement from ratiocination finally guarantees not her creative authority, but her aesthetic materiality; in "The Ebony Tower," a similar estrangement in Breasley comes together with significant artistic achievement. The difference here is one of gender. Breasley's inarticulacy has a qualitatively different meaning from Sarah's, not only because he is an established artist, but because his masculinity permits (in Fowles's terms) his association with such artistic authority in the first place.

Thus the formless instinctiveness and the creative power, which in *The French Lieutenant's Woman* are separated conceptually and valorized separately in different individuals, can be connected here because of the artist's gender. In this way Breasley indirectly reveals the condition under which Sarah's enigmatic sensitivity might have issued in sustained creative power. That condition is maleness.

Also, Breasley's verbal ineptitude and his lack of a linguistic role in the story do not signal any corresponding reduction of artistic status. His painting is a creatively viable alternative form of articulacy which *The French Lieutenant's Woman* does not make available to Sarah. As a painter, Breasley is supremely articulate, and Diana crystallizes this when, interpreting Breasley, she tells David that "art is a form of speech" (46). It might not be too facetious to suggest that Breasley's paintings, with their "constant recomposition and refinement away from the verbal" (26), give a kind of transhistorical shape to Sarah's formless and unutterable "language." But even if we reject this idea, Breasley's association with the shaping power of the artist remains operative in the story, and his indifference to the literal meanings of his work recalls Conchis's commitment to the energy of the unanswerable.

It is, in fact, the unusual equation in this story between mature male creativity and inarticulateness that allows the relationship between artist and critic to be foregrounded in relation to David's verbal skill and Breasley's mastery of the alternative language of paint. This is represented in painterly terms as a clash between Breasley and Williams on the opposing merits of representational and non-representational art.[12] In *The Ebony Tower*, aesthetic values once again reflect and interpenetrate with sexual and moral ones. To communicate this, Fowles reworks those elements of romance that fuel his own artistic imagination: Williams is indeed a kind of knight-errant seeking adventure in a foreign land. He travels through a forest to face ordeals in a remote spot, and if he passes the tests of his chivalry and integrity, he may rescue a damsel from her entrapment by an enchanter and claim her as his own. Breasley's attack on David's artistic and critical credo is one of these ordeals of courage. Surviving it, he finds himself, like Eliduc, torn between two women who represent (in typically Fowlesian terms)

12   For a discussion of the political implications of this debate in the context of twentieth-century art, see Huffaker, pp. 117–18.

two different styles of life and of art. It is interesting in this regard that Fowles sees himself as unable to think fictionally except in terms of hunt and quest.[13] In "The Ebony Tower," his exploration of his own imaginative roots re-creates the enchanted enclosure as Broceliande; the "little forest womb" (90) of Coëtminais joins the *domaines* of earlier fictions, and David's self-discovery involves an elusive woman who embodies the values and vision of life for which the Fowlesian hero, as we have seen, is compelled to search.

But as my discussion of other aspects of "The Ebony Tower" has suggested, to read the story only in terms of its existential elements is to reduce it to a rather straightforward variation on both *The Magus* and *The French Lieutenant's Woman*.[14] It is also to reduce the story's involvement with art and creativity to a simple replacing of Conchis's Greek "metatheatre" with Breasley's private art gallery in France. The very sophistication of Fowles's relationship to his mediaeval source material suggests complexities at work in "The Ebony Tower" which undermine any predictable thematic symmetry, and one reliable way of discovering such complexities or submerged contradictions in a Fowles text is to scrutinize that central figure, the heroine.

Diana combines Sarah's inscrutability with the almost surreal coolness of Julie Holmes. Like Miranda she is an art student dependent on the lascivious tutelage of a mature artist whose establishment she — again like Sarah — helps to run. Diana is, in brief, one of those all-purpose women so indispensable to Fowles's fiction: part live-in maid, part muse, and part mistress, she even

---

13 Fowles, "Hardy," p. 35.

14 Fowles's admitted wish to demystify *The Magus* by means of "The Ebony Tower" invites this kind of reading. See Kerry McSweeney, "Black Hole and Ebony Tower," *Queen's Quarterly* 82, No. 1 (1975), 152–66; and *Four Contemporary Novelists*, pp. 111–21. Arnold E. Davidson has come closest to challenging the view of the book as a conventional variation on themes in two articles: "The Barthesian Configurations of John Fowles's 'The Cloud,'" *The Centennial Review* 28, No. 4/29, No. 1 (1984/85), 80–93; "*Eliduc* and 'The Ebony Tower': John Fowles's Variation on a Medieval Lay," *The International Fiction Review* 11, No. 1 (1984), 31–36. Loveday also reads the stories in terms of their ambiguities and contradictions rather than their symmetries (pp. 82–102).

serves the intellectual purposes of the narrative by assuming a symbolic function. As David comes to realize, his failure to claim Diana as his lover signals not only a loss of sexual nerve, but a moral and aesthetic inadequacy manifested in both his comfortable marriage and his safe art: "It was metaphysical: something far beyond the girl; an anguish, a being bereft of a freedom whose true nature he had only just seen" (102). David begins "[s]lowly and inexorably" to perceive "that his failure that previous night was merely the symbol, not the crux of the matter. . . . Bungling the adventure of the body was trivial, part of the sexual comedy. But he had never really had, or even attempted to give himself, the far greater existential chance" (109).

But if Diana represents on one level the link between sex, art, and existential authenticity, her behaviour in this symbolic role is, like Sarah's, by no means unproblematic. Ranged against Beth Williams as a romantic option threatening to involve David in the hazardous freedom of illicit love and a concomitant breakthrough into artistic integrity, Diana appears to need rescuing from an over-sheltered world. Fowles implicitly makes another structural reference here to *Eliduc*, but unlike Guilliadun, Diana must remain with her fatherly protector as a kind of domestic-servant-cum-vestal-virgin, for she is as important to Breasley's art as Sarah becomes to Rossetti's. This is not because she helps Breasley in the studio — the story makes clear that her talents are inferior to those of both Henry and David[15] — but because her sexuality, and indeed her very physical body, are a kind of objective correlative for the representational truth which the old man's art strives to express and achieve.

To David, Breasley claims that his art is based on fidelity to "reality," to "human facts" rather than ideas (46). He also makes clear that he defines reality with uncompromising literalness: "Pair of tits and a cunt. All that goes with them. That's reality. Not your piddling little theorems and pansy colours. I know what

---

15   We are told, for example, that Diana's sketch of teasels is "impressive if *rather lifeless*" in its accuracy (24, emphasis added). The drawings she later shows David are "lacking in individuality," and she herself compares her paintings to "bad David Williamses" (85). Agreeing with her, David sees the paintings as resembling his "in a more feminine, decorative kind of way" (86).

you people are after, Williams" (42).[16] By invoking the female as
both an irreducible physical entity and a kind of metaphor, Breasley
communicates to David his sense of the crucial involvement of art
with "the human body and its natural physical perceptions" (111),
as well as his corollary of this, art's obligation to deal with human
experience rather than with mere intellection. As Diana glosses:
"Art is a form of speech. Speech must be based on human needs,
not abstract theories of grammar" (46). The implications of this
are twofold and they place us at the core of "The Ebony Tower."
On the one hand, Fowles is insisting once more on the instrumentality and sheer materiality of women in relation to art. On the
other, we see a connection established between the availability of
women for appropriation as artefacts, and their identification with
that quintessential inarticulacy — the definitive lack of shaping
power — upon which the expressive capacities of the artist thrive,
whatever his medium. For the sake of clarity, these two related
issues of sex and language are best discussed separately.

When Breasley explains to David the origin of the name
"Mouse," he does so by creating a collage of the word "muse" and
a drawing of the pudendum (79). Given the old man's tendency to
exterminate by "constant recomposition" any "clumsy literalness"
(26) in his art, we might see this as a representation of Diana
almost equivalent to that nude drawing of Sarah which Charles sees
at Cheyne Walk. In "The Ebony Tower," the female body is palpably and literally the stuff of art, the "reality" from which it is made.
It both symbolizes and embodies artistic truth; and female sexuality,
moreover, not only suggests artistic inspiration, but *is* that inspiration.

This spectrum of associations dominates the central
scene of the story, the woodland picnic. Here David observes that
the nudity of the women seems "to still something in the old man"
and to create in him "a kind of quiet pagan contentment" (59).
Although Breasley spends most of the afternoon asleep, the impression left here is of an old master quietly communing with the sensual source of his power. Furthermore, the availability of the body as

---

16   This suggests, of course, that the story defines the human body as
      implicitly the female body. The male physique is never made available
      to the artist in the same way — a point which I consider later in my
      analysis.

the stuff of art is signalled in the text by a repeated tendency of the narrative voice to place the characters literally within frames, thereby turning Breasley's art gallery into a place of "meta-art" directly comparable with Conchis's theatre. Diana sits "as if her mind were somewhere else — in a Millais set-piece, perhaps" (22); at dinner the "lamplight made the scene like a Chardin, a Georges de la Tour" (37); the bathing women make David think of "Gauguin; brown breasts and the garden of Eden" (59), while later he sees Beth as the Princess of Trebizond in Pisanello's *St. George and the Dragon* (99). Through this persistent allusiveness, human beings come to embody paintings, existing as, in, and for masterpieces. The women especially make themselves available to the imaginations of the men who watch them as living, contemporary re-creations of great works of art: Breasley does a drawing of Anne which parodies "that famous Lautrec poster of Yvette Guilbert" (67), while he himself is more often perceived in relation to other artists than in terms of whom or what the artist paints. Thus Diana's sexual elusiveness is counter-pointed, like Sarah's, by the availability of her image for inclusion in pictures. These are not so much the pictures that make up Breasley's *œuvre*, for his favourite subject is Anne, but those that make up Fowles's *œuvre* — "The Ebony Tower" is itself a kind of literary picture within which Diana has the distinct edge on Anne as the artist's favoured female subject.[17]

Breasley also tends to see his experience, and especially his experience with Diana, in terms of pictures. He uses the painting *Roman Charity* to describe their relationship to David: "Know that thing? Old geezer sucking milk from some young biddy's tit. Often think of that" (25). In fact, one of the particular virtues that Diana and the Coët *ménage* seem to possess is this ability to facilitate thinking in pictures rather than in the disconnected fragments of colour and texture to which David is accustomed: he makes no other drawing in the reductive, minimalist style of his sketch along

---

17   The relationship between Diana and Anne could be a reworking of the kind of heroine/maidservant relationship popular in mediaeval romance. In *Yvain*, for example, the beautiful lady Laudine is manipulated by her shrewd and good-hearted maid, Lunette, into accepting Yvain as her husband. In any event, the more conventionally attractive Diana is set up from the start as the story's leading lady; the punkish, practical Anne is clearly never in line for the hero's affections.

the road (3). In terms of cognition, if not actual practice, David turns away from abstraction quite early in the narrative and his visualizing imagination directs itself with reference to the paintings he knows best.

Both he and Breasley then project these pictures back onto their experience as a sort of self-fulfilling prophecy, and this process enables them metaphorically to take possession of Diana, as well as the less desirable Anne, while her physical unavailability remains undisturbed. Diana thus retains the essential impenetrability of the Fowlesian heroine, apotheosized in Sarah, while offering herself up in various transmutations for contemplation as art, and for utilization in the service of art. Her two names are a perfect shorthand designation of her ambiguous function. The divine chastity of "Diana" exists in contradistinction to the blatant sexuality of "Mouse." The former refers to the physical inviolability which she retains despite Breasley's attentions and David's overtures; the latter suggests the kind of promiscuous availability which helps define her as both the artist's subject and the *objet d'art*.[18] In "The Ebony Tower," then, that all-important sexuality of the muse, which Fowles would later depict so literally in *Mantissa*, combines an Olympian aloofness with the whorishness traditionally associated in Bestiaries with small, furry animals like mice and weasels.[19] Diana thus becomes identified with the weasel crushed by David's car — itself a version of the bereaved, magic weasel from *Eliduc*. Once again, Fowles reconceives an image from the *lai*, assimilating it to his personal thematic concerns and effectively making it his own.

---

18   The story's presentation of paintings as both feminine and fleshly is confirmed in an unobtrusive textual detail: Breasley identifies his "Kermesse" canvas as female when he says, "She's playing coy. Waiting, don't you know" (24). This harmonizes with an earlier comment that David had not seen the *Moon-hunt* "*in the flesh* since the Tate exhibition of four years previously" (18, emphasis added).

19   See Beryl Rowland, *Animals with Human Faces: A Guide to Animal Symbolism* (Knoxville: The University of Tennessee Press, 1973), pp. 158–60. Also Huffaker's footnote, pp. 145–46. The book's pervasive references to mediaeval literature make it appropriate to refer to Bestiaries in this context.

The constant presence of paintings in a story so much about paintings indirectly signals the constructedness of both written and visual art. It is a metaphor for Fowles's own narrative method in "The Ebony Tower" and a sign of the story's involvement with the complexities of the creative process. Fowles too is concerned to create masterpieces and to build his own works out of, as well as in the inevitable presence of, the works of other artists. David's analysis of Breasley's *Moon-hunt* is paradigmatic of Fowles's technique too, and this helps to identify Fowles and Breasley:

> As with so much of Breasley's work there was an obvious previous iconography — in this case, Uccello's *Night Hunt* and its spawn down through the centuries; which was in turn a challenged comparison, a deliberate risk . . . just as the Spanish drawings had defied the great shadow of Goya by accepting its presence, even using and parodying it, so the memory of the Ashmolean Uccello somehow deepened and buttressed the painting before which David sat. It gave an essential tension, in fact: . . . behind the modernity of so many of the surface elements there stood both a homage and a kind of thumbed nose to a very old tradition. (18)

This is clearly a *mise en abyme* of method, a useful summary of that relationship between Fowles and his literary influences which we have seen operating in his *œuvre*. But here this paradigm may be applied not only (as we will see later) to the structure and movements of the literary macrocosm, *The Ebony Tower*, but to those of the literary microcosm, "The Ebony Tower," within which the specific and conscious re-creation of a famous painting has pride of place: the picnic scene is remarkable for its reworking, in another medium and another age, of Manet's *Luncheon on the Grass*.

It is appropriately Breasley himself who makes the analogy: "Gels suggest a little *déjeuner sur l'herbe*. Good idea, what? Picnic?" (51). He directs us here to perceive this lyrical interlude, which combines nude women, clothed men, and rural serenity, in the perspective of great art. Fowles evokes the early Impressionist scene quite as deliberately as, and perhaps more emphatically than, he evokes scenes, configurations, and images from mediaeval romances like *Eliduc* and *Yvain*. Clearly this story both examines and performs the act of artistic imitation, with its contingent processes of restatement and transmutation. The result is a careful overlay in the text of mediaeval resonances with mid-nineteenth-century ones, which have themselves been imported from the Renaissance: Kenneth Clark points out that Manet's design for the *Déjeuner* goes back to Raphael's *Judgment of Paris*, which was based on classical models and which is known to us now only through an engraving by Marcantonio.[20]

If we combine this with Clark's comments on mediaeval attitudes to the nude, we gain an important insight into the intentions of the narrative here. Clark contrasts the frankness "with which the antique world accepted the body" to mediaeval reticence about it:

> It ceased to be the mirror of divine perfection and became an object of humiliation and shame. The whole of medieval art is a proof of how completely Christian dogma had eradicated the image of bodily beauty. That human beings were still conscious of physical desire we may assume; but even in those subjects of iconography in which the nude could properly be represented the medieval artist seems to show no interest in those elements of the female body which we have come to think of as inevitably arousing desire. . . . [The bodies of] the first full-size, independent nude figures of medieval art, the *Adam* and *Eve* at Bamberg, . . . are as little sensuous as the buttresses of a Gothic church.[21]

This suggests precisely that aspect of mediaeval art which it seems to me Fowles, for all his admiration of Marie, Chrétien, *et al.*, is most eager to avoid: its de-emphasis of sensuality and its tendency

---

20   *The Nude: A Study in Ideal Form* (New York: Doubleday & Co., 1956), p. 179.

21   Clark, pp. 401–403.

to treat love, under the auspices of Christianity, more in its romantic and spiritual aspects than in its physical one.[22]

Given his own existential and atheistic concerns and his
conception of women, it is essential for Fowles to centralize the
female body in his work and to treat sex with a physicality that
Eliduc's intense but chaste passion for Guilliadun does not admit.
He must modify his rather austere generic model on this point in
order to convey the mysteriousness and spiritual intensity of mediaevalized love in combination with a sensuality more appropriate to
the classical era or to modern art. Manet's particular blend of
modernity and classicism suits Fowles's thematic and structural purposes ideally here: Manet's modernity consists in the frankness and
informality of early Impressionist treatments of the nude, but his
artistic moment falls before the disturbing fragmentation of the
body which characterizes early twentieth-century art. His appropriation of classical models puts him in touch with the candour of pre-
Christian attitudes to the body while potently suggesting that the
Déjeuner, like "The Ebony Tower," is a series of reworkings and
borrowings involving Raphael and his mediator Marcantonio, as
well as Manet himself. One of the ways in which "The Ebony
Tower" explores the nature of art is by highlighting it as a construct
of artefacts made and mediated by other artists.

It is in terms of Manet and his artistic ancestors that we
must see the unaffected nudity of Diana and Anne, as well as the
combination here of clothed and unclothed figures. But despite
this, the reader cannot avoid observing that the scene is quite pruri-
ent as well as lyrical. Peter Prince quotes the following extract as
evidence of Fowles's sly slaughtering of the proverbial two birds:

> The lights of the Mouse's skin were bronzed where
> the sun caught it, duller yet softer in the shadows.
> The nipples, the line of the armpits. A healed scar
> on one of her toes. The way her wheaty hair was dry-
> ing, slightly tangled, careless; and a smallness, a

---

22   Fowles has angered mediaevalists like Hieatt by his cavalier treatment of
     Marie's involvement with Christianity and Christian ethics. Declaring
     religion to be "responsible for the ending of *Eliduc*, but not much else"
     (124), he apparently prefers to see Marie as a "clear-eyed realist" (Hieatt,
     353) — a twelfth-century Jane Austen — rather than as a woman deeply
     implicated in and committed to the dominant value system of her age.

> Quattrocento delicacy, the clothes and long skirts she
> wore were misleading; . . . [s]he sat sideways, facing
> the lake, and peeled an apple; passed a quarter back to
> the old man, then offered another to David. (61)[23]

Having surrounded this description and this scene of nude bathing
with profound reverberations from the realms of art and literature,
having directed us to view it in the now impeccably respectable perspective of early Impressionist painting, and having compelled
together the refined formalities of Marie de France and the relaxed
sensualities of Manet, the narrative allows that hint of voyeurism
and the quietly lascivious to register — protected, as it were, by the
unimpeachable credentials of the highest art. In this way, Fowles
achieves again that marriage of convenience between intellectual
respectability and the bestseller lists, between fine art and the cen-
trefold, which marks his *œuvre*.

  This accomplishment is not undermined by the fact that
David joins the women for a swim. The narrative voice never dwells
on his body as it does on theirs. Quite simply, David's body is not
offered for exhibition at all: he may be naked but we as readers cannot "see" him, for he is not described (71–72). Instead it is the
female body — both symbolic and literal, as form and as flesh —
that absorbs the attention of the narrator, just as it absorbs that of
the artists within the story and, by implication, the artist outside and
in charge of that story. For by framing these characters, both naked
and clothed, in an artefact of the author's devising, the narrator is
practising what his narrative preaches, and here the other implications of women and the body in this story become important.

  The particularly literal link which "The Ebony Tower"
establishes between the female body and art cannot be separated
from its valorization of Breasley's kind of sophisticated representational art — the art that remains loyal to "reality" — and its
scorn for abstract art as the pusillanimous embodiment of an over-
theoretical intellectualism and hence, inevitably to him, of sexual
impotence. Suspicious of reason and science, Fowles seems to side
with his surrogate when he has Breasley attack David: "Footsteps of
Pythagoras, that right? . . . Castrate. That's your game. Destroy. . . .

---

23   Prince's witty and irreverent review of *The Ebony Tower*, entitled "Real
      Life," appears in *New Statesman*, 11 Oct. 1974, 513.

Experimental. My arse. High treason, that's all. Mess of scientific pottage. Sold the whole bloody shoot down the river" (37, 42–43). The associations established here are complex. If, as the presentation of Diana implies, the female body is literally the artist's inspiration and his material, and if, as the character of Breasley implies, the artist's creative power need not depend on his skill with words, then what the story is apparently seeking to valorize is verbal inarticulacy itself. Not only does the inspirational power of the female body rely on its inarticulacy, its ability to bring "pagan contentment" to its observer, but the power of the visual artist, Breasley, is unvitiated by the kind of inadequacy with words that he exhibits.

In "The Ebony Tower," female physicality and the power of the artist who gives shape to it are alike in their involvement with what is not written and what remains not entirely available to language. It is David, who stands in the story for bad art and its corollary, criticism, who turns away from "reality" as the story defines it into mere ideas. His failure to claim Diana thus becomes in effect an inability to ally himself spiritually with the female body in either its literal or symbolic capacities. In this story a commitment to words is presented as a commitment to reason and abstraction. Reduced to its lowest terms, this means incapacity with the female and what she symbolizes, rejection of the muse, and a spiritual alliance with homosexuality.

It is from this perception that the haphazard excremental energy of Breasley's language comes: his obscenities are usually anal and he repeatedly asks David if he is a "bumboy" (44–45). Breasley expresses art's betrayal of itself and of "reality," its sell-out (as he sees it) to language and reason, in homosexual terms — as the betrayal of "true" sexuality and hence as a kind of sexlessness: the "[t]riumph of the bloody eunuch" (41). The anal exuberance of Breasley's language thus serves a double purpose: its schoolboyishness suggests the kind of innocence that links him to the "Celtic green source," the body of myth and folktale which nourishes him; its cartoon homophobia equates great art with heterosexuality, bad art with the homoerotic. So it is David, the man of words and concepts, who comes to perceive his art as fitting a "critical-verbal vocabulary" (108), and to recognize this as, in Breasley's phrase, the "triumph of the eunuch" (110). His initiation consists in glimpsing the freedom of the unwritten, the non-verbal and all it implies, as "the laboratory monkey allowed a glimpse of his lost true self" (110). His punishment is, finally, to look at his own words in the draft introduction and to find them "hopeless. Phrases and judgments that only a few days previously had pleased him . . . ashes, botch" (112).

But the story's overt presentation of language as unambiguously negative is problematic. Breasley's commitment to the non-verbal is not by definition a commitment to inarticulacy *per se*. His painting, as I have argued, is a form of articulation in itself, and this allows Fowles to experiment in "The Ebony Tower" with the possibility of the creator as verbally inept *without* separating him from the shaping power of the artist. Breasley's mastery of another medium means that he can, in a sense, share the inarticulacy of the Fowlesian heroine without partaking of her powerlessness. Furthermore, the story's attempt to valorize verbal inarticulacy as not only compatible with but crucial to creative power is strikingly ironic given that this valorization is itself accomplished through the words and narrative formulations of a writer, John Fowles. This unresolved disjunction in "The Ebony Tower" illuminates again that ambiguous response to authorship which characterizes Fowles's work. It suggests a deep desire for wordlessness operating within the larger context of a strong commitment to language.

This reading of "The Ebony Tower" helps us to perceive connections with the other pieces in the volume, which explore the various tensions and conflicts revealed in the title story. However, my analysis of Diana's role is not meant to imply that Fowles is moving his heroine into a position of authoritative creative power vis-à-vis art. Diana is another of Fowles's poignant apprentices: she has cut short her career at the Slade, does little work of her own, and is being pressed, much as Paston presses Miranda, to stop painting and marry an artist.[24] Like that of her predecessors,

---

24 We should note here that for Davidson Breasley is an ironized magus-figure — rather like G.P. — whose sense of reality is narrow and dubious, who uses art to justify sexual exploitation and who sees sexual prowess as a measure of artistic greatness (*"Eliduc,"* 35). What works against this view is the whole tone of the story, with its evident admiration for Breasley as a respecter of mediaeval literature and an honest, active admirer of physical form. It is not until the inverted strategies of "The Cloud" that Breasley is ironized at all, and then only indirectly. Davidson's reading focuses on only one story, and over-emphasizes narrative subversion.

Diana's relationship with art is complex but passive, and it must
remain so for her role as muse to be fulfilled. It must also remain
so for her role as mouse to be fulfilled, for her sexuality is not crucial in itself or in terms of its self-expression, but in its appropriation
by the artist. This suggests once more that for Fowles artistic
enterprise is a masculine activity, and here the book's governing
image, the ebony tower, takes on its crucial significance. If the title
story identifies anti-art as abstraction/criticism and equates it with
homosexuality, then the ebony tower becomes an image of the
black or destructive phallus — that is, of phallic power misdirected
and, inevitably, of artistic power misapplied. "The Cloud," as we
will observe, returns implicitly to this spectrum of associations,
which it further explores and develops.

• • •

        To move from "The Ebony Tower" to *Eliduc* is effec-
tively to apply the epigraph of the former to the latter, for it is difficult to pick one's way through the forest of literary problems here.
A volume of short stories includes a translation by the author of
another, earlier author's work. This is preceded by a short essay on
the life and merits of that earlier author, which includes a directive
that we see the stories before us as "variations" on her themes.
Why, then, is the work of the earlier author placed second rather
than first in the volume, when her function as literary model has
been so plainly asserted? Apparently presented with a puzzle, the
reader, assuming a critical function already discredited in "The
Ebony Tower," tries to answer these questions in the light of
his/her knowledge of Fowlesian indirections.
        It is understandable that an author should wish to cen-
tralize his own work in his own volume. For Fowles to have used
Eliduc as a curtain-raiser would have thrown too much emphasis on
Marie, suggesting an influence more pervasive than he intends
when he distinguishes between "structural" and "emotional" similarities. But the placement of the *lai* has other implications, which
Arnold Davidson has observed: "By giving precedence to the
retelling of a much earlier original, Fowles dis-orders compositional
sequence to a definite end." To then read *Eliduc* is to reread "The
Ebony Tower," and the earlier work becomes an ironic commentary

on the later one.[25]   This throws into question the idea of literary reworking which Fowles emphasizes in "The Ebony Tower," by suggesting that the latter is not so much a retelling of *Eliduc* which filters it through a contemporary consciousness, but the exact opposite.   *Eliduc* becomes not only a rereading of "The Ebony Tower," but an effective reworking of it, reversing the process of literary imitation to which the title story seemed committed and making "The Ebony Tower" the ancestral original of *Eliduc*. If the two stories mirror each other — and Coët has been described as a mirror (108) — it is singularly difficult to perceive which work is on which side of the glass.[26]

Here Fowles returns to those notions of disrupted chronology analyzed in the previous chapter in order to effect, in a more specific and complete way, the kind of appropriations undertaken in *The French Lieutenant's Woman*. For Davidson, the ambiguous relationship created by this ahistorical manoeuvring means greater flexibility for Fowles. One story can "reverse the narrative direction and attendant details of the other yet retain the same essential narrative configuration."[27]   Thus David's trip to France counterpoints (and is counterpointed by) Eliduc's trip to England; both stories deal with a "traditional love-triangle plot" in an atypical way, for in both a basically decent and a basically dishonest male protagonist has his choice made for him by one of the women. In each case she advocates her opposite, mistress or wife, and the result is despair for David, harmony and peace for Eliduc.[28] Davidson's observations are acute, but his conclusions are perhaps simplistic. For if the structure of *The Ebony Tower* implies a violation of the historical relationship between Marie de France and Fowles — a violation unacknowledged anywhere in the text — and if this ahistoricism undermines the notions of artistic re-creation and importation implied in "The Ebony Tower," then Fowles is effectively presenting his own story as a model for Marie's. For the

---

25   Davidson, "*Eliduc*," 31.

26   Davidson, "*Eliduc*," 34.

27   Davidson, "*Eliduc*," 34.

28   Davidson, "*Eliduc*," 35.

purposes of this book and within its covers, then, Fowles's imagination becomes a directing force in relation to Marie's — not accidentally the imagination of a woman — and his artistic creation becomes a point of departure for her own.

It is significant in this regard that the translation which Fowles includes here is his own. Translations are themselves ambiguous documents. Discrepancies between translations attest to the freedom which a translator can claim in changing and rearranging a work. The words we read in *The Ebony Tower* are not, in any sense we can be sure of, the words of Marie de France; they are only her words as rendered to us and interpreted by John Fowles. They are in a sense *his* words, and it does not seem too far-fetched to see Fowles's act of translation as, at least in part, an act of appropriation. In a wider structural context, this functions together with the placement of *Eliduc* to suggest a deliberate shifting of artistic control from the ancestor to the descendant, from the literary parent to the progeny.

The salient fact here is, of course, that the literary parent is a mother. For the generic premise of *The Ebony Tower*, its own fascinated involvement with mediaeval romance and specifically with *Eliduc*, offers Fowles a contradiction: if the title story, like his novels, carefully places women in a complicated but passive relationship with art, where does one place a woman who has produced, even in the (male) author's estimation, artistic masterpieces of her own? In this volume, it seems, Fowles struggles to confront not only the anxiety of influence in general, but the problem of achieved female creativity, both as a phenomenon and as part of the tradition of fiction within which he places himself. Those female creative forebears edited out of *The French Lieutenant's Woman* return in *The Ebony Tower* in the person of Marie de France; she represents for Fowles the paradox of the woman artist, who may not appear in his own work but whose appearance in history, like her artistic achievements, cannot be denied.[29]

---

29   Sarah Benton has shrewdly observed in this regard: "The woman whom John Fowles would have most feared meeting is Jane Austen," whom he deeply admires. Austen — and here Benton quotes Fowles — "would see through every pretension — and then record it for posterity!" Apparently Fowles's admiration for the woman author is always shot through with unease. See Benton, "Adam & Eve," *New Socialist*, No. 11 (1983), 18.

But her presence and power, like those of her male counterparts, can be manipulated, and at this point in *The Ebony Tower*
Fowles solves his dilemma by an act of narrative repossession. He
can kill Miranda and control Sarah through elaborate narrative
strategies; he can mastermind Catherine's inexplicable disappearance from "The Cloud." But as an historical figure, Marie de
France is simply not available in the same way. So, in a manner
which suggests Clegg's treatment of Miranda and the authorial
compromising of Sarah, he recasts this mother of the text as his
own literary offspring, and appropriates her words through
achronological structuring and the acts of translation and inclusion.
Because Marie is female this process of appropriating a predecessor
can be far more thoroughgoing than it was in *The French
Lieutenant's Woman*. One of her most substantial literary works, as
well as her very identity, is entirely recast and re-identified as
Fowles's own creation in *The Ebony Tower*. Thus Marie de France is
incorporated into the *œuvre* of John Fowles; a recipient of his gal-
lant condescension,[30] the woman takes her place *within* the text,
and the shaping power which produces that text is transferred symbolically from her to him. Effectively Marie becomes like Diana,
one of whose functions is to interpret Breasley's ineloquent insights
to David: she too is set up as a woman whose words are at the service of an artist for whom *she* mediates, rather than the other way
around. Thus Fowles, having it both ways, first interprets Marie via
translation in order to control her, and then projects her as the
interpreter of a wisdom and a vision which she herself does not
originate. In short, Fowles turns Marie de France into one of his
own fictional characters.

This process of repossession and fictionalization is
borne out by the comments which critics have made on Fowles's

---

30   For an example of Fowles at his lyrically chivalrous best, see his
      Foreword to *The Lais of Marie de France*, trans. Robert Hanning and
      Joan Ferrante (New York: E. P. Dutton, 1978), pp. ix–xiii. Describing
      Marie as "this seductively humane and intelligent Frenchwoman," he
      asserts that she, "once known, like a spring day in the Anjou of the royal
      family to which she may have belonged, . . . will not be forgotten"
      (p. xiii). In terms of imagery and tone, this is very different from the
      narrator's anxious approach to the "shadow" of Hardy in *The French
      Lieutenant's Woman*. It suggests the relative ease with which the female
      forebear, unlike the male, can be repossessed.

translation of *Eliduc*. Both Hieatt and Morse have pointed to the vitality and accessibility of Fowles's rendering, as well as its rather unscholarly attitude to its "original."[31] Morse observes that Fowles, choosing to abandon Marie's couplets, imparts an informality to her language, a brevity and simplicity to her syntax.[32] If we compare some extracts from Fowles with some from the translation by professors Robert Hanning and Joan Ferrante, we can observe this, as well as an interesting shift of emphasis in Fowles's version.

Just after her meeting with Eliduc, Guilliadun confesses her feelings to her page. Hanning and Ferrante translate as follows:

> "By my faith," she said, "this is terrible. / I have gotten myself into a sorry mess. / I love the new soldier, / Eliduc, the good knight. / Last night I had no rest, / I couldn't close my eyes to sleep. / If he wants to give me his love / and promise his person to me, / I shall do whatever he likes; / great good will come to him: / he will be the king of this land. / He is so wise and courtly / that, if he does not love me with real love, / I must die in great sorrow."[33]

Fowles's translation sounds somewhat different:

> "Dear God," she says, "I'm in such a state, I've fallen into such a trap. I love the new mercenary. Eliduc. Who's fought so brilliantly. I haven't slept a wink all night, my eyes just wouldn't shut. If he's really in love with me, if he'll only show he's serious, I'll do anything he likes. And there's so much to hope for —

---

31   Hieatt, 351–52; Morse, 22, 28–29.

32   Morse, 23–24.

33   Hanning and Ferrante, p. 205, ll. 337–50. I am aware that to compare one translation with another is in a way to defeat the very point I am trying to make here: an academic translation is as subject to distortion as any popular one. Unable to avoid this problem, I have judged it reasonably safe to assume that a scholarly rendering is more likely to keep strict faith with an original, although Fowles would undoubtedly accuse me in this of misplaced critical partisanship.

he could be king here one day. I'm mad about him.
He's so intelligent, so easy-mannered. If he doesn't
love me, I'll die of despair." (129)

Apparently Fowles has rendered Marie's words in terms of his own
stylistic traits; for example, his attachment to the sentence fragment
and its peculiar shorthand effect is evidenced here. More generally,
he has shifted her language in the direction of modern colloquial-
ism ("I'm mad about him"), emphasizing less the decorous passion
of Marie's Guilliadun and more the intense emotionalism of a
woman whom Fowles sees not as a well-behaved and bewildered
daughter, but as a "wayward princess" (121). In her first interview
with Eliduc, Fowles's Guilliadun behaves like a coquette, "stealing
looks at him," finding him "attractive" and "close to her ideal man"
(128). At this point Ferrante and Hanning have her "look[ing] at
him intently, / at his face, his body, his appearance; / she said to
herself / there was nothing unpleasant about him. / She greatly
admired him in her heart."[34] Morse glosses this as follows: "Marie's
Guilliadun is a conventional modest heroine surprised by love;
Fowles's is already on the lookout."[35]

Hieatt has observed Fowles's tendency to perceive the
lai's basic triangle in terms of strong sexual passion and a corresponding de-emphasis on those ties of faith and loyalty so crucial to
mediaeval society's conception of itself.[36] This is implied in the
rather lurid presentation of Guilliadun, whom we are encouraged to
see as revealingly dressed,[37] and the somewhat sensationalistic treatment of the love affair. For example, in Fowles's version, Eliduc

---

34   Hanning and Ferrante, p. 204, ll. 300–303.

35   Morse, 26.

36   Hieatt, 352–54. On this point Fowles's translation does not entirely
     accord with his "Personal Note," wherein he does acknowledge the
     importance of such ties (123).

37   In order to conjure up a visual image of Guilliadun, Fowles refers in a foot-
     note to the *lai Lanval*, which gives a description of the heroine's appear-
     ance: "She was dressed like this: in a white linen shift, loosely laced at the
     sides so that one could see the bare skin from top to bottom" (130).

goes to Guilliadun's room to say goodbye, and she clings to him
"passionately" (134), whereas according to Ferrante and Hanning,
she "greet[s] him six thousand times."[38] For Fowles, he addresses
her in emotional language: "You sweetest thing, oh God, listen —
you're life and death to me, you're my whole existence. That's why
I've come. So that we can talk about it, and trust each other"
(134). For Ferrante and Hanning this is: "By God . . . my sweet
love, / listen to me for a little: / You are my life and my death, / in
you is all my comfort. / That's why I am consulting you, / because
there is an understanding between us."[39]

By contrast, Fowles treats Eliduc's wife Guildelüec in a
rather more distant way; his language loses some of its idiomatic
vibrancy when it deals with both Eliduc's marriage and his role as
vassal. Thus, when Hanning and Ferrante render Eliduc's feelings
about his marriage, there is no noticeable change in tone relative to
their rendition of his affair: "[F]or he remembered his wife / and
how he had assured her / that he'd be faithful to her, / that he'd
conduct himself loyally."[40] Fowles's language is vaguer, and he does
not include the strong words "faithful" and "loyally": "He remembered his wife, and how he had promised to behave as a husband
should" (128).

Equally strong words suggesting the importance of fealty
are used in Ferrante's and Hanning's version when the king of
Brittany summons Eliduc home: "Because of his great need, he was
sending for Eliduc, / summoning and begging him — / in the
name of the alliance that bound them / when the king received
homage from Eliduc — / to come and help him, / for the king
needed him badly."[41] Again, Fowles suggests a weaker bond —
"[I]n the name of the trust that had existed between them ever
since the knight first paid homage to him" (132–33) — than that of
intense passion. Eliduc, we are told, loved Guilliadun now "to the
anguished depths of his being" (133), rather than just "painfully,"

---

38   Hanning and Ferrante, p. 214, l. 656.

39   Hanning and Ferrante, p. 214, ll. 669–74.

40   Hanning and Ferrante, p. 205, ll. 323–26.

41   Hanning and Ferrante, p. 211. ll. 565–70.

as Hanning and Ferrante see it.[42]   It seems logical to conclude, as
both Morse and Hieatt do, that Fowles is suppressing Marie's concern with loyalty in favour of an emphasis on desire, and that by so
doing, he is effectively compelling more of a parity between himself
and her than necessarily exists. In Fowles's translation, Marie de
France sounds like John Fowles and also shares his concern with sex
as existential imperative and hence as instant priority.

"The Ebony Tower" itself supports this view, for it edits
out Guildelüec's equivalent, Beth Williams, almost entirely. She is
allowed no heroic deed of sacrifice and restitution comparable to
Guildelüec's, and exists in the story as little more than an unde-
sirable option. Insofar as "The Ebony Tower" is a reworking
of *Eliduc* — and Fowles's own strategies make such a claim ambiguous — it all but eliminates Guildelüec and *her* relationship with
Guilliadun, makes nothing of the fact that the *lai*'s other title is
Guildelüec and Guilliadun, and focuses principally on the
erotic/existential problems of a twentieth-century Eliduc, David
Williams. As Hieatt observes: "[Marie] was overwhelmingly concerned with man's unfairness to woman. Fowles is almost exclusively concerned with the problems of men, even when he devotes a
major part of the narrative to looking at a woman's point of view, as
he does in . . . 'The Cloud.'"[43] One could also say that *The Ebony
Tower* effectively manages to appropriate Marie's work by virtue of
method as well as structure: not only is Diana a version of Eliduc's
mistress, but Guilliadun is herself a version of Diana, brought into
line with the contemporary woman's frustrated intensity through
an act of authorial re-emphasis.

But Fowles in the role of translator raises other prob-
lems: a translator is only a *kind of* creative artist, and here Fowles's
Eliduc, like his "Personal Note" and the title story, engages with
the difficult issues of language and the nature of artistic power.
This part of *The Ebony Tower* presents us quite literally with the
artist in the role of critic, as Fowles not only reads and critiques
Marie de France, but writes a short biography of her and offers his

---

42   Hanning and Ferrante, p. 212, l. 573.

43   Hieatt, 357–58. To this end as well, the figure of the liegelord to be
     obeyed and served is transposed into the vaguer, more mystical one of
     the sage to be imitated.

own interpretation of the historical context for the mediaeval romance: "The mania for chivalry, courtly love, mystic and crusading Christianity, the Camelot syndrome, all these we are aware of" (118). The author seems to move here into that unhappy position occupied not by his explicit surrogate, Breasley, but by Breasley's anti-type, David. He becomes both the creator and explainer of art, and hence, according to the story's definition of these terms, a living paradox — or more simply, a second-rate artist. If art and criticism are antithetical here, then *Eliduc* and its "Note" postulate a tension and constitute an acknowledgement of the difficulties involved in occupying both positions. It is not illogical to claim, in fact, that Fowles's efforts to fictionalize Marie de France and assimilate her work into his own are based on an attempt to turn the role of critic or reader into that of artist, and so to deal with the pressure of other artists' creativity.

This is why, it seems to me, there is so much emphasis in *The Ebony Tower* on transformation. On the level of imagery, Marie's magical weasel becomes the mortal weasel of the title story. On the level of character, Diana, a "bit of 'seventies bird" (32), becomes a *princesse lointaine* waiting for her lover in the woods (106). In the last story, a woman tries to project herself through narrative as just such another lost princess, but is transformed instead into a cloud. On the level of genre and plot, a detective tale becomes a love story in "The Enigma," and a thriller becomes a cryptic piece of surrealism in "Poor Koko." Conradi claims that Fowles's fiction concerns itself with the effecting of impossible liberations;[44] in *The French Lieutenant's Woman*, for example, Fowles attempts to liberate the modern novel from its Victorian precursors and, in *The Ebony Tower*, to liberate his own work from that of a mediaeval forebear. To this end, I would add, his books seek to accomplish transformations essentially impossible except through the agency of the imagination, and they consistently invoke narrative (identical, for the purposes of my discussion, with fiction) as a kind of magic able to inaugurate such changes. It is narrative that can turn Marie de France from literary ancestor to descendant; here, perhaps, is another reason for Fowles's absorption in a genre, the mediaeval romance, which insists on the magical rather than the merely logical or possible.

---

44   Conradi, p. 15.

Like the very existence of Fowles's *œuvre* and Marie's, the attribution of magical properties to narrative suggests that it too is art, and that words (the components of narrative) possess transformative power. Once again, Fowles's dealings with Marie imply a contradiction of terms set forth in "The Ebony Tower," where words and the "crossed wires" (101) they there represent are established as the property of anti-art and the medium of the anti-artist. But again, this particular opposition is not one that a man of words and a creative artist like Fowles can allow to go uncontested. For literature, like history, brings together articulacy and art, not only in the troubling figure of the woman writer, but in the act of writing itself and the creation of art through words. Thus the *Eliduc* part of the book, by implicitly recognizing that the artist can deal in words as well as in paint, moves the volume from visual to written art; it begins to reformulate that central opposition between artist and critic in the direction of a dialectic between words and action, on the one hand, and between different kinds of words, on the other.

These dialectical manoeuvres provide the paradigm which governs the next two stories: "Poor Koko" presents the man of words as critic and would-be biographer, and pits him against a man of action whose verbal incapacity pales beside the dazzling eloquence of his deed. The thief is a variation on the figure of the non-verbal creator, Breasley, with his artistic sophistication reduced to the level of gesture. He is a perverse performance artist, and the transformative power of his art is directed, significantly, at turning a book to ashes. But if for both David Williams and the superannuated biographer of Peacock the word literally becomes ash, for Mike Jennings in "The Enigma" one kind of word becomes another. As the rational and inductive mind of the critic, here imaged as the detective, gives way to the visionary imagination of the incipient novelist, Isobel, one kind of story literally becomes another. The end of "The Enigma" seems to present a paradox triumphant, as a woman writer — herself another version, perhaps, of Marie de France — reveals to us through a different kind of language the mysteriousness of truth and the truth of mystery.

But the very story itself, as well as the dense obscurities of "The Cloud," reinstate this figure as a contradiction. The latter story, as we will observe, also effectively replaces the dialectic between word and word with a more fundamental dialogue between language and meaning. In a way, Fowles's tendency to experiment with narrative personae manifests itself in his "Personal Note," where he performs the duties of both critic and literary biographer of Marie de France. The result is an ambivalent relationship between the author as artist and as critic, and this appears in his translation as a contradiction. On the one hand, Fowles assumes critical authority, thanking an Oxford professor, in a footnote, for his learned help;[45] on the other, he produces a translation too racily popular to be really academically respectable, as Hieatt's reaction suggests.

This ambivalent relationship with criticism, this simultaneous flirtation with the academy and the Book-of-the-Month club, informs much of Fowles's work; it dominates the central confrontation of "Poor Koko" and the qualified victory which that story awards to its critic-protagonist. The narrator here is also a literary biographer — of Peacock, one of Fowles's favourite writers.[46] He seems to be another authorial surrogate, a parodic one, and Fowles's self-mockery is conveyed in this narrator's unwitting presentation of himself as complacent, solipsistic, and unaware of his own ridiculousness.

He sees his absorption in books, therefore, as a tasteful refusal to engage with life: "I have never pretended to be a man of action. . . . [N]or can I deny that books — writing them, reading, reviewing, helping to get them into print — have been my life rather more than life itself" (147). Intellectually as well as physically myopic, he does not perceive the air of absurdity which hovers around his own literary endeavours: he is proud of his silly-sounding book, *The Dwarf in Literature*, a "most successful potboiler" which he chattily admits was not "quite the model of objective and erudite analysis it pretended to be" (147). This kind of cosy false modesty undermines the narrator, for he alludes without self-irony to his own narratorial unreliability even as he is about to present an interpretation of an action that he wants us to

---

45   "I must thank Dr. Nicholas Mann, of Pembroke College, Oxford, for help over some particularly difficult lines" (123).

46   See Fowles, "I Write," 17.

perceive as both brilliantly astute and true.[47]   He is, as Kerry McSweeney has observed, "a second-rate, back number man of letters . . . [who] has the appearance of literary distinction without the reality."[48]

By means of this untrustworthy narrator, Fowles focuses the story on an act of interpretation, of "reading" the "text" of an action. This relates "Poor Koko" thematically to the pieces preceding it while further exploring the link between critical endeavour and power. The narrator, a man who "live[s] by words" (185), is ironically betrayed by his very vocabulary into unwittingly exposing the power-hunger at the root of his involvement with writing: "I felt so eager to *kill off* the final draft [of the Peacock book], to have my fascinating and still grossly underrated subject *alive* on the polished page" (152, emphasis added). This is the language of the collector, eager to convert vitality into living death, and in its setting and sadistic details, "Poor Koko" is a clear variation on Fowles's first published novel.

If the narrator is, implicitly, a Clegg-like anti-artist, then this story sees the conflict between critic and artist as brutally competitive and based on certain hidden agendas. For the old man, who projects himself as custodian and protector of "the word, its secrets and its magics, its sciences and its arts" (186), is blind to his own use of it as an instrument of punishment. Claiming to "trust" and "revere" language (185), this man not only is unreliable as a narrator, but cannot perceive that his own involvement with language is based more on aggression than reverence. His very act of interpretation reveals this, for he "reads" the thief's actions in a way that flatters his own vanity and corrects the balance of power between them. Humiliated by the intruder's treatment of him, aware of his physical puniness and inability to defend himself, the narrator retaliates in his own medium by resurrecting his destroyed book, and by reading the incident in terms that arrogate lasting

---

47   Loveday's reading also identifies the narrator with Fowles, and sees the
       narrative itself as a victory over the burglar. Loveday places the unreli-
       able narrator within his own literary/critical category as a "dwarf in liter-
       ature," and declares it difficult for us to share the narrator's certainty that
       he has found the meaning of his ordeal (p. 100).

48   McSweeney, *Four Contemporary Novelists*, p. 117.

power to himself — terms that both proclaim the might of the word and focus that might in the person of the literary critic. Thus he mentions his tendency to indulge in "the characteristic malice of the physically deprived" (147), admits his desire for revenge (176), and effectively accomplishes that revenge when he concludes his tale with the pompous categorization of himself as a "word-magician. I presented a closed shop, a select club, an introverted secret society; and that is what [the thief] felt he had to destroy" (186).

"Poor Koko" sees the critic's action in reading and rewriting a text as essentially aggressive, vengeful, and self-serving. Presenting the narrator as both an author and critic, the story is haunted by the exigency that the artist himself is forced by the very nature of art into those acts of criticism that Fowles's work actively mistrusts.[49] Nevertheless "Poor Koko" constitutes a bitter and clever comment on the critic's need to appropriate the artist's imaginative creations, whatever they may be, through his endless endeavour to render the mysterious intelligible. The narrator here can turn a shameful defeat into a triumph by explaining the thief's action, and thus appropriating and controlling him: he refers to the intruder repeatedly in the possessive, as "*my own* specimen of youth in revolt" (166), "*my* thief" (183), and "*my* young demon" (186, emphases added). The story is, furthermore, a comment on the act of translation. It ends with a literal translation of its own epigraph: "Too long a tongue, too short a hand; / But tongueless man has lost his land" (187). This cryptic couplet highlights again the contrast between language and action, "tongue" and "hand," while proclaiming the man of action, the "tongueless" one, as finally dispossessed in the loss of "his land." The translation thus supports the reading offered by the narrator — a reading aimed at depriving just such a "tongueless" one of power — and its inclusion implies

---

49   In the interview with Halpern, Fowles expressed his sense of the clash between literature and criticism in especially Breasleyesque terms, as a dichotomy between art and science. His comments here, whatever their general reliability, are apposite to the whole endeavour of *The Ebony Tower*: "There's always a dimension in art that science hasn't yet evolved a science to describe and analyse. It's a sort of quantum of mystery, which you cannot really pin down by scientific means. An *n* quantity. I simply refuse to believe that literary criticism is more important than literature. A bad novel is humanly more important than the very best criticism" (43).

that the story itself is a kind of translation, dominated by the suppressed desires to manipulate and to possess.[50] "Poor Koko" becomes a sort of allegorical summary of Fowles's own endeavour as critic/reader of Marie de France: just as he creates *his Eliduc* and presents *his* Marie de France, so the Peacock biographer turns a performance artist and his savagely effective production into *his* story and *his* young man.

Thus the narrator's efforts in "Poor Koko" to project the critic as an all-powerful word-magician are ironically compromised by the story's own strategies, and the authorial self-awareness which these imply — that quiet but persistent sense that the artist himself must read and rewrite — propels Fowles to yet another variation, this one sweeter and more melodic. "The Enigma" takes up the problem of creativity and the word in a different key as Fowles, escaping that horrible image of the burnt book, examines language not in tension with gesture but in league with it. As Isobel Dodgson (whose surname seems to associate her with the imaginative fantasies of Lewis Carroll) undertakes an act of creative interpretation aimed at preserving the essential mystery and individuality of Marcus Fielding's deed, language ceases to be the tool of the aggressive anti-artist and modulates into the medium of the apparently true artist. Deliberately annexed to art rather than to criticism, the word here can reveal truth and effect transformations both magical and beautiful.

One such transformation takes place on the level of style and genre. The analytical, ratiocinative methods and attitudes of the critic/author/narrator in "Poor Koko" are echoed in the early stages of "The Enigma," as Fowles apes the documentary mode of the conventional detective story:

---

50   For his own interpretive purposes, the narrator deliberately ignores the thief's intelligence, his literary sensibility (162), knowledge of antiques (159), and serious attempts at political analysis (163). The narrator prefers to see himself as easily intellectually superior to the intruder, who is presented as just a hooligan — largely by virtue of his inarticulacy, his sense of the old writer as "just saying words, man" (160). The latter smugly claims: "I knew any attempt at serious argument with this young buffoon would be like discussing the metaphysics of Duns Scotus with a music-hall comedian" (159).

> The commonest kind of missing person is the adoles-
> cent girl, closely followed by the teen-age boy. The
> majority in this category come from working-class
> homes, and almost invariably from those where there
> is serious parental disturbance. There is another minor
> peak in the third decade of life, less markedly work-
> ing-class, and constituted by husbands and wives try-
> ing to run out on marriages or domestic situations
> they have got bored with. (191)

It is under the auspices of this popular sub-genre that the story initially operates: Fielding's disappearance is treated as a "case" to be
solved through logical deduction and official investigation.
Ostensibly devoted to rendering the mysterious intelligible, "The
Enigma" — like "Poor Koko," which draws on the thriller for its
effects — focuses on the attempt to read and interpret the text of a
human action. Mike Jennings, with his leads and tabulations, is the
equivalent of the critic, who believes in the availability of textual
meaning to intellectual endeavour and who tries to locate this
meaning through the discovery and interpretation of clues. But
the process of interpretation changes qualitatively when Isobel
Dodgson appears. A budding novelist, she begins to read the text
of Fielding's disappearance with the perception of an artist. Her
stroke of interpretive genius is, in fact, to perceive the deed as literally a text and to approach the incomprehensible action from an
aesthetic rather than a logical point of view: "Let's pretend everything to do with the Fieldings, even you and me sitting here now, is
in a novel. A detective story. Yes? Somewhere there's someone
writing us, we're not real. He or she decides who we are, what we
do, all about us" (236).

By thus jettisoning the merely feasible or possible and
bringing Fielding's actions within the purview of the artist, Isobel
breaks the stranglehold of criticism, of reason itself, and thereby
alters the story's dominant generic influence. The narrative
exchanges its documentary mode for a lyrical one, and becomes in
effect a love story: "The tender pragmatisms of flesh have poetries
no enigma, human or divine, can diminish or demean — indeed,
it can only cause them, and then walk out" (247). With this telescoped reference to Marcus Fielding, John Fowles, and the *Deus
absconditus*, the enigma of sexuality replaces that of disappearance;

the story deliberately shifts focus in order to preserve an unsolved mystery and declare itself in favour of indeterminacy. In this way it revises the aggressively closed ending of "Poor Koko" by using the unintelligible, the textually unavailable, to undermine the certainties of the detective/critic.

Departing very clearly from the premises of "The Ebony Tower," the story also allies language with the imagination of the artist by highlighting its ability to offer explanation without dogma and, apparently, to interpret without the desire to control. For Isobel never declares the absolute truth of her reading, and the shift in narrative emphasis suggests how ultimately unimportant this reading is. It implies, moreover, that the act of interpretive reading is itself unimportant in this story, for the narrative seems to have created Fielding simply in order to create the love between Isobel and Mike.

It is here, as incorrigible critics, that we find our own clue to what troubles the apparent intellectual serenity of "The Enigma." In a sense, the book's two middle stories interlock: both are set in England rather than France; both emphasize popular literary forms at the expense of the courtly romance; the second revises and completes the first by introducing a cool and intelligent artist who balances the pomposities of the anti-artist. But if we look at "The Enigma" as part of a continuum of ideas which *The Ebony Tower* persistently re-explores, we find within it tensions and contradictions that may not manifest themselves clearly until "The Cloud" — a story which also centres upon a character's disappearance from the text that contains and constitutes her. For we cannot help noticing how Isobel's reading is implicitly devalued by the very transformation which it effects: as the mystery of Marcus Fielding is made less important by the foregrounding of the love affair, so the discoverer and preserver of that mystery, Isobel, becomes less important in her capacity as reader. She does in fact go the route offered to both Miranda and Diana: she abandons, within the frame of the narrative, her role as artist and creative reader of texts, in order to play the role of lover to a man who sees her (as Fowles himself seems to see Marie de France) as part deity and part pin-up, an "unlikely corn-goddess" (236) who may not be wearing anything beneath her dress (242).

The story effectively recasts Isobel in terms of her sexuality and not in terms of the artistic power which she seems to possess. Insofar as she represents another creative woman in *The Ebony Tower*, and is a possible narrative reincarnation of Marie de France herself,[51] her creativity is denied by being superseded, pushed away from the reader's attention along with the text which she makes her own. And even here Isobel is not really allowed the dubious but effective power which the reader/critic accrues to himself through the act of interpretive rewriting. Marcus Fielding never becomes the "creation" of Isobel as the thief becomes that of the Peacock biographer or Marie becomes that of Fowles, for it is behind Isobel that the presence of Fowles is most strongly felt, and this is communicated through the story's central irony. When Isobel declares, "Nothing is real. All is fiction" (236), she inevitably emphasizes her own status as a character in Fowles's fiction, and this revelation of the puppeteer's strings places her actions as artist/reader under the direct influence of his authorial presence.

Unlike the old man in "Poor Koko," she is given no first-person narrative to create, on one level of narrative operation, the sense of autonomy. Her reading of Fielding's deed may be creative in the marriage it effects between truth and mystery, but it is compromised by its own ironic context. This makes both the deed and the man who performs it into the property not of Isobel Dodgson, but of John Fowles. Like that of Diana working on Breasley's masterpieces, Isobel's fledgling creativity is colonized by a mature artist; in imaginatively repossessing Fielding, she appropriates him not for herself but for her author. At the end of "The Enigma," Isobel's position is strikingly similar to Diana's. De-emphasized as an artist, she has been defined principally as a mistress, for the story, despite its apparent faith in language as integral to art and words as the legitimate medium of the artist, allows only another qualified victory — this time to that ever-troubling figure, the creative woman. In terms of the book's

---

51   Fowles's assessment in his "Personal Note" of Marie's effect on "European literature" applies to Isobel as a description of what she achieves within the story. Like Marie, Isobel grafts "her own knowledge of the world" onto "old material," introducing thereby (so Fowles would have us believe) "sexual honesty and a very feminine awareness of how people really behave" (120). The talents of one "fictional" character are also those of another.

dominant metaphor of transformation, that point in the text at which the artist and critic might be reconciled is heavily circum-scribed, and that character who might represent such a reconcilia-tion is deeply compromised.

If "Poor Koko" and "The Enigma" are influenced by the thriller and the detective story respectively, the ending of "The Enigma" implicitly interrogates detective fiction conventions by means of indeterminacy. This insistence on the unsolved mystery foreshadows the generic doubling-back of "The Cloud," which returns to France, to the ambience and configurations of "The Ebony Tower," and by extension to the mediaeval romance. The full symbolic significance of the romance for Fowles becomes clear here. Through indeterminacy he asserts the creative power of mys-tery in "The Enigma": if the artist is to use language, he must not over-use it and become too articulate. Here the tendency of the romance to defy rationality and baffle explanation makes it an appro-priate generic symbol for the artist's visionary, imaginative power. For Fowles the rich suggestiveness of the romance lies in its refusal to make itself and its meanings entirely available to cognition. The obscurities of "The Cloud" imitate effectively the impenetrability of the romance; the story does not yield up all its meanings for analysis or explanation, and in this way it deliberately frustrates critical endeavour. For if *The Ebony Tower* sets up a dialectic of genre between the romance and the detective story, it is the romance, reworked into a kind of literary and psychological conundrum, that dominates the book at the end.

There are many parallels between "The Cloud" and "The Ebony Tower": both stories feature the French countryside, an isolated home, the forest, and a pool in its depths. Both present three women, two of whom are close: Catherine and Diana are sen-sitive and frustrated, Bel and Anne are more practical and worldly-wise, Sally and Beth represent behavioural options questioned by both the heroine and an important male character. Peter and David are morally ambiguous figures who experience some conflict of loy-alty between a socially orthodox sexual relationship and the lure of an illicit one. The inevitable similarities to *Eliduc* as well as to *The Magus* and *The French Lieutenant's Woman* suggest how crucial this psychosexual configuration is to Fowles's artistic imagination. These textual parallels are further signalled through an important echoed image. In "The Cloud," the picnic site is temporarily

invaded by "a fisherman, a peasant come fishing, in rubber boots
and faded blues" (263). This figure has appeared at an earlier
picnic, where David Williams glimpsed "an angler, a line being cast,
a speck of peasant blue" (74) after his swim. This image reveals the
perspective in which the stories are to be placed and their interrelationship understood.

In "The Cloud," the angler combines with the specific
mention of a kingfisher, "a flash of azure" (260), to foreground the
dense mesh of allusions to *The Waste Land* which constitutes much
of the story's narrative substance.[52] By evoking at once Eliot's
kingfisher, Jessie Weston's fisher-king, and the poem which synthesizes them, Fowles alters our perception of the story's generic
matrix: what we have here is a direct reference less to the mediaeval
romance than to the other, later text which, like Fowles's own,
reworks the romance and its Celtic elements into a literary form
appropriate to its time. "The Cloud" is preoccupied, then, with the
intelligibility of genre in relation to history; Fowles is restructuring
and recombining traditional features of a genre to make it comprehensible in terms of twentieth-century experience. We seem to be
back not only with the historico-literary endeavour of *The French
Lieutenant's Woman*, but with the informing question of "The
Ebony Tower" and the motivation behind the intellectual acrobat-
ics of *Eliduc*: the difficult issue of literary parenthood and the

---

52   These have been exhaustively traced and discussed by Raymond J. Wilson,
      III, in "Allusion and Implication in John Fowles's 'The Cloud,'" *Studies
      in Short Fiction* 20, No. 1 (1983), 17–22. I am using the presence
      of these allusions to make critical points quite different from Wilson's;
      I quote only a few examples here of these references to Eliot's poem.
      Catherine at the water's edge grieving for a dead man (265) echoes
      Eliot's reference to Ferdinand "Musing upon the king my brother's
      wreck / And on the king my father's death before him" (III, 191–92).
      Catherine emphasizes the waste land geography of "silent cliffs above,
      scorched lifeless planet, windless sun" (276). Bel with the butterfly
      orchids she found a year ago (258) echoes Eliot's hyacinth girl. Paul with
      his rolled up trousers (262) recalls Eliot's often-repeated Prufrockian per-
      sona, while Peter, a television director, is an updated version of one of
      Eliot's "loitering heirs of City directors" (III, 180). As in *The Waste
      Land*, heat and stoniness are the geographical equivalents of emotional
      barrenness and, in this specific context, a loveless sexual encounter sums
      up the sterility and alienation of a world.

artist's relationship with his predecessors' works.[53]

By filtering "The Cloud" through *The Waste Land*, Fowles is doing more than acknowledge that he is neither the first nor the greatest to rework Celtic material; he is raising to the level of a theme the very strategy of reworking itself and examining his own importations, into his *œuvre* and his time, of historically defunct but artistically resonant forms like the mediaeval *lai*. The textual irony of "The Cloud" thus consists in its radically ambivalent status as a reworking not only of a courtly romance, but of its own ambiguous "original," "The Ebony Tower." In the possibility that this status may be not only ambivalent but logically unstable and intellectually untenable, we see Fowles recognizing that the process of artistic re-creation may be ultimately self-defeating.

It is not surprising, then, to find that "The Cloud" displaces the title story — as that story has itself already, in some senses, displaced *Eliduc* — in the direction of irony and parody. Breasley, the mature artist, is replaced by a dead poet present only in his absence; Diana becomes the disillusioned Catherine, and the kindly Anne transmutes into the complacently bovine Bel, who abandons her sister at the end. Instead of a "dishy" (105) art critic, "The Cloud" offers the vulgar, pretentious Peter and his ox-like sidekick Paul. These two represent, in a parodic sense, the critic debased even further, into a parasite on other people's ideas, and the artist debased into a mere popular entertainer. In terms of this apparent pattern of inversion, "The Cloud" presents not a failed quest but an absent one. Even the central figure of the knight-errant, alias David Williams, is eliminated from this story. The cynicism behind "The Cloud" (and its loss of generic faith) is shown in

---

53   In this connection the recurrence in *The Ebony Tower* of relationships of failed parenthood becomes interesting. As father surrogate, Breasley does not pass on the true wisdom of the artist to his substitute son David, and the Peacock biographer fails his surrogate child in the same way. Maurice and Jane cannot get on with their son Richard, and Peter Fielding explicitly rejects his father's values. Timothy C. Alderman formulates this pattern as a failed relationship between the master/magician/parent figure and the servant/initiate/son figure, in "The Enigma of *The Ebony Tower*: A Genre Study," *Modern Fiction Studies* 31, No. 1 (1985), 135–47. Alderman also applies these categories to Fowles's relationship with Marie de France, regardless of differences in gender. His conclusions are dissimilar from my own.

the splitting of this figure into two ineffectualities, Peter and Paul, whom Catherine identifies with the two little dicky-birds of the children's rhyme: "All the Peters and all the Pauls. Won't fly away" (298).

Furthermore, these paradigms of ironic inversion suggest that, while the title story projects the image of the ebony tower as a symbol of bad values and wrong meanings, "The Cloud" offers the literally inverted image of the black hole as a symbol of no values and meaninglessness: "Where all is reversed; once entered, where nothing leaves. The black hole, the black hole" (299).[54] The symbolic opposite of the ebony tower is not so much the ivory one but the void, and this is why the story emphasizes not just transformation, but transformation in the direction of absence, of literal gaps in the text. Catherine has lost her husband and is herself "lost" at the end of the piece — a textual death which parallels his physical one; romance motifs are not only adopted and adapted but eliminated, as if the end-product of such literary reworkings is the draining away of significance from these motifs — a process that makes the quest perversely present in its absence.

This is also why the story emphasizes fragmentation and incoherence, associating these specifically with Catherine: she is aware of having lost her "sense of continuity" (260) and of perceiving her experience in terms of isolated vignettes or "islands" (261); Bel's hat has "fenestrations, an open lattice around the crown" (262)[55] which reminds Catherine of "[n]uclei, electrons" and the dying Ophelia chanting "snatches of old tunes" (262–63). In Catherine's consciousness, absence and fragmentation, with death as their ontological equivalent, are brought together. It is through

---

54   It is important to remember here Breasley's definition of the ebony tower, as glossed by Diana: "Anything he doesn't like about modern art. That he thinks is obscure because the artist is scared to be clear . . . you know. Somewhere you dump everything you're too old to dig?" (54).

55   Davidson extends this image to cover what he calls "fenestrations in the text," the deliberate undermining of certainty in relation to landscape and human groupings. He also sees the copious literary allusions in the story as "openings ever opening onto something else (and thus correlative to the abyss of indeterminacy and irrationality that is Catherine's life)" ("Barthesian Configurations," 84). My own argument draws on some of his ideas.

her too that the literary-critical equivalent of absence and fragmentation, deconstruction, is emphasized in the story — not as any formal system, but as a way of reading and writing as well as of experiencing. Eschewing specific reference to either the theoretical premises or the exponents of deconstruction, Fowles seems to work here with his own imaginative sense of what deconstructive processes imply. Catherine represents in the narrative the idea of disjunction. As the widow of a poet, she is the living emblem of a broken connection — a connection insisted upon as crucial in "The Ebony Tower" — between the artist and his nourishing material, the woman. To use the kind of terminology which the allusions to Roland Barthes make appropriate, Catherine is a sign without a referent and a fitting symbol for the disintegration of meaning of which "The Cloud" is so persistently aware.

For it is in this story, where images of dissolution hover, that Fowles implicitly confronts the collapse of certain stylistic and structural premises which have sustained his textual endeavours in this volume and others: if the method of art is appropriation through re-creation, the symbolic endpoint of this process is Catherine, a disintegrating consciousness and free-floating sign. In her Eliotian inability to connect anything with anything, we find a metaphor for the demise of meaning in a jumble of signs all clamouring for priority. This effective loss of significance to incoherence is what Catherine seems to have in mind when she mentions the death of fiction as an aspect of her own internal dissolution and that which she perceives in the waste land of contemporary life: "Pollution, energy, population. . . . The dying cultures, dying lands. Europe ends. The death of fiction; and high time too" (298). The implied replacement of the ebony tower with the black hole is thus a *mise en abyme* for the fate of the narrative in its entirety. As so often in Fowles's work, what happens *in* the text is what happens *to* it, and in this last story *The Ebony Tower* becomes its opposite, disappearing into the abyss of non-meaning as its methodological and structural underpinnings give way.

The very limits of art are here the very limits of narrative art, and the painter whose spirit presides over this textual fragmentation is not Pisanello or Goya, those old masters of integrated form whom Breasley loved. It is not even Manet and the formal coherence of early Impressionism, for "The Cloud" replaces the sensual *Déjeuner* with a trivial, domesticated paddle and crayfish hunt,

more Prufrockian than picturesque. It is instead Seurat[56] and the
Neo-Impressionist infatuation with disintegrating or potentially dis-
solving shapes that provide the visual equivalent of Catherine's
experiencing consciousness: "The voices, movements; kaleidoscope,
one shake and all will disappear. . . . Nuclei, electrons. Seurat, the
atom is all" (262). In "The Cloud" thinking in pictures becomes
thinking in pointillism; this implicates the story in those interrogations of form and perception associated with modern art — especially with modernism and postmodernism as Fowles conceives
them.

　　　　The story's involvement with the indeterminacy of form
and the threatened demise of meaning confirms that preoccupation
with the tenets of modernism which the pervasive influence of Eliot
already suggests. Furthermore, "The Cloud" replaces the detailed
visual allusiveness of "The Ebony Tower" with an almost obsessive
literary allusiveness. Besides the dominating and overt references to
Eliot and Barthes, there are others to *Hamlet, Antony and Cleopatra*,
Arnold's poetry, Jane Austen, and Voltaire, as well as indirect textual
echoes of Angus Wilson and Katherine Mansfield.[57] This concludes

---

56　Davidson notes the implied opposition in the text between Seurat and
　　Courbet, who is mentioned early on in the narrative (247). The two are
　　identified respectively with fragmentation and coherence as principles of
　　landscape art ("Barthesian Configurations," 83–84). In this story,
　　Fowles also associates Seurat symbolically, and perhaps idiosyncratically,
　　with deconstruction, viewing him as a radical precursor of contemporary
　　disjunctions.

57　*Hamlet* is echoed repeatedly, particularly in the epigraph and in Bel's
　　musings about Catherine (294). *Antony* is implied in Bel's image of
　　Catherine "playing Hamlet to an asp" (306). Arnold's "The Scholar
　　Gipsy" is read in the text (294–95), and "To Marguerite" is suggested in
　　the imagery of islands which Catherine uses to describe experience. The
　　children's names, Emma and Candida, recall the titles of novels by Austen
　　and Voltaire respectively. McSweeney points out the various ways in
　　which "The Cloud" recalls the short stories of Angus Wilson, in "John
　　Fowles's Variations in *The Ebony Tower*," *Journal of Modern Literature* 8,
　　No. 2 (1980/81), 313–14. Loveday sees the story as emulating "the
　　impressionistic 'spirit of place' writing of Katherine Mansfield," and also
　　as referring indirectly to the works of Woolf, Lawrence, and H. G. Wells
　　(pp. 98, 160).

the gradual thematic shift from painting to language in *The Ebony Tower*, signalling the story's absorption in writing while moving it deliberately closer to the technique and themes of *The Waste Land*. The latter functions as a kind of literary metaphor for the process of disintegration under examination in "The Cloud": both poem and story feature a series of individual voices, each one a discrete experiencing sensibility, which effectively destroys any real sense of narrative focus and replaces it with repeated images of alienation and the failure to communicate. This principle of fragmentation is expressed culturally in the implied vision of history as a "heap of broken images" (I, 22), and aesthetically in the perception of art as a series of bits and pieces taken from pre-existent artworks. Thus *The Waste Land* and "The Cloud" are alike governed by the need to shore up fragments against a ruin both personal and cultural, and by the pressure to acknowledge those fragments as not of the author's own making.

In Eliot's battle to find a viable place for the artist within history, Fowles finds an image of his own anxious involvement in the clash between tradition and the individual talent. The corollary of this is *The Waste Land*'s pervasive recognition of art as inevitably made out of other art, and forced by this exigency to examine life under the auspices and the time-honoured authority of other previous examinations. Through *The Waste Land*, then, Fowles thrusts to the fore precisely his dilemma with Marie de France, consciously exposing his own technique through an invited comparison with Eliot. If the previous stories have explored an implied dialectic between artist and critic, deed and word, and different kinds of words, "The Cloud" reformulates this by acknowledging, in the evocation of both Eliot and his poem, the artist's inevitable engagement with criticism. If art is built out of other art, then the artist cannot choose but be a reader, bound to interpret and explain even as he seeks a pure, spontaneous, symbiotic relationship between his art and life. It is in Eliot that the artist and critic seem to come together, as a figure of inevitable compromise rather than of harmony or transcendence, and it is through *The Waste Land* that Fowles focuses his story less on the critic/artist conflict than on the process of mediation itself.

On the level of internal narrative action, Catherine becomes important here, for, apart from Fowles, she is the story's major mediator and promulgator of fictions. Like Isobel, she herself tells a story within the story which contains her; like Fowles, she has edited and translated a work by an important author, the *Mythologies* of Barthes. But Catherine is an emblem of disintegration in the text. Her alienated consciousness is, as I have shown, a metaphor for that anxiety about meaning which preoccupies both Eliot and Fowles. Her involvement in the uncertainties and formal interrogations of modernism is suggested in her tendency to quote *Hamlet* as *The Waste Land* appropriates it, as well as the original play. Thinking of the crayfish, Catherine muses eccentrically: "Oh, that's a beauty. Bags him tonight. Hurry up please it's time. Goonight Bill. Goonight Lou. Goonight. Goonight" (264).[58]

Catherine's feelings of disconnection express themselves not only in her allusions to one work, *The Waste Land*, which deals with disconnection, but in her dim awareness that she herself is inhabiting another such work, "The Cloud": "Yet still one lies, as in a novel by an author one no longer admires, in an art that has become obsolete, . . . as if one had done it before one had, knowing it planned, proven, inevitable" (298). Like Isobel she textualizes experience, and this makes her, despite her apparent authority as reader/translator/narrator, another figure of compromised creativity. Again representing an articulate woman story-teller, Fowles insists that she herself is part of a story, and by emphasizing the narrative frame as well as the action it contains, he imposes upon Catherine a strong authorial presence which undermines the power of her creativity: "And Catherine lies, composing and decomposed, writing and written, here and tomorrow, in the deep grass of the other hidden place she has found" (299).

This affects our perception of Catherine as translator and interpreter of Barthes, for behind Catherine's reading of *Mythologies* we sense Fowles's: it is *he* who appropriates Barthes and assimilates

---

58   The story's loosely associative, stream-of-consciousness narrative could itself be an allusion to another great modernist, James Joyce, while the overall structure of the book as an agglomeration of pieces both discrete and thematically linked recalls yet another one, the Faulkner of *Go Down, Moses*. It is worth noting that Bel reverses the pattern of her sister's literary perceptions, finding the equivalent of *her* experiencing consciousness in what Fowles sees as the thematic and structural certainties of nineteenth-century poetry: hearing her husband read "The Scholar Gipsy," Bel is filled with a sense of "[h]ow all coheres" (295).

his ideas to the artistic endeavour of *The Ebony Tower*. As reader of Barthes and effective re-writer of *The Waste Land*, Fowles brings two authors concerned with the making and breaking of myths into the framework of his story. Using *Mythologies* as a kind of witty heading, Fowles suggests that if he, like Eliot, is attempting to promulgate an anti-myth of irresolution and disintegration, this personal myth must be formulated not only in the shadow of Eliot and in imitation of modernist technique, but in the presence of Barthes and his postmodernist awareness of myth-making as an inevitable but ideologically dubious activity.[59] And here, even as Fowles updates and revises some of modernism's concerns, the singular irony of his own position becomes clear: just as Barthes knows that the exposure of entrenched and false mythologies cannot free one from the need to mythologize,[60] so Fowles knows that to perceive art as a series of appropriations is by no means to free oneself from the need to appropriate. Even as he uses *The Waste Land* to comment on his own art, Fowles himself appropriates Eliot and, in a peculiar act of narrative self-consumption, repossesses himself through an ironic re-writing of "The Ebony Tower." This layering of strategic ironies effectively returns the book to its beginning and poses again the insoluble problem of literary originals and their reworkings.

---

59   In the Preface to *Mythologies*, Barthes gives his motive for analyzing "some myths of French daily life" as a desire "to track down, in the decorative display of *what-goes-without-saying*, the ideological abuse which, in my view, is hidden there. Right from the start, the notion of myth seemed to me to explain these examples of the falsely obvious"; and he goes on to attack the various ways in which ideology is presented not as "History" but as "Nature," in *Mythologies*, trans. Annette Lavers (London: Paladin, 1973), p. 11, emphasis in original. Having already spoken of "The Cloud" in terms of irony and parody, it is no contradiction to speak of it now in terms of myth. As Frye asserts: "Ironic literature begins with realism and tends toward myth, its mythical patterns being as a rule more suggestive of the demonic than the apocalyptic, though sometimes it simply continues the romantic tradition of stylization" (p. 140).

60   As Barthes himself puts it, "[I]s there a mythology of the mythologist?" (p. 12). To which Fowles, in "Hardy," would seem to reply: "Beyond the specific myth of each novel, the novelist longs to be possessed by the continuous underlying myth he entertains of himself" (p. 32).

This disturbing mixture of narrative solipsism and canni-
balism in "The Cloud" accounts for the story's pervasively negative
mood, and it seems to suggest the point at which narrative, at least
in the hands of John Fowles, ties itself up in its own complexities
and outsmarts itself. In acknowledgement of this, the story emphasizes deconstruction as the logical destination for modernist anxiety
about meaning, and the appropriate expression of the contemporary artist's troubled self-awareness. Catherine's understanding of
Barthes is essentially deconstructive, based on a perception of language as able to conceal and suppress the truth, and thus to subvert
the notion of meaning altogether. As she explains:

> A sentence is what the speaker means it to mean.
> What he secretly means it to mean. Which may be
> quite the opposite. What he doesn't mean it to mean.
> What it means as evidence of his real nature. His his-
> tory. His intelligence. His honesty. And so on. . . . I
> think people like Barthes are more interested in mak-
> ing people aware of how they communicate and try to
> control one another. The relation between the overt
> signs, whether they're verbal or not, and the real
> meaning of what is happening. (279, 280)

Through Roland Barthes we are returned symbolically to "The
Ebony Tower": "The Cloud" enacts the horrific possibilities of that
formal incoherence which Breasley fears — that limit at which signi-
fier and signified, utterance and meaning, part company, and art
vanishes in a welter of self-referring and self-consuming symbols.
Only now does it become clear why Breasley's persona, like his
slang, is so retrograde in its *passé* roguishness: this is Fowles's
attempt to keep the artist innocent of postmodernism and its bitter
knowledge, its sense of the abyss as an inevitability rather than an
option.

It is in terms of this principle of disintegration, itself
embodied in Catherine, that Fowles reprimands once more the creative woman while attempting to extricate himself from the consequences of his own vision. For Catherine's inset tale is an effort at
self-transformation through art: like the narrator of "Poor Koko,"
she tries to change her experience by calling upon the "magic" of
words, and attempts to project herself as a wistfully mediaevalized

lost princess. But the word has no magic for Catherine. Like all authors, she must work against the inevitable ironizing of literary form, the loss of generic relevance, and the failure of narrative, in the final analysis, to effect ontological change. Thus instead of a prince she finds the crass Peter, and she engages not in the anticipated union of long-separated lovers, but in a brutal *misalliance* among the rocks.

But Catherine's own status as a fictional character has been insisted upon, and her experience is finally governed by that author from whom she cannot liberate herself. Her initiation into the failure of narrative is in a way a fall from innocence, and it is accomplished by Fowles himself, who not only denies her the power to transform herself through her own narrative, but effects her transformation through and in his own. Sarah too, as we have seen, cannot fully transform herself through her own "art," and is furthermore denied control over the narrative expression of her loss of sexual innocence; she omits the details of her imaginary seduction by Varguennes and it is the narrator who provides them later when she loses her virginity to Charles. In a similar way, Catherine has no control over the expression of her loss of textual innocence — it is Fowles who ejects her, and who transforms her in the direction of literal insubstantiality by replacing her with a cloud. In this story, feminine artistic power is literally vaporized.

This act of authorial control can be seen as an assertion, in the teeth of deconstruction and in defiance of the death of fiction, of narrative's performative power. It is an effort to reclaim meaning, to snatch it back from that vortex of non-meaning, that "vicious spiral . . . a drain to nothingness" (111), which David Williams becomes aware of in "The Ebony Tower." If an author can still convert a character from a presence to an absence, then language (at least in relation to the male author) has not lost its transformative capacity. The need to assert this governs Fowles's refusal to give the sodomizing of Catherine, which precedes her disappearance, the status of a textual certainty. It is this act that, if it were realized in language, would bring together in a savage and literal way the two central images of the ebony tower and the black hole. If Breasley's boisterous anality were to be entirely transformed into the punitive anality of "The Cloud," then misdirected phallic power, the power of the anti-artist, would find its irrefutable destination in the disintegration of meaning. For as the black hole discovered its literal representation in anal darkness, the woman's body would be categorically identified not as the inspiring material of art, but as the very locus of that meaninglessness which stalks the text. Threatened by the abyss, she would herself become it. Severed from her husband, an artist, Catherine would connect irredeemably with his anti-type, a television producer. The symbolic alliance between the female body and the negative phallic power of anti-art would be complete, effectively assimilating the woman into that swirl of over-clever intellectual manoeuvrings which stand implicitly for meaninglessness in this story.

Himself guilty of such manoeuvrings, Fowles, while perceiving the logical endpoint of his analysis, will not push it this far. It is enough for him to show Catherine offering herself up to the death-forces in implied awareness of the kind of betrayal that her intellectual power and her articulacy constitute. When Fowles has her invite Peter to a sexual act primarily homosexual, he implies that the articulate, fictionalizing woman has effectively made herself into a man by usurping the functions of the phallus. This sexual disloyalty of the talented woman highlights "The Cloud"'s concern with notions of purity and corruption. It is Catherine, steeped in language, who understands Barthes' vision of language as itself corrupt: "[T]here are all kinds of category of sign by which we communicate. . . . [O]ne of the most suspect is language — principally for Barthes because it's been very badly corrupted and distorted by the capitalist power structure. But the same goes for many other nonverbal sign-systems we communicate by" (279).

What almost happens to Catherine is an indication of her involvement with an impure medium — a medium that Fowles nonetheless also persists in seeing as numinous and strong. But the cloud which replaces her seems to purify her through metamorphosis even as it claims for language a magical power undimmed by over-usage. In changing the articulate woman into an insubstantial but eerily beautiful natural form, "The Cloud" evinces that nostalgia for inarticulacy, for an actively creative wordlessness, which permeates "The Ebony Tower." Implicitly denying its own intellectual complexities, as well as Barthes' view of all sign-systems as corrupt, the story seeks to affirm Breasley's non-verbal creativity as a kind of purity, an innocence which Catherine has lost. This is why the Edenic setting of the story also signals an inverted paradise, a lush but sterile waste land, and a fallen world riddled with snakes. The children find a snake during their game at the beginning of the story (253), Peter later sees one on his solitary walk (300), and even the laconic Bel admits that a "few" adders inhabit the area (305).

And yet, if "The Cloud" concludes the explorations of *The Ebony Tower* with a rebellious assertion of artistic power as irreducibly visionary and transformative, it does not do so without anxiety. The book cannot fully escape the implications of its own insights or the emotional force of its own categories. For, if the artist must reshape other artefacts in order to create his own, then no state of aesthetic or generic purity can exist. If art can deal with life only through the medium of other art, then this process of reusing its resources sullies it even as it transforms those resources into new creative models. If language is corrupt and mediation a corrupting process, then the literary artist may be forced back, whatever his bravura assertions, into a paradoxically literal inarticulateness, away from words and what Catherine defines them as: "shards, lies, oblivion" (298). On another level, this means that Fowles's preoccupation with the mediaeval romance, like his attachment to the Victorian novel, can be seen as a longing for a state of generic purity; in *The Ebony Tower*, however, Fowles seems to recognize that no such state exists. On another level, it means an impossible position for the writer, whose medium is words. *The Ebony Tower* is poignantly and passionately engaged with this impossibility, and infused with a doubt as to whether language can govern meaning at all.

The book's concern with power must finally be restated in terms of this paradigm of language and meaning, which "The Cloud," significantly, reduces to a kind of dialogue between words and silence, the presence of language and its absence. This is seen in the repeated emphasis which the story places on the song of birds, and in its concluding identification of the oriole's voice with that of a fictionalized princess who "calls, but there is no one, now, to hear her" (312). At the end of *The Ebony Tower*, then, the word has been questioned, even devalued, and anxiously reinstated before this final equation of the voice of fiction with inarticulate sound. As Fowles's original title, *Variations*, implies, *The Ebony Tower* — even as it fulfills its purposes as a work of prose fiction — is trying on a deeper level of narrative operation to become music.

CONCLUSION
DANIEL MARTIN, MANTISSA, A MAGGOT

Fowles's last three novels indicate the direction his work has taken in relation specifically to his most radical and complex fiction, *The Ebony Tower*; each novel illuminates the ways in which Fowles retreats from the various stylistic and philosophical options suggested by "The Cloud." As a whole, Fowles's latest work implies an effective backtracking with regard to narrative technique, a thematic reassertion of the power of the artist (although *Mantissa* is ambiguous in both these respects), and a reconfirmation of the woman in her passive, instrumental role relative to art, language, and narrative. These last three books may be identified, therefore, in terms of the fictional possibilities they refuse, and considered as a collective "road not taken."

In the last chapter I argued that *The Ebony Tower* contemplates "the death of fiction" and negotiates in its concluding story the brink of the abyss of meaninglessness. The volume concludes with a withdrawal from its own implications, as the symbolic transformation of Catherine affirms the power of the author and of narrative, the instrumentality of the female, and by implication the primacy of art. This amounts to an affirmation of language, a confidence in its ability to express meaning, and hence a determined reinforcement of narrative as a legitimate artistic mode for the promulgation and expression of meaning.

But as I have observed, neither *The Ebony Tower* in general nor "The Cloud" in particular can present its affirmations without anxiety. The ability of language to govern meaning is an issue that has haunted Fowles's fiction from its inception; in *The Magus*, as we have seen, he explores the artist's paradoxical tendency to distrust the modes and methods of the very art which he himself creates. The honesty with which Fowles in *The Ebony Tower* questions both language and narrative as an aesthetic formulation of language thus obliges him to end the book with a reference to birdsong — sound unformulated into words. This is an implicit attempt to valorize utterance *per se* — that unsullied sound which, in its freedom from language, is liberated also from any ambiguous entanglement with issues of meaning, veracity, or cognition. Here is the deep nostalgia for the inarticulate which shadows *The Ebony Tower* and shapes its poised ambivalence. It is a book haunted by the dubiety of books, a narrative uneasy with the strategies of narration, and a structure of words yearning towards wordlessness, towards paintings and music as the manifestations of a purer kind of art.

It is in relation to the various delicate balances of *The Ebony Tower*, and particularly its endeavour to flee the consequences of its own vision, that I would like to examine Fowles's subsequent fiction. After 1974 his work, with the possible exception of *Mantissa*, draws away from the linguistic and narrative peripheries negotiated by "The Cloud." Having pushed himself to the edge of the black hole, where words as "shards" attest to the decomposition of meaning under the auspices of postmodernism, Fowles retreats to the safer ground of more traditional literary form and more accessible narrative structure in *Daniel Martin*. This novel, which makes deliberate reference in its title and basic plot to the great *Bildungsromane* of the nineteenth century, is Fowles's most conventional and most stylistically straightforward novel to date. Refusing the options explored in *The Ebony Tower*, it rejects the death of fiction as the inevitable endpoint of literary art and of narrative self-consciousness in the late twentieth century.

That *Daniel Martin* is committed to recuperation, the healing of that breach between sign and referent depicted in "The Cloud," is conveyed in its famous opening sentence: "WHOLE SIGHT; OR ALL THE REST IS DESOLATION."[1] It is significant that Fowles interrupted work on *Daniel Martin* to produce the stories of *The Ebony Tower*. The relationship between the two works is

---

1   John Fowles, *Daniel Martin* (Boston: Little, Brown and Company, 1977), p. 3, emphasis in original. All other page references appear in the text and are to this edition.

clarified by the fact that *The Ebony Tower* takes as its starting point that principle of "whole sight" which governs the entirety of *Daniel Martin*. Embodying this premise in the title story as the formal coherence of pre- and early Impressionist art, the shorter fictions work away from metaphors of cohesion and unity towards the fragmentation, the artistic and ethical "desolation," that dominates "The Cloud." Thus while *Daniel Martin* seeks to embrace the principle of wholeness and all it implies of structural coherence and the integrity of personality, *The Ebony Tower* progressively explores disintegration as both a narrative mode and a psychological state. It is as if the principle of dissolution, with the death of fiction as its corollary, finds fictional expression in one work while being banned from another.

The rejection of fragmentation[2] signalled in the first line of *Daniel Martin* suggests a commitment to the intelligibility of meaning, the capacity of art to produce and express it, and, recalling everything that Breasley stands for in "The Ebony Tower," the indissoluble link between art and "reality." In *Daniel Martin* Fowles attempts to define that reality more broadly than Breasley's definition of it as female physicality. This is shown in the deliberately encyclopaedic quality of the work, its depiction of Dan as a man who must make his novel out of a complex political and social reality as well as a personal, individual, and sexual one. Also, the many references in *Daniel Martin* to the unsurpassed ability of the novel as a genre to represent reality and human life (particularly in the chapters entitled "Games," "Thorncombe," and "In the Orchard of the Blessed") suggest an effort on Fowles's part to suppress his doubts about language and his mistrust of words. He seeks to de-emphasize the perception — so powerful in both *The Magus* and *The Ebony Tower* — of art as involved chiefly with other art instead of directly with life.

Fowles's choice of form here further clarifies the relationship between the two works while indicating the direction in which he chose to go with *Daniel Martin*. *The Ebony Tower* is

---

2   The novel's oscillation between first- and third-person narrative points of view does not, in fact, undermine this rejection. Dan's controlling perspective dominates both narratorial positions, for the reader is encouraged to see this oscillation as part of the technical experimentation that goes into the creation of his "autobiography."

Fowles's only book of short stories; it explores fragmentation by means of a series of literary fragments. By contrast, *Daniel Martin* is a monumental novel. To view these texts from another perspective, the latter begins where *The Ebony Tower* leaves off, as a series of narrative fragments moving the reader choppily between Dan's English past, his American present, and his projected future in his home country. These apparently disconnected short narratives create a kind of structural pointillism in the opening chapters of *Daniel Martin*, recalling indirectly "The Cloud" and all it implies of the uncertainties of modern and postmodern art. But fragmentation does not dominate the book, which ends under the steady gaze of the Rembrandt self-portrait contemplated by Dan in the Kenwood Gallery: "The sad, proud old man stared eternally out of his canvas. . . . The supreme nobility of such art, the plebeian simplicity of such sadness; an immortal, a morose old Dutchman; . . . a puffed face, a pair of rheumy eyes, and a profound and unassuageable vision" (628).[3] This picture, one of the few artworks alluded to in *Daniel Martin*, is a metaphor for the novel itself, which is also a self-portrait seeking to enshrine that solidity and coherence of form, that unflinching but compassionate realism, usually associated with seventeenth-century Dutch portraiture. The allusion to Rembrandt describes the basic trajectory of the novel, whose retreat from fragmentation is depicted as both the progressive discovery of a sustained narrative voice and an unambiguous commitment to closure.

Dan as narrator finds his true voice during his trip to Egypt with Jane. Here he begins to discover what his story is about and to apprehend his own plot, as it were. In this last section of the book, Dan's love for Jane is revealed as the sustaining but not always visible plot of his life. His union with her is effective in relation to both his life and his novel — that novel which he is planning to write, in one sense, and has already written, in another. The reunion of lovers is thus the culmination of the plot of Daniel Martin and the plot of *Daniel Martin*; it describes the destination

---

3   This portrait evidently has a lasting imaginative resonance for Fowles: it is the same picture that his first artist/critic, G.P., interprets for Miranda in *The Collector*. In both novels, the painting seems to be for Fowles the emblem of art as a great humanistic endeavour. He has described *Daniel Martin* as "fundamentally intended as a defence of the institution of humanism (for all its wants and weaknesses) and of the novel as a humanistic enterprise," in Huffaker, p. 35.

of both a life and the history of that life which we have just read. In this way, the most closed of all Fowles's fictional endings arranges retrospectively the earlier fragmentary chapters into a cohesive whole. The valorization of destination as the legitimate endpoint of a narrative as well as the hidden principle of a life — the asserting of all that *The Magus* refused to assert — integrates the apparent structural randomness of most of the novel. Dan's history is made meaningful and intelligible by an unambiguous ending which throws us back to the beginning of the book, in confirmation of Eliot's dictum: "In my end is my beginning."[4] *Daniel Martin* defines the discovery of identity and the commitment to vocation as acts of narrative patterning. The man and his novel are inseparable; the "last sentence" of Dan's projected book becomes the "first" of the achieved one (629), miming in narrative form Dan's creatively fertile return to his roots.

The Rembrandt self-portrait, because it is the product of an earlier age and expresses what to some is an historically specific and outmoded conception of artistic form, confirms what the presentation of the novel as an ostensible autobiography also conveys: the book's involvement with the past and the ways in which history is shaped into art. Particularly, the painting could suggest that the flight from fragmentation is in effect an escape from modernity into the safety of the past; as such, in the context of Fowles's *œuvre*, it is not really a progression but a kind of generic and stylistic retreat. Significantly, the book ends happily only after the sojourn at Palmyra: only when they have visited "the end of the world" (577, 593) can Dan and Jane seal their love. A place of ultimate nihilism is presented here, as it was in "The Cloud," in terms that recall *The Waste Land*: Dan, arguing with Jane, sees himself as "Tiresias, Muslim style" (593), and the barking dog makes him recall Eliot's "*oh keep the Dog far hence . . .* " (598, Fowles's emphasis). Dan's description of Palmyra strongly suggests the general landscape of the poem: "[A]n endless vista of ruins and isolated heaps of rubble,

---

4   This implicit indebtedness to *The Four Quartets* is appropriate in a novel filled with references to Eliot's poetry. The evocations of *The Waste Land* in particular could suggest the influence of "The Cloud" upon Fowles at the time of *Daniel Martin*. Eliot is especially present in the chapters entitled "Games," "Catastasis," "Flights," and "The End of the World."

like a city stricken in some ancient nuclear holocaust and half buried again in sand. Forbidding square towers stood on a skyline to the west, above the plain" (603). This literary allusion implies that the novel's subsequent events — Dan's break with Jenny, his viewing of the Rembrandt, and return to Jane's Oxford house — represent Fowles's sense of where narrative must go after the formal and thematic apocalypse of "The Cloud." It must go backwards to rediscover wholeness as an aesthetic principle governing form and as an ethical one shaping identity. For this reason *Daniel Martin* consistently emphasizes the re-experiencing of things rather than first-time undertakings, and Dan's middle-age is a pattern of returnings — to England and Devon, to Egypt and Jane, to the writing of literature instead of film scripts. For this reason too the novel rediscovers the traditional *Bildungsroman*: it is the only one of Fowles's novels to depict its protagonist's childhood[5] and his relationship with a biological parent.

These *Bildungsroman* features affirm Fowles's relatively unambiguous commitment here to traditionally mimetic/realist novelistic forms, and his sense of the need to resurrect such forms in the face of the centrifugal forces of postmodernism. This idea of revitalization through return permeates *Daniel Martin*, which describes Dan's efforts to find himself through examining his history and to "disinter," in Anthony Mallory's words, "the person Jane might have been" (177) from beneath the stale encrustations of her marriage. It makes Egypt, land of tombs and archaeology, appropriate as the scene for this exhumation of a woman through the excavation of a long-buried love. In the wall-painting at Abydos, which depicts the erotic energy of Isis bringing Osiris back to life (502), the pervasive metaphor of resurrection is "clinched" and the image of the woman in the reeds, whose symbolic revitalization the book has undertaken, is finally comprehended.

---

5   This does not contradict an earlier note about Fowles's general lack of interest in childhood. Dan's childhood is not treated in much depth, and his most important experiences are traced back only to adolescence and early manhood — that time of awakening sexuality so crucial in Fowles's books. Another sign of *Daniel Martin*'s basic lack of engagement with childhood is Dan's omission — intriguing in his autobiographical novel — of any detail about his school life. Perhaps Fowles felt that the emotional significance of schooldays, at least in relation to a protagonist's adolescence, had been adequately explored in *The Magus*.

Given a novel so dominated by the past, it is not surprising to find Fowles, like Dan, returning to aspects of his own history as well as the history of his *œuvre*:[6] *Daniel Martin* recalls *The Magus*, the revised version of which also appeared in 1977, more than it does *The Ebony Tower*. In particular, *The Magus* is suggested in the reappearance of that ambivalence towards the hero's moral growth which characterized the presentation of Nicholas Urfe; although it is more of a conventional *Bildungsroman* than *The Magus*, *Daniel Martin* is also unable fully to commit itself to the idea of progress so central to the *Bildungsroman* form. Thus it seeks to depict Dan's life as a process of development — and to confirm this thrust towards progression by means of closure — while giving its deepest emotional allegiance not to progress and futurity but to regression and the past. This is seen in the novel's tendency, despite its clear marking out of Dan's destination in time, to present the artist's life less as an evolution through history and more as a myth of return.

This involvement with regression and unease with those imperatives of growth that shape the novel of education are evident in *Daniel Martin*'s odd blend of political analysis and wish-fulfilling romanticism. The fate of Dan's Oxford generation is considered in detail, and its failures seen largely in socio-economic terms as a succumbing to money and the media. At the same time Oxford itself — like Thorncombe, Tsankawi, and Kitchener's Island — is presented nostalgically as another version of the *domaine*. Both Dan and Jane associate Oxford with a dream-world, and for Dan the holiday in Spain proves that the Mallorys and the Martins can "be happy (as at Oxford) only in the unreal, not the real" (139). Attempting to engage with history as action and process, *Daniel Martin* is simultaneously obsessed with the *domaine* as a lost Eden, and it is this notion of the mythic and timeless place, exempt from the vicissitudes of history, that Dan in fact uses as an organizing

---

6   Huffaker discusses Fowles's life in relation to the novel in his chapter, "John Fowles, *Daniel Martin* and Naturalism" (pp. 15–43). Fowles's literary past is further suggested in the book's Middle-Eastern section, which reads at times like a vivid travelogue. This reminds us that the first work that Fowles submitted for publication was a travel book with a fictional section. See Singh, 187. The novel's archaeological imagery is significant in relation to both author and character.

principle of his story.[7] *Daniel Martin* is literally crammed with *domaines*. From Thorncombe to the Nile Valley and even to the anti-*domaines* of the Krak des Chevaliers and Palmyra, Dan's life-story is built around these sites, which he (like his author) presents as mythic and timeless. These places implicitly deny the importance of politics and undercut the novel's evidently admiring references to socially responsible thinkers like Marx and Gramsci. Despite its overt presentation of Dan as a man inhabiting a historico-political context, then, the novel is covertly determined to lift its hero out of history and return him to his dehistoricized past as to a kind of paradise regained, a place of innocence and plenitude to which the scarred adult consciousness can retreat.

This sense of history as myth and evasion is reinforced by the novel's handling of its women characters. On a superficial reading, it appears that Fowles has altered the usual relationship between the *princesse lointaine* and her more accessible opposite. Jenny McNeil is presented as a debased "goddess" and "ikon" (621), for she is a divinity only in the corrupt world of Hollywood — a world which Dan repudiates along with the kind of creative work, scriptwriting, that Jenny-as-muse presides over. By contrast Jane, the awkward and dowdy North Oxford mother, is the kind of politically responsible, "authenticity-obsessed" (544) person that Dan is (apparently) trying to become. It is she, with her indefinable capacity for "right feeling" (609), who inspires what is presented as Dan's weightier artistic ambition, the writing of a novel. But this apparent realignment of female forces is deceptive. Jane, far from being a middle-aged Alison reunited at last with her grown-up Nick, is an emblem of the book's pull towards regression and an idealized past. Embodying Dan's personal and narratorial destination in the novel, Jane is the focus of the pattern of returnings in the text. She represents reunion with a lost woman, specifically with the lost mother whom, for Fowles, every male artist seeks to recover through repeated creative acts. Thus Jane reminds Dan of

---

7   In the chapter "The Sacred Combe," Fowles traces the literary ancestry of Dan's obsession further back than even *Le Grand Meaulnes* to "Restif de la Bretonne's [eighteenth-century] masterpiece, his romanced autobiography, *Monsieur Nicolas*" (272). The pervasive influence of Restif and his idea of *la bonne vaux* on Fowles is signalled in the allusion to *The Magus*, another "romanced autobiography" of another "Monsieur Nicolas."

his "vanished mother" (482), and his final reunion with her in that *domaine*, Oxford, which they shared when young is a symbolic return to the womb. Dan's apparent maturity, typified in what seems to be a serenely adult love, is in fact profound regression, a literal and metaphorical enactment of the book's perception of destination and origin as inseparable.

Jane's ordinariness is thus misleading, for she is herself a myth, the representation of femininity as a kind of timeless essence. In fact, Jane is more of a *princesse lointaine* than Jenny. Identified with the goddess Isis (477), she combines the mystery of Julie Holmes and the self-deprecating stubbornness of Sarah Woodruff, while recalling that lost maternal image which is the very model of the Fowlesian *princesse*. As in *The Magus*, the accessible woman can be made desirable only by her displacement in the direction of the idealized and archetypal. It is this basically unchanged conception of femininity that lies behind the unconvincing presentation of Jane's political views and aspirations in the novel. Her interest in social justice, Marxism, and the Communist Party remains disconnected from her emotional life and behaviour, and one of Dan's implied tasks in Egypt is apparently to rid Jane of such socially extensive and historically enmeshed notions of her self and her efficacy. Thus her political hopes dwindle into local politics and the Labour Party (625), while she assumes her role as Dan's mistress/mother and the guardian of his burgeoning artistic flame: "She was also some kind of emblem of a redemption from a life devoted to heterogamy and adultery, the modern errant ploughman's final reward" (561).

It is through his novel, then, that Dan controls Jane's incipient independence by transcribing and typecasting her as his muse. The closed ending seals the process whereby Dan, ever a scriptwriter, scripts Jane by locating her precisely in his life and his text, as both the inspiration and the substance of art. And like other Fowlesian heroines, she possesses the anti-intellectual sensibility so crucial to her role. Dan, a writer and "word man," nevertheless finds reassuring the fact that his connection with Jane exists in a realm of inarticulacy: "Behind what they said, lay on both sides an identity, a syncretism, a same key, a thousand things beyond verbalization" (561). Verbalization is instead the province of Jane's antitype, Jenny McNeil, a variation on the articulate and potentially creative woman encountered before in *The Collector*, *The French*

Lieutenant's Woman, and *The Ebony Tower*. Jenny's attempts at narrative are included by Dan as "contributions" to his own novel. The term "contributions" (231, 429) delineates Jenny as another aspirant woman narrator, compromised and controlled by masculine narratorial manoeuvring. Titled, edited, and located in his own text by Dan, these fragments do not add up to a novel any more than Diana's sketches in "The Ebony Tower" constitute an *œuvre*. In their context, these "contributions" are literally narrative mirrors which reflect Dan. Despite their histrionic criticisms of him, Jenny's fragments are at the service of Dan's narcissism, and Jenny acknowledges that she has no "copyright" (434) over her own work.

Jenny's narratorial authority is further undermined by her sense of Dan as the source of her writings — "[I'm] telling you all this nonsense you first told me" (236) — or by her assertions that what she writes is untrue. About her third "contribution" she declares: "It's not true, Dan. You mustn't believe a word of it" (417). This suggests that Jenny, like Sarah with Rossetti, is less a creator than an amanuensis, while the association of her writing with lies, in a novel concerned with valorizing fiction as a form of truth-telling, devalues it automatically. Far from being Fowles's most sustained and honest attempt to present a female narrator, then, Jenny is another woman writer whose work, like that of Marie de France, is appropriated by a male author for inclusion in his own text. Like Miranda's, her creative efforts are punished by Dan's repudiation of her, and she is ejected from both his life and his book.

Jenny recalls Catherine from "The Cloud" in the slight suggestion of punishment by sexual ordeal in her last "contribution" (429–43). Here she presents herself as the lover of Steve, a shallow actor resembling the corrupt producer Peter, and as the potential lover of Steve's girlfriend Kate. The woman writer is again associated with what Fowles apparently regards as sexual debauchery, and with homosexual behaviour — specifically here, lesbianism. It is no accident that Jenny, like Catherine, is linked with "shards" — not only the pieces of narrative she offers, but the pottery fragments which she collects at Tsankawi (329). In *Daniel Martin* the female writer again stands for those principles of dissolution antipathetic to "whole sight" and rejected by the novel. At the same time her efforts at narrative foreground her not as a writer but as a mistress. Like Sarah's story about Varguennes, Jenny's narratives are aimed more at seduction than self-expression, for she writes not to find her identity, but to lure Dan back. Like Isobel Dodgson's, it is Jenny's sexuality that counts and not her creativity. In these ways she recalls other ambiguously creative Fowlesian heroines while prefiguring the latest one, Rebecca Hocknell. Fowles's presentation of the women in *Daniel Martin* suggests the conservatism of the novel, which clings to old configurations even as it tries to assert, through a new political orientation,[8] its engagement with notions of progress and growth.

I have said that in *Daniel Martin* the quest for self becomes a journey away from the future, back to the archetypal woman loved and lost, the relationship and the life that should have been. In this, Fowles's most nostalgic novel, the ultimate paradise regained is the mother's body. It is this fully indulged fantasy of maternal recovery that makes the book both Freudian and biblical in its emphasis. The novel deals with the Oedipal struggles of the artist in a literal and wish-fulfilling way. Instead of foregrounding the clash between the artist and his progenitors, the text depicts the apotheosis of Dan-as-artist through implied equations between his art and that of earlier masters. Dan stands before the Rembrandt, "dwarfed" (628) by genius, even as the existence of the novel we are reading proves that he too has produced a self-portrait designed to embody the principle "[n]o true compassion without will, no true will without compassion" (629).

In the same way Dan's reading of Lukács' essay on Scott is indirectly self-aggrandizing. It equates him with the famous novelist while also presenting him implicitly as the co-object of a great critic's attention. Thus Dan quotes two extracts from the essay, one describing Scott as a humanistic "honest" Tory, and the other describing his typical "hero" as a mediocre but decent "average English gentleman" (551). Dan then recognizes himself in both these descriptions: "Mirrors: he knew why he had marked those passages and who was really being defined: and it was neither Scott

---

8   Fowles's most explicitly political fiction, *Daniel Martin* fails in its analysis, I think, because the author tries to present his own private themes and configurations as a socio-political agenda — to impose, as McSweeney observes, "a personal fantasy on the national psyche" (*Four Contemporary Novelists*, p. 147).

nor Kitchener: but his own sense of defeat" (551). Dan's admiration for Lukács signals a shift away from deconstruction as the literary/critical aesthetic which dominates "The Cloud" to the critical equivalent of "whole sight"; it is the "humanism" of Lukács that Dan and Jane respect (390), and Lukács' view of the realistic novel as weighty, serious, replete with life, socially engaged, and under strong authorial control that *Daniel Martin* seeks to express and ordain.

In *Daniel Martin*, the artist battles less with his creative forebears than with his literal father and a significant father-surrogate, Anthony Mallory. Like the narrator of "Poor Koko," Dan defeats these enemies partly through narrative, presenting them in his novel as a narrow-minded non-entity and a failure respectively. Equating Anthony with the "claustrophobia of academic life" (176), Dan, who had years earlier usurped his projected place in Jane's bed, goes on to replace this "father-substitute" (69) there again, and to become the true husband that the fusty don could never be. This presentation of Dan as a son victorious partly through the power of the word affirms that faith in language to which the sheer length and detail of *Daniel Martin* further attest. Fowles's desire for the inarticulate surfaces here only indirectly, as a yearning response to Bach's music (561) and as a defining feature of the female *objet d'art* and muse.

This view of male individual development as a chronicle of narcissistic maternal rediscovery associates *Daniel Martin* with the myth of the Fall. If Dan is the archetypal son reunited with his lost love, the eternal mother, and if this reunion is made possible through the symbolic recovery of the past as a lost Eden, then the story of Oedipus, the Book of Genesis, and even the New Testament come together in *Daniel Martin*. The narrative enacts the regaining of paradise in a religious or biblical sense as well as in a psychological or emotional one. We have seen that Dan's life and his novel are inseparable. Like the life of Christ (as told in the Bible) in a more orthodox sense, both the man and his book aim to heal the breach of the Fall and enact a process of salvation. In this way *Daniel Martin* turns the authorial figure — Dan — into a kind of god whose power, by symbolically reinstating Eden, can effectively redeem the "death of fiction." After the apocalypse of "The Cloud," Fowles's most comprehensive and discursive novel offers a multifaceted resurrection.

• • •

    Both *Daniel Martin* and *A Maggot* suggest a strong pre-occupation with various forms of Christianity in Fowles's later work. But this is not true of his strangest novel, *Mantissa*, which is difficult to characterize in itself and to assess in relation to the rest of his *œuvre*. In terms of form, it is not so much radical or experimental as bizarre: the novel exists entirely as a highly contrived psychomachia which offers us no sense of what the world beyond Miles Green's mind is like. This absolute internalization suggests the twin fixations of the book: textuality and fantasy.[9] More specifically, *Mantissa* considers the imaginative relationship between artist and text, and the extended sexual reverie which (in this case) simultaneously gives birth to and constitutes the text. In its dealing with these two related subjects, the novel bypasses entirely those issues of realism — the responsible depiction of identifiable human reality in fiction — that formed part of *Daniel Martin*'s overt thematic concern. Instead, Fowles's first fiction of the 1980s chooses vehemently to exclude external reality from the arena of narrative action. It is both obsessively cerebral and libidinous, insisting on repeated acts of sexual congress while locating those acts in Miles Green's own brain. It is odd to find Fowles, who tends repeatedly to see sexuality (and especially female sexuality) as a needed antidote to over-intellection, focusing so narrowly here on what we might expect him to find both unappealing and limited: sex in the head.

    But *Mantissa* is full of contradictions which tease without always illuminating. The problem with fathoming Erato and her various transformations is not that the sources and workings of creative inspiration are complex, but that the project becomes boring. By the time Miles and his muse reach their moment of glorious union, it is difficult for the reader to remain engaged with either the characters or the novel's ideas about textuality and self-reflexivity in fiction. These latter simply restate Fowles's belief in

---

9   Woodcock discusses the novel as erotic fantasy (pp. 147–64); Fawkner (pp. 131–44) and Pifer emphasize its concern with textuality. See Drury Pifer, "The Muse Abused: Deconstruction in *Mantissa*," in *Critical Essays on John Fowles*, ed. Ellen Pifer (Boston, Massachusetts: G. K. Hall & Co., 1986), pp. 162–76. While *Mantissa* seems to be Fowles's least acclaimed fiction, both Fawkner and Pifer regard it as central to his work.

the mysteriousness of artistic creativity, the inadequacy of rational analysis before this mystery, and the duty of the contemporary author to signpost the fictionality of his texts. Thus Miles laments: "Serious modern fiction has only one subject: the difficulty of writing serious modern fiction."[10] In the face of this, Erato, who apparently represents the numinously creative aspect of Miles's brain, proves herself triumphantly enigmatic, elusive, and unconcerned about the very art that she inspires. She has not even read Miles's books, refers to her "admirer" Aristophanes as "Charlie" (177), and complains about the personal hygiene of Shakespeare (162). Despite the uncharacteristic comedy, this is very familiar ground for Fowles: he has explored these issues more dynamically in *The French Lieutenant's Woman* and *The Ebony Tower*. For all its stylistic exhibitionism, there is a tiredness about *Mantissa*, an air of ideas recycled rather than re-explored. The novel is thus appropriately unrealistic in one way, for it is Fowles's most mannered work, less an energetic re-invention than an imitation of self.

Nevertheless *Mantissa* does comment further on the ideas which this study considers. The novel's involvement with creativity and the relationship between art and gender cannot be ignored, although its treatment of these themes means that in one way *Mantissa* deserves its title: "'An addition of comparatively small importance, especially to a literary effort or discourse'" (188). We should note, then, that *Mantissa* foregrounds quite aggressively that ambiguous relationship between writer and critic which preoccupied Fowles so much in *The Magus* and *The Ebony Tower*, but which he chose to de-emphasize in *Daniel Martin*. Miles begins with the knowledge, both damning and liberating, that Nicholas Urfe had so painfully to acquire: the artist/author is inevitably a critic/reader, and creativity involves the negotiating of areas already staked out, both by other artists and by those who interpret them. Miles is the author obsessed with interpretation, a veritable *critic*-as-artist, who seeks through symbolic intercourse with the muse to create a text free of the burden of interpretation and quite literally unavailable to criticism. This is why Miles sends up so frenetically those "academic readers" (120) who believe "that writing *about* fiction has become a more important matter than writing fiction itself" (118–19,

---

10   John Fowles, *Mantissa* (Toronto: Collins, 1982), p. 118. All other page references appear in the text and are to this edition.

emphasis in original), while trying to produce his own "Unwritable
. . . Unfinishable . . . Text without words" (161).

The impossibility of generating such a text — uninter-
pretable because unwritten and hence irrefutably non-existent — is
what haunts Miles and drives him on, like his creator, to endlessly
revise himself. If the author is inevitably an interpreter, he can at
least interpret and criticize his *own* work. In this way he may be
able to retain some control over his texts. On one level this masturbatory exercise ensures that Miles's text can stay unwritten, for it
exists in fantasy form only; on another, the very existence of the
book *Mantissa* suggests the ontological impossibility of the unwritten text. The title itself thus becomes a critical response to the
book, a comment by Fowles on Miles's desperate attempt to
exempt his own text from the critical scrutiny which both despise.
Like *The Ebony Tower*, then, *Mantissa* insists on the inevitable inter-
dependence of artist and critic while trying, as *The French
Lieutenant's Woman* also tries, to find a place where the text can
retain a kind of purity, a freedom from ratiocinative explanation,
and (in this novel) an inevitable, vital connection with "real life"
(118).

As we have observed, this state of textual purity and freedom — this "real life" — is usually identified in Fowles's work as a
woman's body, and symbolically guaranteed in the dissociation of
woman from language and intellect. Thus Erato maintains her elusiveness through unpredictable and restless metamorphoses; not
quite graspable by the artist, she must necessarily also elude the critic, for they are one. Inspiring the great artists of the past, she
remains unconcerned with their words and only engages with them
sexually — Miles describes her as "a hot night out for every pen-
pushing Tom, Dick and Harry" (91). Erato is the woman who
inspires language without ever taking possession of it. She and the
satyr Mopsus, whom she evidently prefers to her other, more literary lovers, apparently create the Greek alphabet by performing the
sexual act in twenty-four different positions (82). This suggests
that female sexuality is crucial to language and hence to the text,
while language itself, once "created," becomes the property of
those men who make love to Erato. Clearly Erato is to Miles what
Diana is to Breasley: not only the muse but the substance of his art.

Despite her attempts at narrative, Erato is quintessentially without artistic or linguistic efficacy. The poverty of her own

language in the novel is striking. She speaks either in clichés or in
the coy idiom of a spoilt, upper-class English schoolgirl: her parents
are "Mummy" and "Daddy," her "musical uncle" is "an absolute
pansy" whom she dubs "Aunt Polly," and her sisters are "frightfully
soulful and intelligent and all the rest of it" (73). Erato manifestly
prefers sex to art and dismisses the masterpieces she has inspired.
Speaking of Verlaine she says: "I'm not just an idiot pair of nymphs
in some fancy Frog poet's afternoon off" (81). This contemptuous
attitude to the artists of the past emphasizes Erato's absolutely
compromised and controlled status as a figure existing only within
Miles's imagination. She is entirely at the service of the narcissism
and solipsism which the very setting of the book proclaims. Miles,
in fact, uses her to bolster his sense of his own importance with
regard to the threatening presence of other artists: if the muse has
chosen Miles, then he must obviously rank as the equal of her
other, only ostensibly more brilliant lovers. In *Mantissa*, the process whereby a novelist/narrator aggrandizes his ego by effectively
placing himself among the greats recalls *Daniel Martin*'s attitude to
literary parenthood, but *Mantissa* foregrounds this theme with
obsessive intensity.

Furthermore, Miles insists that, while the muse may be
necessary for the conception and birth of the text, her relationship
to that text is predictably passive. Although she — or her sexuality
— is essential for its production, the text is, paradoxically, what
gives life to her. In *Mantissa* this notion of the male-directed text
as literally constituting the woman is given an added twist. If
Miles's text remains on one level unwritten, then Erato exists only
in his mind; she is an erotic fantasy conveniently doubling as a
respectable metaphor for creativity. If, on the other hand, Miles's
text is inevitably written as Fowles's novel, then Erato's complaints
of being used by men for their own imaginative purposes are thoroughly apposite. The very novel proves that to embody the muse is
merely to appropriate her again, and Erato's laments serve only to
highlight how emphatically *written* she is.

It is in this context that we must place Erato's own for-
ays into narrative. Her first story, of her seduction by Mopsus, is
luridly told and accompanied by Miles's own imitation of the satyr's
action: he attempts to make love to Erato while she narrates
(77–82). In terms of the structure of the novel as an internalized
drama, Miles here is titillating himself by allowing this imaginary

woman to talk about sex in ways which he enjoys. His accompany-
ing caresses further convey the purpose of this spuriously independent act of feminine narration: its true aim is to invite once more the
seduction it describes. Thus *Mantissa* gives us no sense of female
experience expressed in language framed and controlled by a
woman. Erato's sexuality may be crucial to textuality, but the
manipulator of language and the designator of narrative voice is
Miles. Like Catherine in "The Cloud," Erato cannot narrate without indisputably calling attention to her controlling author(s); like
those of Jenny McNeil, her pieces of narrative are at the service of
voracious masculine narcissism.

   This presentation of the female would-be narrator in
terms of a fantasy of narratorial transvestitism is extremely cynical
and it culminates in the deliberately absurd idea of Erato as the
author of the *Odyssey:* "To cut a long story short, Miles, [she says] I
did once scribble a little something down . . . under a pseudonym,
of course" (171). Again, this fantasy of hairbrained female authorship is an aspect of Miles's intellectual masturbation, a debunking of
a great literary forebear, Homer, in terms which he finds personally
titillating. Erato herself further debases her efforts by emphasizing,
like Sarah and Jenny before her, the ineptitude of her linguistic and
narratorial efforts. Of her "little something" she says: "It wasn't
perfect by any means. . . . It was terribly primitive and naive in
many ways. I got all the places muddled up, for a start" (171,
172). For Miles this ineptitude is the muse's crucial feature. Like
Breasley, he needs to feel that the sources of his art are not only
female but inarticulate, even if these sources are on one level an
aspect of his own psyche. For *Mantissa* is different from *Daniel
Martin* inasmuch as it returns to that anxiety about language which
the longer novel de-emphasized. Miles's impossible fantasy of the
unwritten and unwritable text is fundamentally a wish to repudiate
words, even as his ongoing and difficult infatuation with the muse
suggests a hopeless attachment to the very words he mistrusts.

   If the basic concerns of *Mantissa* are standard in Fowles's
work, new (or unusually emphatic) narrative elements are the sheer
desperation of the artist's confrontation with self-reflexivity in fiction, the cynical handling of sex in the novel, and the peculiar
despair — a sort of bitter self-consciousness — which hangs over
the ending. As Miles returns to the mental limbo in which the
book began, the bird in the cuckoo-clock moves into focus,

> as if obliged one last time to reaffirm its extraneity, its
> distance from all that has happened in this room, and
> its underlying regard for its first and aestho-autoga-
> mous (*keep the fun clean, said Shanahan*) owner; or as
> if dream-babbling of green Irish fields and mountain
> meadows, and of the sheer bliss of being able to shift
> all responsibility for one's progeny . . . stirs, extrudes
> and cries an ultimate, soft and single, most strangely
> single, cuckoo. (196, emphasis in original)

An emblem of the objective reality which has been excluded from
the narrative action throughout, the clock is also a bone thrown out
to critics of *Mantissa*. They are the ones, Fowles implies, who will
decipher the allusion to Flann O'Brien and thus take "responsibility"
for the "progeny" of both author and character, the text. In
Mantissa the problem of literary parenthood is not re-explored but
lampooned: the critic becomes a sort of sour foster-father to the text
generated by his irresponsible alter ego, the artist. The clock is a
depressing comment, then, on the rigidity with which texts are dis-
sected by the criticism machine in our time.[11] The silly bird seems
to sum up the trivializing work which will soon be undertaken with
regard to the novel, and of which this study itself is inevitably and
ironically an example. The title thus becomes not only an acknowledgement of that work, but an attempt to forestall it by proclaiming
the triviality of the novel at the outset.

    In this way *Mantissa* is a very ambiguous document; at
once self-mocking and self-ingratiating, it is a text that seeks, rather
like *The French Lieutenant's Woman*, to expose and to protect itself
simultaneously — and to effect that very protection *through* exposure. This parodic element in the novel is strengthened by the ironic allusiveness of the ending, which recalls the birdsongs that have

---

11   Fowles's anti-academic sentiments continued to inform his thinking about
     literature in the 1980s. Interviewed by James R. Baker, he criticized
     novels "where you feel you are being lectured to by a history professor
     who is accurately reflecting some kind of general view. . . . This, I find, is
     a mistake many academics seem to make — that you must carefully plan
     and reason as you write." He regards the critical quest for literary influ-
     ences as "idle thumb-twiddling on some campus, trying to find some-
     thing to write about," in "An Interview with John Fowles," *Michigan
     Quarterly Review* 25, No. 4 (1986), 667–68.

ended other novels by Fowles: *The Magus*, with its suggestion of Keatsian suspension at the end, and *The Ebony Tower*, with the oriole's cry evoking a nostalgia for the aesthetic purity of wordlessness. Here these birds are degraded into an absurd little mechanism; the parody in *Mantissa* is more derisive, although no less ambiguous, than that in *The French Lieutenant's Woman*.

This derisiveness surfaces again in the one truly radical aspect of *Mantissa*: Fowles's blatant exposure of the kind of gender relations at work in *all* his books as in some ways misogynistic. In this novel, structured as a sexual fantasy and reading (as David Lodge has observed) like something out of *Penthouse*,[12] Fowles reveals his valorization of feminine inarticulacy and instrumentality as a kind of pornography. *Mantissa* acknowledges that its author's view of artistic power is also a vision of female sexuality which lends itself to both the pornographic banalities of a Frederick Clegg and the more pretentiously obscene imaginings of a Miles Green. Thus Miles (whose sensibility can be racist as well as sexist) projects his ultimate fantasy woman as yet another version of Erato:

> She is Japanese: modest and exquisitely subservient in kimono, exquisitely immodest and still subservient without it. But incomparably her greatest beauty and attraction is linguistic. The very thought of it makes something inside Miles Green curl with ecstasy. With her, any dialogue but that of the flesh is magnificently impossible. . . . His infinitely compliant woman, true wax at last, dutiful and respectful, uncomplaining, admiring, and above all peerlessly dumb — . (189–90)

This suggests that whatever the wordless woman may mean in relation to art — and we have seen that her meaning is complex — her fundamental reality is a sexuality pornographically conceived and open to exploitation. *Mantissa* interrogates the implied sexual agenda of Fowles's corpus with a brutality not evident since the sadistic machinations of *The Collector* and *The Magus*. Here is the woman ultimately reduced, not only as the material for art and anti-art, but as a sex-slave unencumbered by metaphorical significance or symbolic function. The enclosed setting of *Mantissa* is a narrower and

---

12   Quoted in Woodcock, p. 147.

even more obsessively solipsistic version of *The Collector*'s basement room; in its fascination with woman as degraded icon, the mind's eye of Miles Green surpasses even the punitive camera lens of Clegg.

This image of Erato as geisha effectively deconstructs the pro-woman stance apparently endorsed in Fowles's earlier novels. Both resembling and departing from "The Cloud" in its association of deconstructive gestures with gender relations, *Mantissa*, in exposing itself, also exposes the basis of a vision of women, and the pervasive imagery of nudity in the novel acquires a satirical dimension. For Miles, that masculine guilt which, as Woodcock believes, tends to inform Fowles's treatment of sexuality is swift to effect retribution: Miles is immediately changed into a satyr with stringy calves, shaggy black hair, and cloven hooves (191). This picture of the bestiality of the masculine is intentionally disturbing and repulsive; Daniel Martin's hubristic portrait of himself as Rembrandt becomes Miles Green's savage image of the artist as "ithyphallic" (192) monster. At the end of the novel, then, Fowles returns to that need, so evident in *The Magus*, to punish the artist while encouraging and protecting his narcissism in various ways in the text. Exposing Miles is itself a protectionist strategy, forestalling critical attack on Fowles's protagonist just as attack on his text is similarly forestalled. In *Mantissa* the author/hero and his novel are at once reviled and coddled, subjected to ridicule and preserved from it. By asserting with melodramatic intensity that, in spite of all, Miles (like his author) *does* know and recognize himself, *Mantissa*, like *The Magus*, reconstitutes and promotes the male egotism which spurred its examination of gender relations in the first place.

● ● ●

If "The Cloud" contemplates the limits of narrative, and *Daniel Martin* strives to deny those limits and what they suggest about the "death of fiction," *Mantissa* in a sense contemplates another kind of abyss: the possibility that the contemporary novelist, in parodying genre and questioning fictional convention, must finally come to parody himself. Miles Green is a deliberately absurd character whose inner frenzy is perhaps a sardonic comment on the portentous and self-inflated figure of Daniel Martin. In the late

1970s and 1980s, Fowles was increasingly preoccupied with the writer as a species of psychotic, or at least as a being plagued by neurosis and the possibility of schizophrenia.[13] Considered in tandem, *Daniel Martin* and *Mantissa* can perhaps be seen as manifestations of an ambiguous desire at once to glorify the artist as a magician and to satirize him bitterly as a fool. This ambiguity stems from Fowles's fascinated but reluctant engagement with the demand of postmodernism for self-reflexivity in fiction and profound self-consciousness in the novelist. The febrile and hyperactive imaginings of Miles Green come partly from this burden of self-awareness, the ongoing *Angst* of the novelist whom history has pressganged into metafiction: "The reflective novel is sixty years dead, Erato," he blurts out, "it's a *reflexive* medium now, not a reflective one" (118, emphasis in original). In parodying Miles, then, Fowles comes dangerously close to undermining what is vitally important to him — the authority of the artist.

It is perhaps this sense of self-consciousness as debilitating and potentially absurd in its effects that leads Fowles, in his latest novel, *A Maggot*, back to the kind of narrative approach or format which he adopted much earlier in *The French Lieutenant's Woman*. In his newest work he again scrutinizes the past with a contemporary eye, presenting an interpretation of an earlier century which is also a commentary on the powers of fiction. By reverting to his old technique of interweaving in one narrative two historical perspectives, Fowles moves away from the self-satire of *Mantissa* and reaffirms the authorial obligation to self-consciousness without mockery or cynicism. Once again, he goes back to strategies explored previously in his career to assert the power of both novelist and novel. And by means of this formal regression he examines, perhaps paradoxically, the possibility that their enduring strength lies in their ability to adapt and evolve.

In *A Maggot*, then, Fowles uses the eighteenth century as he had earlier sought to use the nineteenth: to discover a view of

---

13   Fowles refers to "the benign psychosis of the writing experience" in "Hardy," p. 29. In the interview with Baker, he declares that all "novelists are neurotics and schizophrenics, at the very least" (668); to be a novelist, "[y]ou badly need a thoroughly split personality" (670). The obvious paradox here is that the artist, Fowles, should be so consciously aware — and so apparently in control — of his own psychoses.

the past unvitiated by nostalgia, and to contemplate history as potentially the agent of positive change rather than as the guarantor, for the novelist at least, of regressive escape. In attempting to do this, the book also emphasizes the capacity of the novelist to capture truths which evade the historian: the story of Rebecca and His Lordship takes place between the lines, as it were, of the official, popular historical chronicle provided by the *Gentleman's Magazine*. It is the novelist who can capture the spirit of the times, while the historian can only record facts. Through the intercutting of his own text with the contemporary factual one, Fowles emphasizes his awareness of his own narratorial roles and undertakes to engage with the generic past of the novel as a responsibly self-aware postmodernist writer. In all these ways *A Maggot* returns to the historical and generic revisionism of Fowles's third novel, while seeking to avoid what I earlier called the generic nostalgia of *The French Lieutenant's Woman*, as well as the wish-fulfilling excesses of *Daniel Martin*.

Fowles imitates here a documentary mode, the question and answer form of legal deposition, which he combines with a few letters, the quotations from the *Gentleman's Magazine*, and some third-person narration. These different forms make *A Maggot* into both a courtroom drama and a truncated epistolary novel, while the discursive third-person narrations allow Fowles to act as a sort of fictionalizing historian, offering his views on events and people in both their eighteenth- and twentieth-century contexts. Speaking of John Lee, the narrator observes: "Like so many of his class at this time, he still lacks what even the least intelligent human today . . . would recognize — an unmistakable sense of personal identity set in a world to some degree, however small, manipulable or controllable by that identity."[14]

A Maggot is thus a loose but effective mixture of styles which implicitly defines the author as at once an historian/critic and an artist. Like Defoe, Fowles here is forced to read the text of history in order to produce his narrative. He finds room and scope for his own imagination despite the apparent fixity of historical fact. As a creator unhampered by mere facts and operating in the interstices between them, the author of *A Maggot* synthesizes critic and

---

14   John Fowles, *A Maggot* (London: Jonathan Cape, 1985), p. 389. All
      other page references appear in the text and are to this edition.

artist, historian and fabulator, by offering us a factual chronicle inter-
leaved with his own fictionalized vision of an era.[15] Like the narrator of *The French Lieutenant's Woman* but without his predecessor's
flamboyant anxiety, the author here can also in effect rewrite the
"text" of an earlier century and so symbolically repossess it.

     Furthermore, *A Maggot* imitates the style of *The French
Lieutenant's Woman* by adopting aspects of different genres — the
inquest, the epistolary and picaresque novels — and manipulating
them from the standpoint of twentieth-century knowledge. This
rediscovery by Fowles of an old technique implies that his retreat
from the threatened nihilism of "The Cloud" has returned him to
his own well-travelled literary landscapes. Like Daniel Martin exca-
vating his personal past, Fowles in this phase of his career is investi-
gating the history of his *œuvre*. Also like Dan, he seems pulled in
two directions at once — towards a mythologized past and a timebound future. We cannot know, but it is possible that Fowles's self-
conscious return to earlier books is part of an effort to break new
ground by retraversing old territories. In any event, he seems to
express this conflict in *A Maggot*'s central image of the spacecraft
becalmed momentarily in the eighteenth century. In its symbolic
bringing together of past and future, its capacity to be both a maggot and a module, the mysterious ship suggests both archaeology
and aeronautics. As such it captures the conflicts of an author still
wishing to colonize the past as a *domaine* and to confront it as the
bringer of perceptible change.

     In *A Maggot*, Fowles adopts a contemporary perspective
on the past in order to explore further the quest of narrative for a
language commensurate with experience. In this way the novel proclaims indirectly the indissoluble relationship between narrative
and human reality while reflecting Fowles's ongoing preoccupation
with the relationship between language and meaning. This is clearly
seen in Rebecca's attempts to render the incidents in the Devonshire

---

15   Fowles, who eschews the scholarly study of history, admires Defoe as "a
      superb narrative novelist" who can "fake history" and so use it for his
      own fictional purposes. Fowles's informal approach to the age with
      which *A Maggot* deals suggests that scholarship has nothing to do with
      his sense of the artist as historian: "As an historical period it bores me in
      many ways: I can't be bothered to analyse Walpole's régime as a proper
      historian would," in Baker, 666–67.

cave intelligible and comprehensible to Ayscough. The ironic impact of these incidents comes from the perceptual abyss which is so suggestively opened between Rebecca's experience and her efforts to communicate it in a language which has not yet evolved the means for her to do so. Possessed of the experience but without the vocabulary to frame it, Rebecca inevitably seems to lack the wherewithal to grasp the full meaning of what has happened to her. Like that of the narrator in *The French Lieutenant's Woman*, the author's twentieth-century perspective here colludes with the reader's to suggest a level of comprehension unavailable to the characters. It is we who, having at our disposal a language congruent with certain realities of the twentieth century, can recognize Rebecca's "maggot" as a spaceship (368), her wall of "gleaming stones" as a control panel (369), and her unbreakable "window" as a video screen or hatch for observing the landscapes of different planets (371). Like Sarah Woodruff, then, Rebecca stands for a kind of experience which is literally displaced because it remains as yet uninaugurated in time.

This cognitive gap between Rebecca and the reader (as well as between character and author) identifies time as the bringer of change and hence of literary or generic obsolescence. The "maggot" disrupts historical sequence: it is an achronological invasion from the future into the time frame of the novel. As such it stands for the inevitability of process, and Rebecca's transformation from whore into madonna confirms the reality of change which the book asserts. *A Maggot* attempts to engage with those notions of personal development, progress, and alteration evaded so consummately in *The Magus*. At the same time it deliberately disrupts chronology in the service of contemporary metafiction. As in *The French Lieutenant's Woman*, the interpenetration of past and future emphasizes the instability or constructedness of the novel's time frame and hence the fictionality of the narrative. In this way *A Maggot* achieves the textual self-reflexivity of the postmodernist novel while avoiding the parodic desperation of *Mantissa*.

This manipulation of chronology has a generic aspect as well, for the high-technology science fiction of our own century here invades a narrative which, although stylistically eclectic, follows the basic shape of the picaresque novel. Once again, Fowles highlights the incapacity of older literary forms to remain relevant to twentieth-century experience, or to reflect the various directions of the twentieth-century literary imagination. The idea of generic evolution is somewhat more coherent here than in *The French Lieutenant's Woman*, for Fowles's attachment to the fictional forms of the eighteenth century seems less visceral and nostalgically intense than his attachment to the nineteenth-century novel. The deliberate incursion into science fiction, like Rebecca's quest to find words that will match her experience, suggests the declared faith of Fowles's latest novel in the ability of narrative and language to evolve as the experiential horizons of humanity expand in history.

This implied belief in growth offers an optimistic counter to the nihilism of "The Cloud," but it should not be taken entirely at face value. Fowles is still obsessed in his latest work not only with notions of timelessness, but with the limitations, as well as the capacities, of language. This is seen most clearly in the ambiguities that continue to cluster around the figure of the heroine. On one level, Rebecca stands for the affirmation of historical process, for she leaves behind her the unhappy life of the bagnio and finds a sense of purpose as a Quaker. But the ways in which Rebecca changes do not wholly suggest a movement towards either liberation or independent self-definition. Escaping the tyrannical discipline of Mother Claiborne's, she allies herself with the equally controlling and disciplined order of James Wardley. The regimented spirituality of an ordered virtue replaces the equally regimented sensuality of an orthodox vice. On another level, then, Rebecca duplicates not only Sarah's historically ambiguous status but her peculiar and ambivalent imaginative status as well. For Rebecca, while prefiguring the "proto-feminism" of her daughter, Ann Lee, and the Shakers, also evokes that eternal woman dissociated from the emancipations effected by history through her removal from time and assimilation into myth. She is at once an individual and an archetype, yet another embodiment of that changeless model of the feminine which continues to haunt Fowles's imagination.

The specific myth to which Rebecca is assimilated is the Christian one: she is presented as a sort of Protestant madonna and her vocation is apparently to bear the reincarnated redeemer. *A Maggot* thus qualifies Rebecca's involvement with ideas of growth and development by displacing her in the direction of archetype. This displacement assimilates Rebecca (like Sarah) to ancient notions of femininity while also identifying her as a precursor of the modern woman. Rebecca's paradoxical capacity to suggest both a new woman and an eternal one indirectly undermines the novel's commitment to historical change, for Fowles is still portraying women not so much as individuals but as fantasies, the generalized incarnations of a timeless femininity.

It is interesting to note in this connection that the novel is dominated by both the mythic figure of the madonna and the fairy-tale one of the misunderstood prince. His Lordship (whose name also suggests Christ Our Lord) seems to stand for the fantasy-motif of the foundling, the unhappy child's sense of himself as a true aristocrat misplaced at birth by noble parents. His obtuse and villainous father, the Duke, evidently regards him as a "changeling" (449), a darker variation of this motif. The central events of the novel enact the effective redemption of His Lordship and his wish-fulfilling reunion with the noble beings who are his "true" parents. Through this element of regressive fantasy — a poignantly idealized treatment of the parent/child relationship — Fowles acknowledges again that imaginative pull towards the fabulous which has always vitiated his relationship with realism as a literary mode, and with process as an ontological reality: "[M]any novelists, not least the present one," the narrator declares, are "baffled, a child, before the real now; far happier out of it, in a narrative past or a prophetic future, locked inside that weird tense grammar does not allow, the imaginary present" (389).

In its ambiguous relationship with the principle of change that it seeks to valorize, *A Maggot* resembles *The Magus*, and it is His Lordship, rather than Rebecca, who plays the role of Conchis. He is the possessor of arcane wisdom, and her salvation, her discovery of faith and vocation, is really a byproduct of his apotheosis. An all-wise prophet, His Lordship is taken alive into a science-fiction heaven. In view of this it is difficult not to feel that Rebecca's experience in the cave is not really her own: without the wisdom and the vocabulary to comprehend, she cannot grasp its full meaning. Like Sarah, whose lack of self-comprehension confers interpretive power on both Charles and the narrator of *The French Lieutenant's Woman*, Rebecca may have had the experience, but it is His Lordship who seems to understand it. Once again in Fowles's fiction, masculine knowledge directs intuitive female susceptibility.

Rebecca's efforts at comprehension lead her to the metaphors of religion. She turns her experience into a sentimental

personal myth based on the tenets of Christianity and a sort of revi-
sionist Marianism: "Then was it as I walked in Paradise, in life eternal and happiness everlasting," she tells Ayscough, "[t]hese two
men were one, the only one, the man of men: our Lord Jesus
Christ, who died for us, yet was resurrected. . . . Holy Mother
Wisdom, 'tis she the bearing spirit of God's will and one with Him
from the beginning, that takes up all that Christ the Saviour
promised" (378, 379). By contrast His Lordship's achieved comprehension leads to his departure with the craft and its inhabitants,
an initiation into futurity which, in Rebecca's terms, constitutes the
direct experience of grace: " '[T]was as if his face was become one
with He I had seen in the meadow in June Eternal, that does forgive all sins, and to all despair bring peace" (383).

Like *The Magus*, *A Maggot* postulates a magician-figure
who generates a difficult "text" which baffles and challenges a reader.
But Rebecca is no Nicholas Urfe; she is another of those deceptive
Fowlesian heroines who appear to be different from their predecessors. Presented as a myth-maker in her own right, Rebecca is
perceived by Ayscough as the creator of a new language: "Thou art
bishopess, woman, why, thoud'st dare to make a theology of thy
foolish fancyings, thy flibberty-gibberty dreamings with thy June
Eternals here, thy Holy Mother Wisdoms there — what right hast
thou to coin such names, when even thy fellow conventiclers know
them not?" (427). This combines with Fowles's apparent efforts in
the novel to reformulate the Christian myth in feminist terms —
with "Holy Mother Wisdom" as an aspect of the Trinity and the
idea of a female saviour — to suggest a new direction in his thinking
about femininity: Rebecca, whose words foreshadow the Shaker
belief in the second incarnation of Christ as a woman, tells John Lee,
"[W]hen the Lord Jesus come again, He shall be She, and the mother must know Her name" (453).

But Rebecca is not what she seems. The metafictional
strategies of the novel prevent us from sharing Ayscough's view and
crediting her with the power to create a language. *A Maggot* develops an effective split between two different languages: the ratiocinative "alphabet" (317) of Ayscough and the instinctual one of
Rebecca, which attempts to express the inexpressible, an experience
"[s]o great it may hardly be said in words." Rebecca confesses:
"I knew not then how to say it in words; I know not still" (414).
But the novel itself forces the reader to view this alphabet of the

incommunicable as not only derivative but ironic. From the twentieth-century perspective which the book insists upon, Rebecca's "names" suggest not the ability of one individual to wield and control language, but the limitations of language in time. Her words are an index of what language cannot yet do, rather than an unambiguous sign of her own power. Thus Rebecca's "alphabet" becomes for the reader not a new language but a non-language, an ineptitude with words created and guaranteed by history itself.

This indirect preservation of the relationship between women and inarticulacy in Fowles's work is further strengthened by Rebecca's lack of true artistic or visionary power. Although she is set up, like Nick, as the reader of a "text," her act of interpretation is not literary, as she does not express her experience in a text of her own making. Her attempts at both narrative and theology are unconvincing, given the technique of the novel. Not only does Ayscough control the questions put to Rebecca, but her answers to him remain fragmentary and listener-directed, like Jenny McNeil's "contributions." They cannot constitute an independently controlled text any more than they can add up to a developed and cohesive creed. Instead Rebecca assimilates her experience to religious dogma and the creative act which affirms her vocation is physical rather than imaginative — she gives birth to a child. In this way the apparent feminization of the Christian myth becomes merely a displacement of the heroine in the direction of the sacerdotal: the handmaid of genius becomes the handmaid of the Lord, and significantly, the man responsible for her transformation (as perhaps for her child) is given no name other than "His Lordship."

• • •

Rebecca Hocknell is an important character because of what she almost becomes rather than for what she is. Like Sarah Woodruff, she stands for Fowles's repeated efforts to create a female magus, to approach women as creatively, linguistically, and artistically powerful. In this Rebecca draws together the ideas in Fowles's work which this study has examined: she represents an image of feminine power defined in physical and instinctual terms, while her intellectual and creative potential remains suggested but unrealized in the novel. *A Maggot* ends with the birth of Ann Lee, who articulated a vision by founding a church. This powerful woman is not part of the narrative and Fowles, who admires her, seems to approach her as he earlier approached Marie de France, by a process of fictionalizing — not Ann herself here, but her ancestry. Rebecca could thus be Fowles's attempt to engage, however indirectly, with Ann Lee as a potent and authoritative woman, although not an artist. Perhaps his future work will see the conversion of Ann from significant absence to tangible presence — a conversion that could create new fictional possibilities by redefining creativity along less gender-specific and hence less circumscribing lines.

For the circumscriptions, ambiguities, and contradictions that characterize Fowles's treatment of women must also illuminate another level of self-reflexivity relevant to and operating upon his texts. This is the level of specific critical self-consciousness, where the difficulties of the critic who attempts a feminist or feminist-orientated reading of Fowles's work are perceived. I have commented occasionally in this study on the obviously ironic position of the scholarly critic vis-à-vis Fowles, given the latter's consistently anti-academic stance and the debate between art and criticism conducted in his fiction. The position of the feminist critic is even more ironic, although less obviously so. She (for such a critic is most likely to be a woman) must negotiate both the implied admiration which Fowles (like many readers) evidently feels for his heroines, *and* those strategies that restrict these heroines within male-defined bounds — bounds that seem at times not only to condition but to create the attractiveness of these women, and thus to encode them as masculine fantasies. In other words, the feminist critic may sometimes feel that Fowles's fictions were not really written for the female reader. And this sense of unease is frequently complicated, as I have suggested, by the textual designation — both overt and misleading — of the heroine as emblematic of different kinds of liberation. The Fowlesian woman seems at once to repel and to invite, even to flatter, feminist scrutiny, just as the Fowlesian text both entices and frustrates the efforts of *any* critic to decipher it. But the situation of that Fowles scholar whose practice draws on feminist principles is uniquely and perhaps insolubly problematic, for the drama of chastised female creativity demands her participation while indirectly rebuking her own creative efforts. She may find herself, as I have, caught between admiration for Fowles's artistry and suspicion of what that very power implies — both intrigued and unnerved by the contradictions that her analyses discover.

This book has argued that these contradictions and their resonances can be explored through the study of power as a kind of extended theme in Fowles's fictions. We might say that contradiction becomes for him almost a narrative mode in itself, so pervasive are the paradoxes and so persistent is the sense of divided loyalties in his work. This suggests not intellectual pusillanimity, but hyper-awareness; it delineates a creative imagination at once anxious and poised, a literary sensibility eager at times to compel itself into moral or aesthetic positions which in other ways — emotionally and psychologically perhaps — it finds uncongenial. It is finally, then, in terms of paradox that we must view not only Fowles's explorations of gender and sexuality, but of the nature of artistic power as well. His sense of the artist's creative heritage as both forbidding and inspiring leads his fictions to express admiration for and hostility towards the authoritative ancestors of the postmodernist text; his vision of women as both necessary to art and potentially threatening to the artist governs his fictional presentation of feminine "power" as somehow at once irrefutably present and effectively absent. In a similar way, too, his *œuvre* manifests that crucial tension between language as, in one way, corrupt and unworthy of the artist and, in another, as his sublime and magical tool. In the light of the various disjunctions and ambiguities emphasized in this study, Fowles's recuperative quest, at this point in his career, for greater structural and thematic stability in his work is sure to produce narrative configurations both compelling and disconcerting, fascinating and problematic.

BIBLIOGRAPHY

Adam, Ian, Patrick Brantlinger, and Sheldon Rothblatt. "*The French Lieutenant's Woman*: A Discussion." *Victorian Studies* 15, No. 3 (1972), 339–56.

Alain-Fournier, [Henri]. *The Wanderer (Le Grand Meaulnes)*. Trans. Françoise Delisle. Boston, 1928; rpt. Clifton, New Jersey: Augustus M. Kelley, 1973.

Alderman, Timothy C. "The Enigma of *The Ebony Tower*: A Genre Study." *Modern Fiction Studies* 31, No. 1 (1985), 135–47.

Allen, Walter. "The Achievement of John Fowles." *Encounter* 35, No. 2 (1970), 64–67.

Auden, W. H. *The Enchafèd Flood: The Romantic Iconography of the Sea*. London: Faber and Faber, 1953.

Auerbach, Erich. *Mimesis: The Representation of Reality in Western Literature*. Trans. Willard R. Trask. Princeton, New Jersey: Princeton University Press, 1953.

Bagchee, Shyamal. "*The Collector*: The Paradoxical Imagination of John Fowles." *Journal of Modern Literature* 8, No. 2 (1980/81), 219–34.

————. "*The Great Gatsby* and John Fowles's *The Collector*." *Notes on Contemporary Literature* 10, No. 4 (1980), 7–8.

Baker, James R. "An Interview with John Fowles." *Michigan Quarterly Review* 25, No. 4 (1986), 661–83.

Bal, Mieke. *Narratology: Introduction to the Theory of Narrative*. Toronto: University of Toronto Press, 1985.

Barnum, Carol M. "An Interview with John Fowles." *Modern Fiction Studies* 31, No. 1 (1985), 187–203.

————. "The Quest Motif in John Fowles's *The Ebony Tower*: Theme and Variations." *Texas Studies in Literature and Language* 23, No. 1 (1981), 138–57.

Barthes, Roland. *Mythologies*. Trans. Annette Lavers. London: Paladin, 1973.

Bawer, Bruce. "John Fowles and his Big Ideas." *The New Criterion* 5, No. 8 (1987), 21–36.

Beatty, Patricia V. "John Fowles's Clegg: Captive Landlord of Eden." *Ariel* 13, No. 3 (1982), 73–81.

Bellamy, Michael O. "John Fowles's Versions of Pastoral: Private Valleys and the Parity of Existence." *Critique* 21, No. 2 (1979), 72–84.

Benton, Sarah. "Adam & Eve." *New Socialist*, No. 11 (1983), 18–19.

Berets, Ralph. "*The Magus*: A Study in the Creation of a Personal Myth." *Twentieth Century Literature*, 19 Apr. 1973, 89–98.

Berger, John. "Goya: the Maja, dressed and undressed." In his *The White Bird*. Ed. Lloyd Spencer. London: Chatto & Windus, 1985, pp. 86–91.

Bergonzi, Bernard. *The Situation of the Novel*. London and Basingstoke: The Macmillan Press, 1979.

Billy, Ted. "Homo Solitarius: Isolation and Estrangement in *The Magus*." *Research Studies* 48, No. 3 (1980), 129–41.

Binns, Ronald. "John Fowles: Radical Romancer." *The Critical Quarterly* 15, No. 4 (1973), 317–34.

————. "A New Version of *The Magus*." *The Critical Quarterly* 19, No. 4 (1977), 79–84.

Bloom, Harold. *The Anxiety of Influence: A Theory of Poetry*. New York: Oxford University Press, 1973.

Boccia, Michael. "'Visions and Revisions': John Fowles's New Version of *The Magus*." *Journal of Modern Literature* 8, No. 2 (1980/81), 235–46.

Boston, Richard. "John Fowles, Alone But Not Lonely." *New York Times Book Review*, 9 Nov. 1969, Sec. 7, 2, 52–54.

Bradbury, Malcolm. *Possibilities: Essays on the State of the Novel*. New York: Oxford University Press, 1973.

Byrd, Deborah. "The Evolution and Emancipation of Sarah Woodruff: *The French Lieutenant's Woman* as a Feminist Novel." *International Journal of Women's Studies* 7, No. 4 (1984), 306–21.

Byrom, Bill. "Puffing and Blowing." *Spectator*, 6 May 1966, 574.

Campbell, James. "An Interview with John Fowles." *Contemporary Literature* 17, No. 4 (1976), 455–69.

Carter, Angela. *The Sadeian Woman: An Exercise in Cultural History.* London: Virago, 1979.

Churchill, Thomas. "Waterhouse, Storey and Fowles: Which Way Out of the Room?" *Critique* 10, No. 3 (1969), 72–87.

Clark, Kenneth. *The Nude: A Study in Ideal Form.* New York: Doubleday & Co., 1956.

Conradi, Peter J. "*The French Lieutenant's Woman*: Novel, Screenplay, Film." *Critical Quarterly* 24, No. 1 (1982), 41–57.

———. *John Fowles.* New York: Methuen, 1982.

Davidson, Arnold E. "The Barthesian Configurations of John Fowles's 'The Cloud.'" *The Centennial Review* 28, No. 4/29, No. 1 (1984/85), 80–93.

———. "Caliban and the Captive Maiden: John Fowles's *The Collector* and Irving Wallace's *The Fan Club*." *Studies in the Humanities* 8, No. 2 (1981), 28–33.

———. "*Eliduc* and 'The Ebony Tower': John Fowles's Variation on a Medieval Lay." *The International Fiction Review* 11, No. 1 (1984), 31–36.

Ditsky, John. "The Watch and Chain of Henry James." *The University of Windsor Review* 6, No. 1 (1970), 91–101.

Dixon, Ronald C. "Criticism of John Fowles: A Selected Checklist." *Modern Fiction Studies* 31, No. 1 (1985), 205–10.

Dixon, Terrell F. "Expostulation and a Reply: The Character of Clegg in Fowles and Sillitoe." *Notes on Contemporary Literature* 4, No. 2 (1974), 7–9.

Docherty, Thomas. "A Constant Reality: The Presentation of Character in the Fiction of John Fowles." *Novel* 14, No. 2 (1981), 118–34.

Dworkin, Andrea. *Pornography: Men Possessing Women.* New York: G.P. Putnam's Sons, 1981.

Eagleton, Terry. *The Rape of Clarissa: Writing, Sexuality and Class Struggle in Samuel Richardson.* Oxford: Basil Blackwell, 1982.

Eddins, Dwight. "John Fowles: Existence as Authorship." *Contemporary Literature* 17, No. 2 (1976), 204–22.

Edwards, L. R. "Changing our Imaginations." *Massachusetts Review* 11, No. 3 (1970), 604–608.

Falconer, Graham. "Straightening Out John Fowles." *Queen's Quarterly* 92, No. 2 (1987), 332–40.

Fawkner, H. W. *The Timescapes of John Fowles.* Toronto: Associated University Presses, 1984.

Fiedler, Leslie. *Love and Death in the American Novel.* New York: Stein and Day, 1966.

Fleishmann, Avrom. "*The Magus* of the Wizard of the West." In his *Fiction and the Ways of Knowing.* Austin and London: University of Texas Press, 1978, pp. 179–94.

Foster, Hal, ed. *The Anti-Aesthetic: Essays on Postmodern Culture.* Port Townsend, Washington: Bay Press, 1983.

Fowles, John. *The Aristos.* New York: New American Library, 1970.

———. *The Collector.* London: Jonathan Cape, 1963.

———. *Daniel Martin.* Boston: Little, Brown and Company, 1977.

———. *The Ebony Tower.* Toronto: Little, Brown and Company, 1974.

———. *The French Lieutenant's Woman.* London: Jonathan Cape, 1969.

———. "Hardy and the Hag." In *Thomas Hardy after Fifty Years.* Ed. L. St. John Butler. London: Macmillan, 1977, pp. 28–42.

———, foreword and afterword. *The Hound of the Baskervilles.* By Sir Arthur Conan Doyle. 1902; rpt. London: John Murray, 1974.

———. "I Write Therefore I am." *Evergreen Review*, No. 33 (1964), 16–17, 89–90.

———. *A Maggot.* London: Jonathan Cape, 1985.

———. *The Magus.* London: Pan Books, 1966.

———. *The Magus: A Revised Version.* London: Jonathan Cape, 1977.

———. *Mantissa.* Toronto: Collins, 1982.

————, introd. *Mehalah: A Story of the Salt Marshes.* By S. Baring-Gould. 1880; rpt. London: Chatto & Windus, 1969.

————. "My Recollections of Kafka." *Mosaic* 3, No. 4 (1970), 31–41.

————. "Notes on an Unfinished Novel." In *Afterwords: Novelists on their Novels.* Ed. Thomas McCormack. New York: Harper & Row, 1969, pp. 161–75.

————. "On Being English but not British." *The Texas Quarterly* 7, No. 3 (1964), 154–62.

————. *Poems.* New York: The Ecco Press, 1973.

————, introd. *The Royal Game and Other Stories.* By Stefan Zweig. Trans. Jill Sutcliffe. London: Jonathan Cape, 1981.

————, and Frank Horvat. *The Tree.* London: Aurum Press, 1979.

————. "Weeds, Bugs, Americans." *Sports Illustrated*, 21 Dec. 1970, 84–102.

Frank, Joseph. *The Widening Gyre: Crisis and Mastery in Modern Literature.* New Brunswick, New Jersey: Rutgers University Press, 1963.

Frye, Northrop. *Anatomy of Criticism.* Princeton, New Jersey: Princeton University Press, 1957.

Glaserfeld, Ernst von. "Reflections on John Fowles's *The Magus* and the Construction of Reality." *Georgia Review* 33, No. 2 (1979), 444–48.

Grace, Sherrill E. "Courting Bluebeard with Bartók, Atwood and Fowles: Modern Treatments of the Bluebeard Theme." *Journal of Modern Literature* 11, No. 2 (1984), 245–62.

Griffin, Susan. *Pornography and Silence: Culture's Revenge Against Nature.* New York: Harper & Row, 1981.

Gross, David. "Historical Consciousness and the Modern Novel: The Uses of History in the Fiction of John Fowles." *Studies in the Humanities* 7, No. 1 (1978), 19–27.

Halpern, Daniel, and John Fowles. "A Sort of Exile in Lyme Regis." *London Magazine*, 10 Mar. 1971, 34–46.

Hanning, Robert, and Joan Ferrante, trans. *The Lais of Marie de France.* Introd. John Fowles. New York: E. P. Dutton, 1978.

Harris, Richard L. "*The Magus* and 'The Miller's Tale': John Fowles on the Courtly Mode." *Ariel* 14, No. 2 (1983), 3–17.

Harrison, Fraser. *The Dark Angel: Aspects of Victorian Sexuality.* London: Sheldon Press, 1977.

Hieatt, Constance B. "*Eliduc* Revisited: John Fowles and Marie de France." *English Studies in Canada* 3, No. 3 (1977), 351–58.

Holloway, Watson L. "The Killing of the Weasel: Hermetism in the Fiction of John Fowles." *English Language Notes* 22, No. 3 (1985), 69–71.

Holmes, Frederick M. "Fictional Self-Consciousness in John Fowles's 'The Ebony Tower.'" *Ariel* 16, No. 3 (1985), 21–38.

Holmes, Richard. "Crystallizing Powers." *London Times*, 9 June 1977, 12.

Huffaker, Robert. *John Fowles.* Boston: Twayne Publishers, 1980.

Hussey, Barbara L. "John Fowles's *The Magus:* The Book and the World." *The International Fiction Review* 10, No. 1 (1983), 19–26.

Hutcheon, Linda. "Barry N. Olshen, *John Fowles.*" *English Studies in Canada* 7, No. 1 (1981), 116–20.

————. *Narcissistic Narrative: The Metafictional Paradox.* Waterloo, Ontario: Wilfrid Laurier University Press, 1980.

————. *A Poetics of Postmodernism.* New York: Routledge, 1988.

————. *A Politics of Postmodernism.* New York: Routledge, 1989.

Jefferies, Richard. *Bevis.* 1930; rpt. New York: E. P. Dutton, 1956.

Johnson, A.J.B. "Realism in *The French Lieutenant's Woman.*" *Journal of Modern Literature* 8, No. 2 (1980/81), 287–302.

Karl, Frederick J. *The Contemporary English Novel.* New York: Farrar, Straus and Cudahy, 1962.

Kennedy, Alan. *The Protean Self: Dramatic Action in Contemporary Fiction.* London: Macmillan, 1974.

Kofman, Sarah. *The Enigma of Woman: Woman in Freud's Writings.* Trans. Catherine Porter. Ithaca and London: Cornell University Press, 1980.

Laughlin, Rosemary M. "Faces of Power in the Novels of John Fowles." *Critique* 13, No. 3 (1972), 71–88.

Lever, Karen M. "The Education of John Fowles." *Critique* 21, No. 2 (1978), 85–100.

Lindblad, Ishrat. "'*La bonne vaux*,' '*la princesse lointaine*' — Two Motifs in the Novels of John Fowles." In *Studies in English Philology, Linguistics and Literature Presented to Alarik Rynell.* Ed. Mats Rydén and Lennart A. Björk. Stockholm, Sweden: Almquist & Wiksell International, 1978, pp. 87–101.

Lodge, David. *Working with Structuralism: Essays and Reviews on Nineteenth- and Twentieth-Century Literature.* Boston: Routledge & Kegan Paul, 1981.

Loveday, Simon. *The Romances of John Fowles.* New York: St. Martin's Press, 1985.

Lovell, Terry. "Feminism and Form in the Literary Adaptation: *The French Lieutenant's Woman.*" In *Criticism and Critical Theory.* Ed. Jeremy Hawthorn. London: Edward Arnold, 1984, pp. 113–26.

Lukács, Georg. *The Historical Novel.* Trans. Hannah and Stanley Mitchell. London: Merlin Press, 1962.

Magalaner, Marvin. "The Fool's Journey: John Fowles's *The Magus.*" In *Old Lines, New Forces: Essays on the Contemporary British Novel, 1960–70.* Ed. Robert K. Morris. Teaneck, New Jersey: Fairleigh Dickinson University Press, 1976, pp. 81–92.

Mansfield, Elizabeth. "A Sequence of Endings: The Manuscripts of *The French Lieutenant's Woman.*" *Journal of Modern Literature* 8, No. 2 (1980/81), 275–86.

McDaniel, Ellen. "Fowles as Collector: The Failed Artists of *The Ebony Tower.*" *Papers on Language and Literature* 23, No. 1 (1987), 70–83.

McSweeney, Kerry. "Black Hole and Ebony Tower." *Queen's Quarterly* 82, No. 1 (1975), 152–66.

———. *Four Contemporary Novelists: Angus Wilson, Brian Moore, John Fowles, V. S. Naipaul.* Kingston and Montreal: McGill-Queen's University Press, 1983.

———. "John Fowles's Variations in *The Ebony Tower.*" *Journal of Modern Literature* 8, No. 2 (1980/81), 303–24.

Mellors, John. "Collectors and Creators: The Novels of John Fowles." *London Magazine* 14, No. 6 (1975), 65–72.

Michael, Magali Cornier. "'Who is Sarah?': A Critique of *The French Lieutenant's Woman*'s Feminism." *Critique* 28, No. 4 (1987), 225–36.

Mickel, Emanuel J., Jr. *Marie de France.* New York: Twayne Publishers, 1974.

Miller, Nan. "Christina Rossetti and Sarah Woodruff: Two Remedies for a Divided Self." *The Journal of Pre-Raphaelite Studies* 3, No. 1 (1982), 68–77.

Mills, John. "Fowles' Indeterminacy: An Art of Alternatives." *West Coast Review* 10, No. 2 (1975), 32–36.

Morse, Ruth. "John Fowles, Marie de France and the Man with Two Wives." *Philological Quarterly* 63, No. 1 (1984), 17–30.

Mortimer, Penelope. "Into the Noösphere." *New Statesman,* 6 May 1966, 659–60.

Murdoch, Iris. *Sartre: Romantic Realist.* New York: Barnes & Noble, 1980.

Newquist, Roy. "John Fowles." In his *Counterpoint.* London: George Allen & Unwin, 1965, pp. 218–25.

Olshen, Barry N. *John Fowles.* New York: Frederick Ungar Publishing Co., 1978.

———, and Toni A. Olshen. *John Fowles: A Reference Guide.* Boston, Massachusetts: G. K. Hall & Co., 1980.

———, and Janet E. Lewis. "John Fowles and the Medieval Romance Tradition." *Modern Fiction Studies* 31, No. 1 (1985), 15–30.

———. "John Fowles's *The Magus:* An Allegory of Self-Realization." *Journal of Popular Culture* 9, No. 4 (1976), 916–25.

Palmer, William J. *The Fiction of John Fowles: Tradition, Art, and the Loneliness of Selfhood.* Columbia: University of Missouri Press, 1974.

———. "Fowles' *The Magus:* The Vortex as Myth, Metaphor and Masque." In *The Power of Myth in Literature and Film.* Ed. Victor Carrabino. Tallahassee: University Presses of Florida, 1980, pp. 66–76.

———. "John Fowles and the Crickets." *Modern Fiction Studies* 31, No. 1 (1985), 3–13.

Pifer, Drury. "The Muse Abused: Deconstruction in *Mantissa.*" In *Critical Essays on John Fowles.* Ed. Ellen Pifer. Boston, Massachusetts: G. K. Hall & Co., 1986, pp. 162–76.

Pike, E. Royston. *Human Documents of the Victorian Golden Age, 1850–1875.* London: George Allen & Unwin, 1967.

Poirier, Suzanne. "*L'Astrée* Revisited: A Seventeenth-Century Model for *The Magus.*" *Comparative Literature Studies* 17, No. 3 (1980), 269–86.

Presley, Delma E. "The Quest of the Bourgeois Hero: An Approach to Fowles's *The Magus.*" *Journal of Popular Culture*, No. 6 (1972), 394–98.

Prince, Peter. "Real Life." *New Statesman*, 11 Oct. 1974, 513.

Rackham, Jeff. "John Fowles: The Existential Labyrinth." *Critique* 13, No. 3 (1972), 89–103.

Rankin, Elizabeth D. "Cryptic Coloration in *The French Lieutenant's Woman.*" *Journal of Narrative Technique* 3, No. 3 (1973), 193–207.

Raper, Julius Rowan. "John Fowles: The Psychological Complexity of *The Magus.*" *American Imago* 45, No. 1 (1988), 61–83.

Ricks, Christopher. "The Unignorable Real." *New York Review of Books*, 12 Feb. 1970, 24.

Robinson, Robert. "Giving the reader a choice — a conversation with John Fowles." *The Listener*, 31 Oct. 1974, 584.

Rose, Gilbert J. "*The French Lieutenant's Woman*: The Unconscious Significance of a Novel to its Author." *American Imago*, No. 29 (1972), 41–57.

Rowland, Beryl. *Animals with Human Faces: A Guide to Animal Symbolism*. Knoxville: The University of Tennessee Press, 1973.

Rubinstein, Roberta. "Myth, Mystery and Irony: John Fowles's *The Magus.*" *Contemporary Literature* 16, No. 3 (1975), 328–39.

Runyon, Randolph. *Fowles / Irving / Barthes*. Columbus: Ohio State University Press, 1981.

Sage, Lorna. "John Fowles — a Profile." *The New Review* 1, No. 7 (1974), 31–37.

Salys, Rimgala. "The Medieval Context of John Fowles's *The Ebony Tower.*" *Critique* 25, No. 1 (1983), 11–24.

Scholes, Robert. "The Illiberal Imagination." *New Literary History* 4, No. 3 (1973), 521–40.

———. "The Orgastic Fiction of John Fowles." *The Hollins Critic* 6, No. 5 (1969), 1–12.

———. *Structuralism in Literature*. New Haven and London: Yale University Press, 1974.

Singh, Raman K. "An Encounter with John Fowles." *Journal of Modern Literature* 8, No. 2 (1980/81), 181–202.

Sollisch, James W. "The Passion of Existence: John Fowles's *The Ebony Tower*." *Critique* 25, No. 1 (1983), 1–9.

Tarbox, Katherine. *The Art of John Fowles.* Athens: The University of Georgia Press, 1988.

Thorpe, Michael. *John Fowles.* Berkshire, England: Profile Books, 1982.

Troyes, Chrétien de. *Yvain: the Knight of the Lion.* Trans. Burton Raffel. New Haven: Yale University Press, 1987.

Wainwright, J. A. "The Illusion of 'Things as they are': *The Magus* versus *The Magus: A Revised Version*." *Dalhousie Review* 63, No. 1 (1983), 107–19.

Walker, David H. "Remorse, Responsibility, and Moral Dilemmas in Fowles's Fiction." In *Critical Essays on John Fowles.* Ed. Ellen Pifer. Boston, Massachusetts: G. K. Hall & Co., 1986, pp. 54–76.

———. "Subversion of Narrative in the Work of André Gide and John Fowles." In *Comparative Criticism: A Yearbook.* Ed. Elinor Shaffer. Vol. II. Cambridge: Cambridge University Press, 1980, pp. 187–212.

White, T. H., ed. *The Book of Beasts: Being a Translation from a Latin Bestiary of the Twelfth Century.* London: Jonathan Cape, 1954.

Wight, Douglas A., and Kenneth B. Grant. "Theatrical Deception: Shakespearean Allusion in John Fowles's *The Magus: A Revised Version*." *University of Dayton Review* 18, No. 3 (1987), 85–93.

Wilson, Raymond J., III. "Allusion and Implication in John Fowles's 'The Cloud.'" *Studies in Short Fiction* 20, No. 1 (1983), 17–22.

———. "John Fowles's *The Ebony Tower*: Unity and Celtic Myth." *Twentieth Century Literature* 28, No. 3 (1982), 302–18.

Wolfe, Peter. *John Fowles, Magus and Moralist.* Lewisburg: Bucknell University Press, 1976.

Woodcock, Bruce. *Male Mythologies: John Fowles and Masculinity.* New Jersey: Barnes & Noble Books, 1984.

Zirker, Herbert. "John Fowles." In *Essays on the Contemporary English Novel.* Ed. Hedwig Bock and Albert Wertheim. Munchen: Max Hueber Verlag, 1986, pp. 193–208.